DEAD MAN HAUNT

ALSO BY T. M. SIMMONS

DEAD MAN HAUNT

A DEAD MAN MYSTERY
BOOK TWO

T. M. SIMMONS

 ePublishingWorks!
love what you read.

Book and cover design by eBook Prep
www.ebookprep.com

August 2022
ISBN: 978-1-64457-342-6

ePublishing Works!
644 Shrewsbury Commons Ave
Ste 249
Shrewsbury PA 17361
United States of America

www.epublishingworks.com
Phone: 866-846-5123

ACKNOWLEDGMENTS

A lot of people helped in varied ways with this book. I'll probably forget someone, and I apologize if I do. First and foremost, Deputy Dave Nelson, of the Morris County Sheriff's Department, patiently explained the various local agencies, their available facilities, and how they worked together. Dave also kept me on track as to what they could and could not do within their jurisdictions, what had to be entrusted to larger cities, and how that worked. I could have listened to Sergeant Donnie Vallery of the Jefferson Police Department for hours, and do thank him again for finding that handcuff key so I could get out of the jail cell, despite what my husband wanted! The ladies at the Jefferson Chamber of Commerce answered my questions without blinking an eye. I guess they're used to dealing with ghosthunters and writers. Officers Ron Jones and Ken McKeown of the Terrell Citizen's Police Academy, as well as the great speakers they brought in, were so very willing to answer anything, no matter how sane or insane. See, guys and gals, I told you my curiosity was for my book, not any illegal activities! Thanks to Louise Harper for the wonderful title and the great Louise'isms. Thanks to my first readers, Louise, Alice, Tracy, and Lynn. Thank you, Lynn, for the web site. Thanks to OurLoopers for enjoying my scary stories even if they did give them nightmares and for encouraging me to write more of them. Sorry, Pam, about the gorgeous ghost who crawled in bed with you in our shared room—not!

*When I first published **Dead Man Haunt**, Katrina had just devastated New Orleans and much more of the Gulf Coast. As I prepare this ebook version of my mystery, Irene has plowed up the Eastern Coast of the U.S. She left behind many deaths and is still wreaking havoc on the New England states, states which have never experienced hurricane damage such as this. I wish everyone touched by this disaster good lives and futures. To all the brave rescue personnel, thanks seems a rather simple word for a writer, but it's heartfelt. Please don't forget all the pets who are wandering lost and alone and need reunited with their owners.*

As always, to Barney, my protector from the bumps in the night...sometimes. Ditto always, to Belle, my own Aunt Twila, and Terry. And to the new generation members added to Belle's extended family, and thus, mine: Savanna, Preston, Nevaeh and JoJo.

CHAPTER 1

"Dadblast that man!" Darn it, it's just not satisfying to hang up on someone with today's technology. I slammed the receiver down, then had to grab it up again to disconnect.

"I take it Jack's not happy with our new adventure," Aunt Twila mused from the lounge chair in front of the fireplace. Miss Molly, the head cat in my menagerie, curled on Twila's lap, enjoying negligent scratches under her chin.

"He said we had no business interfering with a scheduled demolition of a dangerous building," I fumed. "We're not interfering! I just want you to see the place before it crumbles under the wrecking ball."

"Just who did you call to get permission for us to tour that hotel?" Twila asked.

"One of Katy's friends," I replied with an it's-of-no-consequence hand flutter. "I had no idea Katy would tell Jack about it."

Twila wasn't about to let me get away with that evasion. "Cousin Katy has some pretty high-placed friends."

"Yup," eighty-year-old Granny Chisholm, my next-door neighbor, agreed from her seat on the sofa across from Twila. Trucker, my

1

hundred-and-fifty-pound Rottweiler, sprawled across the cushions beside Granny. Upside down, of course, his broad belly available for Granny's age-hardened fingernails. "Betcha you called that there senator."

"I did not!" I denied.

"Come clean, Alice," Twila ordered.

"Oh, for—Katy knows a reporter in Dallas who wants to do a feature story on the hotel before the town officials bring in a demolition team."

"And the reporter probably mentioned to the town officials that she didn't have time herself to research the place?" Twila arched an eyebrow. "Insinuated to the powers that be in the small town that it would be a much more favorable story if they cooperated with us?"

I ignored her, reached for my Crown and Seven on the desk, and gulped half of it. Soothing relaxation spread. It ticked me off that my ex-husband could still do this to me, over two years after our divorce. A divorce that was supposedly amicable, might I add. We grew apart, as the explanation goes to the courts. Nothing in common any longer. Too many differences, too many variances in our lives.

"Sorry, Twila," I said. "It's not fair for you to be upset by a fight between Jack and me when you've barely arrived. You like Jack."

Granny snickered, which pulled the roadmap of lines on her face in new directions. I grabbed my drink again to prepare for what I knew, without doubt, Granny was about to say.

"Wasn't my fault Jack had to stay over," I defended before Granny could utter a word through her cackles.

"Oh?" Twila's voice rose with interest. "Jack spent the night?"

"Last week," Granny revealed. "Seen his truck here that mornin', so's I brought over some of my cranberry muffins for their breakfast. Jack 'peared to be real glad to get 'em."

"He spent the night in the guest room!" I spat. "And the reason he had to stay over was because the water pump went out on his truck. I had to take him into Six Gun the next morning to get a new one."

Twila and Granny blatantly exchanged a high-five across the coffee table. Neither one hid the fact that nothing would make them happier than for Jack and me to give our marriage another go.

"It's not gonna happen, damn it," I told them.

"Uh oh." Granny's mouth stretched with a wide grin. "Ten bucks in the trip kitty!"

I slammed my drink down on the desk and grabbed a pen. "IOU" on the scratchpad, I ripped off the top paper and jammed it into the mouth of Casper—a large-bellied jar with a caricature boasting Halloween-pumpkin teeth across the middle.

Granny and I had made a stop-swearing pact a month ago, agreeing to use the money for a trip to New Orleans during Mardi Gras, since she'd never braved that raucous scene. Ninety percent of the bills and IOU's in the kitty were mine, of course, probably plenty right now for a weekend of decadent revelry. I'd already tried to give it up, but Granny refused to accept my offer to forget the no-swear pact and pay her share to N'awlins. Since Mardi Gras wouldn't happen again for ten months, I figured we'd have enough by then to stay at the Royal Sonesta!

Twila rose and took Granny's empty glass before she headed for the bar across the study. There, she asked over her shoulder, "Anyone else ready for a refill?"

"Yes," I answered. "Just bring me another glass while I finish this one."

"Tsk, tsk," Granny chided. "We might haveta start a cut-down-on-the-drinkin' kitty next."

Defiantly, I gulped the remainder of my drink, then said, "Make mine a double this time, Twila."

"Jack still bothers you that bad, huh?" she asked. I didn't miss her surreptitious wink at Granny.

"I'm just pissed that he's trying to stick his nose into another one of our ghosthunts!"

"Ten bucks," Granny said with a smirk as she accepted her fresh drink from Twila.

At that moment, the Casper clock on the mantel, which Granny had gifted me with as a birthday/housewarming present, bonged a "Boo!" on the half-hour. I jammed another IOU into the Casper trip kitty and grabbed my own drink from Twila. The next boo/bongs would be ten in a row. I'd looked all over that clock for somewhere to turn down the volume, even called the manufacturer. No luck, and on sleepless nights, the boo/bongs echoed in the house, forcing me to close my bedroom door.

There were other ghostly objects around my house. Since all my friends and relatives know about my favorite hobby, on every gift-giving holiday, people searched for more ghosts to add to my collection—a collection that mostly resides in cardboard boxes in my closet, the most garish ones at least.

Twila and I see ghosts. We talk to ghosts. We actually hunt ghosts and enjoy the heck out of our quests. We love to prowl old buildings and graveyards, day and night, study the history of them, and occasionally chat with the long-passed occupants of both the buildings and graves. Yet out of the dozens of gone-by souls we chat with, very few ever keep our attention past that one and only conversation.

Patrick, however, a ghost I met recently, had intrigued us into this upcoming adventure, the adventure Jack was so adamantly opposed to. I'd met Patrick when I joined a few local ghosthunters to investigate the historic, scheduled-for-demolition Springs Hotel in the tiny West Texas town of Mineral Springs. He stepped out of the shower in the men's dressing room, six foot of blond nakedness, dribbles of water crawling down his tanned muscles, a white towel draped around his neck. No doubt in my mind he was a ghost, yet what a gorgeous ghost. Patrick winked at me—he could see me every bit as well as I could him. Then he disappointed me greatly when he faded back into his own dimension. I didn't even get a chance to see if he'd show up in a photograph, because I was too rapt to remember the digital camera hanging around my neck.

I'm a writer, an occupation that makes me one of the select few who actually enjoy the profession that puts food on the table, both for me and my animals. Twila lives in Yankee-land, where she still works part-time in a long-term care facility. (We called them nursing homes when we grew up.) She also cares for her mother and husband, a disabled vet. Still, we manage to get together a few times a year to prowl and hunt, and I'd picked up Twila at the airport early this afternoon. We'd driven the four-hour trip back to my lakeside cabin in Six Gun, Texas, excitedly discussing how we were loaded for bear...ghosts.

We initially hadn't planned on doing anything more this trip than revisit some old haunts, check out rumors of new ones, since Twila could only stay a few days. However, Patrick hitched a ride home with me from the hotel that night, and he passed muster with Howard, the Head Ghost in my spiritual boardinghouse, when he agreed to The Alice and Howard Ghost Agreement. All the paranormal residents that I allow to stay around have to read and abide by The Agreement, since otherwise, I'd never get any writing done. Nothing irks an editor more than a missed deadline, and besides, missed deadlines could shoot a hole in my royalty check schedule.

Mischievous ghosts leave themselves wide open to the discipline Twila taught me to deal out when she dragged me on my first ghosthunting trip and drilled the rules of paranormal dealings into me. She was with me when I found this haunted log cabin deep in the East Texas Piney Woods while searching for a new home post-divorce, too. After a couple episodes of leeway-turned-bad news on my part, I learned to heed the rules and make sure my ghosts did so as well. Twila has no sympathy for a wishy-washy ghosthunter discipline-wise. For good reason, and it didn't take me long to understand the method behind her madness.

Patrick continued to hang around for a couple weeks, and he niggled me with the mystery of his life and the old hotel, dropped hints and innuendoes that I passed on to Twila in various conversations. Eventually, both Twila and I grew fascinated with possibly uncovering the truth of at least one of the tales circulating about the hotel in its prime. In return for his vast knowledge of the place, Patrick also insisted that he needed our help on a quest of his own, a quest he continued to be vague about.

I'd known Twila would absolutely adore this hotel, since it was extremely active with ghosts and spirits besides Patrick. That, as much as our mutual fascination about historical buildings, pushed me through the maze of bracing the officialdom who had banned the public from the hotel until I found Katy's reporter friend.

Having an utterly handsome, naked ghost accompany us was a new twist, one Twila and I decided to enjoy to the fullest.

CHAPTER 2

S uch a grand piece of decay. Brimming with ghosts!

From across the street, Twila and I stared at the once-magnificent hotel and released twin sighs of yearning to explore the decrepit structure. It rose above us U-shaped, multistoried, and numerous broken windows shattered any sense that the façade sheltered anything other than wrack and ruin. Atop, a bell tower crowned the edifice, rising alone into the early morning, cloud-spotted April sky. A wide veranda graced the front, where in times gone by natty gentlemen and flapper ladies—or non-ladies—strolled when not partaking of the mineral baths or hidden-room gambling.

Though I'd been here once before, experience taught me that in Twila's company even more fantastic weird happenings would transpire. Her psychic powers far surpassed the fledgling abilities I possessed, since she'd been chasing ghosts years longer than me. The possibility of encountering past residents in her company, more than the building's wonderful history, fired my anticipation for another one of our shared adventures.

Oh, yeah, that and the fact that Patrick had already intrigued us with tales of his life in the hotel's heyday. Former life, really, since he now abided in the afterlife.

Twila raised her camera and snapped several pictures to begin the record of this adventure, and beside her, Patrick materialized briefly. Could a ghost cry, I'm sure tears would have rolled down Patrick's cheeks at the sight before him, even though in his time men characteristically hid their emotions. Come to think of it, so did men today, like my ex-husband, Jack, except when he was pis...angry at me.

Damn...darn! Now I even censored my thoughts so I wouldn't have to pay into Granny's trip kitty!

Patrick stoically gazed at the building he had called home-away when he lived, then faded back into his own realm.

"Gosh damn," Twila mused, since she wasn't part of the trip-kitty pact. "I wish that ghost would put some clothes on when he visualizes. He's so hot, he even makes a long-married woman pant and remember those days when sex took precedence over sanity."

I giggled. "He forgets sometimes."

"Or maybe he knows how much *you* like to ogle that fantastic body." She nudged me and winked.

I grinned in remembrance. "That day in the men's dressing room, over there in the hotel basement? The first time I met Patrick? Jeez Louise. He'd just stepped out of the shower. Had a white towel thrown around his neck. All that naked muscle and dribbles of water crawling down that tanned skin..."

"You've mentioned that several times. If I didn't know better, Alice, I'd swear you were half in love with a ghost."

"Infatuated, maybe," I admitted. "Not in love, but a definite possibili-ty...infatuation. I've seen your eyes bug out when our friend appears, Twila. Ten seconds after you met Patrick at my house yesterday, you forgot he couldn't consume and offered him a Jack and Coke."

"Well..." she mused. "Maybe fifteen seconds. After I got my breathing under control and could think."

Miss Molly and Trucker accompanied us today. Those two animals from my menagerie see ghosts as well as Granny, Twila, and I do, and are always part of any trip Twila and I undertake. Granny Chisholm pet-sat my other cats, an occupation that pads her small pension. Miss Molly hates her leash, so I held her in my arms even though she wore that irritating encumbrance. Trucker sat obediently at Twila's feet, his leash loosely wrapped around her fingers.

"This place does look a lot like that hotel where that *thing* crawled in bed with you," Twila said. "Same architect, you said."

"Me? You were in that bed, too. But all you did was snore while that —that—that...whatever it was. Invisible entity, I guess. While it crawled straight up the bed between us. You didn't even feel the mattress sinking under its weight. Or hear the claws dragging across the bedspread. You just snored!"

"Until you slithered across the bed screaming to the high universe and woke me up."

"I'd like to see you *not* scream if something huge and hairy laid down against your back."

She muffled a giggle. "I'll give you this. I am glad it wasn't me." She snapped another picture. "Beautiful. Sometimes I do wish we could go back in time and experience these places."

It was so much grander in its prime, Patrick mentally thrust into my mind.

Twila's mind, also, I assumed, since she nodded and replied aloud, "Even in all its deterioration, I can see how glorious it once was. Now, are you finally going to tell us why you insisted we come here?"

In good time, Patrick said evasively. First you both need to get a sense of the place. As it is now

...and as it was.

Stubborn ghost. I'm not sure what gives certain ghosts the ability to intrigue Twila and me into these investigations concerning their long-ago deaths. Whatever, Patrick had that ability.

An older woman stepped through a door on the hotel's veranda, peering around as though looking for someone. Us, I assumed, since thanks to Katy's reporter friend, we had an exclusive on the building premises for a twenty-four-hour period, seven a.m. to seven a.m. I shifted Miss Molly and grabbed my satchel of snacks, drinks, and other ghosthunting paraphernalia from the sidewalk while Twila stuffed her camera back and zipped the case. Ready, we started across the street.

The stupid siren split the air and we jumped back onto the curb so fast I nearly lost my hold on Miss Molly, not to mention my bladder. Trucker hates sirens. He set up a howl that raised the hairs on the back of my neck worse than the precursory chill prior to an apparition's appearance, and Twila squatted beside him.

"Shush, Trucker. It's that nasty old deputy Katy's friend told us about."

It was. The SUV pulled over to the curb, and one of those typical cigar-chomping, beer-bellied good old boys emerged in full regalia. Tan trousers above spit-shined lizard boots, followed by a belly that would have defied gravity even more, had it not been for a wide black braided belt and a Western buckle with a longhorn steer holding it up. An extremely long-horned longhorn steer. The shirt ruined the effect, though. Dirty brown and covered in flashy red roses, white mother-of-pearl snaps, it looked like something that would draw scorn even in a backcountry icehouse where beer, pretzels, and microwave pizzas were the fare of the day.

I gaped in awe of the fact that even with the seat pushed all the way back, that mountain of flesh could fit behind the steering wheel. He even kept his Stetson in place while he drove, and right now he tilted the brim down even closer to his warty, red-veined nose.

"You little ladies headin' for the hotel?"

Trucker, raised with love rather than harsh discipline, and normally a mild-mannered Rottweiler, growled low. It amazed me at times that the dog sensed my dislike of certain people, even though I tried to remember my manners.

The cop zeroed in on my dog. "He had his shots? We got an ordinance 'bout that."

Twila bristled and laid a hand on Trucker's shining black head. "We *little ladies* always keep up our shots. Do you?"

The cop licked the side of his mouth as though searching for a missing cigar, but backed up a step. "Heard there was someone comin' here to the hotel today. You know we got proceedings in the works to condemn that place. You get hurt over there, the city ain't responsible."

"The hotel is privately owned," I said. "We understand the risks and are old enough to make our own decisions."

He glanced across the street, then back at us. "Just so's you know. Frankly, I can't see why anybody'd want to go in there. Place's been abandoned for thirty, forty years. Should've been tore down back then."

"With that sort of rationale," Twila said with a stern glare, "I suppose you think the Alamo has outlived its tenure. It's a lot older than this hotel."

" 'Course not!" he huffed. "The Alamo's a gen-yoo-wine piece of Texas history!"

Given the awe in his voice, I expected him to doff his Stetson and lay it across his chest. I suppressed a giggle and turned my back on him before I lost control. Mistake. Behind Twila, Patrick materialized in all his full, naked glory and thumbed his nose at the cop.

Twila sensed the ghost, too. Her brown eyes crinkled and I'd have been willing to bet that the wild imagination we shared was forming identical pictures in our minds: *the cop, astonished and determined to catch a streaker who dared violate his quiet town. A chase. Patrick deliberately slowing down until the cop reached out to grab him, then vanishing into thin air.*

I examined Twila's face, trying to detect whether the cop behind me could see Patrick, but I couldn't glean a clue. She just caught her lower lip between her teeth and stifled the laughter always so near the surface beneath her quiet demeanor—the demeanor she showed people besides close friends, anyway. Miss Molly took that moment of laxity in my hold to crawl up my shoulder and try to escape down my back, claws working seriously on her behalf. I yelped and dragged her free, capturing her front paws in a stern hold as I nestled her back in place.

"We're running late," I said, teeth clenched against the stings of pain on my shoulder.

"Yes," Twila agreed. She tightened her hold on Trucker's leash, nodded a curt dismissal at the cop, and started across the street. Patrick glided up beside her, offering a gentlemanly arm, which she accepted. She and the ghost strolled unhurriedly, Twila in her long paisley skirt and peasant blouse, white sandals, red hair shining in the warm sun; Patrick a solid six foot of tanned, blond male, his backside one of those yummy rumps I loved to gaze at when outlined in a pair of football jersey pants or faded, tight jeans.

I hadn't decided yet if Patrick looked better naked or in the tailored blue-and-white pinstriped suit he deigned to show himself in at times. I didn't mind one iota examining the ghost over and over again while I tried to make up my mind.

I could see Twila's grip on Patrick's forearm, anyway. The cop probably just saw Twila's arm in the air. Whatever. His entire attitude irked me, and I didn't give a diddly damn whether he saw Patrick or not. I headed after Twila, but halted when he said, "You could've had a nice welcome to town, you'd've let us know you were coming."

"Oh?" I asked. I hadn't told the town officials I was part of the last group, either, since I pretty much kept my ghosthunting separate from my writing life.

"You're that writer, ain't you? Alice Carpenter? Seen your picture on them book jackets."

"Yes," I admitted. "But I'm not here promoting one of my books."

"Too bad. Mayor would've made sure you had a better time than what you're in for over there. Hope you ain't afraid of ghosts. Been lots of stories regardin' strange happenings inside there since they closed down that there Springs Hotel."

"Ghosts?" I said with a straight face. "How fascinating!" *Afraid* of ghosts? If he only knew. "From what I've heard and read, there were also a lot of real-life strange happenings at that hotel when it was in operation."

"Now don't you go dredgin' up all them old half-truths and writin' about them," he insisted with a frown that pulled his warty nose down near his top lip. "Lots of folks are still alive here in town who wouldn't be too happy about that."

"Some of the original population from the stories are still around then, are they?"

He jammed his Stetson tighter onto his head. "Good day. I'd say y'all come back again, but I got a feelin' the sooner the two of you have your *tour* and get out of here, the sooner the mayor will breathe a sigh of relief."

A glimmer of consternation flickered in his eyes, as though he regretted his words. But before I could question him further, he slid his mountain of flesh back into the SUV. He'd left the motor running, and he dropped the vehicle in gear and swerved around the corner beside me with a squeal of tires.

"At least you didn't childishly fire off that stupid siren again," I called after the disappearing vehicle. In retaliation, as though he'd read my lips in his rearview mirror, he popped off the siren in a series of short bursts. Across the street, Trucker howled, and I snuggled Miss Molly close and headed for the hotel.

CHAPTER 3

"Awesome," Twila murmured. "You can almost see the ladies in their ball gowns, the men in their natty suits or white tuxedos. I'll bet there used to be a piano in that alcove over there."

We stood in the lobby. The next floor up, the mezzanine, only protruded over half the lobby, which left the ceiling above us soaring two floors overhead. The lobby itself encompassed the entire front of the block-long hotel and stretched away into shadows ahead of us. On either end, dark stairwells led to the mezzanine, and still brilliant green carpets with bright splotches of red flowers covered portions of the marble floor.

Across the lobby front, glass-filled doors and windows with foot-square panes separated the interior from the veranda, the panes grubby and dirt-encrusted. Only dribbles of light filtered in. Several brass ceiling fans hung from the ceiling, corroded and lacking the patina that would have given them more grace. A garland of foot-high wallpaper circled the room above the doors and windows and below the mezzanine railing. Despite decades of exposure to sunlight and cigarette-smoking guests, the faded scenes on it still bespoke elegance. As on my previous visit, I wished I knew more about the true names of all the exquisite décor, but my interior design and architectural knowledge consisted of whether something was, in my opinion, pretty or ugly.

Hallways beside each of the twin staircases led deeper into the bowels of the building. On my earlier expedition, a few of us had explored the ghost-infested former office space area along one hall and the guest arrival area down the other. At the far end of the latter lay the true entrance to the building, hidden from the street so the limousines could discharge guests in privacy.

Our lone guide, who'd introduced herself only as Carrie, wrung her hands and jittered back and forth from one foot to the other. She was a different tour guide than the one we'd had for the other group. Up closer, she wasn't nearly as old as she'd appeared from far away. I put her age at early sixties, well younger than Granny Chisholm.

"Ah...um...would you like to set your things down before we look around?" Carrie asked.

"That would be nice," Twila answered.

"I...um...the pets..."

"They'll stay with us," I said sternly.

"The cat. Well...um...cats need..."

I sighed and finished her sentence, "...litter. Yes, they do, and I've got a portable box for Miss Molly. Trucker will let us know when he has to go out. I've also got a pooper scooper."

She nodded and jittered off towards one of the stairwells. "Then, I'll...um...show you where you can set up a camping area. You...um...know there's no electricity. And only one bathroom works."

Twila drew in a deep breath. When our eyes met, her brown ones twinkled with suppressed laughter. I'm sure mine were full of irritation at Carrie's halting stutters of explanation. Twila always did have more patience than me.

The stairwell curved upward, a handrail on one side, a bare wall on the other. The steps were muted-red brick, still firm and un-crumbling after all this time. Probably handmade, I assumed. We emerged on the mezzanine level, where the same type carpet covered the floor, this time wall-to-wall rather than the large single pieces. Evidently a much cheaper blend of fibers, also, since worn areas indicated more heavily traveled paths and around the baseboards the carpet had frayed and torn. Whatever padding had once been in place must have worn down with the material. I detected hard floor beneath my footfalls.

Carrie kept moving, but Twila and I paused to examine our surroundings on this level. Below us was an unobstructed view of that gorgeous, shabby lobby. On the far side of the mezzanine set the check-in desk, the fine-quality wood still showing a muted gleam under a layer of dust. Message pigeon-holes lined the wall behind the desk, and a gigantic old cash register set to one side. Beyond the check-in area, a doorway opened to a dark hallway, down which I knew from my other visit lay our bathroom. A twelve-pack of toilet tissue lay by the door, and a line of paper trailed off into the darkness.

Patrick visualized in front of the check-in desk. This time he wore his clothing, the blue suit with wide lapels, white shirt with a darker blue tie, black and white spats on his feet. He didn't even glance at us. Instead, he haughtily drew himself up and pounded on a bell on the countertop. Before I could stop myself, I scanned the floor around Patrick's feet, searching for his luggage. Of course, he didn't carry any. When I glanced back at the counter, I expected to see a clerk scurrying up to pacify this impatient guest.

Instead, Carrie hurried up beside us. "Did you hear that?" she asked, staring across from us.

Wow, an entire sentence without an *ah* or *um,* I mused, then naughtily replied, "What? I didn't hear anything."

"The bell at the desk," Carrie insisted. "I...um...hear it every once in a while. But there isn't anyone over there to ring it!"

"We'll keep an ear out," I said, glancing around for Twila and Trucker. They stood over beside the elevators, and Twila was running her hand across the wall.

"Beautiful," she called to me. "You can still see the wonderful green enamel. I'm glad they didn't cover that up when they repainted."

"Don't get too close to that last elevator door," I warned. "It's partway open."

"It's not supposed to be!" Carrie said without a hint of stutter as she hastened over to the bank of three elevators and halted in front of the open one. The cages were protected by wide, crisscrossed brass, one of those contraptions that would fold in and out on itself when the door was opened or closed. Carrie pulled at the open-shut mechanism, but it refused to budge.

"I'll...um...have to call the handyman," she finally said. "We can't leave this open with you ladies here." She pulled a cell phone out of her skirt pocket and dialed while saying, "You two can go ahead into the...ah...camping area just down the hall." She pointed to her left, past the elevators.

I, for one, hurried to obey, since I wasn't too keen on standing there listening to her haltingly describe the situation to their...ah...handyman. I did look back at the check-in desk, but Patrick had evidently received the attention he demanded and checked in.

My satchel strap cut into my shoulder, and Miss Molly had that look on her face that told me her claws would show themselves again soon if she didn't get out of my arms. Most of the time she loves to be held and petted, but now that I thought of it, those times were always on her terms. Cats could be prissy that way.

Twila led Trucker into a large room, with me following. Twila gazed to our right in awe. Another wall of glass-paned doors encompassed the entire area on the right side of the room, which overlooked what could only have been a ballroom in its day. Below us stretched an area unencumbered by any furnishings, every bit as large as the lobby.

I set Miss Molly down, held tightly to her leash, and wandered over to look out the windows. I'm not afraid of heights, but the stark emptiness of the floor below gave the impression that we were higher above it than in reality, and I crept back, away from the windows.

Twila studied the rest of our camping area. A faded blue couch, which looked as though it would send up a cloud of dust if we dared sit on it, was placed against the far wall, an end table beside each lumpy arm. Another small end table was beside a rickety wooden chair nearby, and a Coleman lantern decorated the top of it. We dropped our satchels on the floor, and I rubbed my shoulder in relief.

"Well," I mused, "like I warned you, it's not the fanciest place we've ever visited."

"Oh, but it's so much more!" Twila gushed. "Can't you just see what it used to be like? How every guest was pampered and catered to? How delicious the meals must have been? Just imagine, Alice. Imagine it as it used to be, like Patrick said."

"Yes." Patrick visualized beside the rickety chair, blond hair slicked back and tailored suit accenting what lay beneath. "It was grand. Even at home, where I had a dozen servants at my beck and call, I didn't feel nearly as comfortable as here. At home there were always a slew of problems to take care of, business to attend to. Here, it was total relaxation. As Twila says, fantastic meals. The baths. Masseuses trained in the best schools available night or day. There was even a gymnasium on one of the floors above us, and a bowling alley in the basement. Utter, total freedom from worry and relaxation drew all of us here, in addition to the healthy mineral baths."

"Yeah," I muttered. "And it probably took a few hundred peons to make all that freedom and non-worry happen."

Carrie scurried back in and asked, "Are you settled? Oh...um..." She stared at Miss Molly by my feet and then the dark gray rug on the floor.

I rolled my eyes and knelt by my satchel to unpack, while Twila did the same. I set up Miss Molly's portable litter box and poured in the litter, sliding a glance at Carrie in time to see her nod in satisfaction. I carried the litter box over beside the couch and stuck it beneath one of the end tables. Miss Molly sniffed at the litter box, then turned her nose up.

"I know it's not as big as your box at home," I whispered so Carrie wouldn't hear. "But you damn well better use it if you need to go!" Then I sighed and added another ten bucks to the running tally in my head as Miss Molly stuck her tail straight up in the air and walked off with a subdued cat-growl of displeasure.

Carrie's cell phone rang, and I remembered my own phone in my purse and dug it out to turn it on. The battery indicator showed a full charge, but I knew that wouldn't last. The battery was well over two years old, and I kept forgetting to buy a new one. So I switched the phone off to conserve it. I had a charger in the car, but without electricity at our disposal here, I hadn't bothered to bring the in-house charger.

"Georgie, the handyman will be here...um...in a while," Carrie said, drawing our attention back to her. "He's a marvel with everything. He even...ah...has an electronics degree. But...ah...likes to work with his hands, too."

I noticed that she kept glancing at the rickety chair. Patrick sat on it now, legs crossed nonchalantly, his expression relaxed, eyes half-mast. I started to ask Carrie if she could see Patrick, then changed my mind. If she could see him, she might not want to mention it, fearful that a ghost's presence this early in the tour might send us packing—along with a request for a refund of our substantial prepaid fee.

"Oh," Carrie said. "Where did you...um...park?"

"The lot across the street," I replied, not mentioning that it was the same one I'd used before. For some reason, I didn't want to mention my previous trip to Carrie. "I didn't see anyone to pay, though."

Carrie chewed her lip. "I suppose that will be all right for now. However, there's a parking area behind the hotel that you'll...ah...need to move your car to before I leave. That lot's closed now."

"Whenever you say," I agreed.

"Then...um...we can see the outside grounds first, before we go into the...ah...basement. Before we come back in, I'll show you how to get to the back of the hotel to park. Is that...ah...all right?"

"Fine," Twila agreed.

"The...uh...animals?" she asked.

Miss Molly and Trucker clearly showed their intentions. Trucker sprawled on the floor with a sigh, and Miss Molly curled up next to him. I shrugged and left them there, although I would close the door to the room behind us to keep them in the camping room. No sense mistaking a roaming animal for something else while we toured.

CHAPTER 4

Satisfied with his manipulations thus far, Patrick O'Hara strolled through the door on the seventh-floor suite he always insisted upon during his tenures at the hotel. A private suite, as befitted his bachelor status; his family had their own space whenever they visited during the same period, on a separate floor.

He couldn't let the dismal disarray and erosion of the once-beautiful suite infiltrate his strict discipline on his emotions. Not now. Not with potential assistance in his quest forthcoming. He tried to block out the current condition of the room where he'd spent so many hours of bliss with her. Sitting at the small tea table, knees touching, gazes bespeaking desire and need while they carried on an innocuous conversation totally contradictory to the actual words in their minds...and hearts. Food on the table only a distraction for hands that yearned to touch each other. The phonograph in the corner a convenient prop, the records chosen by him to lure her into his arms to dance, her reluctance a social demeanor to cover her desire to be exactly there.

The loveseat in the corner, long gone now, their favorite place to sit when they abandoned the charade of hunger. Small, cozy, an excuse to be near each other, touch with the pretext of confined space.

Oh, it had been a posh room once, but the décor ruled secondary. She filled the atmosphere with beauty. Yes, her outward beauty. He'd never encountered another woman who could touch her exquisiteness in life...or since death. He admitted the outward beauty attracted his initial attention, but he fell in love with the inward person, the soul. His soul mate.

Soul mate. How often had he scoffed at that term. His male acquaintances also sneered at such a fallacy. Women were for sex, satisfaction, children-breeders when they found one who would do their own lineage and fortunes justice. Wives and mothers and servant supervisors after that. None of them had ever found a woman like her. Had they, Patrick knew without doubt they would have discovered themselves in the same predicament as he did: yearning to spend every moment of the rest of his life with this one woman by his side, her head on the pillow next to him every morning, her gaze meeting his and mirroring the shared love only found once in a lifetime. A home to rush to in the evenings after a long day of providing a sheltered, comfortable life for her. Children born of love, not genetic convenience.

It could have worked, damn it! It would have worked. He'd come to that decision at long last, been on his way back to her with the blessing she'd feared would never come.

Steeling himself, Patrick strode to the bedroom door. Since his death he'd perfected a few powers, powers others he met shared their knowledge of. Although he could easily glide through the barrier of the door, he halted instead. Fists clenched, he hid his reluctant fingers, shoved his hands behind his back. Stared at the barrier. Tried to block the memories that lay behind it.

The memories won. Slowly Patrick pulled his right hand free. Unclenched his fingers. Pointed the index finger at the doorknob while his other hand cramped with the power of the struggle within him.

The doorknob turned, the tumblers clicked. The door swung open...and Patrick closed his eyes. He couldn't look. Couldn't go in there.

Laughter barked behind him and Patrick whirled to face Antonio.

"Get the hell out of here!" Patrick ordered.

21

"Or you'll what?" Antonio sneered. Hands on black-trouser-clad hips, he swung his head to toss an ebony curl off his forehead and glared at Patrick with storm-cloud eyes. "You don't have enough power to keep me from anywhere I want to go."

"But the women I brought with me do," Patrick said. "You won't interfere this time."

"Those two?" Antonio's lips thinned in distaste. "I've seen them. I'll be glad to pit myself against them, should the need arise." He spit, a ghost glob that landed nonetheless near the toe of his silver-tipped black boot. "They are nothing to fear."

"Not even if one of them is as strong as a *curandero?* With powers over entities like us that rival a *hechicera?*" Patrick informed Antonio in a sly voice. The shock on the other ghost's face satisfied Patrick as he continued, "I've done my research—research you couldn't interfere with because you had no idea it was going on. I chose carefully before I gathered my comrades this time."

Antonio recovered his bluster and snarled, "They're nothing but a pair of psychic ghosthunters, like others who have been here before. They'll be as easy to fool and confuse as any of their kin."

"Are you so sure of that?" Patrick smiled with the pleasure of his newfound confidence in finally banishing Antonio's attempts to foil him. "Sure enough to confront them?"

"In my own good time," Antonio promised. "Are you so sure of their help that you can finally enter that room? Face the memories in there?"

Had he breath, Patrick would have drawn it in to shore up his mental fortitude. Instead, the force of memories tugged him and he glanced over his shoulder. He had at least found the fortitude to open the door this time. Yet to enter the space beyond...it yawned dark and full of reminiscences that waited to capture him, break him. To enter yet remained outside the realm of his strength.

With an effort, Patrick smoothed his features and turned back to Antonio. But the other ghost was gone.

CHAPTER 5

"I'll be leaving you an...ah...key for the front door," Carrie explained as she selected one from the ring in her hand. "Best do that before I...uh...forget."

She held out a single key on a chrome key ring toward me, but Twila stepped forward to grab it. She shot me a look that reminded me that she was well aware how keys had a way of coming up missing when I was in charge of them.

Carrie led us through the side door. Outside, I squinted in the bright light after the dimness and pulled my sunglasses from my sundry satchel. We were on a brick bridge lined with interesting pots that looked as though they had once held torches. Carrie started murmuring what I assumed was her canned tour speech, amazingly, without her infuriating, halting stammer: Yes, the owner had patterned this from a place in France he once saw, and she smirked—a canned smirk, if I read her right—as she told us that the owner set out right from the beginning to make his hotel a standard of one-upmanship on a famous hotel in Hot Springs, Arkansas.

"It's surely a lot taller," Twila mused, clicking away with her camera.

"Oh, then you've been to the other one?" Carrie exclaimed, and in response to Twila's assent, continued, "Then you can see how much grander our hotel used to be."

"But that other hotel's still in business," I pointed out.

"Ah...yes," Carrie agreed as we wandered into the swimming pool area. More canned speech on her part about how this was the first outside pool ever in Texas; how the owner had used that feature broadly in his advertisements. Caught up in the details even though I'd heard a lot of it before, I neglected my own camera until Twila nudged me and nodded at my chest.

"Didn't that backfire on him when the woman died in the pool?" I asked Carrie as I obediently snapped a couple pictures.

Carrie froze, then with an effort, turned to us, a bright, false grin stretching her mouth. "You've been hearing stories about the hotel, then?" No stutter there.

"They're all over the Internet," I replied. "Lots of interesting tales."

"Gossip!" Carrie insisted, but for a moment I thought I saw deep anger. "People spread lies and innuendoes about what they don't understand. If they would just listen to the truths..."

Twila was staring up the side of the building. She pointed her camera there, clicked off a frame, and asked, "Is that the window she came out of? It looks like the most likely one, for her to end up dead in the pool like she did. The stories vary. Some conclude that she was a prostitute, others the owner's mistress. Some say suicide, others murder. Would you know?"

Carrie huffed and said, "I really can't talk about stuff like that. I'm here to give you a building history, that's all."

Twila stifled a laugh when Carrie took off at a near trot, saying, "Let me show you where to park."

I thought for a minute Twila was laughing at Carrie, but she nudged me and pointed upwards again. In the window on the side of the building, seven stories up, Patrick leaned out and waved at us. *No, the window beside me,* he thrust into my mind.

Carrie jerked to a halt and slowly scanned the side of the building, up towards the window. But when I followed her gaze, I didn't see Patrick any longer.

"He dissolved," Twila confirmed in a whisper.

"I'd hate for your car to get towed," Carrie interrupted. "This way."

She led us around the building, through a short tunnel, and then up a steep rise to the guest arrival area, on the back of the building for privacy so the esteemed guests didn't have to contend with curious townspeople. Huge doors crossed the back of the building, which curved around on three sides of us. Here, too, vandals had been at work. Scattered broken windows, even completely missing panes and frames. Whoever the owner used as a caretaker didn't do a very good job, either, since there were trash and used buckets where valets and doormen used to greet the guests.

"—or it might not be here when you leave," Carrie was saying when I pulled myself out of the sadness for what had been.

"What might not be?" I asked.

"Our car," Twila answered. "Weren't you listening? The foundation beneath this drive isn't very sound. We'll have to park down in the tunnel."

"Good grief," I replied. "Should we be standing here?"

"For Pete's sake, Alice. We're not as heavy as a car. Or at least, I'm not."

Still, I was glad when Carrie hurried up to the ornate doors and stuck a key in a lock. It took her a few seconds; the door groaned in protest. She finally shoved a shoulder against the one on the right, got the door open and dusted off her hands.

"Close it behind us."

Twila complied as we reentered the building. For a moment I thought we'd walked from daylight into darkness until I jerked off my sunglasses. We were in a shadowed hallway, a pool of water on the floor. Carrie was already nearly out of sight, and we started after her. Twila pulled me to a stop and murmured, "Those aren't Carrie's tracks."

They weren't. Someone had walked through one of the puddles recently. Very recently. The still-clear tracks led down a different hallway than the one Carrie had taken. Twila dug out her flashlight and shone it on the footprints. Large. Men's. Looked like he wore a pair of leather-soled shoes.

"Someone else is in the building," I said.

"Maybe," Twila replied. "Ghosts don't usually leave footprints *that* clear, but it's possible."

"Yoo hoo, ladies!" Carrie called. "Georgie is here."

"The handyman," I said in a relieved voice. "Just the handyman."

Carrie waited for us at the far end of the lobby, at the foot of the second set of mezzanine stairs. As soon as she saw us, she hurried on up the stairwell, leaving us to follow. We did, a little faster than we normally would have, at least I did. Twila lagged behind some, gazing around her, but I wanted to get a look at that handyman.

Carrie and the man I assumed was Georgie, since he squatted by a battered toolbox at his feet, were over by the elevator. 'Course it could have been the bare half-butt that mooned me above his sagging blue jeans that identified the man. Didn't all handymen have that signature identification? He was a large man, dwarfing tiny Carrie even in his crouch. Had to weigh in at nearly three hundred, was my guess.

By the time Twila joined us, I was already sure. But I let her make her own examination of the bedraggled white tennis shoes on Georgie's feet.

Georgie rose with a flashlight in his hand, then peered through the half-open elevator doors and shone it down the shaft. "Uh oh," he muttered.

"What? What?" Carrie insisted. She pushed him aside, grabbed the flashlight from him and stuck her head inside the doors. Her scream echoed down the shaft, bounced off the bottom and returned to permeate the entire mezzanine around us before she collapsed in a heap on the tattered carpet.

Such a loud scream from that tiny body, I mused as Twila and I hurried over to our tour guide. For a few seconds, Georgie stood there shaking his head, muttering something about calling the cops. Then he clasped a hand over his mouth and nearly knocked us down as he beelined for the bathroom behind us.

CHAPTER 6

For a brief second, I wondered how Carrie could still scream when she lay unconscious. Then I realized Trucker's howls echoed from the camping room. Not only him. Miss Molly's eerie cat-screeches accompanied the dog. Torn between my pets and the unconscious woman, I hesitated until Twila nodded an indication for me to check on the animals while she knelt by Carrie.

"Bring back some water," Twila called as I raced toward the camping room.

I barely managed to slam the door shut before Trucker and Miss Molly could escape. Trucker woofed and scratched on the door, but I shouted "No!" as I grabbed one of the water bottles. The dog subsided reluctantly, his head swiveling back and forth from me to the closed door.

I had no idea what was down the elevator shaft—not really. But suspicion indicated something horrible. *Please. Not a dead body.*

Or maybe I verbalized the words, since Patrick visualized beside me and replied, "It is."

I caught myself just in time, right before I threw the water bottle straight at him. "Don't do that!" When he shrugged a *what?* I continued,

"Pop in like that when my nerves are on edge!" Then his words registered. "Oh, God, how do you know?"

"I was down in the men's dressing room a moment ago," he replied.

"Just tell me about the body." I headed for the door. "I've got to get back to Twila." He floated after me, and although I shut the door firmly in his face to keep my pets trapped, he came on through it.

"I wandered around near the elevator shaft," he went on. "It's right behind the kitchen. There's only half of her body visible, though."

The water bottle dropped from my nerveless fingers just as Twila reached for it. It hit Carrie on the forehead, but the unconscious woman didn't budge.

"Alice!" Twila chastised as she picked up the bottle. Then, to Patrick, "There's a woman cut in half in the basement? The elevator doors did that?"

Patrick nodded.

"But there's no electricity to run the elevators," I insisted, then gulped and clapped a hand over my mouth, barely restraining myself from scurrying after Georgie into the bathroom. He hadn't returned, though, and I didn't want to join him in there while we both emptied our stomachs.

"Get hold of yourself, Alice," Twila ordered as she unscrewed the top of the water bottle and poured a small stream on Carrie's forehead. She wiped the water off with her skirt hem. "Get your cell phone and call 9-1-1. Or...here." She grabbed Carrie's cell phone, which the poor woman dropped on the floor nearby. "Use this one. Get some help here."

I punched in "9" before my fingers froze.

"What?" Twila demanded as she patted Carrie's cheek, still trying to revive her. "Call!"

"What will I tell them?" I asked. "*We* haven't seen what's down that shaft. How am I going to explain that we know there's a dead body down there? Tell them a ghost told us?"

"Good point," Twila said. "Maybe you better look down there yourself."

"Like hell!"

"Then go get Georgie," she said logically.

I took a step, then shook my head. "It's dark in that bathroom."

"Take your flashlight!"

I hadn't noticed Patrick leave, but just then he glided out of the bathroom hallway and toward us. "He's not in there. He must have left the building."

"Or gone down into the basement to check on that body," I said, thinking frantically. "Go see, Patrick."

"Georgie took off to go puke just from seeing the body from up here," Twila said. "Why would he go closer to it?"

"I don't know!" I half screamed. "Quit being so logical. Go, Patrick!"

He dissolved and I punched in the emergency numbers with new resolve.

"What are you going to tell them?" Twila asked.

I held up a wait-a-minute finger, because the operator answered, "9-1-1. What's your emergency?"

"We're at the old hotel here in town," I answered. "Our tour guide just looked into one of the elevator shafts and screamed, then fainted dead away. We need an ambulance. We can't wake her up."

Computer keys clacked behind the operator's voice. "Carrie? Is Carrie Carter your tour guide?"

"Yes," I said, not understanding what difference that made.

"Your name?" she asked.

"Alice Carpenter. I'll let the ambulance crew in when they arrive. We've got a key."

"Is someone injured in the elevator shaft?" the operator asked.

"How the hell do I know?" I spat. "I'm not going to look down there and see what made her faint!"

"You'll have to," the operator insisted. "I need to know how many emergency personnel to send."

For a fleeting moment, I thought of handing the phone to Patrick to talk to her. *No go,* my mind told me. For one thing, Patrick hadn't returned from the basement. For another, how the heck would I explain who they'd talked to when the cops arrived.

"Look," the operator broke into my thoughts. "I've got an ambulance on the way. Do you need another crew and squad?"

"I—I—don't know!" I insisted.

Twila sighed and rose to her feet. She took the phone from me and said into it, "This is Twila Brown. I'm here with Alice and Carrie. Let me see if I can tell you what's down the shaft."

She handed me the phone again and retrieved her flashlight. Then she slipped her head through the partially open elevator doors and shone the light downward.

"Put the phone to my ear, Alice," she ordered.

I edged close to her, but kept as far away from that elevator shaft as I could and still stick the phone to her ear. Into the phone, Twila said, "There *is* someone down the shaft. I'm afraid she's dead. It appears the doors cut her in half."

I closed my eyes, but that didn't help me ignore the picture her words formed in my mind. When I realized I held one arm across my stomach, as though holding my own body together, I shuddered and leaned against the adjacent elevator door for a brief second...until it dawned on me that these damn doors weren't the safest things to prop a person up. I jerked away from the door and forced my eyes open while I gulped in a steadying breath.

Twila eventually emerged and nodded at me, then the phone I'd somehow managed to keep extended. "The operator wants someone to stay on the phone with her until the ambulance gets here. And the police now, of course. I'm going down to unlock the front door."

"Not alone, you're not!" I tagged right after her—after I dropped the cell phone as if it had grown a disease. Let the operator try to wake up Carrie for someone to stay on the line with her. They appeared to know each other.

"You're the one who doesn't want to stay alone," Twila said with a smirk as we hurried down the stairwell. "What about Carrie?"

"She's dead to the world," I answered, and regretted my word choice immediately. "She won't be afraid. Uh...she *is* just unconscious, isn't she?"

"As far as I can tell. She's breathing well, but she just won't wake up."

Given Twila's medical training, I gladly accepted her diagnosis. In the distance, sirens wailed, and she unlocked the front door.

"Uh..." I began. "Uh...what...?"

"You don't want to know what I saw down that shaft," Twila finished for me as she drew the door open. "You're not good with blood."

"Oh, God," I breathed.

"But there was something very strange," Twila mused as the ambulance squad pulled up in the street outside the hotel. The siren died—darn that word!—but the lights still swirled.

"What?" I asked, although I really only wanted to blot everything out of my mind. She was *so* right. My stomach often lurched at just the thought of blood, let alone having to smell or see it. I even got queasy when I wrote about it.

"I'll have to tell you later," she answered *sotto voce* as two emergency techs raced up the steps toward us.

Then that police SUV pulled in right behind the ambulance. "Shit," I whispered as the door opened and I recognized the cop who'd irritated us earlier.

"Trip kitty," Twila murmured, and despite my inner insistence that I had a right to curse in this dire situation, the mental tally for the trip kitty climbed higher.

A few minutes later, the medics struggled down the narrow stairway with Carrie on a stretcher, still unconscious. The big-bellied cop eyed Twila and me as we stood in the camping room doorway, each controlling an animal. Twila kept a firm hold on Trucker's collar and I'd resorted to allowing Miss Molly back on the floor, her own leash snapped firmly into the metal loop of her detested harness. The cat did her best to derail me by winding back and forth between my legs, snarling the leash tight.

"I wonder why they can't wake Carrie up?" Twila mused as the cop turned his back on us and said something unintelligible into a handheld radio. "People usually recover from a simple faint fairly quickly."

"Who knows?" I replied as I shook my foot to try to free my ankle from a leash twist and nearly fell on my butt. "Miss Molly! If you don't sit still, I'm going to put you in my satchel and zip it!"

The cop slowly strolled toward us—his pace perhaps an attempt to keep his belly from jiggling. The frown on his face, however, proved a deterrent to any jibes.

"Don't think I got your name earlier," he said to Twila.

"I don't recall you introducing yourself, either," Twila shot back at him. "And shouldn't you be investigating what's down that elevator shaft?"

His frown deepened, and he jammed the radio into his shirt pocket before he pulled out one of those spiral notebooks and flipped it open. "I ain't got time for pleasantries," the cop said. "But I'm Deputy Rover. You?"

Oh, sweet Universe! If he'd said Deputy Dawg, I wouldn't have turned around that fast to hide my near-hysterical chuckles. Under cover of disentangling the cat, I listened to Twila answer him. My hands trembled, an indication there had to be something taking place here that my psychic subconscious was dealing with, hiding until it sprang the reality on me without warning. I never fell apart like this in a crisis, and I'd dealt with my share of bodies, both corporeal and non-corporeal. Something about this situation had me on edge, though, and I couldn't help but wonder if I was picking up a broadcast to me from Twila's psychic senses. Something to do with whatever she was holding back to tell me later.

"Would you like my rank and social security number, too?" Twila said sweetly.

I puzzled over Twila's dislike of the cop for a second. Normally the more tolerant of the two of us, it wasn't like her to be so openly animistic, especially to a policeman. I was the one who usually got us into trouble law-wise.

"You in the service?" Deputy Dawg...uh...Rover asked.

Twila fluffed her hair with her fingers. "Why, thank you, Deputy Duh...Rover. I'm a bit past the age of enlistment, but it's nice of you to notice that I carry my age well."

"I didn't mean...uh...just answer my questions!" he sputtered. "My bein' first officer on the scene means my partners are gonna expect me to've gotten some prelim info when they get here. 'Specially our detective."

"You only have one detective on the force?" I asked in astonishment.

"Small town," he shot back nonchalantly. "Don't have no need for more'n one." A reconsidering look crossed his pudgy face. "Leastways, we ain't 'til today."

Miss Molly dug her claws into the carpet and lunged toward the inner room, and I sighed with frustration and tightened my hold more firmly on her leash.

"You better let her go, Alice," Twila said.

"There's no telling where she'll take off to," I said. "I can't just let her loose. Not with a dead body in the house."

"Only as far as the litter box," Twila insisted.

"Oh," I replied in understanding. Miss Molly hunched her back and squatted, and I gasped as I grabbed her and trotted across the room, where I shoved her inside the litter box. Her cat-voice hiss-merowled in relief.

Even from on the far side of the camping room I could hear new footsteps clump up the stairwell. Two more uniformed policemen joined Deputy Dawg...Rover. One of them definitely caught my eye. Twila's, too, I realized when we shared glances and I recognized the deep appreciation on her face.

One man had to be the police chief, since he wore a spic and span, neatly pressed uniform with a badge clipped to the belt circling his waist. A uniform tailored exactly for him. It fit just so, the shirt angling from a set of shoulders to drool on, the buttons running down his chest and drawing attention to his flat stomach, the trousers tightened just enough to show off his yummy rump and athletic legs. His face fit the rest of him perfectly, I realized, when his George Clooney–eyes scanned both Twila and me with appreciation.

"Ladies," he murmured. "I'm Chief Tyler Grandberg. Ty, to y'all. I hope you're not too upset over all this. Would you care to sit down while my deputy updates Detective Peters and me?"

I swooned in obedience and dropped to the blue couch with a sigh amidst the anticipated cloud of dust. Mentally cursed that ten pounds I wished like heck I'd lost last month during yet another failed diet attempt. Hoped the chief didn't notice.

Twila wandered over to join me. She barely avoided a tumble over the rickety chair, since she kept glancing back. She sank down beside me with more grace than I'd managed and whispered, "I loved *Oh, Brother*."

"I thought he should have gotten what he deserved," Patrick said in a grumpy voice when he materialized beside the couch, hands propped on slender hips and once again as naked as the day he came out of that men's room shower.

"When do you watch movies?" I asked Patrick.

"I have to do something to pass the time," he replied. "And I don't have to buy a ticket."

"Oh, lord." Twila fanned herself with her hand. "Two gorgeous men at once. Be still, my libido." Patrick shot her a mollified grin.

Beyond the open camping room doorway, the chief, detective, and deputy had their heads together beside the elevator. The detective pulled away from the group and strode toward the stairwell. Deputy Rover rather reluctantly tagged after him.

"I guess they must be going down to the basement," Twila said.

"Probably." I kept my gaze on the chief. Well, mostly on that fabulous rump as he squatted and played his flashlight beam around on the floor outside the elevator shaft. "I suppose our tour is over now. Gosh darn it, I wanted you to see this place!"

She arched an eyebrow.

"Not that a dead person isn't more important than a ghosthunt," I hastily reassured her, although she sniffed a delicate snort of disbelief at my defense. Sometimes someone can just know you too darned well!

Grandberg rose with one lithe motion and came towards us. Although I kept my gaze on him, in the corner of my eye, I noticed

Patrick dissolve. The chief glanced at the litter box when Miss Molly emerged and scratched the plastic front of it.

"She always does that," I explained. "Most cats scratch around inside. Mine has to be different."

"Beautiful cat," he said with a grin that lifted one side of his delicious mouth. "Even if she is sort of backwards."

I sighed a smile at him as he stuck his fingertips into his back trouser pockets, his stance drawing that fitted shirt closer to his yummy tummy and thrusting his pelvis forward a bit.

"I understand you two ladies are psychics," he said.

"Why, yes, we are," Twila replied. "How did you know?"

"Ms. Gueydan from Jefferson is a...friend of mine," he explained.

Oh, great, I thought. Another one of Katy's past romances.

"And," he directed to me, "I've heard you're quite a detective yourself. Ran across Jack Roucheau at a conference a while back, and he admitted that you were the one who cleared Katy of that murder rap."

"It was my belief in Katy as much as anything else," I replied. "There was no way she could kill someone. She hesitates to even call an exterminator."

"I suppose you both know that I'll have to take your statements before you can leave."

Twila and I nodded in unison. He smiled at us and strolled back toward the elevators.

CHAPTER 7

"What were you going to tell me?" I asked Twila as soon as we were alone.

She hesitated, then picked up Miss Molly, settled the cat on her lap and stroked her head. "The woman in the elevator. It's weird. She..." Her brown eyes met mine and she frowned. "She wore a dress like the flappers back in the Twenties. And had bobbed hair. You know, that style fashionable then? And long strings of pearls around her neck."

"You're telling me that that elevator shaft cut one of the ghosts here in the hotel in half? That's impossible, my dear."

"Absolutely impossible," she agreed. "All the blood and gore didn't come from a spectral body."

I swallowed my rising gorge again. "I don't want to hear about that part of it! Or see it!"

"I guess you'll have to show me how to use your laptop then."

"Why?" I asked. Twila adamantly refuses to touch a computer. "You always make me download the pictures from your own digital camera because—" Stunned, I sank back into the couch. "Twila! You didn't! You took a picture while you were looking down that shaft and talking to the emergency operator!"

"Several," she admitted with a sly grin. "Remember? You showed me how to use that movie feature, so we could try to catch floating spirit orbs."

I had, I realized. We both saw plenty of spirit orbs—which were a subject of much debate among ghosthunters—with the naked eye. And we loved to capture them on film. But my mind digressed. Taking unauthorized pictures of a crime scene victim was a definite no-no. I glanced at the camera hanging around Twila's neck and grinned. "I'm a bad influence on you."

"Then you'll download the pictures for me?"

"Hell, no!" I savagely shook my head. "But I'll show you how...and how to print them out."

"Without ever looking at the screen, huh?" she teased as she set Miss Molly aside, rose and walked over to her satchel. "Here." She pulled out a small cooler and lifted the lid to expose a bottle of Crown Royal and several cans of soda pop. "I know we don't usually indulge on hunts, but given this building's reputation, I thought we might have to bend that rule this trip. A drink or two later will soothe your nerves so we can check the pictures."

Nodding, I mused, "We'll probably have to find a motel room nearby to do that. As soon as Ty gets our statements, we'll be outta here."

"Maybe not," she said. "He seemed awfully interested in our psychic abilities. I wonder if he's one of those cops who believes in allowing psychics to assist in an investigation."

"Are you picking up anything?" I asked.

"Lots of confusion. As you said, this place is very active...or it seemed to be while we were checking it out from across the street. But can't you feel? It's totally dead now. Except for Patrick, of course."

I tilted my head and let my mind roam as I replied, "*Dead* is a good word. There's a heck of a lot of space around us, though. Could be that anybody here is staying behind the veil." Another thought dawned, and I started to continue, but Twila simultaneously said, "What about the soul of the murdered woman?"

Twila stared at me grimly, undoubtedly sharing my same memories.

The last trip she'd made to Texas was after my plea for help when Katy was accused of murder. Then we'd had another recently departed soul to deal with—a man who died unexpectedly and violently. A ghost who stirred up consistent havoc while he searched for a missing part of his body—his head. Nearly all ghosthunters believed that at times the souls of people who died violently or unexpectedly resulted in some of the ghosts we chased. Logically, it would follow that this dead woman's soul might still be haunting the hotel, rather than crossing through the light.

"Bucky's *head* was missing, though," I pondered. "This woman's body is all there, isn't it? Patrick said the lower torso was in the basement, beside the elevator shaft that cut her in two. You said her upper body was inside the shaft. And many times souls do cross on through the light, even after a violent death."

"True," Twila agreed. "Still, I have a strong sense that she's still around, just not ready to communicate yet. And I can't get over the fact that she's dressed like a flapper. Why would she be roaming around here like that? It doesn't make sense. It's not Halloween."

"Maybe there's a costume ball in town or something. We can ask Ty."

"Unless he's the same type cop as Jack," she said. "One who refuses to give out any information to civilians while he's involved in an investigation."

I sighed in accord. On reflection, I'd realized that Jack's job as a detective involved in high-profile crimes in New Orleans, where we'd met, was part of the reason for our marriage deterioration. He wouldn't —mostly couldn't—share his thoughts with me. His distance led me to fill my time with my own work, writing and ghosthunting. The separation grew until when we actually were together, we didn't have much to share. Too much time passed in between. I wanted someone to share the excitement with while it was fresh and real. Jack wanted to zone out and totally relax following an especially difficult and emotional case. After our divorce, Jack quit his job in New Orleans and moved to a smaller town, Longview, Texas, but even though we remained supposed friends, we never overcame our past problems enough to see if the differences in our new lifestyles would matter in our relationship.

"I rather wish Jack was here," I said. "Given his past experience, I'll bet he could look into this murder a lot better than these small-town cops."

"You can't be sure of that, Alice. We have no idea how good a cop Ty is. Or his detective. Besides, even though Jack was forced to admit that ghosts were real during that murder investigation at Esprit d'Chêne..."

"...he wouldn't be at all happy about getting involved in another investigation connected to ghosts," I completed. "Jack's still pissed that Sir Gary forced him to swallow his disbelief in ghosts."

"Um hum," she agreed, then giggled, despite the seriousness of the situation. "Can't you just imagine Jack if Patrick appeared to him in his birthday suit?"

I groaned. "Let's don't go there. Anyhow, one of the reasons we're here is our promise to Patrick...although he won't tell us exactly what it was we promised. I hate to disappoint him, but we're not going to be much help now."

"Not if you two just sit here chattering!" Patrick materialized once again, hands on those naked hips.

Before I could say a word, Twila erupted in one of her rare fits of temper. "Maybe if you'd deign to appear with clothes on, we could think rationally! If you were like this in life, I'll bet feminine confusion followed you all the time! I'm beginning to believe that you were a narcissist! Still are one!"

Just before Patrick dissolved, a quick grin lifted his beautiful lips. He wasn't suitably chastised by Twila's rebuke, and something told me this new-sprung irritant between the two of them foretold trouble. Twila's belief in disciplining ghosts didn't bode well for Patrick if he continued to annoy her. Plus her flash of temper, when she hadn't seemed overly concerned with Patrick's nudity until now, bothered me. Maybe what she'd seen down that elevator shaft was, in turn, tormenting her more than she let on. Oh, lord, Twila was my stability in situations like this. Maybe we should retreat with or without valor from this predicament, even though it would gall me when Jack found out.

Twila's hand trembled when she cuddled Miss Molly closer and stroked her, and that fired my determination to get out of here for now. Maybe permanently. No long-past mystery or even recent death that could be capably handled by the local police was worth shaking Twila up.

Patrick materialized again, this time wearing his clothing, but when I glanced at Twila to gauge her reaction, she didn't look a bit mollified. Indeed, when Patrick floated towards the couch to sit beside her, Miss Molly hissed at him. Given the fact that my cat had, until now, accepted Patrick's presence without problem, Miss Molly was either picking up on Twila's ire or beginning to have her own doubts about Patrick's association with us. Recalling that at Esprit d'Chêne, Sir Gary had tried to manipulate me more than once—until Twila showed up on the scene—I stayed quiet and let my more adept partner handle this for now.

Twila held up a forestalling hand before Patrick got to the couch. "I've had quite enough of your vagueness," she said. "I have no idea until we talk to the police further if we'll even be allowed to hang around here. But if we do, and if you continue to treat us like women without brains enough to digest more than bits and pieces of the information you want to dribble out as it suits your purpose, then you're shit out of luck. I'd love to see more of this old place before it falls to the wrecking ball, but Alice and I have dozens of other spots we can visit while I'm here. You can wander around in your own realm until you find different suckers to listen to your supposed tale of woe."

"Well!" Patrick said with a huff. "Maybe that would be best! Or maybe it would be better if I just dealt with Alice. Things were proceeding well until you appeared on the scene!"

I gasped, so furious I couldn't get a word out...except three. "Sic him, Trucker!" I spat.

A deep growl erupted, and Trucker leapt for Patrick without hesitation. The terrified look on Patrick's face was priceless, even though Trucker lunged straight through the ghost. The dog landed on all fours, but swiftly turned and gathered himself again.

"Stay, Trucker," I said. He obeyed, but his upper lip drew back to expose glistening fangs and a rumble continued in his chest.

Patrick dissolved in the blink of an eye, just as Twila screamed, "No!" and threw herself off the couch toward Trucker. She grabbed him and even though the dog weighed more than her, her impetus tumbled both of them into a corner. I gazed around wildly and spotted Grandberg in the doorway. His shirt gaped open to expose a shoulder holster, and he crouched in a shooter's stance, the deadly automatic aimed at my dog.

"No!" I echoed. "Put that damn gun—"

Miss Molly took care of it. In a flash, she streaked across the floor, around Grandberg's legs and up his back. Her claws raked his face, and he jerked in reaction, yelped in pain. The pistol exploded and Grandberg dropped it to grab at the hissing, snarling cat as a shower of Sheetrock chunks and dust from the ceiling covered both of them.

I lunged for my cat, enough sense remaining to kick that damned pistol toward Twila as I rescued Miss Molly before Grandberg could hurt her. Miss Molly met me partway, leaping into my arms and mewling piteously as she looked over my shoulder at her friends Trucker and Twila. Cat in arm, I scurried backwards. I could barely stifle my stab of satisfaction when Grandberg jerked a handkerchief out of his back pocket and covered the streams of blood on his left cheek. All the while, though, he glared at us with murderous rage. Damn, was every good-looking man associated with this mess a Jekyl and Hyde? Or had this one for some purpose initially used his charm to disarm us?

The pistol lay in a corner, behind Trucker. I helped Twila to her feet, and she stood beside me, shielding the dog. Quietly, she whispered, "Can they arrest an animal for attacking a cop?"

Wide-eyed, I stared at her and gulped down the first bubble of hysteria. The second one burst free, and Twila's half-sobs, half-giggles immediately joined it. I kept a wary gaze on Grandberg as we both sank to the floor and huddled together in front of Trucker, Miss Molly protectively between us. Both of us struggled to breathe through the shudders and gasps.

"What the hell was going on in here?" Grandberg demanded. "I thought that dog had gone rogue and was attacking you!"

"You didn't think," Twila snarled through gritted teeth. "You just reacted! I'd sure as hell hate to be an innocent bystander in a shootout where you were involved!"

"That dog was crouched for attack," Grandberg blustered. "And you were right in the line of it."

"He was attacking a ghost," Twila shot back. "And he did his job. The ghost's outta here now."

"A...?" He rolled his eyes. "Toss that pistol back over here."

"Come and get it," I snapped.

He took a step forward, and Miss Molly scuttled out of my hold. She stalked around our huddle and stopped in front of the pistol, back arched and tail twitching, blue eyes daring the cop closer. Grandberg reached for the radio on his belt. But before he removed it, he shook his head and collapsed back against the doorjamb, shoulders heaving with laughter.

"I'm sorry," he said after a moment. "You're right. I should've at least tried to figure out what was happening before I grabbed my gun. But this place puts everyone on edge, even without having to deal with a murder. And I didn't see any ghost here."

Neither Twila nor I were about to accept his quick change of attitude that easily. We both rose again, arms steadying each other, gazes wary. "You see ghosts, then?" Twila asked.

"Yeah, sometimes." He shrugged. "We've had lots of calls to this place since I've been chief. Most of the force thinks they're all bullshit, but...well...I've seen a thing or two."

"Are you going to arrest my cat?" I asked.

He chuckled, but this time the laughter died short of his eyes. "No. It was self-defense on her part. Or defense of her friend, anyway," he explained disarmingly. "I humbly apologize. I'm sure you ladies aren't in the best frame of mind, either, given what's happened. Especially if one of the hotel ghosts is giving you problems on top of everything else."

I still didn't trust the man. But I had to admit that he was right about one thing. My mind was a chaotic mess right now, filled with lingering fear for my pets and the aftermath of Patrick's attempt to come between Twila and me. Not to mention the fact that I was starting to believe we'd made a huge mistake coming here. Writing about murder was one thing, but being involved in one like the Esprit d'Chêne case...You could distance yourself from murder on a printed page.

"Let's go home, Twila," I said.

She nodded and we both began gathering up our belongings.

"Uh..." Grandberg walked a little further into the room. "I completely understand how you feel, but I do need to get your statements."

"You can get them somewhere besides here," Twila replied. "We're leaving."

"I'm afraid I can't let you do that," Ty said mildly. This time he removed his radio and spoke into it. "Where are you?"

"Right here." Detective Peters strolled through the doorway, pistol drawn.

"What on earth do you think you're doing?" I asked with a gasp.

"You two were in the building at the time of this murder," Ty said. "We have to question you."

"We're suspects in that woman's death?" I shook my head in denial. "That's about the most stupid thing you've said or done since you got here!"

"Maybe," Grandberg mused. "But that's the way I conduct my investigations. I consider everybody a suspect until I'm proven different."

"So you don't believe in innocent until proven guilty!" I shot back.

"Nope."

CHAPTER 8

"Look," I backpedaled, suiting my actions to words as I edged toward the couch before my shaky legs dissolved. I'd never realized how horrendous being accused of a crime could be, let alone staring down the barrel of a gun. "We'll cooperate. We'll be glad to give you our statements whenever or wherever you want."

Twila remained defiant for a few seconds, but after she stared at Peters' pistol, she fissured and drew in a quaking breath before she joined me on the couch.

"Call your animals over," Grandberg ordered.

"Tr—" I swallowed and continued, "Trucker, come. Miss Molly, you, too." Thank goodness both animals obeyed without hesitation. Trucker sat at my feet but with ears alert. Miss Molly leapt onto Twila's lap.

Twila lowered her head and whispered, "Call Jack," as she stroked the cat. "Now."

"I'd sooner go to jail," I gritted.

Her head shot up and she narrowed her eyes.

"Well, maybe not," I admitted as Grandberg strolled across the room and retrieved his pistol. I breathed a sigh of relief when he re-holstered it and nodded at Peters to do the same.

"I want to make a phone call," I said.

"Oh?" Grandberg asked with a quirked eyebrow. "To whom?"

"Our attorney," Twila said before I could stop her. Good God, didn't she know that a request for an attorney was the one thing that would seal our guilt in the cops' minds?

"If that's what you want, you can do that from the station house," Grandberg said flatly.

"No!" I said to Twila. "The animals. Trucker and Miss Molly!"

"That's right," Grandberg said with a sneer. "They'll have to go to the pound until you get out to spring them. *If* you get out in time. They only hold animals for twenty-four hours at our pound. Not enough room to keep them any longer."

"I...I didn't think," Twila said. Her eyes filled with tears and she gazed forlornly at me and cuddled Miss Molly protectively.

"We'll think about answering your questions without an attorney," I told Grandberg. "But I do want to make a phone call first. A private one."

His eyes flickered around the room. "I don't guess there's any chance of you two leaving here from this place. Okay. Make your call. But Peters and I will be right outside the door."

"That son of a bitch," Twila spat as soon as the two cops left the room. "Somehow he's going to pay for this."

Patrick materialized briefly and said, "Despite our differences, I'll be glad to help you out. I've got my own reasons, though. I'll be around." He dispersed again.

"I suppose Patrick will expect us to apologize to him," Twila said with a sad lift of her lips. "But Trucker and Miss Molly come first. Call Jack."

I grabbed my cell phone from my satchel and hurriedly punched it on. Then realized I hadn't pushed the darn button hard enough to disconnect it earlier. The battery still indicated a partial charge, but it would discharge quite a bit as I used it. Hopefully I could at least get the call in. The signal strength gave me much more pause.

"I need to get close to the window," I told Twila. I rose and sidled

45

over there while Twila cast a worried glance at the doorway. But neither of the cops reappeared.

"I'm buying you a new damn phone as soon as we can get to the store," Twila muttered.

I punched in Jack's number...all but the last digit. Damn, I hated to call him.

"Do it, Alice!" Twila ordered.

I hit the last digit and then send. I wasn't sure whether I was glad that Jack answered after the first ring or not.

"Hey, *Chère*," he said. Caller ID on his end, too, and he continued to use his pet name for me, despite the divorce. "Enjoying yourself?"

"We were...until the local cops decided to question us on suspicion of murder," I replied.

Dead silence met my ears until I was ready to check the phone to determine if I'd been disconnected.

"Jack, please," I said into the silence. "I need someone to come take care of Trucker and Miss Molly."

"Your dog and cat?" he asked in astonishment. "You're being questioned for murder, and you're worried about Trucker and Miss Molly?"

"They want to put them in the pound!" I shouted.

His voice changed into what I'd always considered his official cop one. "Are you at the hotel or the station house?"

"Hotel, right now," I replied. "But I think we're headed for the police station."

"Is that bastard Ty Grandberg there?"

"Uh...yeah, he's outside the room. I thought he was a friend of yours."

"If he said that, he's the biggest liar in Texas and Louisiana," Jack growled. "Put him on the phone." Just then my low-battery beep sounded, and Jack continued before I could say another word, "I'm gonna buy you a new damn phone as soon as we can get to the store, Alice! I'll be there within three hours. Until then, keep your mouth shut and don't trust Grandberg one in—"

"Inch," I finished into the dead phone, assuming that's what Jack meant. "He'll be here in three hours, Twila. He said—"

I bit off my words as Grandberg strolled back into the room and said, "Are you two ladies ready to go?"

"I'm not letting you put my animals in the pound!" I insisted. "If you try, I'll...I'll..." Instantly a vision of Grandberg when he'd nearly shot Trucker appeared in my mind. That shirt open to expose his shoulder holster. That..."I'll place a voodoo curse on your dick that will make it useless for anything except a water spout!" I spewed.

Grandberg's face blanched, and he staggered back a step, guarded gaze on Twila and me. "You're bluffing."

Twila casually lifted her hands, index fingers raised. Slowly she tilted her extended fingers towards each other. Just before they met in the form of a cross, Grandberg ducked back out the door and slammed it behind him.

"You saw that *gris gris* bag around his neck, too, huh?" Twila asked me as she lowered her hands.

"Yeah. But neither one of us know any voodoo."

"I do," she said. "A little, anyway. I learned it from Cat Dancer, Uncle Clarence's love, when we used to visit her in New Orleans. The times when you went out visiting friends and she and I were alone."

"Good," I said. The first real smile, since all this commotion, tilted my lips. "Maybe you should go ahead and use it anyway."

"I might," she said with a nod. "If necessary. But you know how it is with black magic like voodoo. *Three times three come back on thee.*"

"We're in enough trouble without antagonizing the Universe," I agreed.

The door crept open again, and Grandberg blustered back in. Twila's fingers twitched and his gaze zapped to her hands. She worked her fingers back and forth as though relaxing them...or preparing them.

"We've got two choices," he said. "You two and the animals can stay locked in this room until your lawyer shows up, or we can go on down to the station house—"

"Not without my animals," I cut in.

"No. No, no," he said in a placating tone. "We'll let you take both of them with you. And I'd suggest that you choose the station house. We've got a restroom there. If you stay here, we'll have to lock the door."

I swear sometimes my bladder has a mind of its own. Until that second, I hadn't even thought about having to use the bathroom, but now necessity clamored.

"For God's sake," Twila said. "Let's just get this over with. We didn't kill that woman. She was probably dead before we even got here!"

"We won't know that until after the coroner's report," Grandberg said. "But if you're ready to

go...?"

We both picked up a leash and Twila secured Miss Molly this time while I snapped Trucker's on him. Then we started gathering up our supplies again.

"Sorry," Grandberg said. "You'll have to leave your stuff there so my men can search it. It's part of a crime scene."

Twila whirled on him with an angry glare, but when she started to raise her hands, I grabbed them and thrust them back at her sides.

"The more you antagonize him at this point, the harder it's going to be on us," I hissed. "Like you said a minute ago, let's just get it over with. Jack will be here soon."

Reluctantly, she acquiesced and picked up Miss Molly. She strode out of the room without a glance at Grandberg. Trucker balked for a moment, but when I ordered him to heel, he obeyed. In the mezzanine, Twila was already disappearing down the stairwell. Grandberg followed me. In the lobby, Twila disappeared out the door and hurried down the front steps, toward a police cruiser beside the curb, rear door open, lights flashing. Another car waited behind it, the SUV Deputy Rover drove.

Detective Peters replaced the radio mike on the console and slid out of the cruiser's passenger door. I glimpsed another cop behind the wheel as Peters assisted Twila into the back of the cruiser. "Watch your head," he said as he helped her duck inside, the same thing I'd heard dozens of cops say on TV. Then he slammed the door behind her.

"Crime techs are on the way," Peters said with a nod at Ty. "I'll wait for them."

Grandberg grabbed my arm and steered me toward Rover's SUV. "What...what are you doing?" I demanded. "I'm going with Twila!"

"You have to be separated for questioning," he said, that sneer on his face again.

Trucker growled, and Grandberg halted abruptly. He and I played Mexican standoff for about three seconds, but he'd already won. My dog meant more to me than my dignity or being with Twila, and I had no doubt Grandberg would cause me every bit of worry that he could over Trucker if I gave him any further trouble.

"In, Trucker," I murmured. Grandberg slammed the door after us.

I examined the SUV interior, but already knew that I was in a vehicle without any inside door handles. I'd ridden in similar cruisers when Jack or one of his buddies helped me with book research. The steel grate between the front and backseat was the same. Not that I was going to try to escape. I settled back, agreeing with Twila. One way or another, that son of a bitch Grandberg would get his comeuppance for treating Twila and me like common criminals! While we drove down the small-town streets, I mentally tallied up the money I owed the trip kitty as a different focus for my fuming mind.

CHAPTER 9

Sometimes my mouth tends to get me in worse trouble, but after we arrived at the police station, it just slipped out. "Why separate Twila and me after we've already had a chance to talk?" I asked Grandberg.

Guilt flickered across his face—in those eyes that oozed charm when it suited him. Years of research and writing about murder made me well aware of the blunder, let alone living with a homicide cop, not to mention all the cop shows on television these days. Grandberg shouldn't have allowed Twila and me even a short time alone at the hotel. For a moment I chastised my inner smirk at his lapse in crime techniques. After all, he didn't have big-city resources to draw on. Perhaps he'd done the best he could with what he had in the face of such a grisly crime.

Then he grumpily explained that Twila was already undergoing questioning, and guided Trucker and me into a room on the right. He closed the door and sat across the table from me, arms crossed, face stiff with resentment. My teeth clenched and any stir of sympathy directed itself to the victim. She deserved a competent investigation of her murder.

And no doubt it was murder. She wouldn't have—couldn't have—

closed those elevator doors on herself. Yet...Carrie insisted the electricity was still off in the building, as it had been when I went there a few weeks earlier. Didn't elevators run on electricity?

"Just because you're somebody famous, don't think you can get out of cooperating here," Grandberg said. "The law applies to everybody."

Try to tell that to O.J, I fumed inwardly. Not that my own claim to fame in any way rivaled O.J.'s. I figured at least a few thousand less people had read my books than watched the famous trial. My royalty statements proved that. Temper brewed too close to the surface still, though. I didn't dare blurt out what I thought of his snarly comment, not with my own liberty and that of my pets at risk, let alone what could happen to Twila. They could hold us here for any one of various different reasons. I bit my tongue until tears clouded my eyes to control that wayward appendage.

It dawned on me what one thing might be that underlay Jack's dislike of this man. Jack never tolerated an inept fellow officer. Yet instead of Grandberg treating us with a measure of respect, he personified bully mode. Maybe because we were females? Maybe because in his mind the little women in the world needed hard-handed guidance?

He sat there and practiced at least one of the questioning techniques he remembered: let the silence hang. That might work most of the time, since perps were known to rush to fill a pregnant silence and give birth to their protestations of innocence and supposed alibis, or point fingers at someone else. The problem for Grandberg continued to be that I knew what he was up to and had no intention of talking to this buffoon until Jack got there.

The chief cracked first, and I let my satisfaction show on my face.

"You changed your mind about a lawyer?" he asked.

"Not yet," was all I said.

"Then you need to give me your statement!"

I glanced around the room. Not much bigger than a jail cell. No see-through window on any wall where witnesses might listen in on what I said. No camera lens that I could see to record a visual of our conversation. Then I stared pointedly at the table, bare, no recording equipment on it. Just Grandberg and me in the room. Trucker by my side, the only witness.

"What?" Grandberg fumed. "Do you need me to ask the questions?"

"No," I responded.

"Then tell me your end of what happened in the hotel!"

"Why?" I asked.

"B—because you were there!" he sputtered. "I need to know what you saw. Start gathering information for our investigation!"

I sighed, then gave in to the banked anger and slapped my palm on the table. Trucker uttered a growl, and I hurriedly placed my stinging palm on his head as I said, "I know you're a small-town cop—"

"Chief!" he interrupted me.

"Whatever." I waved my hand negligently. "But you must think I'm utterly stupid if you think I'm going to talk to you without a witness to our conversation or a record of it."

He had the grace to flush. "We're a small-budget department. Our only recording equipment is in use in the room where your friend is."

I settled back in my chair. "Then I'll wait until it's available."

"We need to get going on this ASAP," he railed. He leaned across the table and pointed a finger. "Your lack of cooperation will be noted!"

"Where?" I turned my head as I scanned the tabletop and room again.

His jaw clenched and veins in his neck bulged. If he thought his antagonistic attitude would scare me into talking off the record, he had another think coming. I was also worried about how they were treating Twila, given her unexpected personality change. So I confined the multitude of acidic thoughts about what a total moron he was to silence, although my poor tongue protested in agony.

"I can put you in a cell," he spat. "Hold you as a material witness until you get ready to talk."

"Go ahead." I shrugged. "I know a fantastic civil rights attorney. Think your town budget will handle the legal fees on your end? They might have to cut back somewhere else, like on their already tight police force budget."

"You b—" He clamped his mouth shut.

"Now I see why you don't have any recording equipment in here," I said, proud of the nonchalance in my voice.

He surged to his feet so quickly his metal chair clanged and clattered to the concrete floor. Trucker tensed beneath my hand, and I quietly shushed him. Grandberg could do a lot of damage to my dog before Jack could get here.

Someone pounded on the door, and Grandberg stomped over to open it. I only caught a word or two of the whispered conversation, but those words filled me with relief. I was indeed scared spitless, but had too much pride to kowtow to this bully. All right, maybe it was stubbornness. Whatever.

I rose. "I want to talk to Penny."

Triumph on his face, he snarled, "You can't speak to anyone until after your statement."

"Penny will wait as long as necessary."

I did manage to edge to a position in the room where I could see past the small woman clerk who'd brought the news to Grandberg. Penelope Thibedeaux, a/k/a Penny Thornton, ace political reporter, fluttered a four-finger wave, along with a nod of reassurance. She wore her television persona, black hair a riot of casual curls that took an hour to arrange, makeup without a trace of obviousness, brown eyes large and intelligent in her beautiful face. Her suit probably cost a month of her huge salary, skirt ending mid-thigh, sandals to die for on her tiny feet. Barely five foot, she packed more suppressed energy in that small frame than a dozen experienced cops. I wasn't sure how Penny had learned of my captivity so quickly. Maybe through her acquaintance with Katy's reporter friend ... or perhaps a police scanner.

"At least let Penny take Trucker," I insisted when Grandberg started to close the door. "My dog knows and likes her, and she'll take good care of him."

He debated a moment, then stuck his head back out the door and called, "Miz Carpenter wants to know if you'll take her dog."

Evidently Penny agreed, because Grandberg walked over to me and reached for Trucker's leash. I hastily positioned between them. "He doesn't like you. I'll turn him over to Penny."

"If you utter one word..." he warned.

"I won't." I sidled around him and met Penny at the door. No spoken words were necessary. Our looks at each other communicated volumes. Penny accepted the leash with a nod that told me not to worry about either the dog or the situation. I answered with as much gratitude as I could put on my face. Then Grandberg reached around me and shut the door. I wandered back to the chair and sat.

"Are you ready to talk now?" Grandberg growled.

"Not without a recorder," I answered.

"You're a material witness to a crime. Let someone know when you're ready to talk."

Someone?

The door slammed, the next noise suspiciously like a lock turning. My stomach lurched, but I sat stoic...outwardly, at least. Claustrophobia's never bothered me...not so far, although right now that trauma stirred and I clearly understood how locked doors could give a person the willies when they caged you personally.

Once again I scanned the room. Without doubt a camera hid in here somewhere. Buffoon Grandberg might be, but not buffoon enough to spend time in a room male-to-female alone. In a corner, the ceiling vent lacked one crosshatch. Enough room for a camera lens. I stared a moment, bit my lips to keep from sticking my sore tongue out, then settled down to wait. My wristwatch showed at least another hour or so before Jack could possibly get here.

At least Trucker would be cared for. And I had faith in Twila. We shared that same stubborn streak, honed both by heredity and life experiences. She'd protect Miss Molly with the same stubborn fervor.

CHAPTER 10

Patrick visualized on the passenger seat of Alice's Jeep. "May I join you?" he asked Twila. "Since I'm suitably attired?"

She spared him a glance, then focused on the road ahead. The cat sprawled in the backseat, harness looped through a seat belt shoulder strap. She slit her blue eyes briefly before she shifted and snuggled her black face on her rump.

"Just keep your clothes on," Twila said. "I've got enough on my mind right now. And no telling when we'll run across someone who can see you."

"I understand," he murmured. Yet nakedness gained me Alice's initial attention. And yours. "Where's Alice?"

"Still giving her statement, I guess. I told the clerk to let her know I'd be back and pick her up in a little while."

"And where are we going in the meantime?"

"*I'm* headed to Wal-Mart. Put your seat belt on. I don't need to drive by a cop who can see ghosts and...oh, shit."

Patrick met her gaze in the rearview mirror. Red and blue lights swirled on the roof of the car tailing them. Twila flipped her turn signal on and slowed for the upcoming highway exit. "Dissolve," she hissed.

Patrick complied, but remained where he could see what would happen as Twila drove into a convenience store parking lot and halted, the police car right behind her. He stared out the rear window, expecting the officer to alight from the vehicle, but the driver's door remained closed. Twila shifted the Jeep into the gear Patrick understood held the vehicle in place, but left the engine running. In his day, he mused, they had a hand-pulled parking brake, and then sometimes still had to use blocks behind the wheels, should they desire to park on a grade.

What would she think of these modern vehicles? The only time I persuaded her to steal away from her family for a picnic, I had to change a flat tire.

When the cruiser door finally swung out, Twila pushed a button to roll down her window as a female officer dressed in a blue uniform approached. The officer halted a step back from the car window and said, "May I see your driver's license and insurance card?"

"Of course, Officer," Twila responded. She reached for her purse on the console, then hesitated. "My driver's license is in my purse. I think the insurance card in is the glove box."

The policewoman propped a hand on her gun butt, but nodded for Twila to go ahead and retrieve the documents. She unzipped her purse and took out a wallet, then leaned over to open the glove box. Papers and junk spilled out, and she muffled another curse, this one directed at Alice's sloppiness. She unsnapped her seat belt and leaned over to dig through the mess. Victorious, she held up a postcard-size paper and handed it to the policewoman.

"Take your license out of the billfold, please," the officer said when Twila just opened her purse and extended it.

Twila fumbled the license out and the policewoman accepted it, then compared it to the insurance card. "Not your car?"

"No," Twila said. "It belongs to my niece. I'm just using it to run an errand."

"Your niece lives in Six Gun? You're from Ohio."

"I'm visiting. We were just doing some...well, touristing."

"I'll be right back."

The officer took the documents with her and returned to the vehicle. In the driver's seat, she picked up a microphone and spoke into it.

What's she doing? Patrick asked Twila.

"Checking to make sure I didn't steal Alice's car," Twila murmured. "And what are you still doing here?"

I'm controlling my visibility, he assured her.

The policewoman returned to the Jeep and handed the insurance card and license back to Twila. "You've got a taillight out," she said. "I should write you a warning, but I'll let it go if you'll tell your niece to get it fixed immediately."

"I will, Officer," Twila promised fervently. "I promise."

She nodded and strolled back to her cruiser. Eyes on the side mirror, Twila muttered, "Don't do it!" when Patrick started to visualize. "In fact, stay in your own dimension until I give you permission to leave it! I've had enough of you to last me quite a while."

May I at least stay in communication with you? Patrick pleaded.

"Depends on what you say."

The policewoman shut off the swirling red and blue lights and pulled around them to return to patrol. Twila released a relieved sigh.

She didn't see me, Patrick pointed out.

"Shut up."

Twila drove out of the parking lot, turned right, opposite from the cruiser, and continued down the street a block. There she pulled into another parking lot, one quite larger where a huge building with a Wal-Mart sign sat. A car backed out of a parking space near the entrance and, aisle clear in front of her, Twila sped straight to it and parked.

She left the keys dangling in the switch, engine running, and opened the door. "Wait here," she ordered. "I need to leave the air conditioning running for Miss Molly, so she doesn't suffer heatstroke and die on me. I'm locking the door, and I'll unlock it with the extra set of keys when I get back."

Can I just ask you one question first?

At first he thought she would ignore him. She gathered her purse and slid out of the car. Then she stood there and asked, "What?"

When can we talk? There are things I'm ready to tell you now.

"You should have thought of that before some poor woman got cut in half at that hotel. Now you can just wait your turn!"

Distracted, Patrick allowed her words to slide over him without rejoinder. The beautiful Hispanic woman a foot or so behind Twila gasped. She held a baby in her arms, a wide-eyed toddler's hand clutched in her other hand.

Twila stiffened. "You're visualizing!" she whispered in a harsh voice.

"I can't help it. She looks like—" With an effort, Patrick drew back.

Twila fixed a brilliant smile on her face and spun around. "Hello," she murmured.

"Mommy," the toddler whispered as he gazed up at his mother, a puzzled look on his tiny face. "Man dressed funny. Where he go?"

The woman clutched the baby closer and swept the toddler into her other arm. Long black tresses flying, she dodged between two cars in the opposite aisle. The toddler gazed over her shoulder through a fan of hair across his face and waved until the woman arrived at a gunmetal gray SUV. She fumbled the door open and shoved him and his baby sister inside.

"I told you..." Twila heaved a frustrated sigh. "Keep an eye on the cat!" She slammed the door and, back rigid, stalked to the store and disappeared inside.

Patrick thought better of following her, even in an invisible state. Twila could pierce the veil. She'd know if he tagged along. And there were probably scads of children in the store who might catch sight of him should he lose his concentration as he had a moment ago. Instead, he made himself useful and manipulated the mess of papers and junk back into the glove box.

As he waited patiently for Twila to return, though, his mind wandered to his reason for continued being. The woman had been nearly as beautiful as her. Would they have had such cute children of their own? Sparkling brown eyes? Probably. Her brown-eye genes would have overridden his green ones. Black, shiny hair or lighter, given his blondness? A son with his miniature features but her exotic coloring? A daughter with her dramatic beauty but his green eyes set off by her satin skin?

What would their life have been like? By now he supposed they both would have crossed over...died. Yet seeds of their love would have remained. Children of their bodies, born of their joy in each other. He slammed a fist on the dash soundlessly. It passed through the padding and bounced off his own knee. How cruel fate. How cruel the youthful immaturity of a young man's mind. He couldn't even blame Antonio for the outcome. His own stupid actions put fate into motion.

* * *

I used the time alone to go over what happened at the hotel...not much in the way of any clues as to who could have killed that poor woman. Maybe I should have cooperated with that blasted hunk of masculinity. I failed to see why or how, though. He was the one in charge. He should have focused on the crime. Instead, he antagonized Twila and me, threatened my pets. Treated us like garden-variety criminals!

Stewing about that situation wasn't getting me anywhere, so I regrouped. The only living people at the hotel were Twila, Carrie, Georgie, and me. As far as I knew. There were those footprints...

And there was Patrick, as well as floors and floors of vacant rooms, plus a basement, and who knew how many once-living residents. How on earth could a small-town police force search the entire place? Even if they tried, how could they tell anything? Junk lay strewn on floors with faded carpets still in place, wallpaper sagged in formerly grand rooms, hung in tatters in some. Though Twila hadn't gotten any further than the lobby and mezzanine, I'd toured the entire structure during my earlier trip. My tour had actually been the final one before the town officials exercised their authority and condemned the building, closed it to the public, citing fire and building code violations. Only Penny's intervention gained Twila and me access.

So why did they still have a handyman? Georgie had been only a phone call away for Carrie. And why was Carrie available? Who was she?

A former tour guide or someone connected with the absent hotel owner? And how was Carrie? Didn't a person who fainted usually wake up within a few minutes?

The hands on my wristwatch crawled so slowly that I tried to ignore the darn thing, but my gaze drew back to it. I clamped a hand over it as I continued to muse, waited until I was sure at least five minutes had gone by. Nope, only one. Still, I'd been locked in here over an hour.

And darn it, I still had to pee!

CHAPTER 11

I knocked on the door. Tentatively at first, then harder. No response. Finally, I decided the heck with subterfuge and stalked over to the vent. Stuck my face straight up at it and yelled, "I need to use the restroom!"

Two long minutes later, during which I stood by the door and patted my foot, debated whether to throw a metal chair against it for my next move, the lock disengaged. Not Grandberg, though. A tiny woman stood there, five foot of antagonism dressed in a bright red, silky jogging suit. Maybe she was the dispatcher. Tiny she might be, but that look on her face startled me and I stepped back.

"I'll take you to the bathroom," she snapped. "But you make one wrong move and..." She pulled a stun gun from behind her back.

I covered my dismay with a belligerent, "*You* make one wrong move with that piece of equipment, and I'll drag your ass through the courts until you're too old to benefit from social security!"

Her face crumbled, but she kept a tight grip on the stun gun. "I—I'm sorry. But—but—" She drew in a steadying breath. "I'm alone here. I have to be careful!"

"Where's my Aunt Twila?" I demanded.

"I'm not supposed to talk to you. Just go use the bathroom." She nodded at a door on the far wall. "Then you'll have to wait back in there."

My bladder demanded that I obey her, so I did. As far as I could tell in my hurried pace across the room, she was right. I didn't see a sign of anyone else, although two other room doors were closed. Could have been someone behind them, but I didn't dare veer off my straight path to investigate.

When I reemerged from the bathroom, she stood guard, albeit a fair distance away. She motioned the stun gun at the room I'd left. I sighed and trudged in the indicated direction until that stubborn hostility reared again. Quickly, I sidestepped her and, before she could react, plopped my butt down in the chair behind the only desk in the room.

"No!" she gritted. "Go back in the room!"

"I'm not going anywhere until you tell me where Twila is! The way we're being treated is bullshit! There's a murderer on the loose somewhere in this town full of idiot officials and..." The additional worry that had been niggling me surfaced with a vengeance. "And my aunt and I might be in danger! We were there. What if that perp's afraid we know something? What if he's a serial killer? What if he decides to get rid of any possible witnesses?"

Darn, sometimes I hated my fertile writer's imagination. The tiniest worry molehill grew to mountainous proportions in the blink of an eye once my mind acknowledged it. And this situation hardly qualified as a molehill.

The woman glanced around furtively, then asked, "If I get rid of this darn thing, will you agree not to try to escape?"

"I'm not going anywhere," I promised, "until I know where Twila is."

She laid the stun gun on a plastic chair beside the restroom and, wary gaze on me, edged crosswise until she sat in the chair on the other side of the desk. Then she leaned forward and whispered, "Did you see who got killed in the hotel?"

I shook my head negatively, not offering the information that Twila actually took pictures of the body. Definitely not that info. The fear we would get caught with unauthorized crime scene photos continued to roil inside me. The less anyone knew about us having those pictures, the better. As a change of focus, I studied her. Sea-green eyes, but beautiful skin, despite her age. Hair thick and still luxurious, although gray now so I couldn't determine the original color. It coiled around her head in an intricate configuration that reminded me of hairstyles on women in the historical portraits in the old Southern mansions Twila and I loved to visit.

Delicate hands lay on the desk, unmarred with the age spots I expected, nails well cared for and lacquered with clear polish. No hint of arthritic gnarls like those on Granny's finger joints. Of course, she was at least a couple decades younger than Granny.

"What's your name?" I asked when she bit her lips, eyes shadowed with worry.

"Patty," she replied. "Patty Alvidrez. I'm a widow now, and I've lived here all my life. I know just about everybody in town. I'm related to a lot of them."

"You're afraid the woman at the hotel is someone you know, or a relative."

"Yes," she admitted. "Sam would tell me, but he hasn't been back from the hotel yet."

"Sam?"

"Our detective. Sam Peters. This is a quiet town, but we've had our share of trouble. One of those troublemakers was released from prison last week. Sam's been on the lookout for him, and we're keeping our doors locked now."

"Who is this man you're afraid of?"

"Delroy Mitchell. He's an awful man. We all tried to warn my grand-daughter about him, but she was...you know...in love."

I couldn't halt a grimace. Yeah, I knew love.

Rather than my expression irritating Patty, she eagerly confided, "You do understand. I can tell. Of course, as we age, life's experiences do make us more knowledgeable about things we wished we had known as a young person, don't they?"

I didn't care much for her looping me into the same age category as her. She had to have a few decades on me! And I probably looked far beyond my age, given the stress of the past few hours. "You shouldn't worry so much until you know for sure who the victim is," I soothed.

"I hate that," Patty shot back. "Victim! That poor woman in the hotel has a name. A family that's probably worried to death about her."

Chastised, I nodded. Glanced at my watch again. Where the hell was Jack? "I really need to know about Twila," I prodded Patty.

"She huffed out of here with a Siamese cat in her arms. It was a few minutes after I arrived and right before that reporter showed up."

"The cat's Miss Molly. Did she say anything before she left?"

"The cat?"

"No! Did Twila say anything?"

"She asked if there was any place in town to buy a cell phone," Patty replied. "And a litter box. I told her I didn't know of anywhere local but gave her directions to the closest Wal-Mart. Oh, she did say to tell you she'd be back to pick you up."

Oh, sheesh. I'd forgotten Miss Molly's litter box was still in the hotel. I hoped she found the

Wal-Mart before Miss Molly peed on my car carpet.

"This waiting is horrible," I murmured aloud just as Patrick materialized behind Patty, thankfully, fully clothed. I didn't need the distraction of a naked man...ghost or not...right now.

Patty shivered and rubbed her arms through her red-clad sleeves. "Is it just me, or is it getting cold in here? The weather forecast didn't mention a front moving in."

Uh oh. Patty obviously carried a sensitivity to ghosts. The chill...

"Maybe some coffee would help," I urged. "Surely you have coffee here."

"Of course." She rose, then dropped back into the chair. "But it's in the snack area. I can't leave you alone. Won't you agree to go back into the interrogation room and wait?"

Not on your life. But the alternative was to try to have a conversation with Patrick in her presence. Maybe a mental conversation would work.

Do you know what's going on? I asked the ghost.

Twila wants to know if that stuff you buy is called Cat Out.

I hurriedly glanced at Patty to see if she by any chance also heard Patrick, but her eyes only held that pleading look. *I'm shielding her from my thoughts*, Patrick said, as Patty pointed at the open door on the room I'd been imprisoned in and I shook my head firmly.

"I'm not—Cat Out?" I interrupted myself as Patrick's words registered and my gaze flew back to him. "Miss Molly peed in my Jeep?"

"What...how could I know?" Patty asked at the same moment Patrick shrugged those broad shoulders and one corner of his mouth lifted in a grin.

Twila says that if you'd get a decent cell phone battery, she'd have been able to call you herself.

"When have I had time to buy a battery?" I spat. "I've been locked in that darn room over there! Besides, the cell phone's back at the hotel, so a battery won't help right now."

"Who are you talking to?" Patty whispered.

"And we've got a few more pressing worries right now," I threw back at him without bothering to reply to Patty. I also had a few more pressing worries than whether or not she thought I was talking to thin air.

"Who...?" Patty edged out of her chair and glanced at the stun gun. For a senior lady, she could move pretty fast when she set her mind to it. Unfortunately, at least for Patty's mental health, Patrick got to the stun gun first. The ghost curved his palm and the stun gun lifted from the chair just as Patty reached for it. It floated over to Patrick and Patty's gaze followed its path.

Patrick nestled the stun gun under one arm and propped his other hand on his hip. In that wide-lapel, Twenties-style suit, he reminded me of pictures I'd seen of gangsters with their machine guns gripped negligently. I expected Patty to faint dead away and I surged to my feet to catch her. She might break a bone on that hard floor...

Patty didn't faint, though. She stared at the stun gun, then I would have sworn that she scanned her gaze up and down, as though she could see Patrick. Indeed, Patrick examined her in turn. The glint of mischief in his eyes faded into astonishment.

"You—you're..." Patty whispered. Then she slowly backed up, one hand behind her tiny rump, waving as though searching for her chair seat. I hurriedly took her arm and guided her to the security of my vacated seat. She never once looked at me, only kept her gaze in Patrick's direction, a frozen expression of awe on her face.

"Patty," I began, but just then the front door opened and Jack stormed in, six feet of Cajun fury and every ounce of that anger reflected in his deep brown, blazing eyes.

"Where's Grandberg?" Jack asked. "Are you all right, *Chère?*"

A couple years ago, I would have run into those strong arms and buried my head against his neck. Pre-divorce years. Now all I could do...all I had the right to do...

The hell with it. I threw myself at Jack, and he held me close as I buried my face in his neck. Breathed in the comfort of the Jack smell, the feeling of man and solace. Shivered with relief and didn't give a damn that I had no right to be in his embrace. Screw the divorce papers. I needed a man to hold me, and not just any man. Jack. My wonderful, ride-to-the-rescue Jack.

"They were going to p-p-put my animals in the p-p-pound!" I wailed.

"Shhhh. Shhhh," he murmured. "We'll get this straightened out, *Chère.* Then maybe you and Twila will finally realize this ghosthunting business is foolishness."

CHAPTER 12

I didn't knee him in the groin. It took a lot of effort, but I glued my feet to the floor and slowly pushed out of Jack's arms. He hesitantly reached for me, but I shook my head and propped my butt on the desk. Gritted my teeth until I sorted through the thoughts in my head and chose an appropriate one.

"I assume Grandberg's at the hotel, investigating the crime," I forced through clenched teeth. "Twila's off at Wal-Mart in my Jeep." I glanced at Patty, past her. No Patrick. The stun gun lay on the floor.

Patty gazed at me, a deep longing on her face. "Where did he go?"

"Back to his own dimension," I said without thinking.

Jack's razor-sharp mind immediately grasped the situation. "There's another one of your damn ghosts involved here?" he asked in a frosty voice. "One who was just here?"

"He was!" Patty stared at Jack with the same icy expression on her face as his. "Who are you and do you have any identification?"

Jack normally has the utmost respect for his elders, and especially for women. I finally noticed that he wore his customary attire—jeans, boots, and a V-neck shirt with the Longview police symbol on the pocket where he'd clipped his badge. No shoulder holster bulge. His sidearm hung in a hip holster on his belt. He casually set a palm on the protruding gun butt.

"I'm Jack Roucheau," he replied to Patty. "Detective Roucheau from Longview."

"You have no authority here in our town, young man." Patty held out her hand. "I'll thank you to check your gun."

Jack stared at her for a quick second, then laughed. "I think not, ma'am. If you won't accept my law enforcement status, I've still got a license to carry."

Patty drew herself up to her five full feet. "Our town ordinances don't recognize the license-to-carry law," she informed him in a haughty tone. "You'll have to give me that pistol!"

Jack evidently decided to ignore the order. He focused on me again. "You ready to get out of here?"

"She can't leave!" In another one of those unexpectedly swift movements for someone her age, Patty scooped up the stun gun and aimed it at Jack. "Remove your pistol, young man. Now!"

Jack rolled his eyes. "Ma'am, if you think I don't know what that is you have in your hand, you're wrong. You can't hit me with that from over there."

Patty's face crumbled. "I don't even know how to use it!" she wailed.

Ever the gentleman, Jack hurried over to soothe her. The next instant Jack lay on the floor, writhing in pain, Patty over him, a deadly glare on her face. "Want another taste, young man?" she asked, but had sense enough to back away from Jack.

I couldn't decide whether to giggle or scream. Neither won out as I hurried to Jack's side and knelt by him, a peripheral wary gaze on Patty.

"Are you all right?" I asked Jack inanely, more for something to say than anything else.

"Shit no!" he growled. "How do you think I am? You want me to describe how I feel, so you can record the info for one of your books?"

"Um...not right now. Maybe later."

He uncurled his legs and slowly rose to his feet. Both hands on the stun gun, Patty kept it pointed straight at us. Her puzzlement showed on her face and she gnawed her bottom lip.

"You shouldn't be able to get up yet," she said.

"In case you don't know it," Jack snarled, "there's a gauge on that damn thing. Thankfully, you've only got it turned on low voltage."

If he expected Patty to direct her attention away from us and on the gun, he erred. She only responded, "Low was enough to put you down. It can again."

"Like hell." Jack turned to me. "You coming with me or not?"

"Neither of you are leaving here!" Patty insisted.

I didn't have to debate. I grabbed Jack's hand and the two of us ran for the door.

"Don't go, Ms. Carpenter!" Patty called. "I need to talk to you about Patrick!"

I skidded to a halt, although Jack nearly pulled my arm from the socket. "How do you know his name?"

A stubborn pout answered me. "You'll never know unless we talk."

"I—"

Jack scooped me up, and we were out the door, down the steps. I gave brief—very brief—thought to a struggle, then relaxed. Only for that instant, though. Jack dumped me beside his damn Harley and handed me a helmet.

"You rode that darn bike?"

"Get on," he ordered.

"I have to talk to Patty," I insisted.

"About the ghost who was in there?"

"Yes."

"Your choice." He forked the bike and jammed his helmet on his head. The bike rumbled to life and I quickly grabbed my decision. Helmet barely secure, I scrambled on behind him a split second before he dropped the bike into gear and roared off down the street.

"Will they charge me with jailbreak?" I screamed in Jack's ear.

His shoulders heaved under my hands. For a moment I thought he was so angry at me that he might stop the bike and toss me off. But when he didn't respond, I managed to engage the helmet strap with one hand, then laid my head against his back.

Not anger. Deep chuckles of laughter rumbled against my senses.

CHAPTER 13

Jack slowed the Harley at last—possibly in response to my nail gouges in his flat stomach. I chanced a glance to see where we were. Out of town, headed east, back toward Fort Worth. Suddenly Jack swerved onto a freeway exit ramp. When the intersection light ahead changed to green, he gunned the bike through and turned left on the crossover.

"Where are we going?" I shouted.

"Your Jeep's headed the other way!"

Twila. Finally.

The traffic light on the opposite side of the crossover turned yellow, but Jack went on through. We reentered the freeway in the westbound lane, and Jack expertly threaded through the traffic. Not that his skilled maneuvers allayed my distaste for this mode of transportation, especially in this heavy traffic. Wind rushed by us, no steel barrier protected us from the unyielding asphalt beneath the tires. Even the four-wheelers dwarfed the bike, let alone the semis interspersed with their smaller brethren vehicles. Good grief, a semi tire hit me right at eye-level! I blundered when I stared up at one of the truck drivers, and he winked at me, then blasted us with an ear-splitting eighteen-wheeler horn.

My hands constricted in reaction, and Jack incautiously—at least for my peace of mind—removed one hand from the handlebars and eased my grip away from his belly. Tried to, anyway. I

re-secured my hold as soon as he replaced his hand where it belonged, on those flimsy handlebars.

A click in my ear was a prelude to Jack's voice. "Ease up, *Chère*. This traffic's too heavy for me to be distracted by your fear of the bike."

What? I jerked upright, then realized Jack must have bought new helmets, with radio communication. Well, duh.

"That's better," his voice murmured in my ear.

Not for me. I now had a much clearer view of just exactly how closely we interacted with the blurs of vehicles and guardrails and...oh, sheesh. A construction zone with orange barrels shoving the traffic down to a single lane!

Caught between two of those huge semis, Jack braked to the now-crawling traffic. Then he glanced to his right and zoomed between a semi trailer and a towering Hummer, onto the shoulder. Oh, lord, no! What if another driver had the same idea? A driver safely secured in a decent vehicle...a larger vehicle? The hell with it. I buried my head on Jack's back again and prayed.

Jack eased down the shoulder—I could tell that much, since my darn eyes crept open a slit—until he pulled up beside the Jeep. He beeped that silly Harley horn, and Twila bobbed her head at us. The bike dropped back a few feet, and Twila signaled for the next exit just ahead of us.

Thank you, Universe! We're getting off this madhouse road.

I expected Twila to stop at the service station/convenience store at the intersection, but she continued on to an IHOP and drove through the parking lot until she found two adjoining parking slots. Jack pulled in beside the Jeep. Before I could unsnap the helmet and consider whether my shaky legs would hold me up when I got off this blasted conveyance, Twila was at the bike. She extended a sales slip to me. "You owe me some money, Alice."

"Fine. Fine," I said as I shoved the helmet straight up and then over

Jack's shoulder. He caught it...barely. "I'll gladly pay you tomorrow for a hamburger today."

Her stern expression eased at the familiar jibe we used with each other, but not completely. "You look like you've been rode hard and put up wet," she said in a lighter tone. Then she leaned into Jack and kissed his cheek. "Hi, Jack. I'm hungry. Let's go eat."

"Hi, Twila, girl." Jack removed his helmet and hung both of them around the handlebars, straps snapped to keep them in place. "Good choice here. How 'bout some waffles?"

"Yum," Twila agreed. "Blueberry waffles."

"And country ham."

"Hash browns," Twila said. "Don't forget the hash browns."

"Onions in mine."

"Mine, too, although I'll regret it later."

"Will you two quit discussing food when I'm on the run from a murder investigation?" I shouted.

A couple approaching their car two slots down froze, gazes glued to us. "Uh oh," I breathed. Jack and Twila swiveled to see what had caught my attention. "They heard what I said," I explained.

"You shouldn't shout it to the entire state of Texas," Twila chastised.

The man pushed the woman to the driver's door and jerked it open. She tried to stare over the car roof at us, but he shoved her in. She scrambled across the front seat, and he dived in after her and had the engine roaring before a person could blink. She pressed her nose against the side window, but as he reversed out of the parking slot, he jerked her shoulder and pushed her back into her seat. Tires squealing, he disappeared out of the lot.

Jack frowned at me. "Look, *Chère*. The fun's over now. There's no reason for you to worry. You're not on the run. You cooperated and...." His brow pucker deepened. "You did cooperate, didn't you? That woman was just pissed at me because I wouldn't hand over my pistol. Wasn't she?"

"Well..."

"Come clean," he demanded.

"I refused to talk to Grandberg," I admitted. "He treated us all like dirt, even Trucker and Miss Molly. So I decided I wouldn't give him my statement until after you got there."

"You fled the scene of a crime instead of giving a statement?"

"I didn't flee! You carried me off!"

"I thought you just wanted to hang around and talk ghost crap with that woman!"

"I'm still hungry," Twila said in a nonchalant tone. "Let's go eat."

"Well," Jack said with a considering look. "Now that Alice has advertised the fact that she's on the run, maybe we should find a different restaurant. There's a Waffle House down the road a ways. Motel next door. We don't want to hang around here very long, but we can hide the Jeep and bike among the motel cars and maybe buy enough time to eat a bite."

"Maybe?" I asked. "What are we going to do if the cops show up to arrest me?"

Neither one of them paid me any mind. Twila strode back to the Jeep and Jack fired the bike up again. "I'll ride with Twila," I insisted.

He handed my helmet over his shoulder and dropped the bike into reverse. I mentally fumed and sputtered while I snapped the helmet in place, promising dire consequences to Jack for his attitude. But I had enough sense to keep the punishment deliberation mental for now. He controlled that machine that rumbled between my legs, a machine I vowed never again to ride, even if it meant I had to hitchhike!

Sure, hitchhike. Were our descriptions already rocketing through law enforcement channels as APB's? Vehicle license numbers attached? Patty could have followed us out of the police station to get Jack's bike tag number. Or maybe the couple who just left already had their cell phone fired up to report us. How long would I last with my thumb out before I ended up right back in a police station? Maybe cell-bound this time.

Twila and Jack circled the motel to the back, where they parked again. Jack disengaged the kickstand and my grip on his belly, then planted his left foot on the ground. He eased past me, long right leg sliding over the leather seat. I sat there with my knees gripped, hands forlornly seeking safety.

"Better get off, *Chère*." He gently removed my helmet. "Your weight's an added strain on the kickstand."

My body agreed with him. My mind was still back there on the free-way. Visions of monster truck grills snapping at the piddly gnat that intruded in their road space, interspersed with cruisers containing sharp-eyed cops on the lookout. Jack evidently took pity on me, since he secured the helmets and lifted me free of the bike. Unfortunately for the rest of my body, my legs rebelled. Jack chuckled and gripped my rump to hold me steady...and close to him.

That did it. My energy ignited. "Get your hand off my ass," I hissed as Twila approached.

"But it's such a nice ass," he murmured. "And my hand's been there lots of times."

"Not for over two years," I reminded him.

"More's the pity," Jack whispered, a twinkle I recognized in his deep brown eyes before he released me and asked Twila, "You got stuck with the cat, huh?"

She nodded and they both looked at the Jeep, where Miss Molly stood with her nose pressed against the passenger window.

"Did you get another litter box?" I asked.

"Yeah," Twila assured me with one of those smiles we used with each other that warned josh-time-coming. "But it's mortgaged until you pay me for it and the litter."

"I'll pay you, I'll pay you, darn it," I promised with a half-giggle.

I instinctively reached for my purse before I remembered that Grand-berg had confiscated all our belongings. "How'd you manage to get out of that hotel with your purse?" I asked her. Her purse hung on her shoulder.

"I left it in the Jeep." She patted the purse. "And I got out of there with something nearly as important. Come on. Let's eat and I'll show you."

She walked towards the Waffle House next door and Jack took off right after her.

"Miss Molly," I called. "We can't leave her here. It's too warm in the Jeep."

Twila jangled the keys in the air. "I left it running, with the AC. on. She'll be fine."

I toddled after them a few steps until my legs cooperated better and I caught up. "Did you get gas? The tank was near empty when we got to the hotel."

"Because you were too intent on getting there to stop and fill up," she reminded me. "But yes, I got gas. And the sales slip, which I'll add to what you owe me."

We entered the small restaurant and took an isolated booth back in a corner. Twila sat on one bench, Jack and me on the other. Jack and Twila chatted innocuously until we'd placed our orders and the waitress brought coffee. I didn't pay much attention to their conversation. Instead, I kept one hand up to hide my face and furtively examined the three other customers to try to determine if they might be interested in us. Might be the type of people who avidly watched *America's Most Wanted* and made note of any fugitives that needed apprehension.

Two customers were an elderly couple, the other a man at a counter bar stool. The elderly couple was arguing about something, a map spread on the table next to their half-eaten food. The man at the counter appeared more interested in flirting with the waitress than us. Thank goodness. Maybe we would have time to eat. My stomach growled an agreement.

The waitress brought our orders, waffles and ham and hash browns for all three. I didn't even remember ordering, but my appetite must have done it without my conscious thought. I slathered butter and syrup, then cut off a huge waffle chunk, hoisting it dripping to my mouth.

"You shouldn't have done that," Jack said to Twila. "But hell, let's see them."

"Here they are," Twila said. She pulled an envelope I recognized as containing pictures from her purse and handed it to Jack. "The nicest woman at the Wal-Mart photo shop showed me how to use that machine."

"What?" I demanded. I dropped the waffle and fork back to the plate with a clatter. "You got those pictures developed?"

"Haven't you been listening, Alice?" she asked *sotto voce*. "And please don't announce it to the entire restaurant."

No, I hadn't been listening. I'd been...

My gaze froze on the envelope in Jack's hand. He opened that sticky flap. Drew out the blue plastic folder inside...

"Can't we wait until after we eat?" I whined.

"Get a grip, Alice," Twila said, though not in a reprimand. She picked up my fork and offered me the waffle. "Here. Eat. You'll feel better. You always feel better with a full tummy."

I opened my mouth like a baby bird and she inserted the waffle. I took the fork from her and pasted my gaze on it rather than the pictures Jack now flipped through.

"How'd you get those developed?" I asked Twila. I grabbed the knife and sliced off a huge chuck of ham to jam in my mouth next.

"Like I was saying, they have the neatest machine now at Wal-Mart. You just stick that card thingie from the digital camera in it and voilà. A while later you've got your pictures."

I frowned at her. "Grandberg kept our cameras."

"Not the card thingie," she said with a smirk. "I slipped that out and into my pocket before he confiscated everything."

"It's a picture card," Jack corrected her. "You want to see these, Alice?" When my eyes orbed wide, he continued, "Guess not." To my relief, he shoved the pictures back into that plastic holder.

He and Twila dug into their meals, and with those illegal crime scene photos safely out of view, I actually enjoyed mine. Plates empty, Jack waved the waitress over and she refilled our coffee cups. I examined the restaurant as she left our table. The other three customers had gone. Now we were alone. When I picked up my coffee cup, Jack and Twila exchanged surreptitious chuckles.

"What?" I demanded.

"I don't understand how you can write such suspenseful novels, yet be afraid to look at those photos," Twila explained.

"I don't *do* autopsies, either," I informed her. "I can get the information I need from other books, thank you very much."

"Maybe Patrick will recognize the woman," she mused.

"Is that the damn ghost that's hangin' around with you two this time?" Jack asked.

Twila bristled and Jack held up a forestalling hand. "Don't get so touchy. You've put me in a bad situation here, you know. My badge could be in jeopardy, and I'm not real amenable to adding dealin' with one of your spooks to the jumble."

"You're free to leave anytime," I told him in an icy voice. "We'll handle things perfectly well on our own."

"Sure," he said. "Maybe you can talk Grandberg into giving you a cell with Internet access. We can keep in touch in E-mail."

Twila giggled. "You aren't going anywhere, Jack. You know as well as I do that once you get your fingers into something, it takes a dynamite blast to get you out before the situation is resolved."

Jack had the grace to flush.

CHAPTER 14

An hour or so later, we pulled up at the gate to Penny's house. Thankfully for my fugitive status, Penelope lived out in the country, her nearest neighbor a quarter-mile away. Given her semi-celebrity, Penny also secured her property with the best high-tech safety measures available. She owned over fifteen acres, fourteen fenced for the quarter horses her trainer handled under her instructions while she dug into various scandals. Spotless white board fence surrounded the pasture; a ten-foot-high stone wall with an electronic gate protected her house and grounds.

Safely behind the wheel of my Jeep now, I stopped by the intercom panel and signaled our arrival. The bike idled behind us, Jack astride alone. Not that Twila would have been adverse to riding with Jack. After all, her husband, Jess, was a Ride-to-Live, Live-to-Ride biker nut. However, she preferred country back-road riding behind Jess to the more dangerous city streets.

"Come on through, Alice," Penny invited via the intercom. "And that luscious ex of yours, too. Hi, Jack!"

The gate swung open and a video camera on top of one stone pillar swiveled to follow our progress as we drove through. The gate closed behind us and we followed the oyster-shell drive to Penny's house, a hundred yards inside the stone wall. Her beautiful log structure was two-story, and it reminded me of the gorgeous *Bonanza* home. The drive curved past the long front porch, and we parked near the door.

I got out and stretched as I drank in the first glimmer of peace and safety I'd had since Carrie shrieked and collapsed. Immaculate grounds surrounded us, scattered with profusions of helter-skelter plants and shrubs. Penny preferred the gone-wild look rather than the tailored strictness some gardeners practiced. Beds of day lilies, bellflowers, columbines, and other perennials interspersed the shady pines and pin oaks. Plant crawlers from creeping junipers obscured their white-rock defining circles. A profusion of white, red, and pink azaleas lined the porch and pink-blossomed rosebushes climbed trellises on each end. The sweet smell of honeysuckle filtered from a riot of tiny yellow trumpets against the log garage.

I fell in love with this place the first time Penny invited me to visit. We met at a book signing and clicked right away, especially since we'd first found each other in an Internet ghost chat site. Penny, like all my closest friends, believed in ghosts, unlike Jack.

The front door opened and Trucker bounded out, followed by Penny. Before I could brace myself, Trucker's huge paws hit my shoulders, his drool-wet tongue swiped my face. My butt hit the Jeep fender, but I grabbed Trucker around the neck and returned his embrace, then ruffled his ears.

"How you doing, boy?" I asked, although he only answered with another slurp. "Having fun with Penny?"

"He sure is," Penny said as she rounded the Jeep and pushed Trucker away so she could hug me in his place. Trucker immediately bounded away to greet Jack. "Although boss lady Daisy isn't too sure how to handle an animal that much bigger than her." A great fan of the Roaring Twenties era, Penny had named her cat after Gatsby's great love.

"Are you sure you want us here?" I asked Penny quietly.

"Damn straight," she said. "Like I told you on the phone, this is the best place possible for y'all right now. Plus I'll have an exclusive on a great story. I'm getting tired of political scandals. What better way to break into crime investigation than an actual murder all of my own." Suddenly her brown eyes dimmed. "I'm sorry. I didn't mean that like it sounded. That poor woman at the hotel. Maybe I'm not cut out for this type of reporting after all."

"Then having us here—"

"Hush, Alice. You're also here as my friend, so let's not hear any more of that."

Penny patted my cheek, then strode over to Jack, who knelt by his bike, Trucker happily sitting beside him. The two of them greeted each other, then Penny turned her attention to Twila, who still stood by the Jeep's passenger door, Miss Molly in her arms.

"I'm Penny," she said with an extended hand. "You have to be Alice's Aunt Twila. I'm so in awe of what I've heard about you."

Twila ignored Penny's attempted handshake and hugged her with her free arm. "I'm glad we finally get to meet," she said, "but not about the circumstances."

"Let's don't worry about that just now. Come on in."

Penny led us across the porch and inside the huge, high-ceilinged living room with log rafters. She'd mixed a Western style of decorating with feminine touches: beautiful Remington oils that she collected and Native American blankets on the walls, butter-leather brown furniture with earth-tone throw pillows, lacy curtains, ferns and ivies in pottery. Southwestern-patterned throw rugs lay in strategic spots on the gleaming hardwood floor.

Penny settled us in her conversation area in front of the huge stone fireplace. She'd already set out a pitcher and glasses of iced tea on a serving cart. I squeezed a slice of lemon in mine and Jack grimaced. He'd never understood my preference. Jack preferred his tea straight, as he did his bourbon.

Trucker sprawled on the rug and, happy to be reunited with her buddy, Miss Molly curled up at his side. A movement in the corner of the room prefaced Daisy, who stalked over to investigate the new intruder in her domain. Huge, black, and long-furred, her green eyes glowed with cat-suspicion. Miss Molly laid her head on Trucker's outstretched front paws and stared serenely back.

"Daisy, be nice," Penny cautioned.

Daisy halted in mid-stalk and sat down in front of the fireplace. Back to Trucker and Miss Molly, she bathed her already-immaculate self.

"Now," Penny said as she crossed one slim leg and leaned back in her lounge chair. "While I waited for y'all, I checked with one of my sources. It's very weird. The news of a murder at the hotel must be under tight wrap. No one's heard a word about it, except the one transmission a friend picked up on a scanner and relayed to me."

"Whew," I breathed in relief. "Then no one's chasing us."

"Not openly," Jack said, and new jitters cramped my stomach.

Penny nodded agreement. "For all we know, they're just releasing info on a need-to-know basis. My source said she'd see what she could find out."

Twila chuckled. "At least I walked out of the station a liberated woman. I gave them my statement and contact info, and they said I was free to go."

"You're lucky they didn't do a full body search," I grumped. "They'd have found that picture card."

"Picture card?" Penny asked. "You took pictures of the crime scene, Twila?"

"Uh huh," my aunt admitted as she dug into her purse and handed the blue plastic folder to Penny.

I gulped tea and an ice cube slid down my throat. Choking, I spat, and it landed on my bosom. Jack rose from his chair and joined me on the couch. While he patted my back with one hand, he reached for the ice cube with the other. I smacked his errant hand away.

"I'm fine," I said when I could speak. "Just fine. Just promise me that you'll get my pets back to Granny for me when my ass lands in a cell!"

"We're not going to jail," Jack assured me. "If Grandberg even hints at that, he'll be one sorry sucker."

"You've got something on him?" I asked as a different focus from watching Penny flip through those photos. Penny frowned and shook her head as she paused at one picture, then handed it to me. I automatically accepted it...then as soon as I realized what I held, dropped it as though it had grown snake fangs. Unfortunately for my peace of mind, it landed faceup...on my lap.

"No!" I surged to my feet. Tea splattered Jack and Penny and the photo fluttered to the floor...faceup. I froze, while Twila tsk-tsked and handed Jack and Penny linen napkins from the serving tray.

"I...don't...want...to...see..."

Still, I looked. Twila had telephotoed in on this shot. A beautiful face, had it not been marred by terror. Arms flung over her head, fingers clawed. Dark hair bobbed in a Twenties style, and she wore a low-cut, bright green dress, two long strings of pearls with a knot in each flung across her small breasts. Fringes decorated the dress bodice beneath her breasts. A wasp-thin waist—cut in two by the elevator doors.

Not much blood, though. But enough that my knees wobbled at the sight of what there was soaked into the light-colored carpet on the elevator floor. I sought the safety of the couch behind me before it dawned on me that, sitting, I'd be that much closer to that horrible photo. With an effort, I stepped over the photo and scurried around the couch, sat my rump on the back of the couch and swigged my tea to lubricate my dry mouth. Hell, nothing left in the glass. I stared at it forlornly. No way was I going to approach that serving cart to refill it.

"Here."

I screamed...well, more of a distressed chirp, which was all I could force out. Twila snaked an arm around my waist and shushed me.

"It's just tea, Alice." She jiggled the glass in front of me and ice cubes tinkled against the crystal. I accepted her glass and drained it before I handed it back to her.

"Sorry," I managed. "It's just...I don't..."

"I understand," Twila said. "It's not necessarily those photos, although they're definitely gruesome. There's something about her."

"I hadn't even seen her face until now," I insisted. "How—?"

"Why?" she interrupted. "Why is she so silent from the other side of the veil? She's there. She hasn't crossed over. I could sense that, but she's extremely unwilling to communicate with us."

"Maybe—" I cleared my throat and went on, "Maybe she doesn't realize she's...uh..."

"Dead," Twila finished for me. "No, I think she's very aware of that. She's torn somehow between wanting to cross on through the light and leave this dimension behind her and wanting to complete some unfinished business."

"Expose who killed her?" I asked.

Jack snorted and said, "If only it were that easy. All we'd have to do is call on you or Twila to communicate with murdered victims and ask them who killed them. Hell, we wouldn't need detectives at all!"

Used to Jack's negativity about our psychic senses, Twila and I ignored him. But Penny gritted, "The crime-solve rate might be a lot better if some of you nonbelievers would open your closed minds, Jack!"

"Of course," he tossed back at her. I glanced over my shoulder as Jack set his tea glass down on the tray with a thump and threw up his hands. "We could spend our time talkin' to every flake who walks in off the street and insists she knows exactly who killed who. Tell the DAs who prosecuted the case to be careful in *voir dire*. Make sure the jury pool had enough ghosthunters on it to provide a suitable audience for their expert witness—the psychic who would lay out the crime facts in all their gory detail, just like they happened! We wouldn't need witnesses, would we?"

Anger rushed to the forefront of my mind. It didn't quite override the niggle that this was a much better focus than confronting those pictures, though that thought wouldn't leave my mind. But Twila defused the argument before I could jump into the middle of it. She giggled at Jack.

"What?" he semi-snarled.

"I was just remembering what your face looked like when Sir Gary slammed that car trunk down and nearly broke your finger. When you had to admit right in front of us that you actually could see Sir Gary Gavin, the ghost."

"Damn it, Twila. I—"

Feminine laughter drowned out the rest of his words. Mine quickly deteriorated into near hysteria, partly, I'm sure, from tension relief. I gulped a breath, but one look at Twila's face broke my control. Hiccups, one after the other, interspersed the laughter.

"Don't—hiccup—look at—hiccup—me!" I pleaded with Twila.

She knew what I meant. Numerous times shared amusement ended up with both of us rolling on the floor, unable to control our laughter even after our stomachs ached. She obliged and turned her back, but she and Penny shared a glance. Both of them broke out in renewed whoops and Twila collapsed into the closest chair.

I held my breath, just like the old folks told us. *Hold your breath and the hiccups will stop.* "Hiccup!" A pause. Hmmmm. I let out my breath...made the mistake of glancing at Jack. I lost it and tumbled over the back of the sofa, belly down, full length on the cushions, where I whooped along with my aunt and friend.

The three of us finally silenced our merriment. My first thought of Jack, I edged my face over the side of the sofa.

No Jack. Just an empty spot in front of the fireplace. Daisy still sat there, undisturbed by the cacophony, as were Trucker and Miss Molly.

When I met her gaze, Twila shrugged. "I didn't hear him leave, either."

Outside, the bike's engine rumbled. All three of us scrambled to our feet and rushed to the front door, out onto the porch. By then Jack was halfway down the driveway. The bike's rear tire spit a trail of oyster shells in its wake.

"He can't get out the gate," Penny mused. "Wonder what he'll do?"

We hurried down the steps and over to where we could see the gate. Jack slid the bike to a halt sideways in the drive. But not because the gate blocked his way. He was still a good fifteen feet from that. Patrick stood in front of the bike, hands on his hips, head cocked to one side...thankfully, clothed.

The ghost ignored Jack and yelled to us, "Took me long enough to find you! Can I come on in?"

"Who's that?" Penny asked in an awestricken voice. "You girls sure do hang around with gorgeous hunks."

"He's a ghost, and you should see him naked," I answered, then called, "Come on up, Patrick. We need to talk."

"Your wish..." He disappeared in a blink and continued when he materialized by my side, "...is my command."

"Remember that," I ordered to let him know I was still in charge.

I let Twila make the introductions as I stared at Jack. Who stared back at me. Then shook his head and yelled, "Tell her to open this effin' gate!"

I wandered on down the driveway toward him. When I got close enough to talk without screaming—yet still a good distance from the Cajun fury in those brown eyes—I said, "Don't you want to come on back and meet Patrick?"

"No!"

"Then you did see him, huh?" I insisted.

"Just get the damned gate open," he snarled.

I bit my lip. Much as I wanted to make him admit that he'd seen Patrick, I also wanted Jack with me right then. Twila and I could handle the ghost business, but legalities already had me scared spitless. Should I apologize? Might be a good idea.

"We're sorry, Jack. Please don't leave. We just lost it for a minute. You know how Twila and I are when we get the giggles. It was tension relief, not laughing at you. How can we find out who really killed that poor woman before the cops decide I did it? They won't look beyond their noses at anyone else."

"Exactly," he said in a quiet voice. "*Chère,* you're in trouble here because you refused to cooperate. That's what you should be concerned about, not whether this poor woman's soul is uneasy. You can't just write a new scenario like you do in your books and make things turn out the way they should. Cops make mistakes, even good ones. And Grandberg's focus is gonna be on his reappointment. Getting a murderer behind bars ASAP, so the people in his town breathe a sigh of relief and think of him as their savior. Keep him on as chief."

"He won't win the confidence of the townspeople when they find out he arrested the wrong person and didn't keep looking for the real murderer!"

"And how long can that take?" Jack asked. "Months? Years? You read the papers. How many articles have you seen recently about wrongfully convicted men or women released due to new DNA evidence? How long were those people behind bars? Have you got that long?"

Damn my writer's imagination! I visualized myself languishing behind prison walls for years. Cut off from everyone I loved by a pane of bulletproof glass and a telephone sticky with sweat from the hands of other panicky prisoners. Unable to fight for my own rights while some lawyer filed reams and reams of legal mumbo jumbo to try to free me.

Would I be on death row? I searched my mind for research into Texas capital murder law, but couldn't dredge it up through the layers of current stress. One thing I did recall for sure: Texas definitely had capital punishment and executed convicted felons. Old Sparky had been retired at Huntsville, replaced by lethal injection.

I sniffled with self-pity and backhanded my nose. Jammed my hands in my jeans pockets and stared at the oyster shells beneath my feet.

Jack sighed and cut the bike engine, unlatched the kickstand and swung off. He gently pulled one of my hands free and thrust a handkerchief in it. While I blew my nose, he patted my shoulder.

"The best thing I can do for you right now," he said, "is to find out exactly what's going on. Maybe make some waves and let Grandberg know that I'm keeping an eye on him."

"Don't you have to get back to your job?"

"There's that," he admitted. "But things are quiet right now, and I've got some leave time built up. Still, I'm gonna have to watch myself. It's not gonna look good on my record if the POBs find out I'm interferin' in another jurisdiction's investigation. Especially—"

He broke off, but I asked, "Especially if it involves ghosts?"

"No." Jack briefly caught my gaze, then stared back up the driveway. I turned slightly to see Penny, Twila, and Patrick grouped silently as they watched us.

"Then what did you mean?"

"Don't worry about it, *Chère*." He gently knuckled me under the chin. "I promise, I'll stay in touch. Now go on up there and tell your friend Penny to open this gate."

Stubbornly, I held my ground. "Not until you finish what you didn't want to say."

He searched my face for a long moment, then whispered, "Especially when it's a case where someone I care about so much is involved."

Stunned, I shook my head. "We're only friends now, Jack."

"Of course." He winked at me. "We were friends before lovers before man and wife. Full circle. And friends don't let friends down. Go, *Chère*. Let me get on with being your friend."

He swung back onto the bike and revved the engine, then slowly eased the bike up to the gate and let it idle. I gazed at his broad shoulders for another second, then turned and trudged back to Penny.

"Let him out," I said. "He's going to see what he can find out that your sources can't."

Penny nodded. "I'll get the transmitter."

While she hurried back into her house, Patrick mused, "I should talk to him before he leaves. Try to make him understand why you two are helping me."

"He won't have anything to do with you," I cautioned. But Patrick dissolved.

CHAPTER 15

Patrick waited until Jack rode out of sight of the gate before he visualized on the seat behind him and tapped his shoulder. Jack stiffened. The bike's engine decelerated sharply.

"Yo, Jack," Patrick said. "Can we pull over and chat?"

For a moment Patrick thought Jack might try to ignore him, but then the mortal guided the bike onto the side of the road. Still, the engine idled and Jack didn't turn around. Impatient, Patrick prepared to tap him again, but he noticed Jack's face in a tiny mirror beside the handlebars. The mortal was examining the seat behind him.

"It's just vampires who don't show up in mirrors, buddy," Patrick said.

Jack dropped the kickstand and swung off the bike. His right leg whizzed through Patrick without resistance, and the ghost chuckled.

"I'm not your damned buddy!" Jack snarled. "Now get the hell out of here!"

"Can't do that," Patrick replied. "Well, I can, but we need to talk."

"I'm not interested in talking to a gho—" Jack closed his eyes and shook his head. Then he strode a few feet away, flipped his helmet visor up and whirled to face Patrick. "I don't believe in ghosts!"

"From what Alice and Twila say, your supposedly not believing doesn't mean you don't see them," Patrick mused.

"What do you want?" Jack gritted.

"Nice ride you've got here." Patrick smoothed the leather seat Jack had vacated. "Feels nice between a man's legs."

"Then get your own damn bike!"

"It's not the bike we need to discuss."

A car drove into view down the road, and Jack froze. His eyes moved, though, as the convertible drew closer. The woman behind the wheel was blonde, young, a negligent wrist on the steering wheel to guide her path. She wore dark sunglasses, and what Patrick could see of her figure indicated it suited her gorgeous face. He released a low wolf whistle.

"Disappear!" Jack insisted.

"If she stops to flirt, it won't be with me, buddy," Patrick explained. "I'm not visible to her. She's a true nonbeliever."

The blonde waved a red-fingernail-tipped hand at Jack as she blew past them and barely negotiated the curve in the road that hid them from Penny's driveway.

"So you're reading minds now?" Jack demanded.

"No," Patrick assured him. "I don't have that ability. I just watched her face. She turned her gaze straight past me and onto you." He laughed at Jack's puzzled expression, then shrugged. "I'm fairly certain that it wasn't just that she prefers tall dark strangers to well-built blond ones. She didn't see me."

"What do you want?" Jack demanded again. "I've got things to do. In case you aren't aware of it, there's a possibility Alice might be arrested, due to her own stubbornness and my foolishness."

Patrick bit his lip. This wasn't going to be as easy as he'd thought. "Okay," he began. "Let's get something straight right now. I'm just as interested in clearing Alice of suspicion as you are." Reconsidering, he continued, "Well, I guess you've probably got me beat as far as worrying about Alice."

"We're divorced."

"A piece of paper doesn't kill feelings."

"We're just friends."

"Maybe on her end," Patrick said. "But I've seen you look at her when her attention is elsewhere."

"I don't like sneaky spies," Jack hissed.

"Invisibility can be useful," Patrick assured him. "Especially if I can gather info you might need."

"Then go spy on Grandberg. He's the one we need to be worried about." Suddenly Jack groaned and shook his head. "I can't believe this. I'm talkin' to a blasted ghost!" Before Patrick could speak, he went on, "What's your take in this? You're here for some reason. From what I know of how Alice and Twila work, you told them some hokey story to get their help."

"It's not hokey. And they don't know all of it. Though I'm fairly certain I wouldn't even have gotten their attention if the hotel wasn't involved. The two of them are fascinated with historical stuff. People, too."

"You're not tellin' me anything I don't know. Yet."

"Fact is," Patrick mused, "I actually think my quest is nearly over. I've already found someone who can probably tell me everything I want to know."

"Go talk to her, then. After that, hie yourself back into your own dimension."

Patrick threw up his hands, then dismounted the bike and stalked over to Jack. "For someone who thinks he knows so much, you're amazingly thickheaded. Why would I want to live in that half-life dimension? Don't you understand? That's no life!"

Jack leaned in until their faces were only inches apart and said, "You ain't got no life. You're dead."

Patrick backed off and crossed his arms. "Bodily dead, yes. It's my spirit that's caught in this...this...whatever it is. Half-world, half-dead world. It's damn sure not a half-alive world."

"For what it's worth, you've got my sympathy." Jack bypassed Patrick and swung onto the bike. "But I've got living people to take care of. It's not just Alice, either. Twila's married to someone I do call a buddy. My friend, Jess. Since you don't seem inclined to do anything more than stand here and drown in a self-pity party, go ahead and have at it. Alone."

He dropped the bike into gear and roared off. Patrick debated whether or not to follow—no way did Jack have Alice or Twila's ability to restrict him. Yet his shoulders slumped and instead, he wished like hell he could cry in this state.

Damn, it was lonely.

CHAPTER 16

"We have to get back into the hotel."

I gaped at Twila. "Like hell! We're *not* going back there!"

"I have to agree with Alice, Twila," Penny said. "What if you get caught?"

"We have to try to contact that poor murdered woman," Twila explained. "And that's where she is. I'm sure she's frightened, confused. We can't leave her to deal with this alone. Not when we have the ability to help her."

"Ha!" I snorted. "How much help will we be if we get arrested for trespass? Let's don't even consider the fact that I'm a wanted woman."

"There's no security at the hotel." Twila rose from her lounge chair and wandered over to Penny's bar in the far corner. "And I still have that key that Carrie gave us."

"No," I said flatly. "We are not going back there. We'll have to figure out some other way to investigate."

Twila ran a finger down a bottle of Crown Royal on a glass shelf, then removed the bottle. With her back to us—although Penny and I could follow her movements in the mirror—she uncapped the Crown and poured a substantial amount in each of three glasses. She searched the bar counter until she found the ice bucket and plopped a couple cubes in each glass, then opened a can of 7-Up and measured it between all three drinks. Juggling the glasses in spread fingers, she returned to Penny and me and offered them.

No hesitation on my part. I chugged half the drink with my first elbow bend.

"Besides," I said as I kept the glass rim close to my mouth for another swallow, "that key's for the front door. It probably won't open the back door, the one hidden from the street."

Twila quirked an eyebrow at me. "Then you do understand that we have to go back there."

"No!" I gulped more Crown and Seven and continued, "I am not agreeing to that. I was just explaining facts."

"I think you were analyzing the situation," Penny mused.

"You're both full of sh—crap," I insisted. But the expressions on their faces told me I wasn't getting through to them, and I searched my mind for another means to shake some sense into them. Lifted the glass to drink some more, but it was already empty.

Twila handed me her drink.

"I can get a refill," I said.

"I don't drink Crown. You know that. I fixed an extra one for you while I was up."

Sometimes her in-depth knowledge of my frailties really pissed me off. I still grabbed the drink, though.

"Then it's settled," Twila said. "We're going back."

"It's not settled," I insisted. However, the whiskey already spread soothing relaxation through me. Not enough to cloud my judgment, though. "If you two think it's necessary, then go on. I'll hang out here and watch the news reports to see if anything breaks about the murder. Or—do you have a police scanner, Penny?"

"Yes," she admitted.

"Then I'll listen to it for any report of two trespassers picked up at the hotel."

"You're the only one of us who's been in the entire hotel," Twila said. "I need you there to keep from getting lost."

"Ha, ha," I said. "Good try, but I know you aren't going to be physically looking for that poor woman's soul. You'll try to contact her psychically, and you don't need to prowl around the hotel to do that. Your psychic powers are strong enough to reach out all over that building."

"Two psychic powers are better than one," Twila reminded me. "We've always been a team. Always worked well together, too." When I mutinously continued to sip my drink, she prodded, "Haven't we, Alice?"

"Yeah," I admitted. "Look, can't you see that I'm just trying to protect us? We can't help that poor woman if we get arrested."

Twila winked at me. "If you're not living on the edge, you're just taking up space."

"Not fair," I pleaded. "I'm trying to be rational here."

"Death's not rational. Ghosthunting is fun for us. We both admit that. But how many times have we also agreed that it comes with a measure of responsibility. We can't just pop into situations that exist on the other side of the veil and then ignore them. Especially if it's a situation where our abilities might do some good."

"Even if we get arrested, huh?" Thank goodness for this wonderful whiskey. Or maybe not. Here I was, after only two drinks of my favorite bad habit, agreeing to what I'd initially deemed a totally inappropriate plan of action. "We only agreed to look into Patrick's situation this trip," I reminded her.

"And you only agreed to look into Sir Gary's situation when Katy called begging you to come to Esprit d'Chêne," she reminded me right back. "But when Bucky was killed, I came running to help you control a violent ghost. We dealt with both deaths, right?"

"Yeah, but because...because..." I spluttered. "Because we had to!"

She raised that reddish-brown eyebrow at me again. Darn, I hated it when she could stab me with guilt without saying a word. Too close, we were just too close at times.

"And what about Trucker and Miss Molly?" I went on. "What will happen to them if we don't come back?"

"Trucker's going with us," Twila said to me, then went on as she slid her glance to Penny. "There's no need for you to risk the hotel part of this. We need someone on the outside."

"You're probably right," Penny said.

"What about Miss Molly?" I reasoned. "She and Daisy aren't going to get along at all, especially if Penny leaves them here alone to go talk to one of her sources."

"I thought I'd give Granny a call," Twila said, liquefying my last argument. "See if one of her multitude of relatives will pitch in to take care of your other animals while she comes here to help out."

"Oh, stop with the teasing," I told her. "We can't get an elderly woman involved in this mess."

"I'm not teasing."

"Sure you are. Besides, Granny's got no business driving on the interstates between Six Gun and here. That Oldsmobile convertible of hers has never gone over forty miles an hour since she bought it brand new in 1950. And the minimum speed on the freeway is forty-five."

* * *

We took Penny's new Lincoln back to Six Gun. It had limousine-dark windows on all sides. Even then I scrunched down in the seat whenever we passed a highway patrol cruiser. And we passed at least ten during the trip; I counted them from the backseat where I sat with Miss Molly and Trucker while Penny drove and Twila rode shotgun.

I drowsed off finally and dreamed. The judge wore a black-hooded robe that nearly obscured his face. All I could see were two red eyes glaring at me. He droned out my punishment—death by lethal injection, may your soul find mercy—in a satisfied, smirky voice, then banged his gavel and announced, "Court dismissed!"

The gavel noise woke me and I stared through the rear window. We'd arrived at my log cabin in Six Gun. The noise had been Twila and Penny slamming their doors after they got out of the Lincoln. Both of them were already climbing the steps to my upper deck, where Granny waited in the open sliding doors.

I sat there for a minute, torn between the lingering fear from the dream and...another emotion. Shame. Yep, shame. What was I doing cringing and simpering? I'd faced down smarmy reporters who denigrated my fiction writing and accused me of romanticizing crime. Even overcome nearly debilitating stage fright and been interviewed on television. Hell, a time or two I'd even faced hostile paranormal entities and banished them without Twila at my side. I believed in the justice system...for the most part. A small-town cop wasn't going to get the better of me. Wasn't going to stick me behind bars without a hell of a fight.

I wrenched the door open and, Miss Molly in my arms, stood outside. Trucker lumbered out and sat beside me, then stretched out his kinks from the ride. I loved my home and the peaceful atmosphere and surroundings I'd created here since I'd bought the haunted cabin just after my divorce. It sat on over an acre, and the grounds had grown wild and untended for a year or two before I found it.

I'd met one of the ghosts who inhabited the place and obviously made it a hard sell on the first trip down the drive after Twila and I spotted the faded real estate sign on the backcountry road. Even if I hadn't, the jittery real estate lady would have transmitted something weird to me when she gave us the key and agreed to let Twila and me prowl through the house without her. Little did she know the weirdness of the place drew me as much as the potential privacy and chance for a home instead of a cramped apartment. A place where I could have animals and ghosts both.

The upper deck where Granny, Twila, and Penny now waited for me overlooked a small lake across the road. Instead of joining them, I turned and strolled down my driveway, Miss Molly still in my arms, Trucker at my heels. We crossed the road and I sat down on a small bench in a cozy area I'd created on the lake shore.

No breeze today. The lake stretched out smooth and blue, and jack pines, oaks, and various other trees lined the shore. Puffy white clouds reflected on its surface, as did the trees. A month or so ago, only the jack pines were green, the branches of the rest of the trees bare and stark. Now the variegated shades of green from the fully leafed trees made a pleasing patchwork scenery.

At the end of the dock, Howard, the Head Ghost, sat in the rowboat that came with the cabin. He'd kept the boat tied this time, although other times he actually went out onto the lake. Howard loves to fish, although he's a catch-and-release ghost. He left his cane-pole bobber floating on the water and dissolved, then rematerialized on the bench beside me.

"Fish biting?" I asked.

"Nope," said Howard, the ghost of few words. He reached over and stroked Miss Molly's head, and my cat purred with pleasure. Trucker nudged Howard's knee—although his nose passed through it—and the ghost patted the dog, also.

We sat there for a few minutes without conversation and I drank in the soothing solitude and peace, which chased away my last vestiges of stress. There were only a few other houses on the lake, five at my last count, all but one weekend cottages. Granny, of course, lived here year-round in her small clapboard house next door to me. Eventually my mind returned to my current situation, although I faced it with a well of courage this time. And it dawned on me that Howard, a doctor in real life, could answer a couple questions for me.

"How long would it take someone to die if they were trapped between closing elevator doors?"

"A while," Howard replied.

"I thought elevator doors ran on electricity. Plus have some sort of safety mechanism. I mean, I've rushed for an elevator and stuck my hand in between the doors when they were closing. They usually open back up."

He shrugged. "Elevators were before my time."

I thought of the lack of blood in the picture I'd seen at Penny's. "If a person were already dead, how much blood could they still lose?"

"Not much, with the heart not pumping. But some would leak out for a time after death. If it had a place to leak out of."

The poor woman could have been killed elsewhere, then the stage set at the hotel. Stress reviving, I realized I was going to have to examine those photos more closely.

Howard disappeared and materialized in the rowboat. I realized that the red and white bobber was no longer bobbing, the line on the end of the cane pole tight, tip bent. Howard levitated the cane pole and a panfish's nose peeped out of the water. The ghost leaned over the rowboat and gently removed the hook. That darn fish actually floated there for a moment, nose pointed at Howard just like the Incredible Mr. Limpet! Then it leapt up, dived and tail-slapped the water before it disappeared. I laughed aloud. Even fish communicated with ghosts!

I set Miss Molly on the bench beside me, stood and stretched. I was ready now. My home and visit with Howard had replenished me somewhat. Not really ready to look at those photos, I pondered with a grimace. But no help for it.

CHAPTER 17

Penny, Twila, and Granny grouped behind my chair while the computer loaded the photo software and I explained what Howard and I had discussed. Twila had had the forethought to also have the photos stored on a CD disk, and it lay there beside my mouse, waiting to expose the contents. The computer program would allow me to examine the photos in more detail than the prints, but I kept glancing at the CD with distaste, until I chastised myself. What did I expect it to do? Leak blood onto my desk calendar like something in a Stephen King novel?

Program open, I gingerly picked up the CD—and the damn phone shrilled right beside my hand! I dropped the CD with a scream, somewhat satisfied when the other three echoed it in various tones. None of us were as calm, cool, and collected as we let on.

I grabbed the handset on the second ring. "Hello!"

"Oh, Alice, don't be so grumpy," Cousin Katy shot back. "I'm calling with some good news about a gift I have for you."

I hesitated before I thanked Katy. Katy's gifts could range from the desired to the unwelcome, depending on her mind-set when she decided to clean house. Or more accurately, redecorate. Her funds were basically limitless, her greatest pleasure changing the décor in various rooms at Esprit d'Chêne, the family plantation she inherited by default.

"Are you still there?" Katy asked.

"Yeah. Yes, Katy, but I've got company right now and I'm sort of busy."

"Oh, who's there?" Katy asked.

"Uh...Twila and Granny. And Penny."

"How wonderful," Katy cooed. "I'm having a dinner party this evening! It won't be any trouble at all to tell the caterers that I'll have four more guests. Fairly informal dress. And pre-dinner cocktails at seven. I'll look forward to seeing all of you." Fairly informal dress to Katy meant floor-length gowns but you can keep your bosom covered. Before I could refuse, Katy continued, "Put me on your speaker. I'll invite the others myself."

"We can't make it, Katy," I finally got a chance to say. "Sorry, not this time."

"Oh, pooh, Alice. I haven't seen Twila at all this trip. And it's been ages since Penny and I actually got together...beyond the call I made to get you set up at the hotel," she added in a remember-what-I-did-for-you tone. "Granny loves to come to Esprit d'Chêne, also."

"Katy—"

"I just know that Penny will enjoy tonight," she babbled on as though I hadn't tried to interrupt. "A member of the *Times Picayune* board of directors is going to be here. You remember that newspaper, don't you? The big one in New Orleans? I've been trying to call Penny today, anyway. I understand the paper's looking for an investigative reporter."

Sighing, I pushed the speaker button. "Katy wants to talk to all of you."

Inattentively, I listened to the conversation as I inserted the CD in the slot. I loved Katy dearly, but no way would I attend that dinner party. Not tonight, not when I had other important things on my mind. Things like staying out of jail. Katy should understand that. I'd been material in getting her butt out of jail not too long ago!

Just as I pointed my mouse arrow and started to click, the front door-bell rang. I jumped from my desk chair, inwardly disgusted at my relief that the little envelope on the screen was still closed. I hurried out of the study and opened the front door. One of my favorite UPS men stood there, already in his summer uniform of brown shorts and shirt.

"Hi!" I greeted him enthusiastically. "Come on in!"

"Can't this time, Miz Carpenter," he drawled. "Got a tight schedule today. Need your signature here."

I accepted his extended pen and then belatedly looked around to see what package he wanted me to sign for. Nothing under his arm, where he normally carried overnight envelopes. Nothing propped against the steps, where he sometimes set larger parcels that contained a bulky manuscript full of copyedits or galleys or perhaps advance reading copies of my next book. No larger box, either, which might contain my author copies, a box which I'd have to fetch the dolly from the garage to wheel inside.

I guess my face reflected my confusion, because Brown Guy nodded beside the door. "We don't usually carry freight," he said, "but I guess the person who sent this had enough pull to override our rules. Heavy sucker, too."

Pen forgotten in my hand, I stared at the wooden crate propped against the cabin logs. Upright, carefully nailed slats. Darn sure not books or any of the other writing business paraphernalia I'd come to expect.

"Return address is Jefferson," he said. "Would've been easier to bring it here themselves. Cheaper, too."

Katy's gift, I realized. And no, Katy wouldn't think of delivering a gift herself. That wouldn't be socially proper. I scribbled my name, and with a snappy salute, Brown Guy took back the pen, tucked his clipboard under his arm, then hurried back to his brown truck. Hands on hips, I stared at the crate, wondering where on earth I'd stored that dolly this time in my overloaded garage.

Then a hint of excitement stirred. Was it...could it be...? Idiotically, I pried at the slats bare-handed. Broke a fingernail and sucked on the sore digit. Then raced back to my study. Penny sat in my desk chair, one hand on the mouse. Granny and Twila peered over her shoulder.

"You're not talking to Katy any longer?" I asked.

Three heads bobbed negatively, three gazes remained on my computer monitor.

"Are you three going to the dinner party?"

Three negatives again.

"Ugh," Granny said quietly.

"Oh, her parties aren't that bad, Granny," I said.

"Not the party," she replied. "These pictures."

The phone shrilled again, and I vowed once more to remember to turn down the stupid ringer volume. It took a lot, though, I reminded myself, to break my concentration when I was deep in the creative throes of writing. And maybe Penny would take care of those photos to Twila and Granny's satisfaction, and I wouldn't have to do that.

"Hello?"

"I totally forgot," Katy said. "You'll be getting a UPS package."

"It's already here."

"Oh, good! It should look wonderful over the fireplace mantel in your study. Of course," she lowered her voice as though someone might hear beyond the receiver, "I'd suggest you move that Casper clock if you do take my advice and display it there."

I surreptitiously glanced at Granny and knew without doubt now what the crate hid. And no way would I hurt Granny's feelings and move that clock.

"Gotta run," Katy said. "See you this evening!"

My protest fell into dead air, and as I replaced the receiver, I glared at my friends. "I thought you turned down Katy's dinner invite."

"We did," Twila said nonchalantly, then bent closer to the computer screen and pointed. "There. Blow that up, Penny."

"Well, she's still expecting us!" I insisted.

"Not us, just you," Granny said. "You wasn't here to RSVP for yourself."

"Well, thank you very much! I'm still not going!"

Gazes glued to the screen, they ignored me. I sighed and left to find the dolly.

CHAPTER 18

I tarried out on the deck as long as possible. First I removed the slats with a hammer and exposed Grandmere Alicia's portrait. I'd yearned for that portrait of my namesake for years, although I hadn't let on to Katy. I'd had it restored soon after we discovered it in the manor house attic, but agreed it should stay at Esprit d'Chêne, where Katy hung in it the Great Room. Indeed it did suit there, probably better than it would over my mantel. The portrait and I shared a common bond. Guilt stabbed me over my decision to no-show at Katy's dinner party after such an expansive gesture on her part. I'd better come up with a good excuse. I loaded the portrait carefully on the dolly and wheeled it into the study.

"Look what Katy sent me!" I cooed.

They didn't even glance at me. I surreptitiously stared at the computer monitor, but the screensaver was on.

I pushed the dolly toward the fireplace. Suddenly Trucker and Miss Molly surged to their feet. Trucker growled low and the ruff on his neck spiked. Miss Molly hissed, then ducked beneath Trucker's belly and peered between his front legs, a cat-snarl rumbling in her throat.

"What on earth's the matter with you two?" I asked. "It's Grandmere Alicia's portrait. You remember it. From Esprit d'Chêne?"

Unappeased, the two animals maintained their antagonistic stances. When I took a step forward, Trucker curled his upper lip back to expose gleaming white fangs and for an instant, fear surfaced. Not at my dog. Never my Trucker. Whatever had set him and my cat on edge could possibly mean danger. I checked behind me to see if the animals could be agitated about something other than the portrait. They were.

Patrick stood there, but it wasn't that ghost who upset them. Another entity stood behind him, an evil glare on his Hispanic features. He directed his enmity at me for a brief second before he dissolved. Behind him, he left an echo of fiendish laughter.

Patrick whirled at the sound. "No!"

The dolly handles dropped from my nerveless hands and it crashed to the floor, spilling Grandmere Alicia's portrait off.

"Who the hell was that?" I screamed at Patrick. "Why'd you bring him here?"

"I didn't," he said. "He must have followed me."

Penny pushed the desk chair back and rose to stand between Twila and Granny. Faces stricken, the three of them gaped at the doorway, then Patrick, then me.

"Who was that, Patrick?" Twila demanded also. "No more evasion. That man's projecting evil, and if he has something to do with what you've been hiding from us, you better come clean right now! Or I'll shake you silly until you spill everything."

She stomped over to Patrick and, hands out in a pleading gesture, he backed away a step for each one she took. At the doorway, Patrick side-stepped, then peered out into the hallway.

"He's gone," he said in a relieved voice...and turned back to find himself nose to nose with my aunt.

"Spill it," Twila snarled. "That bastard's dangerous."

Patrick nodded. "Yes, and I'll tell you everything. If you'll just give me a chance to catch my breath."

"You don't have breath!" Twila spat. "You're just trying to gather your thoughts and see what you want to tell us, what you don't. Start talking right now, or I'm going to banish you from contact with any of us."

"He's Antonio Quintana," Patrick babbled. "He's Consuela's brother. He's part of the reason I didn't make it back to meet her so we could plan our wedding."

"How?" Twila demanded at the same time that I asked, "Who's Consuela?" Twila waved me to silence and continued to glare at Patrick.

"Whooee," Granny murmured. "I think we better sit down, Penny."

The two of them scurried over to the sofa in front of the fireplace. Well, Penny scurried, a steadying hand on Granny's arm as she hurriedly tottered beside her. Penny settled Granny on the sofa and plopped beside her.

"Can we sit, too?" Patrick asked Twila. "We might as well get comfortable. It's a rather long story."

"And we still got's to figure out how to get that there autopsy report," Granny said.

"What autopsy report?" I asked. "Not...don't tell me you think we need to steal more crime evidence!"

"While you was takin' care of your portrait—" Granny nodded at poor Grandmere Alicia's face, which stared up at us. "—we decided that we needs to find out more info 'bout that murdered woman. Her name. And how she died."

"I don't see how this is all connected."

"It might not be," Twila admitted. "We aren't going to find out, though, unless we have all the facts in front of us. Starting with some facts that are a few decades old."

No, ghosts don't have breath, but Patrick seemed to draw in something. His chest expanded, then he relaxed and floated over to the lounge chair across from Granny. Twila allowed him to sit before she motioned me to join the rest of the group. Before she followed, Twila picked up Grandmere Alicia's portrait and leaned it against the fireplace.

"There," she whispered. "If you've got anything to say, feel free."

We exchanged glances. I'd never told anyone other than Twila how Grandmere Alicia communicated with me at times through her portrait.

"Now," she said with a nod at Patrick. "Let's hear from you."

CHAPTER 19

SEVENTH FLOOR, 1929

"Then you'll meet me there?" Patrick pleaded.

Consuela lowered her gaze and stared at the carpet. The fingers of her right hand twiddled the satin apron hem, rolling and unrolling it. "We should not," she whispered in that throaty accent. "If someone should see us, they will fire me. Your family might see to that."

"They won't," Patrick assured her. "My family wants me to be happy."

"But you know my family," she said. "They will not allow it. Still, I will try to come tonight."

"Sweetheart." Patrick cupped her cheek in his palm, and she sighed and leaned into his touch. "You care about me. I know you do. And I never knew what love was until I met you. We can't ignore this. We'll never find anything this special ever again."

"It is not only the two of us who must be considered," Consuela said. "If it were, then the choice would be easy."

"I don't give a darn about our different cultures," Patrick insisted.

"And it won't matter to my family. If it does to yours, then what does that say about how they feel about your happiness?"

Tears gleamed in her brown eyes, and Patrick immediately regretted his words. "Darling, please," he whispered as he gathered her into his arms. One hand smoothing her luxurious sable hair, he continued, "I'm sorry. About what I said, but not about how I feel. I laid awake for hours last night, imagining my life for the rest of my years without you. Then imagining it with you. The emptiness without you was horrible to contemplate."

Consuela wrapped her arms around his waist. "It would be wonderful. Yes. I, too, have thought about you for hours and days on end. Yet—"

He pushed her back far enough to see her face. She bit her bottom lip and ducked her head, but he tenderly tipped her chin up. "What? What aren't you telling me?"

She shook her head and refused to speak.

"I know your family depends on you," Patrick said. "Your mother, your two young brothers. I understand, and you needn't worry about them. I'm capable of providing for them as well as you."

She hesitated, then said, "That is part of the problem. At least as far as Antonio is concerned. He

...he saw me with you yesterday."

Patrick gripped her arms and growled, "If he physically touched you, I'll kill him."

"No. No, no," she denied. "Antonio does not have to touch someone to make his point. He is head of the family now. He has been in charge since Papa died three years ago."

Patrick guided her over to the settee, where he could hold her even closer. She was so small, so delicate. He hated that black hotel uniform she wore, the shapeless, ankle-length dress, the white satin apron with a ruffle on the bottom. The ugly white-net cap that covered her beautiful hair. He even hated those dreadful shoes with the pointed toes and high tops. Her small feet must hurt her terribly after a twelve-hour day.

"I wish I could buy you a red gown and dancing slippers," he murmured as he traced her full lips with a finger. "Diamonds...no, amethysts to set off your wonderful eyes. A tiara the only adornment for your hair, which you should leave long and swirling."

She pouted against his finger, but a mischievous twinkle sparkled in her eyes. "I am sorry my attire displeases you."

"That's not what I meant..." He chuckled when she tilted her head and giggled. "You knew all along what I meant. I want to give you things that make you happy."

"Things are not what it is about." Consuela pressed a kiss on his palm. "I would love you if you were a poor beggar at the kitchen door. That you are not is one of the reasons Antonio will never agree to our marriage."

"That doesn't make sense," Patrick said. "I can help your family. I can make your life easier."

"*Si,*" Consuela agreed. "But again, that is part of the problem."

"Explain, sweetheart," Patrick pleaded.

She settled back on the settee and tucked one slim leg under her. "You know me only as one of the maids at this place you visit from time to time. Someone you only have to crook your finger to in order to have each and every wish met."

"Never," he denied.

"Shush." She tapped his lips. "You asked me to explain, but you must listen while I do." She continued, "Our family has not always been poor. Indeed, we were not poor when I was born, nor for several years after that. Once we had a large ranch, which our family had owned for many, many years. My ancestors can trace their past to some very noble families. They received their land grant long before the *Tejanos* discovered this part of the world, and managed to hold onto it through several generations of disorder in *Tejas*. At my mother's insistence, I had tutors along with my brothers." She smiled. "Although that did not come about without a serious discussion between Mama and Papa. A discussion which you might even call an argument, which I overheard one night. Papa said girls did not need an education to bear babies. Mama said that if he felt that way, perhaps he would be more comfortable sleeping in the barn. Mama won."

"That's one of the things I noticed about you the first time I saw you," Patrick admitted. "The staff here is very amenable, but you stood out like a shining star from all the others."

"I try not to be...um...uppity," she replied. "It does not make for easy days if those you work with think that you feel you are better than they. It has helped that no one here knows that much about my family. Our ranch was near San Antonio. We only came here after Papa died."

"What changed your circumstances so drastically?" Patrick asked.

"That is what makes Antonio so furious about any thought of you and me," she said quietly. "The man who stole our land from us was a banker, like your father. He befriended Papa, or seemed to. Papa was taken in by him, and when we had a drought for a few years, Papa borrowed money from the man's bank. Just before Papa died, I found Mama listening outside Papa's study door. Her face was terribly white and her hands clenched at her sides. She didn't see me and I moved closer to see what was troubling her.

"Inside, Papa and the banker man were shouting at each other. Papa yelled that he would surrender his land only if he were dead. The banker stormed out the door, and Mama hid behind it as she watched him leave. Two days later, Papa did not come home from a trip he took to town. Antonio found his body in a canyon. He'd been shot four times."

"And the banker showed up with papers showing that he now owned the ranch," Patrick said sagely.

"*Si*. Antonio was determined to fight the banker, but no one would help us. The lawyers he approached all barely glanced at the papers and said they were legal. The marshal and his men came, and they allowed us to take our clothes and a few things that Mama begged them for. Some photos, a bit of furniture so we might have beds on which to sleep when we found a new place to live."

Compassion filled Patrick, but he had no words of comfort. He'd watched his own father agonize over foreclosures his banking officers demanded that he carry out. The difference was that Patrick's father would make sure the families were at least set up elsewhere, even if it took his own money to help them. He would never put a family out to their own devices.

"I can understand," Patrick said. "But we aren't like that man who coldly threw your family out of their home. Father would have helped you."

"There was no help that Antonio would accept other than to stay on our own land. It was his life. His blood. It changed him to lose his beloved ranch."

"He didn't lose it," Patrick said. "Your father did."

"Not in Antonio's mind," she denied. "In his mind, the banker stole it from us. And it is his fault that we now live in a small shack and I have to work here. He found employment at one of the ranches outside of town, so at least he's still able to do what he loves—work with the cattle and horses. But it is work done for another man who owns the land."

Patrick considered her story silently while an idea formed in his mind. He could probably talk her into eloping with him, but that would alienate her from her family. Plus his family—although they would get over it—would at first resent Consuela, not so much for the marriage as for the surreptitious way they slipped off and wed. It would be so much better for her if he could somehow overcome Antonio's hostility and befriend the man.

"Oh." Consuela glanced at the clock on the mantel of the fireplace in the suite. "I am out of time for my lunch." She jumped to her feet. "I must go."

Patrick followed as she hurried to the door. He pressed a palm against it to keep her from opening it, and she gazed up at him, her worry distorting her beautiful face. "I'll let you leave," he promised. "But first..."

He kissed her, softly at first, then gathered her close and unleashed his ardor and love. She responded with her arms around his neck, her body nearly one with his. Then the damn clock chimed the hour and she broke free. Still, she kept her gaze on his as she groped for the doorknob and opened the door. With one last, loving glance, she raced out the door and down the hallway.

Patrick comforted himself with her promise that she would somehow slip away tonight and meet him when he drove out to the small house where she and her family lived. He would park down the road and wait as long as necessary. And he would go see his father the next day.

CHAPTER 20

"And did she come that night?" Granny asked as she eagerly leaned forward.

"Yes," Patrick replied. "And that's when we first...and the only time—we came back to my suite. But I took her home before dawn. Without discovery, so I thought."

On the mantel, Casper boo-bonged and we all swung our gazes to the intrusion.

Twila spoke first. "I love that clock. But it's not working right."

I frowned. "It's not. It's not supposed to go off on the quarter hour, just half-hours and hours."

"Well, it says a quarter past seven," Penny pointed out, although all of us could tell time. "And I need to get home. I probably could try to get what information I can on the phone, but the people I need to talk to will be more forthcoming in person."

"But we ain't heard the rest of Patrick's story," Granny grumbled. "It was just gettin' good."

"It'll have to wait," I said, still pondering the clock's malfunction. Then I happened to notice the portrait and Grandmere Alicia winked at me. Now I understood. She evidently thought we'd dilly-dallied long enough. There was something we needed to do, and we couldn't do it sitting here in my study.

"I need some clothes," Granny said as she struggled to rise from the sofa. "No tellin' when I'll get back home. Penny can go with me to carry my suitcase. And I need t'call my niece and see why she ain't here yet for me to give her your key to keep an eye on your other cats, Alice."

Penny agreeably accompanied Granny, and as soon as they were out of the room, Twila and I shared a glance, then looked at the portrait. "You saw it, didn't you?" I asked softly.

"Yeah. I told her to let us know if she had anything to say."

Now, though, it was only an oil painting propped against the fireplace. Or was it? I thought maybe the twinkle in Grandmere Alicia's eyes was a tad brighter. Could have just been the result of a talented artist, however. I remembered Patrick, and caught him gazing at the portrait, also. He still sat in his chair, but he rose when he realized we were looking at him.

"It's wonderful to be in touch with your family history," he said. "Most of the time."

"We need to hear the rest of your story," Twila said sternly. "I have an inkling about where it's going, but I want to hear it directly from you."

"I thought we had to leave," he reminded her.

"We do. I'm just giving you a heads up that as soon as possible, you're going to be on the hot seat again. So don't use the time in between to pick and choose what you want to tell us among your memories." She paused and glanced at the doorway. "And if you happen to run across Antonio, tell him there's plenty of room on that hot seat for him. That I might just make sure it's hot enough to burn those black britches right off his ass if he tries to mess with me."

"Yes, ma'am," Patrick said in a respectful tone.

"Meet us back at the hotel later tonight," Twila ordered, and the stress butterflies woke up in my tummy. No sense arguing with her, though. We'd just have to take our chances.

* * *

Twila borrowed some black clothing from me before we left Six Gun. We're about the same size clothes-wise. I still thought we looked as silly as characters in a *noir* movie as we slipped through the night from where we'd parked Penny's Lincoln three blocks away from the hotel. We wore black leggings from one of my failed health club eras, long-sleeved, black turtlenecks and black socks and tennis shoes. I even found two black baseball caps I'd bought on Bourbon Street that we could tuck our hair up under. Unfortunately, they both had white lettering across the front, so we'd hid that with black shoe polish. The caps had formerly sported *Suck Heads, not Tails* around a crawfish and *Stolen from a Bourbon Street Whorehouse, where the Customer always Comes First* on them. I do enjoy naughty hats.

I'd given in to Twila's insistence that we dress in black, even though the weather forecast called for possible storms and the dark night would conceal us anyway. Gloomy clouds periodically scuttled across the moon, so maybe the forecasters were right for once. Trucker didn't need any dark clothing, although I'd exchanged his chain leash for a wide, black-nylon one. Even the tan spots on his shiny coat didn't stand out tonight.

Storms, though, were another phenomenon that woke up ghosts, as Twila and I knew from earlier experiences. One stormy night at a haunted plantation house over in Louisiana will forever remain in my mind.

Backpacks, black of course, hung on our shoulders. I'm not sure what Twila packed in hers to replace the satchels Ty confiscated. Probably—hopefully—plenty of her time-honored protective materials, things she'd used for years and knew actually worked. I carried my spare digital camera, extra batteries, an extra flashlight besides the tiny penlight in my hand now, two plastic bottles of water and some sandwiches. Heaven knew when we'd get out of here, and Penny had thought to supply us with some food. We also each carried a hooded black sweatshirt. April it might be, but that building would be cold at night. Both weather cold and supernatural cold.

Oh, and I'd slipped in a few of those small airline-type bottles of

Crown Royal from home. Not the normal ghosthunting fodder, but this wasn't a normal ghosthunt in my mind. I'd foregone anything to mix with the alcohol. That wouldn't matter, should an alcoholic jolt be necessary.

Once we hit the tunnel behind the hotel, Twila stepped out into sight openly. She held Trucker's leash, and he trotted happily beside her. I lagged behind for a few steps, my reluctance heightening. Until I realized my companions were already out of sight around the tunnel bend. Ignoring the slap of my tennis shoes on concrete, I caught up to them in no time.

And nearly barreled right into Twila, since I kept glancing at the huge building looming above us on its last legs. In daylight, it drew us with the mystery of the past. At night, chills crawled up and down my spine and my knees wobbled. When I'd been here previously, I had the company of several friends with whom to share both interest and frights, even chatter now and then. We'd had permission, though, and as far as I knew, none of us were wanted by the cops.

"What?" I asked Twila, who stood on the ramp a dozen or so feet from the back doorway. She shone her matching penlight back and forth across the guest arrival area.

"Thought I heard something," she replied. "Probably just a rat in the trash."

"A rat!" I stepped so close to her that she brushed at me to ward me off. "I don't *do* rats, Twila!"

"I know," she replied. "Or snakes or spiders, either. Neither do I, but things like that congregate around places like this."

"And here all I was worried about was getting caught," I muttered.

"That, too," she agreed. "Remember, we call our ghosthunts *adventures.*"

"Adventures, adsminchures!" I retorted. "I don't think I've ever been this scared spitless. Other than the time that entity crawled in bed with us in Hot Springs. And you just laid there and snored when I yelled for help!"

"Trucker will keep the four- and eight-legged creatures away, won't you, boy? Legless ones, too." She patted Trucker's head and ignored my reminder of that other wretched *adventure*. My dog stared up at her adoringly.

Twila shifted her backpack off, unzipped one storage pocket, and held out something to me. Good. She did bring strong protective measures. I slipped the quince seed bracelet over my wrist as she placed one on hers.

"What else do you have?" I asked eagerly.

"That's good enough for now. If we need more later, I've got a couple other things."

"Why not go ahead and protect ourselves as much as possible right from the start?" I demanded.

She shot me a look that shouted my naiveté. "If we protect ourselves too much," she reminded me, "we won't be able to communicate with any of the entities."

"Works for me," I muttered.

She sighed in exasperation. "Do you want to abort, Alice?"

I debated—very passionately—for a long moment. Then I realized what I'd have to go through for months, maybe years, if I chickened out. At inopportune moments, Twila would remind me of my cowardice, the same tactic she used on me when she first started me down this ghosthunting road years ago. She knew me well enough to work that type of reverse psychology successfully on my subconscious. Like when she would charge off into overgrown graveyards on dark nights after agreeing that I could stay in the car. She knew I'd pitty-pat straight after her rather than wait all by my lonesome. If I finally acceded to my spine-lessness, maybe she would dust her hands of me and never take me with her again! Much as I disliked the frights I experienced at times, they were also addictive. Adrenaline pumping, senses alert. Too, the ego trip of being able to experience things that nonbelievers would never know was a total thrill.

I'd die if I had to give up ghosthunting. It would be as bad as my sales dropping off and never being able to sell another book!

I straightened my back and marched toward the doors. "Coming?" I called over my shoulder.

She giggled. I expected that. What I didn't expect was that the door would swing open for me even before I rattled the latch. Or that when I jumped back to stand inside Twila's protective aura, it wouldn't be there.

I swiveled so quickly that I turned my ankle, although I caught myself before I fell. Twila still stood in the same place, Trucker by her side. I couldn't see her face from here, so I hightailed it straight back to her so I could. Luckily, the ankle turn was minor, and the slight pain faded with each step.

"Why are you back here?" I whispered harshly. "I thought we were going inside!"

"We are," she acknowledged with a nod. "But as you just saw, we need to do this with the proper preparation."

"I never touched that door," I insisted.

"That's what I mean."

I glanced back at the door. It still stood open. "Someone...some*thing* is waiting inside the door for us!"

"I believe so," she agreed.

"Oh, please," I breathed. "Not...Antonio."

"I can't tell," she said. "Whoever...whatever it is, has either already left or..."

"Or?" I prodded.

She glanced at me in pity. "Or is a pretty strong entity."

"Stronger than you?" I demanded.

"I won't know until we meet up."

I hung my head and muttered, "Is abort still an option?"

CHAPTER 21

Twila didn't bother to answer. Perhaps for my peace of mind, she handed me Trucker's leash and approached the doorway slowly. I didn't want to believe that she was actually scared. Cautious I could handle, but I drew my courage partly from her and depended on her staid spirit, guts, and determination to bolster my own.

"We didn't even need the key," I mentioned inanely. Then giggled, more from nerves than humor.

She shone her penlight inside, but the tiny dot of light didn't illuminate much. Same floor, same hallways stretching off into midnight blackness. She centered the light on the area where we'd seen the wet footprints earlier that day—was it still the same day?—and to my amazement, there were those footprints again.

"How?" I whispered. "They should have dried long ago."

"Unless they aren't new footprints," she replied.

I nodded. I understood that part. The footprints could be a lingering trace from another time. If so, then only people with our abilities would see them. Still, they looked so fresh.

Twila walked over and knelt by them. She touched one with an index finger, then jerked it back. "Ugh."

"What?" I asked.

"Remember that time you stuck your hand inside the mist in the bathroom?"

"Ugh," I echoed, and instinctively rubbed my hand against my thigh. I remembered all too well. A cold drop of what Twila explained was probably ectoplasm had adhered to the back of my hand that day. A cold, jellish mass that I could barely restrain myself from wiping off before Twila examined it.

She wiped her finger on her leg and stood, but kept her light focused on the footsteps as they completely disappeared. Faded back into their own dimension. No sense asking Twila how old the footsteps were. I knew that much. They could have been recent or as old as the building. Perhaps even prior to the building. The only firm deduction we could make was that the footsteps came from someone on the other side of the veil, given the ectoplasm that made them visible.

Twila reiterated my deduction. "They aren't from whoever killed that poor woman. Unless that person died at the same time."

Now, there was a distinct possibility, one I didn't much care that she'd deduced. "Which means there could be another body somewhere in here waiting for us."

It wasn't a question, and she didn't bother to answer. Instead of walking down the hallway that Carrie had led us through earlier that day, she moved in the direction the footprints had been pointing.

"Uh...we haven't explored that way this time," I reminded her.

She kept walking, forcing me to follow. "What about when you were here before?"

"I don't recall going this way at all." I gripped Trucker's leash securely, glad for his bulky presence. "Unless...it's probably the same hallway that starts in the lobby. But if I remember right, that one dead-ended before we got back to this area."

"Dead-ended?" She chuckled. "You do tend to have a way with words, Alice. So maybe that's why the footprints were here now."

Her explanation didn't reassure me at all. If the ghost...or entity...was leading us somewhere...into something...it could be good or bad. I rubbed my quince seed bracelet for confidence as we walked down a passageway that seemed to close in on us in the darkness. In fact, once I swung my penlight behind me to make sure that it wasn't...crumbling silently behind us, caving in and trapping us. The hallway eventually did dead-end...at a door. I halfway expected it to swing open for us, but it didn't.

Twila rattled the doorknob. "Hum. I don't suppose by any chance Jack ever taught you the technique to pick locks."

"Jack? Straight and narrow Jack? You've got to be kidding."

"But...?" she asked in face of the fact that I left my answer hanging.

"Well," I admitted. "One of his buddies showed me how to pick locks once. For book research. But it takes a set of special tools."

"And?"

"And I didn't bring the ones he gave me with me."

"No need," Patrick said as he visualized. "Here." He wiggled a finger and the tumblers clicked, the door swung open.

His actions didn't surprise Twila and me; we'd seen another ghost do that. Patrick, however, stared at the door with a pleased expression and said, "He said that would work, but it's the first time I tried it on my own."

"You met Sir Gary while you were at Alice's, huh?" Twila said.

"Yes," Patrick agreed. "He came by one day to visit, but Alice was writing, so we didn't bother her in her study."

"Good thing," I said sternly. "That's the number one rule of The Howard and Alice Ghost Agreement. Never—"

"—EVER bother Alice when she's writing," Twila and Patrick both recited along with me.

"It was interesting to talk to Sir Gary," Patrick went on. "Among other things, he told me that I'll be able to come back and visit for short periods once I do cross over."

"True," Twila told him. "Right now, you're a ghost, but once you cross through the light, you'll become a spirit. Then you can transcend the two dimensions once in a while. As Sir Gary said, however, just for brief periods."

"First you have to pass through the light, though," I explained.

Patrick nodded before he glided through the doorway. Then he murmured something about seeing us in a few minutes and dissolved.

"Thanks for your help," Twila said into the silence.

You're welcome, he thrust into my mind.

The hallway eventually led us back to the lobby area, and I breathed a sigh of relief—at first. We switched off our penlights, since some street light filtered through the dirty windows across the front veranda. Eyes adjusting, I scanned the lobby. An orb flashed from one side to the other, but even my less-developed psychic senses understood it was just one of the many entities who occupied this elderly building. Although there were dozens of passed-on spirits here, most of them were benign and comfortable in their existence. Some were just spirits, not ghosts, spirits who probably felt the urge to come back and sit a spell somewhere they'd enjoyed during their physical stages.

I didn't sense any supernatural darkness here. It wasn't necessarily peaceful, either. Sort of a heavy atmosphere, indicating that beings were present and accounted for. Twila's face held a look of concentration, and I respectfully waited while she silently examined the room. Until—

The leash jerked from my hand and Trucker dashed across the lobby. Lucky for my shoulder joint, I'd held the strap laxly, my awareness elsewhere. What chilled me, though, was that the dog ran noiselessly, almost like a ghost himself. No growls, no pants, no forewarning for whatever Trucker was bent upon attacking. Empty, the lobby offered no interference to him. Nothing visible, anyway. When he reached the foot of the far stairwell, he lunged up three steps, then whirled and bounded back to the floor. Again, he raced across the lobby, this time directly at Twila and me. My feet stuck like glue to the floor, even though mind over matter shouted for me to find a hiding corner. Curl into a ball and hold out the arm with the quince bracelet to ward off Trucker's prey.

The dog passed us in full run, then disappeared up the other stairway to the mezzanine. Twila and I both released held breaths. I could hear her beside me, since I'd evidently sidled close to her again without realizing I'd moved or that my feet weren't inoperable. I tried hard to turn my head and seek her calming gaze, but instead, I tilted my head back and looked up at the balcony above us.

"Where's my dog?" I managed to whisper. I couldn't hear him, couldn't see him. He didn't pass across the mezzanine.

"I don't know," Twila admitted in the same low whisper. "I can't remember..."

"What?"

"There was a door beside the elevators."

I sprinted across the lobby, up the stairwell, a vision of that damned open elevator in my mind. Surely the cops had closed the elevator door. Surely Trucker would have better sense than to nose into it. Unless whatever he chased—whatever we couldn't see—led my dog to his doom.

CHAPTER 22

"Alice!" Twila yelled, although she was hot on my heels. "I didn't mean the elevator!"

I didn't listen. I rounded the end of the stairwell and pounded across the mezzanine until I stood before the elevator doors. The *closed* elevator doors, the crisscross gates secure. I swooned in relief and plopped down on the floor.

"Don't get too comfy," Twila ordered. "Trucker's not here. And he didn't cross the mezzanine, or we would have seen him. He evidently went up this stairwell."

I craned my neck toward her voice, then remembered the penlight and clicked it on. I still couldn't see much, but Twila stood in front of another door between the elevators and the doorway to the room where we'd set up camp so briefly. An *open* door.

"That's one of the stairwells that leads to the upper levels," I said as I forced myself to my feet.

"Oh?" she asked. "It's awfully narrow."

"They're all like that," I explained. "And you've got to be careful. Some of the steps are crumbly."

"Huh," she replied with a snort. "Are you insinuating that our weight will make them dangerous? Your dog weighs a lot."

I wasn't about to compare our weight to Trucker's. I'd avoided the scales for several months now. And it wasn't because I accidentally-on-purpose kept forgetting to buy a new battery for the digital display. I peeked around her and shone my penlight up the stairwell, even though I knew what I'd see. A narrow passageway, deteriorating steps, no handrailing. Ragged concrete walls that would scrape off elbow skin if you inadvertently brushed against them. Which I'd done a time or two on my earlier visit. In days gone by, maids and other employees used these stairwells to traverse between floors, in addition to the one freight elevator. The one that had killed that poor woman, and in an earlier time, a hotel employee.

"There's not room for us to go side by side."

"I'll go first," Twila said, to my relief. Still, she obviously couldn't help adding, "I'd like to get to the next floor before morning, and you'd probably stop and study each step."

"So?" I grumbled. "I told you, they're dangerous."

Just then Trucker yipped above us. Twila rushed up the steps two at a time, and I kept right up with her.

The doorway at the top was open, and we rushed through, then halted in another hallway junction. One led ahead of us, one to the left. Directly in front of us was the gymnasium, empty now of all the equipment available for the guests. The penlights didn't even begin to illuminate the stark darkness in the cavernous room.

"Screw this," I muttered, and shifted my backpack off. The Velcro tore loose with a harsh sound in the stillness, and I felt around in the pocket until I found my large lantern light. I pushed the *On* switch and panned the light around the gym.

"That's awfully bright," Twila said.

"We're in the inner hallways," I replied inattentively. "No one outside can see this light." The beam fell on Trucker. He lay on his side by a pile of trash. "Ohmigod," I screamed.

We both reached him at the same instant and knelt beside him.

Heart thundering in fear, I pulled his head onto my lap and stroked his fur. Trucker opened his eyes and whined.

"Where are you hurt, boy?" I asked. Trucker, of course, didn't answer. Instead, he groaned and surged to his feet. "Maybe he was just tired from his run."

My anxious glance at Twila begged her to confirm my thought. Then I grasped Trucker's collar to hold him beside me while I shone the beam over his head, his back, down his legs. Even crouched and examined his stomach. No blood anywhere. I set the light down and smoothed my hands over him. Still, I didn't find any indication of injury.

"What happened to him?" I asked Twila.

She picked up my light and rose to shine it around the room, back toward the doorway, then in a circle around to the right, along the wall. At the corner, she continued the path on that wall. Halfway down the right wall, a bright flash reflected back at us.

"I thought so." Twila took a step, but I grabbed her leg. The black tights stretched in my fingers for a second, then she stopped. "I need to go examine that, Alice."

"Why? You know what it is. Some invisible barrier someone...*thing* put up. Trucker must have bounced off it and had the breath knocked out of him. We've read about stuff like that, but never encountered it."

"Exactly," she agreed. "We have to see what it is. Dominate whatever entity did this."

"What if it's a vortex?" I whispered in fear. "Or more correctly, a barrier to a vortex. They won't want us messing with it."

"All the more reason *to*."

She sternly pulled her leg free and walked toward the barrier. The reflected flashlight beam outlined her in the darkness. Outlined Trucker and me, also, since I wasn't about to let Twila approach that oddity on her own. The dog and I padded right after her.

Suddenly the flashlight beam penetrated straight to the far wall with no interference. Whatever had blocked it was gone. We halted a couple steps back from where the blockage had been, and Twila reached out her free arm to wave it ahead of us.

"No vortex," she confirmed. "Someone playing around with powers he isn't real adept with."

"Antonio?"

"Maybe. If so, he's got another strike against him on my shit list."

"Mine, too. He was able to lead Trucker into it because Trucker doesn't understand it takes concentration to fight something like that."

She shone the flashlight on around the room. Nowhere did it meet any other resistance in the vast space. Then she switched the light off.

"Uh..." I whispered.

"Shhhhh."

Twila stood there silently for several long seconds. I knew she was concentrating, trying to tune in and get a feel for what we were facing. Not necessarily the dangers of stumbling around a deteriorating building full of tangible pitfalls such as weak floors or unsturdy walls. We faced that, of course. But additional danger lay in forces from a nonphysical realm.

I coped with the darkness and inner dread as long as I could. Longer than I could, really, well aware that I should be helping, not hurting, her concentration, but that my fear would hinder more than assist. I gritted my teeth and stoically endured. Finally...

"Can't I at least turn my penlight back on?" I whined.

"Might as well," she replied all too nonchalantly. "We need to go on up to the seventh floor."

Aw sheesh. I gulped. All along I'd known we'd end up there. All along I'd dreaded that even more than actually breaking into the building under cover of night.

CHAPTER 23

"That's where she's waiting for us, isn't it?" I asked Twila as she turned her penlight back on and handed me the lantern flashlight.

I couldn't see her nod in the darkness, but she placed a comforting hand on my arm. "I'm proud of you, Alice. Even though you were scared to death, you followed my concentration and got the same thought I did."

"Not willingly," I admitted. "And my legs are just as unwilling to go up there."

"But you will."

"Yes, damn it," I muttered. "I will."

"We'll take a short break first," she said. "Let's sit over by the door and have a drink."

"Sounds good to me."

"I meant water, Alice," she said, a laugh in her voice. "Just water for now. We need our senses about us."

She led Trucker and me back to the doorway, found a somewhat less dirty spot on the floor, and removed her backpack before she sat. I did the same and leaned back against the wall...after I'd shone my own penlight on it to make sure an eight-legged invader hadn't taken up residence ahead of us. One had, but evidently it had dined on all the available insects and moved on. I found a paper napkin in among the sandwiches and brushed the half-shredded web away, then settled back and tried to relax. Trucker sprawled beside me and laid his head on my leg.

Twila's next words negated any hope of relaxation to replenish my store of courage. "Call Jack," she said.

"What?" I jerked upright. "I know he won't know where I'm calling from on the cell, but—"

"The point is to tell him where we are," she cut in sternly.

"Bull sh...crap!" I shook my head. "He'll blister my ears with a rant about ten dozen reasons why we shouldn't be here!"

"But he *will* know where we are," she pointed out.

"Granny and Penny know," I said stubbornly.

"If we need someone to come after us, Granny's only option would be to call Jack anyway. And who knows where Penny is. She said her sources preferred to meet with her in person."

"Yeah, but—but—" I couldn't come up with any sort of counter to her sage advice.

"You did bring the new cell phone I got you, didn't you? The one you still owe me money for?"

"Yes!" I said. "I wasn't stupid enough to come back here without a decent cell phone. But calling Jack...can't we just call Granny at Penny's and let her tell him?"

"I want to know a couple other things. Things Granny won't know but Jack might. Call, Alice."

"Uh...how much do I owe you? We might as well settle up while we wait." I pulled my backup billfold that I'd retrieved in Six Gun out of the backpack.

She snickered. "You're just putting off the inevitable. We'll settle up later. Call."

I heaved a sigh, reluctantly replaced the billfold and dug the cell phone out. Grimly punched in Jack's number, hit SEND, then handed the phone to Twila.

She chuckled, but accepted the phone.

"No, it's not your *Chère*," she said after a second. "It's Twila. We're at the hotel, and Alice is afraid to talk to you."

I swerved my penlight at her face, and she shaded it with her hand as she moved the phone an inch or so back from her ear so I could hear the tone of Jack's voice, if not make out his words. Just as I thought, he sounded like he wished he could reach through the phone and throttle us both.

"Yes, Patrick's around here somewhere," Twila said in answer to something on Jack's end. "But shut up for a minute, Jack, and answer a couple questions for me."

She fluttered her hand at me and I finally slid the penlight to the side, although I kept it focused near enough to read her face. Her lips quirked into a grin.

"Naughty, naughty, Jack. You're lucky we aren't the type to sue for verbal police brutality." I closed my eyes briefly and shook my head. She continued, "Doesn't matter if you're on duty or not. Look, you can't do a thing about us being here at the moment. So if you don't want to put us in even more danger, give me the information I want."

She paused for a few seconds, then said, "Jack? Are you still there?" Evidently he was, because she asked, "Have you heard anything from the hospital about Carrie?"

She nodded, then said to me, "Carrie's still catatonic. The doctors can't understand it, and they're thinking of transferring her to a psych ward." Then, into the phone, "What about the identity of the woman who got killed here?" To me, she said, "They still don't know who she is. No one's reported a missing woman to fit her description and her fingerprints aren't on file."

"Lots of people's prints aren't on file," I replied.

She turned her attention back to the phone. "Have you been in contact with Chief Grandberg?" A moment later, she continued, "Oh?

Well, we'll just see about that. Right now I wanted to let you know that we're heading on up to the seventh floor here."

She smiled again and pulled the phone away from her ear a little further this time. I could make out a few of Jack's words: stupid, asinine, idiotic. A curse that I knew from experience only crossed his lips right before his temper exploded past restraint bounds. That particular curse also heralded the possibility of flying objects. Twila calmly held the phone out to me.

"Huh uh!" I defiantly stuck my free hand behind my back. "You're the one who wanted to talk to him, not me."

"I just wanted you to turn off the phone," she said, her smile still in place. "I'm not sure which button to push."

"END," I informed her, determined not to be the one to disconnect Jack. "Did Jack say where he was?"

"No, but from the tone of his rant, I assume he's a little too far away to get here in time to stop us from going any further into the hotel."

I shoved the phone into the backpack, then handed Twila one of the water bottles and found one for myself. The water wasn't cold any longer, but it still went down wet. After I quenched my thirst, I cupped my hand and squirted some water in it for Trucker to slurp.

I really didn't want to know. Yes, I did. No, best left alone. "What did Jack say about Grandberg?" I blurted.

"He thinks we're a couple of charlatans," she said, "who should be in a circus sideshow."

"We'll see about that!" I echoed her as I surged to my feet.

She rose and said, "I think it's probably safe enough for a while for you to use that larger light."

Agreeably, I exchanged the water for the lantern. My hand brushed the sweatshirt and on second thought, I pulled it out. "It's going to get colder as we go further up," I told Twila. "Better put these on now."

Seconds later, we cautiously crept out into the hallway, back to the stairwell. Since Twila had proven her courage over mine earlier, I drew deep into my well of determination—all right, stubbornness—and pushed past her to lead the way. Trucker, though, would have none of it. He shoved his bulk past me and I stifled an ouch.

"What?" Twila asked.

"Hole in my sweatshirt elbow," I grumbled. "I hit against the wall when Trucker squeezed by."

"Stop," she said when I tried to follow Trucker's pull against the leash. "Let me see."

I commanded Trucker to sit and held my arm out to her. After she examined it in her penlight beam, she turned away for a moment, then crouched beside her backpack.

"Why aren't you carrying your backpack on your back?" I asked.

"I want it readily available in case I need any of the protective devices I have with me," she explained, firing my trepidation. Then she uncapped a small tin and smoothed something on my elbow that immediately soothed the sting.

"Aloe," she said. "I've also learned to carry some first-aid supplies when I'm around my accident-prone niece on a ghosthunt."

I grimaced, but held back my smart-ass retort. Gripping Trucker's leash tightly so he couldn't escape again, I said, "Go on, boy. But not too fast."

He rose and walked up the steps. I shone the lantern light beam ahead of him and we counted the floors we passed. Four. Five. Six. The closer we got to that eerie seventh floor, the more the lump of dread in my throat thickened. Only the dog ahead of me and the presence of Twila behind me kept me going.

Nearing the seventh-floor landing, I noticed none of us were too eager to reach our goal. Twila dropped back a step. Could be that we were somewhat tired from the climb, but I couldn't fool myself with that thought. Even the flashlight beam weakened against the stygian darkness. Then the beam flickered out, leaving us in that total blackness except for Twila's tiny penlight beam. Six stories of emptiness below us, seven above us. Empty rooms, but thousands of tons of building. A veil that might or might not divide us from the beings who could transcend it.

"Shit," I whispered. Would have yelled, but a whisper was all I could manage past the foreboding weight in my chest.

"Turn it back on," Twila said quietly.

"It burned out," I insisted.

"Flick the switch."

I did. The light shone again. I damned well hadn't turned it off. My thumb had been glued unmoving to the handle with the rest of my fingers. "Take that," I muttered to whoever had messed with the switch.

Behind me, Twila whispered, "Yeah."

Two more steps and we stood on the landing. I halted, and even Trucker sat, appearing reluctant to move through the door, although his ears were alert as he gazed into the hallway. I shivered even with the sweatshirt on. Not only the atmosphere had grown colder but, as I predicted, the temperature.

"I think we need to lay some ground rules before we go out there," Twila murmured.

"Just tell me what you want me to do."

"Not for us," she said with a wry chuckle that didn't set my mind to ease at all. I also caught the underlying disquiet, the tenseness in her stance. "For whoever's waiting for us on this floor."

"Ha," I whispered. "As if they...he...it's going to play by the rules we lay out!"

"They won't," she agreed, confirming another fear niggling my mind. More than one entity grouped out there. "But they'll know in advance what we won't tolerate."

"Where on earth did Patrick get off to?" I asked. Anything to delay going out onto that floor. I'd told Twila what had happened to us there before.

"He'll show up sooner or later." She reached for my light and set it on the stairwell floor beside her backpack, then took my hand. She rested her other hand on Trucker's head and I did the same. Circle complete, she spoke.

"We're here in peace, but if peace isn't your intention, be forewarned that we do not fear you. You believe you have a purpose for being as you are. You may well be right or wrong, or you may be evil, a value you chose in life. If the latter is the case, your capabilities now will not be strength enough against ours. This is how it will be."

She paused, drew in a breath and continued, "You may visualize. You may speak. You may explain yourself and we will listen. We agree to try to help you, but should you not like what we have to tell you, it will do you no good. We know you have certain powers, but ours are stronger. We will not hesitate to use them against you, should the need arise. You have a choice in that. That choice is banishment or accord with us."

"So mote it be," I whispered with her.

CHAPTER 24

Torn, Patrick waited outside the door to the seventh-floor suite. Alice, Twila, and the dog emerged from the stairwell, but didn't appear eager to explore any further. They only stood there and played their flashlight beams around. A good thing, too, since piles of rubble littered the hallway and doors swung loose where hinges had rotted free of the wooden doorjambs.

Eventually Alice would recall which suite he'd described to them in his memories. She'd been in this suite on her previous trip for a few seconds, until Antonio chilled and frightened her group without revealing himself. Patrick had noticed her immediately among the group and decided to contact her. He hadn't expected her in the men's shower room, but when opportunity presented itself, one needed to take advantage of it. Plus, he'd shown himself at the suite window that morning, should Alice need a further nudge to her recollections.

He'd waited in the suite since he left Alice and Twila in the downstairs hallway, but no one showed up to ease his loneliness as he strolled among happier memories. Not Consuela, although he'd tried as hard as ever to contact her. Not even Antonio. No doubt the bastard was around, though. He wouldn't forego thwarting any chance Patrick had to find the only love of his life again.

He really needed to go back and talk to that woman at the police station. But what if Twila managed to contact his beloved while he was gone? Worse yet, what if they needed his help and he wasn't there for them? He'd led them into this, his yearning to find Consuela after all these years of fruitless search overcoming the knowledge that Antonio would do his damnedest to make sure that never happened, as he had in life.

It would probably take Twila and Alice a while to do...whatever they had in mind. Surely he'd have time to research a bit on his own, now that he had a new path to follow. It wasn't that far from here to the police station, and in this condition, he could get there and back a lot quicker than a mortal, who had to depend on gasoline-powered transport. He entered the suite one last time and longingly walked through it. Nothing. Making up his mind, he willed himself away from the hotel.

In the police station, he realized his mistake. Patty wouldn't be there now. Mortals in positions like hers worked shifts. A pretty young woman barely out of her teens sat in front of the phone bank and radio equipment, reading a paperback book. Remaining invisible, he moved to her side and glanced over her shoulder, then snickered. Something like that would have been banned in his time, or at least hidden beneath a cloth cover. The models on the book gave every indication that inside a reader would find not only a love story, but scenes left to the imagination in earlier times.

The young woman shivered, and Patrick realized he'd been so engrossed in the book cover that he'd nearly crossed into her dimension. He corrected the oversight, and although she hurriedly scooted her chair back and scanned the room, she couldn't see him. She went back to her book, and Patrick bit his bottom lip in thought. There should be a file around here with Patty's information in it, her address. The town hadn't changed that much since the early part of the last century. He should be able to find her house...if he could determine where she lived.

Since no one could possibly be offended, he shed his clothing. Not that it encumbered him. He'd enjoyed the freedom of movement when he lived, especially when he would sneak out at night and relish his family's swimming pool. Moving naked through this adjacent dimension gave him the same sort of pleasure, plus reminded him of those nights at home.

A closed door on a side wall offered no resistance to him, of course. The small office was utilitarian, a row of file cabinets against one wall, a desk with one of those computers on it, a chair for the chief, and two uncomfortable-looking, hard plastic visitor chairs in front of the desk. A small credenza against the other wall held one of those facsimile machines he recognized from television and a row of large notebooks propped upright with metal bookends.

Patrick studied the bank of file cabinets. Enough light entered the window behind the desk so he could read the labels, but none of them looked promising. He walked around behind the desk. The first drawer slid out, and he willed on the reading lamp on the desk. Nothing interesting in here. Snacks, a salt and pepper shaker, some small plastic packages labeled mustard, catsup, relish. The rest of the drawers opened to reveal other non-interesting contents...except one. It obeyed his concentration, however, when he focused on it and disengaged the lock.

Ah, yes. Files with names on them. He manipulated them one by one until he found the label *PATRICIA ALVIDEZ*. So that was her last name. It didn't ring a bell in his mind, but generations had passed. No other files had that first name, so this had to be the one he sought. He floated the file out of the drawer and onto the desk, where he opened it and read the page stapled to the left side of the folder. Memorized it and then replaced the file. The street address was familiar. It was only a block over from the other one he knew so well.

"Chief Grandberg," the young woman in the outer office said. "I didn't expect you in tonight."

"Last time I thought about it, I didn't need your permission to come in here, Janet."

Grandberg appeared in fine fettle, Patrick mused as he relocked the desk drawer and turned off the lamp. Or maybe he treated all his employees that way. The doorknob rattled and then the door swung open. Grandberg switched on the overhead light, slammed the door shut, then strode over to the credenza. Patrick shielded his visibility and glided back against the window, still close enough to see why the police chief had found it necessary to return to the station this time of night. In fact, Patrick thought as he considered the situation, why wasn't the man already here? After all, he was supposed to be spearheading a murder investigation.

Grandberg picked up some papers from the facsimile tray and stood there as he read them. Patrick moved closer and grimaced when he recognized an autopsy report. However, he forced himself to read the name on it.

"Jane Doe, my ass," Grandberg muttered at the same time Patrick read the name. "You may have been gone five years, but..." He ran his finger down the page until he stopped on a paragraph labeled identifying marks, then tapped his finger against the words, *butterfly tattoo, upper left breast.*

"Mary Ann," Grandberg whispered. He tossed the papers onto the credenza. They scattered, and the first page fell to the floor as Grandberg stumbled over to his desk chair, where he sat and buried his face in his hands. Grief-stricken sobs shook the man's shoulders.

"No," he moaned. "Why, Mary Ann? You were free."

Grandberg threw himself back in his chair, swiveled it toward the window and pushed his fingers through his hair. Then he froze and ever so slowly turned his head toward the credenza. For a moment, Patrick thought he'd once again inattentively allowed himself to partially visualize. However, Grandberg's gaze slid past him and centered in the corner of the room.

The murdered woman stood there. She was beautiful, what there was of her. The top portion of her, head to waist, hovered above the floor. She stretched out a hand towards Grandberg, then disappeared.

"No! Don't go!" The police chief surged to his feet and raced around the desk. Evidently, though, he got a grip on his emotions quickly. He halted and held his hands out as though to ward off the now invisible woman's image. Then he backed away from the credenza and collapsed in his desk chair.

Patrick stifled a stab of sympathy for the man. He recognized the longing on his face. But since he couldn't read Grandberg's mind, Patrick continued to tarry in the office, hoping the mortal would speak aloud again. Instead, Grandberg pulled a key ring from his pocket and opened the locked door. He shoved the confidential files to the front of the drawer and pulled out a half-full bottle of Jack Daniels from behind them. Not bothering with a glass, he unscrewed the cap and took a long swallow.

CHAPTER 25

Even Trucker's steps lagged as we approached that seventh-floor suite. The room both drew and revolted me, and I assumed Twila experienced the same *come-no-don't* sensation. She flicked her searching gaze around rather than focusing on the door. Antonio was definitely on my mind, but I also sensed a deep sadness, which I didn't think came from the dark ghost. It could have, I supposed, although the brief contact we'd had with him indicated more anger in his personality than anguish.

At last we had no choice but to enter the room. "Come on," Twila whispered.

"I—I'm ready," I stuttered.

"Not you...although I'm proud of your courage. Something tells me that Patrick should be here. You can bet Jack's riding like a bat out of hell, also, trying to intervene."

She drew in a breath, held it, whooshed it out, then the action twice more—her grounding technique, combined sometimes with her pre-trance preparations. I damn sure didn't want her to go trance-like on me right now! Her compliment on my courage didn't even begin to negate my need for her complete physical and mental presence right here beside me within hand's reach.

"I love you to death, Twila," I muttered furiously through my trembling lips. "But I swear, if you even half leave me right now, I'll jerk your ass right back out of whatever semi-state you go into!"

She whispered a chuckle in return. "I know, Alice. I won't leave you. But I have to follow my senses. And they're telling me right now that we should not go in this room without Patrick."

I plopped down on the dirty floor, as much in relief at the delay in entering that room as the fact that it gave my wobbly legs a different sort of relief. "Then we'll just wait for him, okay?"

Trucker offered a silent agreement as he laid down beside me, woofed a sigh, and snuggled his head into my lap. I stroked a hand down his broad back, and the slight shiver in his muscles indicated his trepidation. My tinge of relief escaped somewhere in the dim hallway recesses at the dog's uneasiness in addition to ours.

Twila joined me on the floor, cross-legged in front of me. She cupped my chin and turned my face toward her, away from the eyestrain of searching the darkness. "Listen, Alice," she soothed. "The ghosts can*not* hurt us. Oh, they can scare the shit out of us and, depending on how much they've developed since their deaths—"

"They?" I interrupted, not bothering to lower my voice. "Just how the hell many entities are waiting inside that room for us? I told you. When I went in there before, I only lasted about ten seconds. Something evil snickered so vilely that I barely had time to race out into the hallway. And I lost my damn lunch when I tossed my sandwiches out of the plastic bag so I could puke in it! For the remainder of the night, the rest of the group I was with wouldn't even talk about coming back to this floor."

She leaned back and crossed her arms. "Tsk, tsk. You must owe that trip kitty at least a hundred dollars by now."

"Screw the trip kitty! I sure won't be going to Carnival with Granny if I'm stuck in a mental ward babbling nonsense! Or in jail!"

Trucker lifted his head and whined. Twila tensed before she slowly swung her head around to follow Trucker's gaze. Three relieved sighs echoed when Twila shone her penlight in that direction. I swear, Trucker also sighed.

Patrick floated toward us at a snail's pace, the troubled look on his face illuminated in the light. He was naked again, that towel around his neck, the dribbles of water easing paths down his golden tan. Suddenly Trucker scrambled upright and growled, low, vicious. Twila surged to her feet, and confusion crowded my mind, but not enough to keep me there on the floor alone. I clumsily pushed myself up, staring back and forth between Patrick and my companions.

"What?" I asked.

"Keep back," Twila warned. "That's not the real Patrick."

"Patrick's not real anyway," I insisted.

The ghost floated closer to us, and Twila kept her light on his face, although she held her left arm out in front of me and backed me up with her as she retreated. Trucker balked for a moment, continued to growl, but yielded to my forceful tug on his leash. As he got closer, I realized the Patrick-ghost...image...whatever it was, didn't appear to realize we were there. He...it...

"What is it?" I whispered to Twila.

"I think it's a previous image of Patrick," she explained. "It could be why..." Her voice trailed off as Patrick floated to the suite door and continued on inside.

"Why what?" I asked.

"Why he's having trouble crossing over," she replied. "There's some real confusion here. I believe Patrick is torn between more than whether to cross over or not. There's someone on the other side of the veil that he wants to be with, but something on this side that he needs to understand."

"What's Antonio got to do with it?"

"I don't know," she admitted. "I think we need to do a séance."

"Here?" I croaked. "No way! Twila, you know better! There are way too many entities here for us to mess with in a séance!"

She nodded an agreement. "It would definitely test my powers."

"And what if they failed? What if...what if we found out that some of our beliefs were in error? That ghosts really can kill people? Especially if a bunch of them gang up on us? Huh, Twila? What if?"

"Calm down your writer's imagination," she said. "I'll be careful. If it looks like I'm out of my depth, we'll terminate the séance."

"What if we can't?" I insisted. "What if it's too late and we've released someone...some*thing* that doesn't want to be terminated?"

"I've got a protective device that I haven't used yet," she assured me.

"If you haven't used it, how do you know it works?" I demanded. "Twila, listen to me. I've got all the confidence in the world in you, but—"

"You don't sound like it. You sound very doubtful."

"Maybe I'm echoing your own doubts."

To my terror, she nodded an agreement. "But Patrick's in there now. You have to admit, my thought about that was on the money. We were supposed to wait for him."

"You don't know for sure that's the version of Patrick your senses meant!"

"No," she agreed again.

The thundering fright in my mind heightened and I shrieked. But that wasn't like me. I'd never give in to that sort of embarrassing hysteria in front of Twila, not if I could help it. The shriek rebounded off the walls around us. Not me. I glanced at Twila, her face transfixed as she stared down the hallway. The puny penlight faded out way too close to us to illuminate anything. Trucker sidled against my leg, and this time his shudders left no doubt in my mind that he was as terror-stricken as we were.

The evil laugh died, but even before my ears cleared of the echo, a moan whispered. Pain. So much pain. No way to tell if the ghost...entity...whoever...*what*ever it was cried in physical pain or mental anguish. The moan broke off in a whimper, then dead silence. Weighty silence. It crushed against us as though every floor above us exerted a downward pressure.

The tiny phosphorescent orb appeared at the far end of the hallway. I blinked my straining eyes, for an instant believing I'd imagined it. Still there. It bobbed up and down, zigzagged back and forth,

then...

Enlarged. So fast that one moment it was only a pinprick, the next a huge, towering, wavering, and ebbing circle. Suddenly it transformed into a whirling dervish of white mist filled with snapping, blinking, multicolored lights. The upper portion widened, the lower formed into a slithering tail. It looked like a white tornado hovering between the two doorways at the end of the hall.

Then it moved.

Its tail flicked right. The door on that side slammed open with a crash.

Left. That door slammed and broke from its hinges.

The damn thing destroyed four more doorways before we broke free from our terror, and then only when the thing slapped its tail forward and sent one of the doors sliding down the hallway, straight at us.

"Run!" Twila shouted as she pushed me toward the stairwell.

Patrick considered reading more of the autopsy report that Grandberg left on the credenza, but the distaste that idea left in his mouth overrode his curiosity. Besides, he needed to find Patty. He wanted Twila and Alice with him, however, when he spoke to the woman. If she confirmed what he hoped...well, he was torn. Did he really want to know? Still, that had been his goal for decades now. Hadn't it? Alice and Twila had alleviated his loneliness so much, given him a measure of support with their ability to see and communicate with him. Granted, once in a while they argued with him, but after so many years of wandering alone, he appreciated their presence.

He left Grandberg with his friend Jack Daniels. At the hotel, he approached from the off-street tunnel. He halted, though, halfway to the entrance and added clothing to his body. Before he started onward,

Jack roared into the tunnel on his motorcycle. Patrick heard the sound before the bike appeared, and Jack raced straight at him, then evidently caught sight of Patrick. He swerved around him, and the bike's muffler struck sparks from the concrete before Jack regained control and got the bike upright. Jack skidded it to a halt a few feet away, facing Patrick.

The cop killed the engine, shoved the kickstand down and dismounted. He wore his helmet, but the face shield was up, his face murderously enraged.

"I could have killed you!" he snarled.

"Someone already did that," Patrick replied with a haughty sniff of contempt at the cop's grip on reality.

Jack closed his eyes and shook his head before he said, "What do you mean? You think someone murdered you?"

Patrick straightened arrogantly. "My Buick Master 6 was top of the line, only a month old. That scruffy Tin Lizzie had no business even being on the same roadway as me. I should have blown his doors off with ease. Besides, I'd just had the car serviced the day before I died. I wanted it to be in tiptop shape for my anticipated honeymoon trip."

Jack removed his helmet and propped it on the gas tank. Although deep night now and the hotel towered far above them on three sides, they stood in the middle of the concrete drive, which was large enough for vehicles to enter and circle around to leave without any problem. Storm clouds were gathering overhead, but the bike's headlight also still shone.

"You were drag racing?" Jack asked, a tinge of interest in his voice. "Way back then?"

"Racing, yes, that I'll admit to. The drag part...that should have been the term applied to that decrepit Lizzie. Compared to the comfort in which I traveled, it dragged down the road."

"Definitely," Jack agreed. "Those old Tin Lizzie's only had a four-cylinder, in-line. What? Twenty horsepower or so?"

"Twenty-one," Patrick informed him with a sneer of contempt. "My Master 6 had six full cylinders and seventy-five horses under the hood!"

Jack leaned against the bike and crossed his arms. "How'd it go down? The race?"

Patrick almost laughed at Jack's eagerness to hear the tale, but a stir of long-tamped smugness at his vitality when he lived, and even a certain arrogance as to his superiority over some of his acquaintances, surfaced. Indeed, he'd never truly forgotten how full of youth and vigor he'd been while he lived. The undeniable masculinity of his existence. The blood pumping through his veins and the flush of youth, with his entire life ahead of him.

And...he had to admit, he missed the camaraderie of other males. The late-night bachelor gatherings over bathtub gin despite Prohibition. Such a joke, Prohibition. The friendships and even the boasting and competition. He sighed. He'd had no one to enjoy just being a male with now for...oh, a little over seventy-five years. He even missed sharing locker room dirty jokes!

"I was on my way back here that night," Patrick said in that male confidence-sharing tone he'd missed so much. "After speaking to my parents about my engagement to a wonderful woman. I felt I should speak to them in person, rather than by a wiregram or phone. My father and I also had a discussion about another matter pertaining to this."

"The drag race?" Jack prodded.

Patrick glanced overhead as a few preliminary drops of rain fell. They hit Jack's head, but didn't bother him. "I was in a wonderful mood," he explained, ignoring Jack's eagerness for him to get to the gist of the story, just as he would have made one of his companion males wait back in his living days. "Happy, content, so very glad I'd finally received an answer from her. That she'd agreed to share my life. I wasn't concentrating as I should on the highway, I suppose, just dawdling along. There was a car following me, but I didn't pay much attention to it until it drew far too close to my rear bumper. Its headlights made it difficult to see, so I pulled as far to the right as possible, hoping the driver would pass me. He didn't."

Patrick snorted. "I got a good enough glimpse of him on a curve to see what he drove. It was one of those runabout models. Not even a newer model, one that had been around for a few years. He had the ragtop and windows up. I doubt he'd washed it in a month of Sundays, and there was even a coat of dirt on the windows, so I couldn't make out the driver. Finally I sped up somewhat and watched for a place to pull completely off the road and let him by. I didn't want him to spoil my good mood, intrude on my happiness. However, on a straight stretch, he pulled beside me, but didn't pass. He matched my speed and beeped that silly horn at me. Beep, beep. Beep, beep. I waved my arm out the window and motioned him to get that blasted contrivance on around me."

"It was a black runabout, I suppose," Jack said. "As I recall, Henry Ford said you could have one of his cars in any color you wanted, as long as it was black."

"An ugly beast," Patrick said. "My Master 6 put it to shame. The 6 was black, but oh, the chrome and wheels it had. Quite showy, if you want to know the truth. And there was no comparison to the engine sounds. Why, that Lizzie sounded just like its name, a piece of tin struggling down the road. Or a bucket of bolts. My car growled like a sleek tiger on the prowl."

"Sort of like a hemi," Jack said with an agreeable nod.

Patrick sighed in remembrance. "A nice rumble. Rather like that machine you're so fond of. I'm glad I got to ride on it."

"How did you end up racing?"

"It wasn't my idea," Patrick said defensively. "He kept pace beside me until we came to an intersection. I, of course, being a cautious driver, stopped to make sure no vehicle was approaching up or down the other road. At times those elderly pieces of junk operated without headlights at night. Why, I even recall reading about a wreck once where this besotted driver was headed home after drinking at a friend's house until late in the night. His headlights were burned out, so he tied a lantern on the front of his car. Another driver thought he had adequate distance to pass when they met on a dark road, but instead, his car plowed right into the drunk. The fool had tied his lantern to the passenger side of his vehicle!"

"Idiots," Jack agreed.

"Anyway," Patrick said with a frown of recollection, "the Lizzie driver halted at the intersection, also." He stepped over beside Jack and propped himself against the bike...although it was more for show than support. He assumed that since the other man accepted his nearness, it bespoke of his continued fascination with the story, so he told Jack, "Just like this. Right beside me. Then the fool actually revved his pitiful engine at me. What's a man to do?"

"Show 'em your taillights," Jack acknowledged with an approving nod.

The rain grew into a drizzle, but even when a streak of lightning bounced across the sky, Jack only swiped at his hair and kept his gaze on Patrick. After a fleeting look at the roiling clouds, Patrick went on, "It had been threatening rain earlier that evening, and the rain did break through at that point. Not too hard at first, but I ignored that pathetic challenge beside me and took a moment to switch on my wipers."

Jack shifted his rump to give Patrick a little distance, probably because of the chill his presence gave off, but the cop's rapt attention remained riveted, as though not to miss a word. For a moment, Patrick allowed himself to re-experience that long-ago night. The darkness beyond the headlights, the lonely road, the challenge and his own assurance that his was the more manly vehicle. Two sets of testosterone itching to show each other how ineffectual it was to dare taunt the other one.

Patrick laughed aloud and beside him, Jack chuckled. Then Patrick wrapped the fingers of his left hand around the imaginary steering wheel in front of him, positioned the right hand on the imaginary gear shift. He planted his right leg out as though on the Model 6's gas pedal, his left on the clutch.

"Then I snickered to myself and floorboarded the gas feed and did just that. Showed that Lizzie my taillights! Errr, rummmm!" he growled, then jammed the imaginary gearshift upward and popped the imaginary clutch. "Errrp, rummmm, errrrr! The tires screeched, the smoke from them engulfed his Lizzie. I sped off so fast, I was a hundred feet down the road before he even crossed the intersection. I laughed quite freely at how quickly I made that bucket of bolts eat my exhaust."

"I remember those days," Jack said. "When you thought you were immortal and the way to prove your manhood was to have the biggest, baddest, fastest engine around. Made the chicks sit up and take notice, too. But there was nothin' like seein' your challenger's headlights dwindlin' in the rearview mirror."

"That was part of the problem," Patrick admitted. "I was snickering to myself about how easy it was to leave him behind. Trying to imagine what on earth ever gave him the guts to think he could take me on. But I'd traveled this road frequently, and suddenly I remembered a sharp turn ahead. I slowed, satisfied that even if he caught up to me, he'd been given his reprisal for daring to test my superior vehicle."

"So he caught up?"

"Yes. And the idiot did try to pass me again. But he cut back towards me before he got completely around. I instinctively hit the brakes and wrenched my vehicle away from him. But the steering only responded for a split second, then completely disintegrated. His rear fender hit my front one. I remember the crash noise, then my car tumbling down an embankment. Next, I was looking down on the wreck. I was there on the ground, down in a gully, and I saw no sight of the other vehicle. I'd been thrown from the car, but then it rolled and landed partially on me. I was there," he repeated quietly, "but I was also above the wreck, looking at myself."

"Did the investigation confirm that the steering was deliberately sabotaged?" Jack asked.

"I don't know. It was a while before I realized what had happened, that I'd died in the crash. I had a few other things on my mind at first, and by the time I was able to navigate through this shadowy new existence without confusion, the car had been destroyed in a wrecking yard."

"Then you can't be positive it wasn't an accident. And you never did get a look at the other driver?"

"No, I never saw him clearly."

Jack frowned, then wiped his face again and glanced overhead as though in surprise at the rain. When he looked back at Patrick, that disgusted look was on his face again. "I am standin' here in the rain, supposedly talking to a ghost about drag racin'," Jack muttered. "A ghost who's tellin' me how he died. Next thing you know, a swarm of men in white coats will appear and drag me off to the loony bin."

Exasperated, Patrick said, "*You* asked *me* to tell you what had happened. And I did. Who did you think you were talking to? Or do you habitually go around talking to people you don't admit are there?"

Jack reached over and turned off the bike's headlight. Then he shoved himself upright and strode towards the entrance doors. "You comin'?" he asked over his shoulder.

"Who? Me? The person who's not there?" Patrick called as he followed him. "Are you asking if I'm coming? How can I come with you if I'm not here?"

"Shut up! Just shut up." Jack tested the doors and found them open. As he went on inside, he said, "All right. You're here. But I ain't a damned bit happy about the fact that I have to admit that! Now, where are Alice and Twila in this monstrosity of disintegration?"

Patrick froze, head cocked as he stared overhead and listened. "Did you hear that?"

"I don't hear a thing. Just you."

"Something's wrong," Patrick said.

"There's a hell of a lot wrong with this situation," Jack said angrily. "Which facet of it are you referrin' to?"

"They're in danger! Hurry!"

Patrick raced down the left hallway. He heard Jack pounding behind him for a few steps, but when he entered the lobby, Jack wasn't with him. Patrick stared around the empty lobby for an instant before he heard Jack's voice yell, "Where the hell did you go? I can't see a damn thing!"

Patrick slipped back down the hallway a ways and yelled, "Turn on your flash! Bear to the left!"

A dim light appeared in the distance, and Patrick retreated into the lobby. Nerves fidgety with fear, he strained his senses, yet now he could sense nothing. Hear nothing, except Jack's hurried footsteps as he raced into the lobby to join him.

"Where are they?" Jack demanded. "Alice and Twila."

Patrick pointed overhead. "Up there somewhere. We only have to search every floor."

CHAPTER 26

We didn't stop until we raced down that entire stairwell, clear to the mezzanine level. At some point during our mad scramble, I dropped my backpack, as well as Trucker's leash. My dog burst through the doorway only a split second before me, with Twila right on my heels. We didn't stop there—not that close to those ghastly elevators. We barreled out into the open and collapsed into a huddled heap, hanging onto each other and the dog for dear life.

Then a beam of light illuminated us. Twila and I both screamed and scrambled away from it...until I realized we were heading for those elevator doors. I snatched Twila by the jacket and detoured her along with me to the reception desk. We both grabbed the dusty wooden surface and panted for breath.

"I'm going to start back at the gym as soon as I get home!" I said between gasps. "This ghosthunting business takes more physical ability than I've got sometimes."

Someone ran up the stairwell beside the desk. We unlocked our grips on each other and backed away, toward the bathroom hallway behind the desk, hands out in front of us to ward off the new threat. I rushed into the bathroom before it dawned on me that I'd be trapped.

We should have run down the other stairwell! Gotten the heck out of here!

The blackness closed in on me, but I sprinted around the corner anyway, into a stall, and slammed the door. Whispered, "Twila? You out there?"

No answer. I checked my pockets for the flashlight, then remembered I'd stuck it in my backpack. Which was somewhere in the upper stairwell where I'd dropped it to lighten my load and run faster. Another cell phone down the drain, also.

Utterly black in here. Claustrophobic black. Darkness with a weight to it. And multiple floors filled with ghosts over my head. Not that I was afraid of ghosts! But that other entity...a ghost, or something else? Had it been content to scare the bejeebers out of us and chase us out of its territory? Or had it followed us? Was it lurking in this solid darkness? Was that someone breathing? Ghosts didn't breathe! Did other entities?

Where the hell did Twila go? She was the expert and I needed her. Now! The penlight. I had mine somewhere...

"Alice!" Twila called. "It's Jack and Patrick. You can come out now!"

Oh, for Pete's sake. Now Jack would realize just how scared I got at times. Believe I lied to him whenever I gushed about Twila's and my ghosthunting *adventures*. Still, I was willing to face that in order to get out of this darkness. I pushed the stall door open...and stubbed my toe on a large, soft mass of...something. Stumbled and pitched forward with a shriek of terror. I hit the tile floor with a jolt of pain, but didn't tarry. Rocketing to my feet, I flew forward...and hit the wall before I remembered the hallway curved to reenter the mezzanine.

I bounced back and took off down the right direction, toward the welcoming pale light ahead of me. When I burst out, Jack and Patrick were standing over by the elevators around Jack's flashlight beam, Twila several feet back from them.

"In—in—in there," I babbled, finger pointing back down the hallway. "Another body! Someone else is dead! Like we were afraid of when we got here earlier!"

The three of them hurried to me...just as Trucker emerged from the bathroom hallway. He sauntered up to me and sat, then lifted a large paw to my thigh and whined as he stared up into my face. I sagged in relief and cupped his muzzle with both hands. "You. That was you I tripped over in there. Oh, Trucker, how many times have I told you not to lie down where it's dark and I can't see you?"

Twila chuckled, but not real loud. "He was just following his mommy to protect her from the bumps in the night."

"And I very much appreciate that," I said truthfully to both her and my dog. "But I thought...oh, never mind. I should have realized. I've tripped over him now and then at night, when I'm half asleep and my darned bathroom nightlight's burned out."

"I don't imagine you were thinking too clearly in there," she murmured sympathetically as she patted my arm.

"I wasn't. And now I have to go back in there and pee. Can I borrow your flashlight, Jack?"

"You came in here without a light?" he asked.

"Of course not," I denied. "But I dropped my backpack somewhere along the stairwell."

"Just how far up in this decrepit building were you two?"

I ignored him and jerked his flashlight out of his hand. As I turned back toward the bathroom, Trucker's leash firmly in my other hand so I could keep track of him, Twila nudged me. "You've got something wrapped around your leg."

I shone the light down at my feet and the beam illuminated a tangle of toilet paper trailing a good six feet behind me. Cheeks flushing in embarrassment, I unwrapped myself and tossed the paper aside.

"Tsk, tsk. Don't mess with Texas," Twila reminded me as she gathered the paper up and handed it to me to dispose of in the bathroom.

"My hands are full," I said with a haughty sniff and stomped away. Well, stomped as well as I could with my legs nearly crossed to hold back my desperate bladder's need. Still, I cautiously examined the entire hallway and each and every one of the three stalls before I entered one...and left the stall door open. Now what? Leash in one hand, flashlight in the other. Bladder clamoring now that my mind knew relief was just a squat away. A zipper and snap to deal with...no, I recalled. I had on those tights with an elastic waist. I bent to set the flashlight on the floor...

...and yelped when something touched my ass. Swung around in my squat so fast I could see a trail behind the light and shone the beam on the toilet tissue holder that jutted out from the stall wall. Sighed, and leaving the flashlight on the floor, beam shining, stood and thrust my fingers into the tights to jerk them down and plop on the toilet seat.

Trucker laid his huge head on my left leg for an instant, then reached up and slurped my face. I hugged him tightly until I finished, then it dawned on me that the tissue holder had been empty. I glared at it. Didn't bother that empty roll one bit. Then I recalled a box of replacement rolls...out at the head of the hallway.

"Trucker, be a good boy and fetch me some toilet paper, will you?" I whispered.

"No problem," a voice answered, and I managed to stifle this yelp just in time, as soon as I recognized Jack's voice. Not that I really thought my dog had learned to talk!

Jack handed me a roll of tissue and I jerked the stall door closed as soon as I grabbed it. "Go away! I'll be out in a minute."

"We need to talk, *Chère*."

"In a minute," I gritted.

"We can wait," someone else said. Patrick! Damn it, was everyone here in the bathroom with me?

"Go on, get out of here," Twila said. Yep, every blasted person in our group was standing outside that stall listening to me pee! "I'll wait for Alice and we can talk outside in the mezzanine."

Someone's footsteps sounded, Jack's I assumed, since Patrick wouldn't make any noise. I sighed and finished up, flushed the commode and opened the door. Twila wasn't standing there. "Twila?"

"Just a sec. Hand me the tissue, will you?"

I complied, handing the roll through her open stall door. A moment later, we both stood at the sink, twisting knobs until I remembered... "There's no water here, just in the stalls."

"I forgot, too," she said.

I picked up Jack's flashlight and started back down the hallway, but she grasped my arm. "Who

...or what...was that up there?"

"Me? You're asking me what that entity was?"

"At first it looked like a vortex manifesting. We've seen portals like that before, where the spirits cross back and forth. The ones we've seen even have those lights in them. But that thing...that tail...the way it...none of the ones we saw were ever able to wreak havoc like that. It attacked us, Alice!"

"Could it have been Antonio?"

"I don't know. We didn't hang around long enough to get a good sense of what was going on."

"You're the senior ghosthunter here. If you don't know what the hell it was, then maybe we better get out of here for a while and regroup."

"My thoughts exactly," she replied, and the fear I'd kept at bay since we encountered Jack and Patrick—okay, sometimes it *does* help a woman to know there's a strong man around—descended again with full fury.

"That seventh floor is malevolent," I reminded her. "The time I came with my friends, the entire bunch of us refused to stay there more than ten seconds. And when one of the group played back the EVP on her recorder, there was a nasty voice on it, threatening to kill us if we didn't leave. Thank goodness we were gone by then. That seventh floor is also where the poor woman jumped to her death. Or...was pushed."

She nodded in the dim light cast by the flashlight in my hand.

"Uh oh," I said. "I think the batteries are going dead. Let's get out of here before we're in total darkness."

I didn't wait for her agreement. I gripped Trucker's leash and trotted down the hallway, around the corner, and out into the mezzanine. Jack and Patrick were over by the elevators again. Without discussion, the two of us went over to the reception desk and hiked our butts up on it to rest. Trucker glanced once toward the elevators, but then he laid down at our feet.

I clicked off Jack's flashlight to save whatever battery strength remained, then set it beside me and dropped Trucker's leash. He stayed put, and I didn't blame him. Hopefully, he was resting from the mad scramble down the stairwell. Enough light from the streetlights outside filtered in from the block-long bank of grimy windows in the lobby area so we could see down here on the lower floors. I thought of my backpack up in that stairwell somewhere, but wasn't about to mention it again. Someone might decide I needed to retrieve it.

And I was *not* going back up there. Forever! We'd just have to figure out some other way to help Patrick and the murdered woman.

Feet dangling, I asked Twila, "What next?"

"I still think whatever we need to find out is here in the hotel," she said quietly. "But frankly, I'm pooped."

"If you're pooped, then don't depend on me," I assured her.

"We might have to, Alice."

"What?" I tore my gaze away from the elevators and gaped at her. "My powers still need to be developed!"

"They won't develop unless you stretch them. We're a team, and when I'm drained, you need to take over."

I gulped. "And do what?" I asked, the words torn from my clogged throat.

"As I mentioned, probably a séance," she said, the last thing I wanted to hear. She slipped an arm around my waist. "I know it's scary, Alice. Still, we can't just walk out and forget this quest. We're too involved. I can't dismiss the fact that we saw that version of Patrick up there, a version we knew wasn't real."

"Ghosts aren't real...not physically real," I broke in, although she knew that as well as I did.

"I've never seen anything like that before," she went on as though I hadn't spoken. "And I can't shake the feeling that maybe Patrick's eternal rest is in deep jeopardy if we give up."

"Can't Patrick wait a few more years?" I whined.

"I suppose he could. Yet we took on a certain responsibility when we agreed to help him. Sure, it was a fun thought to have this gorgeous, naked ghost along on a ghosthunt adventure. But did you ever stop and think that maybe Fate brought him to us?"

"I suppose Fate murdered that poor woman," I grumbled. "Just to complicate things for us."

"You know that's not true. But let's stop and look at—"

Jack and Patrick strolled...and floated...towards us, and she fell silent. I bit my lip to hold back a giggly thought. Jack continued to lambaste our ghosthunting, denigrate the existence of ghosts, yet he'd been chatting with Patrick for several minutes. Right now, though, I wasn't about to get into that age-old argument with him. His Cajun temper might flare and off he'd go, leaving us alone.

"Patrick knows who the murdered woman was," Jack said. "And I don't think she was killed here."

"Someone cut her in half somewhere else and staged this?" I asked, recalling my talk with Howard.

"Looks that way," Jack replied. "And I think that autopsy report probably clears you beyond doubt, Alice. She had to have been dead a while before she was left here."

"Probably?" I focused on that one word. "Probably doesn't even count in horseshoes, Jack."

He chuckled and continued, "Well, to get rid of that last doubt, we'll have to find out who actually did kill her."

"We need to contact her," Twila said.

"I've told you—" Jack shut up, then blew out a frustrated breath. "All right, if you insist on goin' down this road again, let me remind you what happened the other time you pulled me into one of your ceremonies to ask a murdered person who killed him. He didn't know. He'd been attacked from behind and had no idea who the perp was."

"We don't know that happened this time," I insisted, then glanced at Twila and continued, "Not that that means I'm agreeable to a séance. Especially if it means going back up to that seventh floor!"

"I don't think Mary Ann's up there," Patrick cut in. "In fact, she's not even here in the hotel. I saw her a while ago, over in that police chief's office."

"Mary Ann is the woman's name?" Twila asked.

"It is," Patrick confirmed.

"Well, that does it for sure." I scooted off the desk and glared at all three of them. "We're not about to troop over there to talk to Grandberg and let him lock me up!"

CHAPTER 27

W e didn't even have to go inside the police station. Jack left his bike sheltered beneath the overhang at the rear hotel entrance, and we collected Penny's Lincoln. Ty Grandberg sat outside on a patrol car hood, smoking a cigarette and staring into the night as Jack pulled the Lincoln into a parking slot right beside the patrol car. Grandberg took a long swallow of whatever was in the plastic cup in his hand at the same moment Jack turned off the key. Twila and I stayed in the backseat with Trucker, protected from discovery by the dark-tint windows, but both Jack and Patrick got out of the car. Jack had to open the driver's door, of course, but Patrick just slid through the passenger one.

Jack propped his forearms on the Lincoln's roof and stared across it at Grandberg. "Got a minute?"

Twila and I both swiveled our heads in time to see Grandberg flip his cigarette in an arc into the street. He remained on the hood as he replied, "It'll take longer than that. And we're not talking until you bring that ex-wife of yours in to give me her statement. I'm also considering filing charges against her for taking off like that."

"See?" I said as our heads swiveled back to Jack, although we could only see his flat stomach and jean-clad legs down to mid-thigh.

He grunted something, then said louder, "You remember that law enforcement convention in N'awlins a couple years back?"

"So?" Grandberg said.

"You even flunked the SWAT team skills. I sure wouldn't want to count on you for backup."

"I was hung over that day."

"Yeah, from hanging out at that transvestite bar on Bourbon Street the night before."

"I—I didn't look at the sign over the bar!" Grandberg sputtered. "She —he—it was standing in the doorway when I walked down the street!"

"Had me a camera," Jack said. "Lost a bet to a buddy and promised him I'd send him some pics of naked boobs, I run across any gals willing to pose for me that night."

"You—you didn't!"

"Caught both shots," Jack mused. "The one where you kissed him and the one where he pulled off his wig and pointed overhead at the bar sign. Haven't done anything with the pics yet. But that same buddy of mine's got a Web site a lot of cops visit...I want your assurance that you won't try to detain Alice. Either for questioning or on suspicion."

"I was just pissed at her superior-than-me attitude," Grandberg hurriedly assured Jack. "Playing hardball with her. She didn't do it, and I'm not going to bother her other than getting her statement."

"Quit it," Twila whispered. "I'm getting dizzy." I realized we'd been ping-ponging our gazes as we listened.

Jack said, "I know she didn't, but what confirmed it for you? Autopsy report?"

"Time of death is never conclusive, Roucheau. You know that. Who's your friend?"

"You can see him?" Jack asked, a measure of astonishment in his voice.

"Shit," Grandberg spat. "Another damn ghost. I've had enough ghosts for one night."

"Mary Ann." Patrick's voice this time.

"You were in my office?" Grandberg asked.

"When Mary Ann appeared," Patrick confirmed. "What did you mean when you asked her why she came back? You said she was free."

"It's a long story," Grandberg said, then swigged from his cup again. "Or...maybe not long enough." He heaved his cup into the street. "My sister's life wasn't nearly long enough."

"Mary Ann was his sister," I said to Twila. "Oh, the poor guy. It must have been horrible for him to go investigate a murder and find that the victim was his sister!"

"You're talking about the guy who you thought might put out a warrant for your arrest," she said in reply. "Have you forgotten that?"

"Well, no," I admitted. "Still..."

Someone opened the car door beside me, and I stared up into Grandberg's face. Streetlights burned brightly outside, and I flinched away from both a lingering fear of his authority and the desolation on his face. An ominous growl grew in Trucker's throat, but Grandberg only stepped back from the door as though in slow motion. He wobbled a bit, so I made a quick assumption that the cup he'd tossed wasn't his first drink of the night.

"You two can get out," he said. "Three, I guess, if you count the dog. I canceled the BOLO and never did seek a warrant. We have to find out who really did murder Mary Ann."

We? He had an entire police department at his disposal, albeit a small one. And he could call in more assistance, should he need it. Nevertheless, the news that I was a non-fugitive delighted me. I slid across the leather seat, out the door, and Trucker and I faced Grandberg. Trucker wasn't too happy with my stern hold on his leash, and I looped it around my hand tightly, then laid my other hand on his head to calm him.

"I expect an apology," I muttered. "I've never been chased by legal authorities before."

"I apologize," Grandberg said with a sigh. "Not for doing my job, though. For being wrong about my deductions." Then he said to Jack, "Those pictures?"

"Maybe they'll get lost after we get done here," Jack replied. "Maybe."

By now, Twila had joined me on my side of the car, and she asked Grandberg, "How did Mary Ann seem when you saw her?"

He backed up unsteadily and propped his rear against the patrol car. I glanced around for Jack and Patrick, but Jack was still in the same position, same spot, and I didn't see Patrick.

"Sad," Grandberg told Twila. "Once we find the murderer, I want you and Miz Carpenter to help her find peace."

Ah, so that was why he wanted our help, at least mine and Twila's.

Jack snorted. "Those two seem to think that should be a dual focus. That maybe your sister can tell us who murdered her."

"Could be." Grandberg nodded a contradiction to Jack's skepticism. "She isn't amenable to talking to us, though. And..." His voice trailed off and he stared at the star-spotted sky overhead. The storm had moved out, and millions of tiny dots sprinkled the black blanket above us.

"And?" Twila prodded. However, when Grandberg didn't answer, she went on in a soft voice, "You only saw half of her, didn't you?"

Grandberg choked, and I instinctively reached out a hand to comfort him. The next thing I knew, he was in my arms, head on my shoulder, arms crushing me. Sobs and shudders shook his body. I had sense enough to release Trucker's leash when Twila took it from my hand, and while I patted Grandberg on the back and murmured soothing nonsense, she led Trucker a safe distance away. Far enough that he couldn't lunge at the man in my arms. His growls died and he obeyed her order to, "Sit."

Grandberg's closeness confirmed what had been in the plastic cup. Whiskey fumes surrounded me as he cried. At long last, he drew back and rubbed the heels of his palms over his eyes, then dug his fingers through his hair, which disarrayed it to the point where a black wave dropped to his forehead. He angrily brushed it back and stepped away from me.

To Jack, he said, "I have no problem with you reading the autopsy report. But I can just as easily tell you what it says. She was killed somewhere else. St—stabbed in...in the heart. She lost a lot of blood at the site where she was killed."

"You know where it happened?"

"Not yet. And..." Grandberg cleared his clogged throat. "Yet there was enough blood left in her body that she bled some more in the elevator."

Horrified at what I just knew he was going to say next, I eased away from the poor man, over beside Twila and Trucker. Jack walked around the front of the car to Grandberg. He flicked his head at us in an indication to move out of hearing distance, but neither Twila nor I complied. I didn't want to hear, but if we were going to get to the bottom of this, we had to have as many facts as we could gather.

Jack shrugged at our refusal to move and said to Grandberg, "What did they use?"

"A saw," Grandberg replied in a quiet, ravaged voice. "Probably something like they use in a butcher shop."

"There's no electricity in that building," Jack said. "How'd the perp stage it to look like the elevator doors did it?"

"I don't know," Grandberg replied.

"Douglas," I murmured, and as both cops stared at me, I explained, "There's a story about the hotel. I think it happened back in 1948. A man named Douglas was an elevator operator there. There's more to the story, but basically, Douglas got fired over something, but he came back to visit a couple friends late one night. Down in the basement. Somehow —either by accident or intention—he got caught in the elevator doors and they severed him in half."

"Is that a true story, *Chère?*" Jack's tone held a measure of derision. "Or one of y'all's made-up, heard-it-from-a-ghost ones?"

"It's true," Grandberg broke in before I could censure Jack. "So whoever our perp is, it's someone familiar with the hotel's history."

"Well, that takes in probably half of Texas," I pointed out. "Especially since there are scads of stories about the hotel on the Internet."

"Not necessarily," Jack disagreed. "We need motive and opportunity. But first we need to trace the vic's last hours."

"Mary Ann," Grandberg insisted. "Her name's Mary Ann, not the victim!"

"Sorry," Jack said. "Mary Ann."

Sympathy for the two of them stabbed me. Cop training instructed them to distance themselves from a victim, both for their own emotional health and in order to keep a clear, investigative mind. After an especially gruesome case, though, Jack had left his job in New Orleans and moved to Longview in order to save his sanity. I knew Jack didn't mean to sound cold, given the identity of the murdered woman.

Jack leaned against the Lincoln and crossed his arms. "I know it's going to be hard for you," he told Grandberg. "But you know the drill. We're going to have to know what's going on here. Why your sister was here. What did Patrick mean when he said that you'd indicated your sister was free?"

"And what's Carrie got to do with this?" Twila asked. "Why did it affect her like that?"

I'd forgotten all about poor Carrie. Patty, too, for that matter. How tangled all this was! Every time we tried to focus on one plot point, another intruded. If this had been one of my books, I'd have been pulling my hair out trying to weave it all together. Patrick's quest, Mary Ann's death. All the entwined relationships that tempted yet confused us.

"Carrie's still out of it," Grandberg said. "And I think I need another drink."

Twila handed me Trucker's leash and ducked into the Lincoln's passenger door. She emerged with her backpack and set it on the trunk. I had no idea how she managed to hold onto everything, while I strew possessions from one end of a ghosthunt to another! I throttled my irritation at my own untidiness and her clarity of focus, though, when she pulled out the bottle of Crown Royal and a few of those plastic motel drinking cups.

She'd just handed each of us a drink—straight for her, Jack, and Grandberg, warm 7-Up in mine—when Patrick materialized. I courteously started to hand Patrick my cup before I recalled that ghosts didn't eat or imbibe. Besides, I needed it worse than he did. I gulped half of it before it dawned on me that Patrick was naked.

"Put some damned clothes on," Jack snarled.

Patrick glanced down at himself as though surprised at his nude body. A split second later, he was dressed. Jack rubbed a hand across his face, then downed his entire cup at once. Twila had poured everyone at least two jiggers; I'd watched her. And when Jack held his cup out again, she set her own drink down and poured more for him.

One of us had to drive. Reluctantly, I put my drink aside on the Lincoln trunk, but Twila handed it back to me. "I'll drive," she said in a soft voice. "I think we need to get back to Penny's." She nodded down the street where an SUV was pulling around a corner, the one I recognized as the deputy's. "Where we have some privacy and can recuperate."

Grandberg said, "All of you get back in the car. I'll handle this."

Jack started around the front of the car, but Twila beat him to the driver's door. I snapped my fingers at Trucker and ordered him into the car. As he obeyed, I grabbed the backpack Twila left behind in her hurry to keep Jack from behind the wheel. Once in a great while I could overcome my disorder trait! I slid in beside my dog, and Patrick materialized over by the other window. Outside the car, Jack shrugged and got into the front passenger seat. He closed the door as the SUV pulled up behind the Lincoln, and I watched in the outside mirror as Grandberg approached his deputy, who rolled down his vehicle's passenger-side window.

"What's up, Chief?" Deputy Rover asked. "What are all them folks doin' out here this time a'night?"

"Nothing for you to worry about," Grandberg said. "Anything going on in town?"

"Guess not," Rover said. "Janet dispatched a call a while ago about a possible prowler. Old Miss Smith swore a naked man was standing outside her neighbor's house." He lowered his voice, but I still heard him say with a snicker, "You know Old Miss Smith. She was prob'ly hopin' the prowler was there to see her, bein' naked an' all."

"Did you do a search? Or just sit in your vehicle and shine your spotlight around so you didn't get out of breath?"

"I looked, Chief," Rover whined. "Wasn't even a twig snapped or a sign of a footprint beneath that tree Miz Smith claimed he was under. And Patty Alvidrez was sittin' out on her back patio. It was her house Miz

Smith said the prowler was watchin'. Patty would've seen him, iffen he'd been there."

Not necessarily. I slid my glance to Patrick, and he nodded. "But I didn't get a chance to talk to Patty. That deputy showed up just as I started across the yard, and Patty told me to come back later."

"You could have just gone on in the house," I insisted.

"She very specifically told me to come back later," he repeated. "I think she's the key to my entire quest, and if I antagonize her, who knows what she'll do."

I chuckled in remembrance, then realized Jack was listening to our conversation. "Patty's the lady in the station there who knocked you down with the stun gun," I explained.

"She did what?" Twila said. "That little lady?"

Twila and I snickered, and Jack swiveled to stare out the windshield. He finished off whatever Crown was left in his cup, then handed it over his shoulder to me without looking.

"Refill?" I asked. "But remember, Texas has an open container law."

He must have considered it for a moment, since he didn't reply at first. I started to stick the cup in the pouch behind his seat, but then he said, "Yeah, hit me again."

I just could not control myself. I giggled and said, "With booze or a stun gun?"

Grandberg tapped Jack's window, and Twila turned the ignition key so he could roll it down.

"I'm going back over to the Alvidrez place with Deputy Rover to have a look around. I doubt the prowler's connected to the murder, but I want to check it out anyway. There's not much I can do otherwise, until I meet with my men in the morning. The county sheriff's promised to help out, too, so he'll be at the eight o'clock meeting."

"You're not driving," Twila said from behind the steering wheel, an order, not a question.

"I'll ride with my deputy. He's sober...right now."

"Mind if we tag along?" Jack asked.

"I thought we were going back to Penny's," I interrupted. Even though Grandberg had assured me that I was no longer a fugitive, I wasn't eager to confront Miz Patty Stun-Gun. She might not have heard yet that I'd been absolved of crime.

Patrick nudged me, but all I got was a cold chill in my side. He got my attention. "I believe we should stop by Patty's first," he whispered.

While my attention was diverted, evidently the rest of our group decided the same.

"Seat belts, everyone," Twila ordered as she started the engine and shifted the car into reverse. We complied—well, Jack and I did, not Patrick and Trucker—and she backed out and followed the SUV down the street. After five minutes or so, when we'd left town and drove down a desolate county road, I refilled my drink and sipped the warm though relaxing liquid, until...

At first it was just a crack ahead of us. Then a splintering noise. I stared through the windshield, and Twila eased up on the gas as the SUV in front of her slowed. Suddenly another crack split the air and, in front of the SUV, illuminated by the headlights, a huge tree whooshed across the road.

Twila slammed on the brakes. Tires squealed, but the Lincoln rear-ended Rover's SUV with a resounding impact. My body snapped against the seat belt restraint, and my drink spilled down the front of me. On the floor, Trucker thumped against the front seatback, then scrambled up between Patrick and me, unhurt.

"Shit!" I spat, and my mind decided to work again, although considering our predicament, it hustled down a stupid path. The mental trip-kitty tally dinged as I wiped at my breasts and peered into the front seat where Twila and Jack fought with twin airbags. Crown Royal fumes filled the inside of the Lincoln, both from my spilled drink and probably Jack's.

"Is everyone all right?" I asked.

Twila escaped her airbag first. Instead of answering me, she pushed open her door and got out, evidently uninjured, as was Jack, who followed her a second later. Jack left his door ajar and strode to the SUV passenger side. Branches from the fallen tree obscured the entire front of the SUV, and Jack pushed one tangle of limbs aside to open the door. The dome light illuminated the shattered front windshield, but given the high seatback, I couldn't tell anything about the occupants. The rear hatchback window of the SUV was also shattered completely, only a bare window frame left.

Twila couldn't get close enough to the driver's door to open it. Another huge limb lay against it, and the partially crushed roof supported the one above it. "Are they all right?" she called to Jack.

"Yeah," he answered as he helped Grandberg out of the vehicle. I watched through the shattered rear window as the deputy maneuvered his bulk over to the passenger seat and eventually tried to emerge from the car. It took Jack and Grandberg both to assist him out.

By then, Twila was back at the Lincoln. She stuck her head in the driver's door. "Are you and Trucker okay?"

"We're fine," I assured her.

"Wish I could say the same for Penny's car." She shook her head. "Dig in my backpack and find my red bag of first-aid stuff. I'll check on Grandberg and the deputy and see if they've got any cuts or bruises."

She left to do just that, and I scanned around me for the backpack. It was on the other side of Trucker, and when I reached for it, Patrick wiggled a finger and floated it around the dog's head and onto my lap. I started to unzip one of the pockets, but something back in the underbrush on the side of the road the tree had fallen from caught my gaze. My mouth opened. I tried to shout a warning, but only a squeak of terror emerged.

"Great Gatsby's Ghost," Patrick whispered beside me.

CHAPTER 28

"G—g—g—go!" I choked at Patrick. "W—w—w—warn them!"

"Not me." He shook his head. "The cops have the guns."

The Rambo-man faded back into the underbrush, a hulking seven foot of camouflage clothing, some sort of camouflage netting over his head and face, sturdy hiking boots on his feet. And an Uzi-looking rifle in his hands, an assault rifle, I'd heard that type of gun called. Two bands of shells crisscrossed his chest.

Trucker leapt over the seat and out the driver's door. That broke my paralysis, and I screamed, "Catch him, Twila!"

She didn't hesitate or question me. As a hundred and fifty pounds of snarling, snapping dog lunged for the underbrush, Twila lunged for him. She splatted belly-first on the ground, but captured the end of the leash in one hand. Trucker dragged her a few feet, but by then, I'd plunged straight through Patrick, ignored the cold chill that enveloped my body, opened the door and scrambled out.

Jack scuttled across the Lincoln's hood and reached Twila at the same moment I did. I grabbed the leash from Twila's slipping grip and hauled back. "No!" I ordered. "Stay!"

Trucker plopped his butt on the ground, though he continued to

172

stare into the woods and snarl, white teeth gleaming beneath his curled-back upper lip. Jack helped Twila to her feet, and as she brushed at the dirt and twigs, he asked, "Are you hurt?"

"I've been better," Twila said. Then, "Put your damn guns away before your shaky fingers accidentally pull a trigger. Whatever Alice and Trucker saw is long gone."

I glanced at the SUV. Both cops leaned on the hood, side-by-side amidst the tree branches, pistols gripped in firing position, aimed at the underbrush. Well, Rover's corpulent body took up most of the hood space, but Grandberg had squeezed in beside him somehow.

"What was it?" Grandberg demanded. "What's wrong with that dog?"

"Who," I corrected, and pointed at the underbrush. "Didn't you big bad *trained* cops see him? Some sort of guerrilla-type soldier."

"Real?" Twila asked.

"I think so," I replied. "The only chill I felt was when I dove through Patrick."

"Patrick who?" Rover asked.

Uh oh. The deputy couldn't see Patrick. Or...I reconsidered as I thought back over the past fifteen minutes or so. Patrick had been in the Lincoln when the SUV pulled up. But he'd been standing outside it seconds earlier, when the deputy drove toward us. Either Rover really couldn't see him, or had just missed him. Where was he now? I'd left the door open, and the ghost wasn't on the seat.

Grandberg holstered his pistol and edged out of the branches as he told Rover, "Let's get over there and see if we can figure out who blocked this road." At least he sounded a little more sober now. "Then we'll have to figure out some way to get the cars free. That Lincoln bumper's jammed right under our vehicle."

"I already seen snakes this spring," Rover warned as he reluctantly followed Grandberg.

"What did he look like?" Twila asked me.

"Huge! Seven foot or more. I thought it was a monster standing there."

"Oh, for..." Jack rubbed a hand down his face. "Now Big Foot's showed up. You've had too much to drink, *Chère*."

"Big Foot doesn't wear camouflage!" I glared at him. "And you've had a lot more to drink than me."

He had the grace to look away, but he muttered, "It takes a drink or two at time to handle some of the things you get involved in."

Hurt stabbed me, but my temper flared anyway. "You can leave anytime. I've gotten along fine without you before. Even while we were married!" I never cry. Well, hardly ever. And when I do, nine times out of ten the tears are angry ones from an out-of-control temper seizure.

I stared around at our small group. Evidently drawn by Jack's and my harsh words, the cops watched us instead of examining the tree. They both wore embarrassed yet rapt expressions. Embarrassed, I supposed, as people are when privy to an argument that should be taken private. Rapt as they waited to see what Jack would say next. Not surprising, since men only knew two ways to handle an angry woman: stomp off or retreat behind a television screen. Decent men, anyway. Others struck back, sometimes physically. Jack would never do that, of course, but the closest television available to him was back at Penny's and neither of the vehicles could move until they got the bumpers untangled. If the Lincoln was even driveable.

And I doubted Jack would take off down the road alone, lose face in front of the male species by retreating in the face of my wrath. I stifled a smirk of one-upmanship as my anger cooled, until...

Twila murmured a sympathetic sound and rubbed a hand across my shoulders. Her touch shattered the last vestiges of my temper, along with my control. I dissolved in a shudder of sobs that rivaled Grandberg's earlier. Before Twila could react, I clapped both hands over my mouth and scrambled into the Lincoln's backseat again.

Face buried in my lap, I clasped my arms around my knees and wailed. I wasn't sure for what. The lost marriage? The poor dead woman? I couldn't get those pictures out of my mind. Jack's disbelief in ghosts, even though he admitted he could see them? More likely, that part of my lament came from that exact thread of this ludicrous predicament. He admitted his paranormal sensibility, at least as far as being able to see ghosts, yet denigrated mine.

A tiny corner of my mind not taken up with misery rather expected Twila to join me and offer a tad more sympathy, but the handkerchief nudged at the side of my face felt large, bandanna-like, rather than the tissues the two of us carried. Large, also, the arm that encircled my waist. Then two strong hands lifted me and pulled me against a nice, broad male chest.

Jack's. Even with my eyes closed, I recognized his scent, his planes and valleys. I'd finger-traced that chest a few times, curled a nail in the black, silky hair many times. Snuggled my face into that strong neck a gazillion times...as I did now.

"I'm sorry, *Chère*." He dropped a kiss on the top of my head. "I spoke without thinkin'. You're right. I've had one drink too many. I just...it's just...damn it, why does that ghost show up naked?"

I giggled. I couldn't help myself. My tears dried and I pushed back...albeit reluctantly. Jack didn't even know the half of what was going on, but he'd hung in there for Twila and me. I wiped at my face, but Jack tugged the handkerchief from my hand and tenderly traced the soft cloth beneath each of my eyes, down both tear-tracked cheeks. Then he folded it and covered my nose.

"Blow," he said with a chuckle, as though speaking to a small child.

I did, then took the handkerchief from him and shifted to stick it in my jeans pocket. "I did see a man in camouflage. Probably you didn't see him because you men were looking at the collision. Plus, he blended in with the underbrush pretty well."

"He couldn't have been the prowler then," Jack said, "since he had on clothes."

I laughed into his twinkling, deep-chocolate eyes, then gnawed my bottom lip for a second. "The first time I saw Patrick, he was naked. He's obviously not a man who's ashamed of his body."

"Yeah," Jack said with a snort. "Or maybe he thinks that attracts the women. It got your interest, since you're still hangin' around with him."

"You're jealous of a ghost?"

"No!" he denied. "Besides...well, I don't have any right to be jealous of who you hang around with these days. Or what you do. Whatever happened to the grocery guy?"

"Cory?" I asked, although I'd bet money Jack remembered his name. Jack had attended the crawfish boil at Uncle Clarence's to celebrate the conclusion of the previous ghost-involved murder situation at Esprit d'Chêne. And even before the party, Cory had told Jack that he intended to court his ex-wife. As I recalled, Jack hadn't objected, either, to Cory's stated intention or his presence at my side that afternoon. And Jack hadn't brought a date to the party. I'd overheard him tell Katy that someone named Jolene couldn't make it that day...

"Was that his name?" Jack asked with a shrug. "Cory?"

"Uh huh. Cory's fun. But I think he's still carrying a torch for Katy."

"If he was usin' you to make Katy jealous, I'll..." Jack sighed. "Guess I don't have any right to do that, either."

"I don't think that was it," I couldn't resist saying. "Cory really does want to find someone else. I'm not enough like Katy, though."

I thought I heard him mutter "stupid Cory" under his breath, but he'd turned to gaze out the windshield. The front of the Lincoln bounced, and when I sat up to see over the seatback, Rover had grown a couple feet. Oh, he was jumping on the Lincoln's bumper, a jiggling mass of flesh as he evidently attempted to detach the Lincoln from the SUV. A shriek of metal split the air and Rover tumbled onto the Lincoln's hood. I flinched when the metal dented inward under his weight.

"Hope Penny's got good collision insurance," Jack said.

Rover slid headfirst toward the passenger side of the car, and Grandberg barely managed to push his deputy sideways so he could turn and tumble feet-first to the ground. The dent in the hood remained for a second, then popped out with a thud. The paint cracked around the edges of it.

I gasped. "The police department's insurance better pay for these repairs! It wasn't Twila's fault!"

"Rear-end collision's the fault of the rear-end driver," Jack explained from his cop lore. "That driver's supposed to keep his vehicle under control."

"I...you..." I sputtered. Then, "Men! You all stick together."

Jack slid across the seat. "I better get out there and see if I can help." He paused. "You all right now?"

Gaze caught on his rugged face and a trace of his scent still surrounding me, I nodded. He got out and left me to admit that more than a trace of scent lingered. That Jack feel, both physical and mental, infiltrated the backseat.

"Nope," I whispered. "Been there, done that. Not a road to try twice. Don't care what Granny and Twila think."

I slid out the door and joined the men and Twila. The bumpers were free now, but shards of red plastic from the SUV's brake lights littered the Lincoln's bumper. And when I examined the front of the Lincoln, splinters permeated one headlight, the other one stared skyward. Amazing. Both headlights still shone, despite the damage. I groaned again, but car repairs would have to wait.

Something rustled in the underbrush and Trucker woofed. The men were discussing our next move, so only Twila and I jumped and stared fearfully at the side of the road.

"Oh," I said. "What a pretty kit—"

Trucker sprang...but not at the side of the road. In two bounds, the dog hightailed it into the Lincoln.

"Skunk!" Twila shrieked. Then she followed Trucker. I barely caught the door before she slammed it in my face. With an oomph of exertion, I shoved Twila into Trucker and both their weights across the seat to give me room to shut the door.

Next thing I knew, three other doors closed. Twila reached over Trucker and jerked the one beside him shut. Grandberg grabbed the steering wheel to keep Rover's bulk from shoving him out and pinned himself between door and flesh when he managed to close the driver's door. Jack thudded the passenger door closed.

Outside, the baby skunk wandered on out of the underbrush. Two more babies followed it, then there came the mother. A huge mother. She must have weighed thirty pounds or more! She stalked out after her babies, that tremendous, fluffy tail held high in a flagstaff.

Twila pressed against me, and we both stared out the window. "I'll bet a skunk that big packs a powerful set of scent glands," she said.

"She has to turn her butt to us," I explained from reading research. I'd never had the unfortunate experience of actually encountering a skunk in the wild. "Stand on her front legs and hike her rump up at her target."

"Where's the keys for this car?" Grandberg asked over the seatback.

"Uh oh," Twila murmured. "Uh...I must have dropped them when I saw the skunk."

"Shit." This time it was Jack. "We can't start the car without the keys."

Rover dug in his pocket, pushing against Jack until he shoved back in self-defense. "Damn it, Deputy. Sit still."

"I got my car keys," Rover said. He dangled them on a pudgy finger.

"Fine," Jack said. "I'll just get in the backseat with the women and you can go out there and start your vehicle. Try to drive it on through that tree."

"Not me!" Rover held the keys out to Jack, but he shook his head.

"What's the skunk doin'?" Jack asked, since he couldn't see our side of the car. "Maybe she'll take her babies on along for their evening stroll. A long stroll. Way down the road."

Twila edged close again and we peered through the dark glass.

"No such luck," I said. "Her babies are chasing crickets, and Mama's sitting there proudly watching them."

"Yeah," Grandberg said. "And there are dozens of crickets hopping around. It'll take them an hour to catch them all, way those babies are going at it."

"Dog'd run 'em off," Rover said.

"Trucker's not going out there!" I jerked back from the window to make my point firmly. Twila pulled back to avoid me, but not fast enough. The back of my head smacked into her nose and she moaned in pain.

"Oh, no!" I reached for her, but she slid over beside Trucker, one hand out to ward me off, the other cupped over her nose. "Are you bleeding? I'm so sorry, Twila."

"Nyt yer foot," she mumbled. "Shed muffed kikker." I interpreted that to mean it wasn't my fault, she should have moved quicker, but my main worry was...

"Please tell me I didn't break your nose," I said through my guilt.

She dropped her hand and stared down into her palm, while I anxiously stared at her upper lip. Breathed a sigh of relief when I didn't see any blood.

"Dot dose," she said. "Fit fung."

"Oh. Is it bleeding?"

"What did she say?" Jack asked.

"It's not her nose," I explained in a patient and less concerned voice. "She bit her tongue."

Twila stuck out her tongue, and I switched on the dome light and leaned close. "No blood, so the pain should ease in a minute. Do you want some water?"

"Huh huh," she said, mouth still open, tongue protruding. She also nodded, so I didn't have to interpret this time. I retrieved her backpack and started to hand her the bottle of water I got out of it.

Just as something scratched the door beside me.

Water bottle and I both lunged at Twila, but she thrust the backpack between us and held me off. While I glanced fearfully over my shoulder, she grabbed the water bottle from my hand.

"The skunk's trying to get in the door," I whimpered.

"Yep," Grandberg said. Nose pressed to his window and a small fog of mist around his mouth, he gazed downward. "Mama. And I only see two babies. Weren't there three?"

Mama evidently dragged her claws down the side of the door again —I didn't move over to my window to confirm Grandberg's observation. The noise irritated my nerves worse than fingernails on a chalkboard, not to mention the visual I had of the further destruction on Penny's car.

"What are we going to do?" I asked.

"The dog—" Rover tried again.

"Use your brain," Jack interrupted him. "Who's gonna give Trucker a ride after he tangles with a skunk?"

"We'd just haveta give him a 'mater juice bath," Rover said. "Had me a hound once that couldn't tell the difference between a skunk and coon. 'Mater juice works real well."

"And just how do we get the dog somewhere we can buy some tomato juice?" Jack asked.

"Well, we can't sit here all night," Grandberg added. "Someone needs to go out there and run those skunks off."

Every single one of us said, "Not me," at the same moment. Including Trucker, if I interpreted his grunt correctly. I finally chanced an apprehensive glance out the window, although I knew there was no blasted way that skunk could get to me. Consciously I knew it. Unconsciously, I cringed and my nose wrinkled in anticipation of the smell just at the sight of the animal. Which now strolled beside the Lincoln, nose to the ground, tail bannered in what I took as a definite warning. Uh oh. There were the car keys.

I must have spoken aloud, because Grandberg said, "Yeah. And she's picking them up."

"It's not the keys she's interested in," I said. "She's chewing on that leather key chain emblem. And...no! No, skunk! Don't do that!"

"What?" Jack asked. "I can't see a damn thing from over here."

"She's leaving!" I told him. "With the keys! But...but I still only see two of her babies. Surely she won't leave without the other one."

"Never heard of skunks knowin' how to count," Rover said. "Mebbe she don't know one's missin'."

Grandberg pounded on his window and yelled, "Here, skunk! Get back here with those keys!"

Mama stopped on the edge of the underbrush. Then I saw the third baby, peering out at her. With the leather tag firmly in her mouth, Mama shook her head slightly and the keys wiggled. Probably jingled, too, but we couldn't hear the noise inside the car. Baby Three wandered out of its shelter and Mama switched directions and headed back toward the car.

"Good skunk," Grandberg said. "Now, just drop the keys and go on your way."

Mama didn't mind him at all. Instead, she waited until all her babies were gathered around her...then stood on her hind feet and jumped up on the SUV bumper. A second later, everyone in the Lincoln had a clear view of her as she crawled through the SUV's broken rear window.

"Hey!" Rover yelled. "Get outta my patrol car!"

"I'll be glad to let you out to make her obey your order," Jack said. He pulled the door handle and opened the door a few inches.

"N—nah," Rover said with a shake of his head. " 'Mater juice'll prob'ly work on the car."

"Sure?" Jack asked, just as Mama stuck her head back out the SUV window. No keys this time, but her mouth worked as though chewing something.

"You got food in your patrol car again?" Grandberg asked Rover.

"Just some donuts," Rover whined. Then said to Jack, "You better close that door."

Jack started to. Then he glanced downward and back up, a horrified look on his face.

"What?" Grandberg asked as I instinctively leaned across the seat-back toward Jack in concern.

Jack didn't have to answer. The tiny baby skunk scurried across his lap, straight up his chest, and perched on his shoulder. *Then* Jack shut the door.

CHAPTER 29

Trucker lunged—but not baby-skunk-ward. A black and tan blur dove across Twila, straight onto my lap. Tried for my lap, anyway. He hadn't fit there since he hit three months old. He tried now, though. He shoved me against the door, and the armrest bit into my back. He laid his huge head on my shoulder, and I wrapped my arms around his shivering body and peered past him.

Baby...whatever number it was...sat on Jack's shoulder. Motionless, Jack stared out the windshield. Trucker blocked my view of Twila, but Grandberg had a horror-stricken expression similar to Jack's as he eyed the baby skunk. Rover still stared at the SUV, evidently unaware of...was it only the last two or three seconds? Still, he obviously had no idea the baby sat barely six inches from his ear, since he was shorter than Jack. He muttered, "Never heard of skunks likin' jelly doughnuts," as he watched...

...Mama slide feet-first down the hatchback door. She jumped to the ground, gripped one of her babies by the neck ruff, picked it up and carried it...yep, straight back into the SUV.

"How soon do baby skunks develop scent glands?" Jack whispered.

Rover shrugged his massive shoulders and replied, "Not 'til 'bout six months, I think. Buddy a'mine caught one once. Took it to the vet to get it de-scented and vet said it was 'bout three months old. Purty thing. Smart, too. He taught it all sorts of tricks."

By then, Mama had her second baby secured in the SUV, perhaps munching happily on jelly doughnuts. When she reappeared in the rear window again, I pushed Trucker to the floorboard. He buried his nose between my legs and whimpered. Twila had shoved herself into the corner on her side of the seat, as far away from the baby skunk on Jack's shoulder as she could get without leaving the car, and Grandberg was pressed against the driver's door in the same pose.

Baby yawned, and Jack asked Rover, "How old do you think those babies are?"

Mama was sniffing around outside my door now, probably looking for Baby Three. Who said skunks can't count? Oh, that was Rover. Hopefully, however, he knew a bit of skunk lore, since he told Jack, "Two months, mebbe three. Them's 'bout the same size as the one my buddy had when he first caught it."

Jack and Grandberg evidently took Rover at his word. Both of them relaxed somewhat. Not Trucker, though. His comprehension of English was limited to the commands he'd learned in obedience school. He kept his head buried, nose protected.

"It's getting hot in here," Twila murmured. "Too many bodies inside this closed up car."

"You're the one who dropped the keys," Grandberg reminded her.

She glared at him. "And your deputy caused the wreck and got us into this mess."

"Whoever dropped that tree in front of us caused it," Rover added.

Grandberg shook his head and said, "Never argue with women's logic."

Jack cautiously lifted his right hand and reached for Baby Three. Something bumped against the bottom of the car beneath my feet, and I glanced out the window. No Mama on that side of the car.

Jack carefully grasped Baby Three by the ruff. The movement evidently caught Rover's attention, and he looked around...straight at

Baby Three. So what if he'd just informed us Baby Three couldn't possibly spray him with foul-smelling liquid at its young age. He squished Grandberg against the driver's door again.

"Get it!" Rover yelled. He batted a pudgy hand at the baby as Grandberg thumped a fist against Rover's head and gasped for breath. Jack captured Baby Three and then transferred it to his left hand. As the little thing dangled, Jack reached for the door handle...and bumped his forehead on the window pane as he stared outside.

"She's over here now," he said. "I can't open the door, or she'll get in." That must have been the bump I heard, Mama making her way beneath the car.

Jack handed the baby across Rover to Grandberg, and Rover shifted to press against Jack.

"Put it out over there," Jack ordered as Grandberg gasped for breath and fumbled for the driver's door handle. Then Jack shoved Rover away with a "Get the hell off me!"

Grandberg got the door open. Jack got Rover off him. Rover shoved into Grandberg just as the police chief bent out the door to set Baby Three down.

Grandberg tumbled out after Baby Three. Worriedly, I peered out my window, but Grandberg missed Baby Three when he fell. Still, I suppose it scared Baby Three, who mewled a sound similar to a kitten in distress. A sound which brought Mama running. Another thump bumped my feet.

Grandberg didn't even try for the protection of the car, since Mama appeared right under the open door. He scrambled to his feet. Mama scrambled to hers...front ones. Tail over her back. But Grandberg was gone, galloping down the road behind us.

"Shut the damn door!" Jack yelled at Rover.

A second too late. Rover shut it...and also imprisoned us in there with the skunk spray that had seeped in.

Trucker abandoned me for Twila, who was further from the odor, and shoved his nose into her crotch. But she didn't let him stay there. Instead, she muttered a curse I hardly ever heard her use unless it was directed at a recalcitrant ghost and shoved her door open. Two seconds later, she was loping down the road after Grandberg, Trucker hot on her heels. I hurriedly glanced through the windshield to see Mama carrying Baby Three into the SUV...and followed Twila.

I hadn't gone a dozen yards before footsteps pounded the asphalt behind me. Jack passed me, his earlier concern obviously gone. I still beat Rover to where Twila and Grandberg stood under a spreading live oak down the road. We grouped beneath the tree, all gasping for breath. Rover's labored breathing drowned out all of ours as he stumbled up and collapsed at our feet. Twila thrust her water bottle into his hands, and he controlled his wheezes long enough to finish it off.

Now what? Again, I guess I spoke aloud, because Jack said, "Damned if I know."

"We might be safe from the skunk here," Twila said. "But some of you didn't get out of the car in time to dodge the smell."

Each and every one of us sniffed the person closest. Grandberg and Twila moved away from the rest of the group, as did Trucker. "It's you three," Twila confirmed to Jack, Rover, and me. So did Trucker. He ducked behind her and crouched to the ground, front paws over his nose as he stared through her legs at us.

"And that giant in camouflage is still out there," Twila reminded us.

"He's probably one of those antigovernment survivalists." Grandberg, in better shape than he instructed his deputies to maintain, breathed easily now, as did Jack. I probably could have, but Twila's words stirred the constriction in my chest—or maybe that tightness was because I tried not to breathe too deeply.

"Anyone got a cell phone?" Jack asked.

"In the SUV," Grandberg said at the same moment I said, "Mine's back at the hotel in my backpack."

"I've got my backpack," Twila said. Of course you do! You remembered to grab it even when you scrambled from the car! "But I don't own a cell phone."

"Mine's in the Lincoln," Jack said with a sigh. "I stuck it on the dashboard."

Rover pointed into the underbrush. "They's a deer trail over there. Leads to Miz Alvidrez's back yard. We can use her phone. Call Becky, our Animal Control Officer, outta bed to catch them skunks."

Grandberg wiped a hand down his face. "And by morning, half the departments in Texas will know she had to drag herself out of bed in the middle of the night to get a family of skunks out of one of my patrol cars. By noon, the rest of the state will have heard the story."

"Maybe Penny will take the skunks into consideration when she sees her car," I said. "Think it's a good human interest story, since we didn't shoot the skunks."

Rover and Grandberg glanced down at the pistols on their belts, and Jack slapped his empty hip and muttered, "Damn, I left mine in the bike's saddlebag." Well, Rover had to shove his belly aside to see his gun. Enough moonlight filtered through the branches to illuminate the disgust at themselves on their faces.

"We wouldn't have let you big bad cops shoot those poor little skunks anyway," I chastised them.

Twila giggled. I joined her. We snickered. Then full belly laughs erupted and we whooped and choked, pointed at the men. Grabbed our bellies and bent over, hysterical laughter ringing out between gasps for breath. Finally my tummy hurt so bad I was afraid I'd collapse beside Rover if this kept up. I straightened and wiped my eyes, as did Twila. The objects of our spectacle of ridicule were gone. Even Rover.

"Shit. Where'd they go?" I asked a now-quiescent Twila.

"I didn't see them leave," she admitted.

Trucker still sat at her feet, though. "Find Jack," I ordered the dog.

He stood and took a step. First, though, he looked down the road toward where we'd left the vehicles and sniffed the air. Then sniffed toward me. Evidently satisfied that the actual skunks weren't too near, even if he could smell them, he trotted into the underbrush, ahead of Twila, so I'd be a ways behind his sensitive nose.

It was dark in them there woods. Trees in Texas are fully leafed by April, and that woods was not only filled with briars, yupon, and prickly holly bushes, but also monstrous trees. The pines and spruce towered straight up, although their needle-covered branches spread in widths ranging from a foot or two to eight to twelve feet at their bases. I couldn't identify the hardwood trees, but everything from pecan to live oak to hickory to trash hackberry trees grew in a Texas woods, every species tall and spreading.

"Don't you have your penlight?" I asked Twila.

"I dropped it back on the seventh floor," she admitted.

All the cops probably had lights. They always carried one on their belts. I peered ahead of us as we stumbled down the faint trail after Trucker, but I didn't see any sign of light. Only more darkness, more jumbled growth encroaching the faint trail we walked along only because it was the least obstructed pathway and Trucker led the way.

"Remember that old graveyard we went to way out in the boonies that night?" Twila whispered.

"Which one?" I asked. "We went to lots of out-of-the-way grave—" Then it dawned on me which one she meant. The one we had to leave our car parked half a mile away from on a dark, moonless night. The one where a corroded gate stuck so tight we had to crawl over the iron fence spiked with sharp points. The one with huge towering trees that would have blocked out any moonlight had there been even a sliver of moon.

The one where our flashlight beams illuminated huge spider webs stretched between the trees and headstones. Webs spun by wood spiders, which can grow up to three inches across their body, twelve inches in diameter if you count their leg spread. I'd seen tarantulas smaller than wood spiders. Supposedly wood spiders were venomless, but my gut feeling was they didn't need venom. They were large enough to capture and eat their prey without resistance, and their frightful appearance kept away human danger to their nests.

"You just had to bring that up, didn't you?" I fumed. "As if both of us aren't already scared shitless!"

"Trip kitty," she muttered. "You probably owe it at least another couple hundred. We won't even try to figure out the cost of what you're going to have to pay for tomato juice right now. Besides, the men went through here first. They'll have cleared any spiders and webs."

"If we're on the right trail," I shot back.

She stopped. So did I, right against her back.

"Darn it, Twila—"

"I can't see Trucker," she interrupted.

"Oh, hell. And don't you dare count that one for the trip kitty!"

"Where the heck is Patrick?" She started her sentence with a semi-snarl, but it ended on a fearful whimper.

"What?" I asked in a tiny whine.

"One of the trees up ahead moved."

"It's...probably one of the men. Waiting for us."

"I suppose you're right. Or Trucker would be raising Cain."

"I can't believe Trucker took off and left us."

"Probably wanted to get away from your smell," she muttered low as she tried to edge away from me.

I caught her jacket, though, and held tight. "I didn't let the frigging skunk smell into the car."

"Not being responsible for it doesn't make it any less odorous," she insisted.

Something up ahead of us snapped. A twig? Someone moving?

"Why didn't you hold onto Trucker's leash?" I demanded. Whispered, really, since my voice wasn't working real well when I tried to force it past the burgeoning panic.

"You ordered him to find Jack. And he took off before I could grab him. Probably to—"

"—escape the smell!" I finished with her, louder now that my irritation flared. "All right. We've badgered that to death. Let's stop arguing and decide what to do."

"Two choices," she said in a more tolerant tone. "Back or forward."

"I vote for back."

"Well, I vote for forward. So we're tied."

Camouflage Man decided for us.

CHAPTER 30

A faint click, then a faint light shone. He stepped out of the underbrush onto the trail in front of us, then crouched to set a camping lantern down. One gloved hand pointed the barrel of the assault rifle at us, the index finger on his other hand at his lips in an explicit warning gesture not to scream. Which I would have done anyway, had he not deigned to speak when I opened my mouth.

"Ah, ah, ah," he muttered in a harsh whisper. "Nice of you two to get separated. Someone wants to talk to you. But if you have to die, I'll also kill the dog."

"What have you done with Trucker?" I whimpered as Twila and I clutched each other and trembled. Not a paranormal entity tremble, either. Staring down a wicked gun barrel was extremely more terrifying than confronting an evil entity. Obviously it overcame my aunt's aversion to my smell, also.

He flicked the gun barrel at the side of the trail. The dim lantern light outlined my dog, who looked like he was sleeping, curled nose to cropped tail. Despite the threat of assassination, I pulled away from Twila and knelt beside him. Warm. He was still warm. Was he breathing? I moaned and gathered his head into my arms.

"Wind was in my favor," Camouflage Man whispered. "I snuck up behind him and knocked him out with a needle full of Domitor I got from an animal doc buddy of mine. He ain't dead, but he ain't going nowhere for a while. You two are, though. And real quiet like."

I smoothed Trucker's head and then laid a hand on his side. Yes, he was still breathing, but only faintly. I stared up at our captor. "What if you overdosed him?"

"I didn't," he assured me. "Now, on your feet."

"I can't leave Trucker here!"

"Alice," Twila cautioned. "Do as he says."

"He won't shoot us," I insisted. "People will hear and call 9-1-1."

"Won't do you two no good, unless they send the meat wagon," Camo Man warned. But he kept his big gun trained on us as he pulled a smaller one, a pistol, from one of his many pockets. A pistol with a silencer screwed on the end of it. "Dog'll come around after while, unless..."

I surged to my feet. "No!" Even in my panic, I somehow kept my voice down. "We'll do whatever you want. Please don't shoot my dog."

"Or us," Twila added.

"Good thinking," he said. "Now, start back the way you came."

With one last worried glance at Trucker, I obeyed. Twila gripped my hand tightly in hers, signaling what I took as both her own fear and maybe an attempt at comfort. I squeezed back in...whatever she wanted to take from it. Then we had to let go of each other as the trail narrowed and I took the lead. Our captor was right on our heels, the lantern light barely penetrating the darkness, but at least it gave enough illumination that we didn't stumble.

We also obeyed his command not to speak. He was the one who broke the silence.

The precursory chill enveloped me just before we reached the asphalt road. Twila and I normally don't communicate telepathically. Not in words, only shared sensations. But I clearly heard her *Yessss* in my mind. Behind us, our captor's footsteps faltered. Twila and I kept moving.

Mary Ann—it had to be her, since only half of a woman's misty shape

—the top half—visualized. A vapor formed first, hovering a few feet above the asphalt, moonlight shining down to illuminate her much better than any lantern could.

"Stop!" Camo Man ordered. "What the hell is that?"

Ah ha, I thought. He can see ghosts.

And a ghost it was. She transformed from a vapor into the same woman I'd seen in those ghastly pictures Twila pilfered. Form and substance, even ultimately color, as ghosts are able to accomplish if they put their spiritual minds to their capabilities. Bobbed Twenties-style dark hair, a face with a stern and forbidding expression this time rather than terror. She still wore the low-cut, bright green dress and strings of pearls, which now lay amidst the fringes streaming down her bodice. All of her visualized...down to the wasp-thin waist.

"Shit," Camo Man whispered.

She spoke. Clearly, discernibly. "Let them go and get the hell out of here, Delroy."

Delroy? Where had I heard that name?

"You're dead!" he yelled as I tried to place that unusual redneck name but failed. Probably because I had a few other things on my mind just then, not the least of which—the silenced gun barrel.

"Yes," she agreed with a regal nod. "I'm dead. You would know, wouldn't you?"

"I didn't do it," Delroy whined.

She sneered at him. "Does that matter? Your hand was in it."

Twila and I edged close to each other and shifted sideways so we could look back and forth between Delroy and Mary Ann. I slipped one arm around Twila's back. The chill deepened to a cold so freezing that I wondered if we actually could move if we got the chance.

Delroy's assault rifle hung from a strap around his neck. I'd seen gun straps like that on hunting rifles and in pictures of marauding terrorists and soldiers. But he still carried the silenced pistol in one hand, the lantern in the other. He dropped the lantern and it landed on its side in a pile of leaves at his feet, light still glowing. Then he gripped the pistol two-handed, pointed at Mary Ann.

"You can't hurt me now!" he spat.

"And you think you can hurt me? Shoot me? Remember, I'm already dead. And as for me hurting you…oh, there are ways, Delroy." She uttered a truly horrendous laugh that echoed and rebounded all around us, then floated toward him.

Zip. Zip. Zip. The silencer muffled the sound, but the pistol bucked in Delroy's hand as he pulled the trigger. Mary Ann, of course, kept coming.

Twila and I went. I picked her right up off the ground and swiveled a hundred and eighty. Shoved her ahead of me through the brush, heedless of the briars and thorns tearing at our clothing. I instinctively ran in a crouch, but I quickly realized Twila didn't understand that need. I grabbed her jacket, but she fought me, and I nearly lost my hold. Desperately, I launched myself at her, caught her backpack, and we both hit the ground, just as…

Zip. Zip. Zip. Thunk. Bullets tore over us, close enough to hit us had we not been on the ground. And close enough that the last one thunked into a tree right in front of us. Right in front of Twila's nose, if my eyes didn't deceive me, although it was far too dark in here to hazard much more than a judgment call when I eased my nose out of her rear end and peered forward.

"Don't move," I whispered.

She didn't. Well, not much. She did stiffen to a near corpse-like state under my hold. Uh oh, wrong word to have in my mind just then. I tried frenziedly to determine our next move.

If we run again, he'll shoot. He'll be able to hear us if we take off, and know which direction to aim his shots.

But he already knows approximately where we are. He'll be coming to find us.

I don't hear him yet, though. Surely I'd hear a man that large crashing after us.

Then that wicked laughter rang out again, followed by a chilling, banshee shriek. We moved. I doubt Twila could help herself any more than I could. We rolled over and scuttled back against the tree, wrapped our arms around each other and quivered and quaked with fear. Through the brush, we could see the lantern. It rose in the air until it shone down on Delroy. He stared at it in horror...or perhaps at the apparition holding it.

Mary Ann floated along with the lantern, one hand out, one finger looped through the lantern's wire handle. From what I knew about ghosts, she probably manipulated the movement mentally, her finger in place just for show. Delroy shot again. At the lantern. At Mary Ann. He kept shooting even after the pistol click, click, clicked when he'd emptied the clip. By then Mary Ann hovered only a foot from him, and she let loose with another banshee wail that sent an icy trill up my spine.

He threw the pistol at her. It clanged against the lantern and bounced off. Disappeared in the brush. I guess he finally remembered the assault rifle, because he grabbed for it. But Mary Ann flicked those two long strings of pearls with her free hand and they looped around his neck.

Delroy whimpered in dismal terror and the lantern light shone on the dark spread on the front of his pants. Urine, I presumed. Couldn't be anything else, unless he carried a squeeze bottle of water under his balls. He forwent the Uzi to claw at his neck. His fingers penetrated straight through the pearls, but obviously he felt the constriction. He choked and sputtered, and when he clawed off that interlaced net mask, I got my first look at his face.

A brief look only, though. With a supreme effort, he wrenched away from Mary Ann. Then all we could see was his back as he ran hell-bent for leather out of there. We could hear him crashing through the brush for a while. Sort of. His terrified screams overrode the noise of his passage. When I had sense enough to look around for the ghost again, she floated in the air right beside us. I drew back with a gasp. So did Twila. But the damn tree behind us forbid retreat.

"Don't worry," Mary Ann said in a now throaty, sexy voice. "You two are safe. I won't harm you."

Twila recovered her ability to speak first. And it didn't surprise me that, even with us both shaking in our tennis shoes, she put on a plucky effort. After all, we were supposed to *discipline* the ghosts we encountered.

"No, you won't harm us," Twila proclaimed. Even there on the ground, staring up at the woman, she somehow managed to project an inflexible demeanor. "You have your ways, yes. But I've had more experience dealing with ghosts than you've had being a ghost. So I'll give you about sixty seconds to explain yourself before I banish you."

"Bravo," I whispered. Mary Ann floated off a few feet and stared at Twila for fifteen of her sixty-second limit, then nodded compliantly.

"Who is he?" Twila asked.

"Talk to Sam about him," she said. "I...I can't seem to stay any longer." She began to fade, and handed the lantern to me. Floated it to me, I should say. "As for me, you know what I need. To be whole, so I can cross through the light intact. Please help me."

"You don't need to be whole." I'd finally found my own sense of speech somewhere beneath the turbulence in my mind. "You can cross in any state you wish."

She shook her head. We could still see the movement, even though her form was now only a gray mist. "I want to be whole. Maybe it's vanity, but vanity was truly one of my sins."

"Your body's at the morgue," I insisted. "Just go back there and reunite."

She smiled sadly. "I have to go. I'll see you both on the seventh floor."

"No!" I insisted. But she wasn't there to command. Even the freezing air began to warm until, within a few seconds, it reached normal temperature.

I surged to my feet and held out a hand to help Twila up. "Wow," I said. "How long is it going to take me to be able to handle things like you do?"

"It's all mind control," she murmured as she brushed at twigs and leaves on her clothing, then picked a few leaves off my jacket. "And not mind control over the entities. Mind control over our own fallibility and instinctive fear of the unknown."

"Well, you sure showed her who was boss," I praised.

"And you sure saved my life," she replied. "One of those bullets could have..."

I smiled and held up a hand, palm out. She gently high-fived me in return. "Partners and buds," we both said in unison.

We hugged briefly, then I hurried over to the pistol. Using the hem of my jacket to preserve any possible fingerprints, I picked it up, then wasn't sure what to do with it.

"Here," Twila said. She gripped the silencer with her own jacket hem and twisted it free of the barrel.

"How did you know how to do that?" I asked. As if her knowledge of how to remove a pistol silencer had a damn thing to do with the situation we were in.

"From TV," she said, then shoved the silencer in my other jacket pocket. I shrugged and pulled her jacket toward me to secure the pistol in her pocket. I grabbed the lantern and started back down the flattened path we'd made during our panic-stricken flee for life.

"Who's Sam?" Twila asked as we pushed aside yupon and stomped down brush that had sprung back up.

"That detective who was with Grandberg back at the hotel," I said over my shoulder. "But let's worry about him after we check on Trucker."

She was right behind me, so I didn't have to yell. But someone was yelling. My name, her name, too, if I heard right. Twila grabbed my arm and jerked me to a halt, then fumbled with the lantern until she found the switch and plunged us into darkness.

CHAPTER 31

"That has to be Jack or one of the cops looking for us," I said. Not loudly, though.

"Are you sure?" she asked. Not loudly, either.

"No," I admitted. "But Camo Man...Delroy...doesn't know our names. Does he?"

"Depends on how long he was watching us. What he heard. He might have been around a while, even back there at the skunk offensive."

"I told you I'm tired of your complaining about my smell—oh, you mean the skunk mugging."

"Mugging. Offensive. Whatever." She peered past me, but neither one of us made a move to take one more step. "Wait. I'll see if I can tune in a little better."

I nodded as she placed the tips of her first two fingers on each hand to her temples, just above her ears. She closed her eyes—well, I assumed she did. I couldn't see her, but that was the normal way we practiced that clairaudience ability. Not that someone like Jack would ever count anything psychic we did as normal.

Finally she sighed and said, "Yeah. It's Jack. Let's go."

196

I turned the lantern back on, and after a few steps, Twila said, "I don't guess Delroy has stopped running yet. He was pretty terrified."

I halted and turned off the damned lantern again. "What if he got his fear under control and is waiting up ahead for us?"

"Alice! Twila! *Chère,* where are you?"

Jack, for sure. We didn't need clairaudience to recognize his voice now. He couldn't be that far away. And through the trees, a flashlight beam bobbed up and down, then swept from side to side.

"Let's let Jack handle Camo Man if he's still around," I said.

"Over here!" Twila shouted, right beside my ear. But relief overrode my annoyance at her insensitivity. "Turn the lantern back on, Alice," she said.

A moment later, we met Jack on the trail we'd vacated posthaste a while earlier. His flashlight blinded me when he shone it directly into my face and kept it there. I slapped at the flashlight, and he finally turned it aside at Twila.

"Are you both all right?" he asked in an anxious voice. "Where've you been? We've been searching all over these damned woods."

"You're the one who left us alone," I reminded him. "If it hadn't been for Mary Ann, we'd probably both be dead right now!"

Not unexpectedly, he ignored my reference to Grandberg's sister, ran the flashlight beam up and down my body, then Twila's. "We were comin' back for you. Are you sure you're both all right?"

"The bullets missed us," Twila said in a cold voice. "Thanks to Alice shoving us both to the ground."

"Bullets? What the hell are you talkin' about? I didn't hear any shots."

I pushed past him, on down the trail, and Twila caught up beside me. "Have you seen Trucker?" I asked as I flashed the lantern at the side of the trail.

"No," Jack replied from right behind us. "I thought he was with you two."

Lantern held high, I paused and examined where we were. There. I recognized that lightning-split oak. I hurried on down the trail another few feet, then dropped to the ground. Trucker stared back at me, then yawned widely, teeth gleaming. I shoved the lantern at Twila and gathered my dog into my arms, all hundred and fifty pounds of him. He laid his head on my shoulder, sighed a dog sigh...and snored in my ear.

"He's still pretty out of it," Twila said as she knelt beside me.

"At least Delroy didn't lie about not overdosing him," I replied. "He'll be okay when the...what did he call it? Domitor. When it wears off. But I'll call my vet at home as soon as we get to a phone."

"Who's Delroy?" Jack asked. "And you said something about a Mary Ann."

I gently released Trucker and allowed him to slide back to the ground. Then Twila and I glanced at each other. She nodded.

We both whipped to our feet and shouted at Jack, "Mary Ann's a ghost! And Delroy's the son of a bitch who tried to kidnap, then kill us!" Amazing. We are so in tune at times. Our words were exactly the same.

"And," Twila continued while I glared at Jack, "it was a ghost who saved us, not a trio of bumbling Keystone Cops!"

"Yeah," I agreed. "A trio of cops who left two defenseless women all alone in the woods to fend for themselves!"

"You two are about the least defenseless women I've ever run across," Jack said. But his voice choked up and he jammed his flashlight into his belt before he gathered both of us into his arms. "I'm sorry. Look, I can't tell you how sorry I am. We were stupid. We shouldn't have left you. It was a macho bullshit mistake in judgment. Look, I'll take you both back to Six Gun—"

Still in tune, we both jerked free and shook our heads. "Huh uh. No way," Twila said. "Mary Ann's counting on us, and it's the least we can do after she saved our butts when you deserted us!"

"Yeah," I stuck in. "Alone with a gun-totting madman in the vicinity!"

"That's exactly what I mean," Jack said in a deadly cold voice. "It's too dangerous for you to stay around here. You're both going home, if I have to hog-tie and carry you."

"You and whose army?" Twila spat. "An army that consists of a drunk police chief and a deputy who doesn't have any more staying power than what it takes to lift a jelly doughnut to his mouth?"

"If that's what it takes," Jack warned. "You can either go home—back to Six Gun—or I'll toss both of you in one of Grandberg's cells and let him hold you as material witnesses."

He meant it. We both knew that. But right now, I wanted to get out of these woods and call Trucker's vet more than I wanted to stand here and argue with Jack so I could continue to shove his incompetence down his throat.

I surreptitiously nudged Twila. "All right," I said. "But we can wait at Penny's. It should be safe there."

"As if." Jack snorted. "As soon as I'm out of sight, you'll enlist Penny's aid and be right back in the middle of this. No, you're goin' home. Far enough away that I don't have to worry about you both sneakin' back here and puttin' yourselves in danger again. This is Grandberg's mess. Let him clean it up."

I shrugged. Twila shrugged. Trucker stirred and grunted. By the time Twila and I knelt beside him again, he was more awake. His brown eyes gleamed brightly and he gathered his legs under him and stood. Wavered a bit, then collapsed.

"You're going to have to carry him, Jack," I said as I looked up at the six feet of Cajun stone will above us.

"I can do that," he said. "That house the deputy was talking about is only a few hundred yards further on. But I want both your promises that you won't try to give me the slip on the way there."

"We promise," Twila and I echoed. I presumed Twila, also, had her fingers crossed on the hand under Trucker's silky ear. I know the two fingers of the hand in my jacket pocket were wrapped one over the other. Besides, it wasn't really a lie. We weren't going to give him the slip between here and Patty's house.

"Just get my dog out of here so I can get him some medical attention and make sure he's going to be all right," I continued.

We moved aside as Jack picked up Trucker. The dog's weight was heavy for even a man in excellent physical condition like Jack. But he shifted Trucker in his arms and headed down the path. Twila carried the lantern this time, and she and I trailed along. We were good girls. It wasn't the right time to be anything else. Besides, we were on the way to Patty Alvidrez's house, where we could get some more important information about what was going on here.

And we were leaving those dark woods behind. I'd have been willing to bet that Frost wouldn't have written such lovely words about these woods! Dark and deep, sure. But lovely? I thought not.

Jack questioned us as we walked. "You said the man who attacked you was Delroy something. I don't suppose he introduced himself to you?"

I let Twila answer that one. "No. Mary Ann mentioned his name."

"Mary Ann?" Jack asked.

"The ghost of the woman who was murdered back at the hotel."

"She wasn't murdered there," Jack corrected. "She was just left there. And I don't suppose there's any sense of me arguing with you about seeing her ghost."

"None at all," Twila shot back.

"So tell me exactly what happened."

Twila explained, in minute detail, from the moment we realized the macho men had abandoned us to the point where Mary Ann scared the piss out of Delroy and he vacated our presence. Once in a while, Jack shifted Trucker, and at one point, the dog laid his head on Jack's shoulder. Trucker opened his eyes and looked at me. I swear I noticed a twinkle in the brown depths, as though he were perfectly capable of walking on his own now but had decided to enjoy the ride.

We emerged beneath a huge live oak on the edge of an alley. Across from us ran a row of rather small homes. Jack glanced at the house on the right, but headed for the one straight ahead. We didn't need the lantern now. Security lights gleamed on the rear of the house, a neat frame, painted white with blue-trimmed shutters on each side of the rear windows. A screened-in porch ran across the back, and the yard was neatly mowed, a line of rosebushes against a wooden-paneled fence on the left, some sort of flowering bushes I couldn't recognize in the dim light along the fence on the right. Monkey grass edged a flagstone side-walk that led to the porch.

At the edge of the sidewalk, Jack sat Trucker down with a grunt. "I know you're awake," he told the dog. "You can at least walk as far as the porch."

I watched my dog closely, but Trucker agreeably ambled up the path, no sign of a waver in his pace.

Jack held out a detaining hand when Twila and I attempted to follow. "We need to talk about what went on out there privately before we let the rest of the community in on it," he cautioned.

"We can't even tell Mr. Police Chief and Deputy Dog?" Twila asked sweetly.

"Deputy..." Jack guffawed. "Rover's not even here. Grandberg called one of the other patrolmen to pick him up and take him to get checked out at the ER. He didn't like the looks of D—Rover when we got here."

"The same hospital where Carrie is?" I asked.

Jack shrugged. "No idea. Anyway, I'm not even sure Grandberg's back here yet. He also called his animal control officer and then a wrecker service to get the vehicles cleared out of the road before some drunk came by and plowed into them. Then we both went back out to look for you two."

Twila sniffed. "Smells like you showered first. And changed clothes."

He shrugged. "Miz Alvidrez had some of her brother's clothes here. I figured I could concentrate better. We need to see if Grandberg's back."

"I'm here," Grandberg said as he pushed open the screen door. He eyed Trucker for a moment, but my dog only walked over to one of the bushes along the fence and hiked his leg. I bit back the demand that he not water Patty's plants. Where else was the poor dog going to relieve himself?

CHAPTER 32

"Have you seen Patrick?" Twila asked Grandberg.

"He's inside. With Patty."

"Probably tellin' her about his drag racin' days," Jack muttered.

When I approached, Grandberg sniffed and backed off a step. "Patty made coffee and sandwiches, if anyone wants some."

"Do we ever," Twila murmured.

She swooped in the door as though she hadn't eaten in a month. My stomach demanded I follow her, but first I called Trucker over. He would only come within six feet of me before he sniffed, then belly-dropped and whined.

"You heard anything about Do—Rover?" Jack asked Grandberg.

"He's fine. Just indigestion and overexertion. I told his wife to take him on home for the night."

I gave up trying to get Trucker to come closer and asked Grandberg, "Where's your other detective? Sam...Peters, I think his last name is."

"My only detective, not other one." Grandberg frowned at me. "I imagine he's trying to get some sleep. Why do you want to know?"

"Mary Ann said we should talk to him," I replied as I kept a close look at his face.

He didn't disappoint me. He blanched for an instant, then grabbed me, evidently unworried now that my smell would contaminate him. "You saw her again! What did she say?"

I pointedly removed his right hand from my shoulder, then his left. "She told us to talk to Sam." And just to see his further reaction, I continued, "She wants us to do a ceremony on the seventh floor of the hotel to help her cross over."

"Then you have to do that," he insisted. "We can go right now."

"*You* can go whenever you want to," I informed him. "I'm getting something to eat, then a bath. I don't give a blast whether my smell bothers you, but it hurts my feelings that my dog won't come to me."

Twila pushed open the screen door and handed me a sandwich and a plastic cup, which I accepted with the same enthusiasm she showed when she left to procure it.

"Patty said Jack used all her hot water, so we may have to go back to Penny's to get that bath," she said as I eagerly lifted the sandwich, uncaring as to the contents. Luckily, I caught the smell before I bit into it. And an idea flashed through my mind. We needed more information here...

To stall for time while I thought this out, I asked Jack, "What did you mean about Patrick drag racing?"

He launched into a tale that Patrick had evidently told him when they ran into each other outside the hotel a while ago. Twila listened closely, and since no one was watching me at the moment, I broke off a piece of the sandwich, then tossed it to Trucker. He scarfed it up, and as Jack told Twila about Patrick saying that he'd hovered over the car wreck, I pretended to gag.

"What's wrong?" Twila asked.

"It's peanut butter!"

"Patty said it was...some sort of jelly," Twila said with a gasp.

I swished a swig of...lemonade, from the taste...around my mouth, then spit it on the ground also.

"I don't care what Patty said," I told Twila when I could speak. "I tasted peanut butter, and you know I'm allergic to some types of nuts."

She and Jack both moved in on me and the porch lights reflected the concern on their faces. "You didn't swallow any, did you, *Chère?*"

I laid a hand on my throat and said, "I think I can feel it swelling already!"

"Where's your EpiPen?" Twila asked. "Never mind. It's back at the hotel, in your backpack. I'll see if Patty has any Benadryl. Come with me so we can wash your mouth out."

I didn't pay any attention to the kitchen when Twila rushed me into the house. The two of us headed straight for the sink, Jack hovering right behind us. Twila turned the water on, and instead of reaching for a cup, she urged my head down. I palmed water and washed my mouth out.

"I think I better go to the hospital," I said.

"Your throat's still swelling?" Jack asked.

I shrugged. He could take it any way he wanted to, since at least it wasn't a lie.

"I'm so sorry," a woman said. "I heard you talking. I used that peanut butter–jelly mixture my grandkids like so much. I had no idea..."

While I wiped my mouth on a kitchen towel that Twila handed me, I turned to see Patty watching us with a worried expression. Patrick wasn't with her, but his whereabouts right now were the least of my worries.

"Y'all can use my car," Patty said. "It's parked out front."

I barely got a chance to nod a thanks to her before Jack grabbed the keys Patty held out and guided me on through the house. Shoved me, really, but I wasn't hesitant. "Trucker," I called over my shoulder.

"I'll take care of him," Twila said. "And get hold of Penny to bring us another car."

"You won't need a car!" Jack reminded her.

It wasn't far through that small house. We went straight through a tiny living room that contained little more than a couch, one chair, and a television, then emerged outside. A nondescript sedan sat at the curb, and Jack unlocked the door and gently, this time, pushed me into the passenger seat.

"How are you feeling?" he asked as I buckled my seat belt.

"Frankly, I think I'm going to be all right," I admitted. "But it even touching the inside of my mouth..."

"We're gonna get you checked out anyway," he said, as I knew he would.

A moment later, we were headed down the back street that came out on a more traveled highway. I thought to ask Jack, "Do you know where the hospital is?"

"Approximately. I saw a sign out here somewhere."

Jack found the tiny community hospital with no problem. He pulled in at the emergency room entrance and ordered me inside while he parked the car. I went, and by the time Jack joined me again, a nurse was taking my insurance information and a white-coated man who appeared young enough to still be in high school was interspersing the admitting nurse's questions with his. I tried to ignore the wrinkled noses on both the doc and nurse. By then, I'd already explained that I was here for my allergy, not my smell.

"I'll check you over," Dr. Powell, as he'd introduced himself to me, said. "But I think you're right. You had a near miss."

"Check her over real well," Jack said. "She's important to us."

Dr. Powell nodded an agreement, and as soon as I signed fifty gazillion places on the ream of papers the nurse handed me—all right, it was only a half dozen places—he took me into an examining room down the hallway and pulled the door closed.

"Alice Carpenter," he said. "The writer?"

"Yes. That's me." That's all I needed. A doctor who knew who I was, telling my reading public that I'd showed up smelling to high heaven like skunk in his ER!

"I've read your books. They're good. When's your next one coming out? Oh, and please take your clothes off from the waist up, if you will."

I started disrobing as I explained, "The next book will be out in October. But there will be a paperback of my last one out in May."

"Scoot onto the table. And here's a gown."

What they call a *gown* in a hospital is my idea of a way to torture patients into sidetracking their minds from those nasty, invasive examinations. He handed me a thin piece of paper that I could have balled up in one fist. But I shrugged the stupid thing on and huddled there shivering as he stuck his icy stethoscope on my back. I jerked, and he murmured an "I'm sorry," but didn't halt his examination.

After he'd sufficiently invaded my poor, cold, embarrassed body, he stepped back and said, "We both agree. You're fine. But before you leave, I'll give you an EpiPen shot to take with you. Your own doctor should have warned you to keep some with you at all times, just in case."

I didn't bother to explain that I normally carried that precautionary drug. I just slid off that table. "How is Carrie, the tour guide from the hotel?" I asked while I reached for my stinky clothes.

"She's fine now," he said, but a frown tugged at his face. "I couldn't find a thing wrong with her. But we're keeping her for observation."

He left me alone, and long before I was dressed, I'd determined to go ahead with my secret plan. This place seemed deserted enough to ally me. If Jack wouldn't cooperate, I'd slip away from him.

I walked out into the ER waiting room area to find Jack involved in a serious conversation with the doctor, who kept nodding his head reassuringly. The nurse smiled at me and handed me a package I recognized as the drug I needed as I passed the admitting desk. Dr. Powell took advantage of my presence when I joined them and slipped away when Jack turned his full attention on me.

"Feel better now?" I asked.

"I should be asking you that."

I patted him on the shoulder and gazed around the waiting room. Dr. Powell had completely disappeared, and the nurse was deeply involved in a game of solitaire on her computer. As I'd already determined, not much business in this small hospital tonight. I took Jack's hand, and instead of moving toward the door, I surreptitiously snuck down the hallway past the examining rooms.

"How do you know which room she's in?" Jack asked quietly.

"Who? I mean, how did you know where I was going?"

"You only know of one person here that I can think of," he said. "That tour guide. Carrie?"

"Uh huh," I admitted. "I got a look at the admitting log while I was doing all that paperwork. I can read upside down fairly well. The nurse logged in that Carrie was transferred from the ER to Room 101. It can't be too hard to find."

"Unless we run into some battle-ax RN who deems it her duty to be part of Homeland Security and run all unsanctioned people off the premises during non-visiting hours," he murmured.

I tossed him a wide grin. "That's where your cop credentials will come in."

He sighed. "And it doesn't matter that I could be put on leave for misrepresenting myself."

"Oh, come on, Jack." I perused a directional sign as I said, "You're not misrepresenting yourself. Not yet, anyway. You haven't pulled out that badge since when you came to the station to get me. And Patty wasn't real impressed then."

He flushed at that reminder, and I giggled and led the way down an intersecting hallway. "Room 101's down this way."

"I can read," he grumbled.

Fate appeared provident tonight. Room 101 was the first room we came to in the section of the hospital housing patients. On down the dark, nighttime hallway, the nurse's desk was bathed in dim desk lamps. And yep, a nurse sat there. A large nurse, one I hoped we wouldn't have to confront and decide whether she had a battle-ax personality or not.

I edged the door to Room 101 open carefully, but like all hospital room doors, the pneumatic lever kept it from creaking and warning of our presence. Jack slid in with me, and I helped the door along as it closed. There were two beds, the one by the door unoccupied and neatly made up for the next patient. Someone had pulled the curtain around the window bed, and there, also, a dim light shone. Plus, a voice murmured. I thought I recognized that voice. Granny already had her head cocked, her bright-eyed gaze centered on the edge of the curtain when I rounded it.

" 'Bout time you showed up. What took ya so long?" she asked. "Been other folks in t'talk to Carrie since she woke up. Even a cop, who made me leave for a while. Hi, Jack."

"What on earth are you doing here?" I asked Granny. Then I noticed the cat carrier with its door open beside her chair, Granny's walnut walking stick propped against the side of it. "Is that Miss Molly?"

Miss Molly answered for herself. She evidently heard my voice, and bounded out of the carrier. But just as quickly, she tried to halt her progress and slid on the waxed floor, then managed to change direction and leap onto the bed. From there, she jumped onto Jack's shoulder and peered around his head at me. Sniffing. Yeah, she sniffed, then ducked back. When Jack gently lifted the cat off his shoulder, she cuddled in his arms and buried her nose in the crook of his elbow.

"I have got to get a bath," I muttered.

"Yep," Granny agreed as she planted her walking stick on the floor and rose from the chair beside the bed. "I'll be right back."

She tottered past us, and I examined the woman on the bed. Her hair frizzed wildly and dark circles marred her face under her eyes. She looked nearly as old as Granny, although not nearly as energetic. Carrie gazed back at me, not catatonic at all now. But she said, "Who are you?"

I started to remind her, but realized she was looking at Jack. He only answered, "Jack Roucheau."

Her hands clasped together on her chest, fingers twined tightly. "What are you two doing here this time of night?"

Instead of answering her, I said, "What happened to your speech? Before you...well...uh..."

"Yes, that's how I sound when I'm out of my medicine," she said with a sigh. "I do the tours at the hotel to try to bring in some extra money, but even that doesn't always stretch far enough."

She looked so pitiful there, I didn't push her to explain what her medical problem entailed. Instead, I let Jack take the lead in questioning. Besides, if I moved any closer to her, she'd probably dive under the bedclothes to escape my smell.

"We'd like you to tell us what you know about what happened at the hotel," Jack said.

Before Carrie could answer, though, Granny teetered back in, followed by a metal cart. The nurse pushed the cart, which contained about six dozen of those single-serving cans of tomato juice.

"We had to raid the kitchen," Granny explained. "But I's seen enuf skunk cases over the years to figger this oughta do it. Gimme your clothes, Alice, and I'll have Nurse Victoria wash 'em. I don't think you got enuf smell that it won't come out."

"I can do all this back at Penny's," I protested.

"Not lessen you can find her," Granny said. She glanced at the bedside phone. "I been callin' her for a couple hours now. Ain't no answer at the house or on her cell phone. And she said she'd come back and get me whenever I wanted her to. Good thing I brought Miss Molly with me! Her and that there Daisy don't like each other a'tall."

"What on earth are you doing here, Granny?" I finally repeated.

"Penny called here to check on Carrie, and that's the first time I knowed her name. Knowed Carrie's mama years ago. Victoria let me talk t'her. I always come when somebody's in the hospital. You know that." Yes, I knew that. Anyone ill could count on Granny Chisholm.

Jack stood back in a corner now, taking all of this in while he stroked Miss Molly. When I glanced at him, he said, "Get your bath, *Chère*. You'll feel better."

"Smell better, too, I suppose," I huffed.

"There's that," he replied.

I sighed and Victoria opened another door, the one on the bathroom. She ushered me inside, pushed the cart in behind me, and then closed us in.

"Don't worry about the smell with me," she said in a girlish voice in complete contradiction to her hefty size. "I'm all clogged up with sinus problems tonight. Shimmy out of those clothes for me, dearie."

As soon as I did and handed them to her, she whisked right out of the bathroom, leaving me to see how long it would take to open all those little bitty cans of tomato juice all by myself!

CHAPTER 33

Patrick eyed Twila warily as she settled on the couch beside Patty and pointed at one of the lounge chairs. He didn't need the support, but he eased himself into it anyway.

"Explain yourself," Twila ordered, then stared at Patty in an indication that the command included her. "I didn't sign onto this ghosthunt to be shot at!"

"Shot at?" Patty broke in. "Delroy! I knew he was around here somewhere."

"That's him," Twila said with an angry nod. "Who is he and what's he got to do with all this?"

Patrick slumped in the chair. "I have no idea who Delroy is, or why he'd be after you and Alice." Confusion mixed with the anger on Twila's face. "I've been trying all this time to find out what happened to Consuela. But Antonio kept thwarting my search."

"Patrick is actually my grandfather," Patty said. "I recognized him at once when he materialized back at the station. I have the photos my family kept over the years."

Twila held her hands up palm out and said, "Wait just a minute." She pointed at Patrick. "You're her grandfather." Her finger traced a line to Patty. "And you're his granddaughter." Back to Patrick. "And for some unknown reason, you didn't want to tell us that your reason for hanging around on this side of the veil was to find out what happened to the woman you loved?"

Patrick whispered, "I tried to cross over, but something held me here. I concluded that I needed to find out what had happened to Consuela after my death. However, I didn't even know for sure that there was anyone to find and ask. Not until tonight, when Patty and I finally had a chance to talk. Antonio sure wouldn't tell me anything."

"Why is he still here, too?" Twila demanded.

"I don't know," Patrick insisted. "I can't say for certain that he caused my death, but I suspect it. However, I did know that if he found out Consuela and I had..." He leaned back in the chair. "Let me finish telling you what happened."

* * *

They didn't mean for it to go so far. But the privacy of the car...the raging need for each other. She wanted him as much as Patrick wanted her. He had no doubt about that. He didn't have to urge her too hard to return to the hotel with him. They both knew what would happen there, and Patrick didn't want his first time with her—her first time at all—to be a hot, sweaty, embarrassing tryst in the car.

A virgin, Consuela gave him her most precious gift in that bedroom a while later. And that filled him with as much awe as her love for him in return. He cuddled her close and draped the soft blanket around her. Their clothing lay scattered around the room, and he wanted her flesh against his with no barrier for a while longer. She fit perfectly against his side, as they had fit together as one only moments before. So incredible. Now he understood the difference between simple sexual relief and lovemaking.

Still, he knew he'd hurt her for a brief moment. And since this had been her first time, he couldn't fathom how she would react. Her reaction meant the world to him, and he held her close, apprehensive while he waited for her first words to him after their joining.

"I love you," she whispered, and Patrick released a sigh of both relief and joy.

He kissed the top of her head, then lifted her chin so he could see her face. "You are my heart," he said. "Forever and ever, beyond the ends of time."

She frowned. "Oh, you should not say that. Fate may laugh at you."

"I mean it," he vowed. "I love you so much that nothing will ever come between us. I'm not afraid of Fate. Fate brought you to me, so she can't be all bad. If, God forbid, something should separate us, I will never rest until we find each other again."

She snuggled against him. "I feel that way, also, but I have learned that a person's world can change without warning."

"No one can foretell the future with certainty," he agreed. "But my life is you now. Without you, I would have no life. Not one that I cared to live, anyway. We'll work things out, my darling. We'll weather everything Fate tosses at us, because we have each other."

She nodded against his chest and traced a fingernail around one of his nipples. "I am new at this," she murmured. "How soon can we have each other again?"

Patrick laughed delightedly and showed her.

* * *

He didn't mention all the details to Twila and Patty, of course. A gentleman didn't tell things like that. But he presumed by their faces that they got the gist of the story.

"You made a vow to Consuela," Twila murmured.

"Yes," he agreed, then continued, "I wanted to talk to Antonio the next day, but Consuela begged me to let her prepare him first. Besides, he had gone somewhere to look for a better-paying job, and she knew he would be tired when he came home. So before I kissed her good-bye that night, I agreed to go ahead and talk to my parents first."

"And?" Twila prodded when he fell silent in his memories.

"And." Patrick heaved a determined sigh. He needed to finish the story this time. "I drove to Dallas and asked for a private meeting with my father first. I was so excited after my talk with him. It was amazing how things could work out. My father knew who had stolen the ranch from Consuela's father. He didn't like the man, called him a robber baron. We worked out a plan to get the ranch back and return it to Antonio."

"That would have been wonderful," Patty said. "But our family never regained title to our land. And Antonio was killed in an oil field blast a few years later. At Spindletop, down by Beaumont."

"Is that what happened to him?" Patrick couldn't dredge up too much sympathy for Consuela's brother. "And my love? Consuela? My rational mind tells me that she has gone on before me, but my heart wants to make sure she's not wandering somewhere, as I am."

"Her headstone's in the graveyard with the rest of the family's," Patty told him quietly. "The only one that isn't there is Antonio's."

Twila opened her eyes. Patrick had been watching her while he and Patty spoke, and at one point, he'd thought her asleep. Something told him, however, that she was listening to every word. Perhaps she was in one of those trances he'd heard about.

She blinked at him and said in a quiet voice, "There was no body to bring back and bury. The blast killed all seven men on the well. An accident with nitroglycerin. Some people believe that if a soul becomes a ghost after a violent death, it is tied to the place of death. But that's not true, and Antonio's presence here helps prove mine and Alice's theory."

He leaned forward eagerly. "Can you see what happened to Consuela?"

"No, she can't," a voice snarled.

Antonio! Patrick sprang out of his chair and faced the other ghost. "You can't stop her," Patrick shouted, fists curled at his side. "She has the ability! Leave us alone!"

"To do what?" Antonio laughed. "Continue bumbling? *I* haven't been able to find out what happened to my sister. What makes you think any of you can? You—" He sneered at Patrick and flipped his hand at him in a dismissing gesture. "You deserted her after you had your way with her. I told her this would happen."

Patrick gasped with disbelief. "I died on my way back to Consuela, and you had a hand in it! If not for you, we would have been married. Lived our lives together."

Antonio advanced on him. "Why didn't you stop? Fight like a man, instead of hiding in your big fancy car? I didn't find you again until after we were both dead."

"You bastard," Patrick said in a deceptively soft voice. "We'll have this out right here and now. It's long overdue."

"No." Twila surged to her feet.

Patrick never took his eyes off Antonio as he said, "You and Patty need to get out of here. Now."

"We're not going anywhere," Twila insisted.

Antonio shrugged, but then he detoured from his path toward Patrick and approached Patty, who still sat on the sofa. He bowed before her, then curved his hand and lifted it upwards. Patty stared at her right hand as it rose from her lap. Then back and forth from her hand to Antonio's face as he gently bent his head and kissed the back of her hand when it reached his lips. She shivered, but didn't pull back.

"You are my blood," Antonio said. "It is for your own good that I ask you to leave."

Patty wobbled her head up and down, then rose to her feet. As though mesmerized, she wandered toward the kitchen. Then Antonio glared at Twila.

"You just made your point," Twila said. "Yours and Patrick's lineage is entwined now. You should work together."

"I will never work *with* him," Patrick spat. "He ruined my life. And Consuela's!"

Antonio whirled on Patrick again. "You are not fit to speak my sister's name!"

Then he lunged. Ready for him, Patrick landed the first blow. Although the dark ghost was larger—had been larger in life—Patrick coldcocked Antonio with a right cross and the dark ghost rocked back on his heels. He didn't fall, though, and the pain in his hand distracted Patrick. He hadn't experienced pain since the moment he died.

He felt it again when Antonio landed a fist in his stomach. With a whoosh, which would have been breath had he had breath, Patrick doubled over. Then flew back when Antonio followed up with a right cross to his jaw.

Patrick landed against the wall and a picture fell...straight through his head. No pain there, he mused as he warily straightened and prepared himself again. Evidently, two entities such as he and Antonio could inflict pain on each other, but physical objects could not. He flexed his fingers, and when Antonio's gaze dropped toward the motion, Patrick attacked.

He battered his head into Antonio's stomach, and a satisfying gasp issued from the other ghost. But far from disabled, Antonio wrapped his arms around Patrick as the two of them fell. In a distant corner of his mind not occupied with the fight, Patrick heard Twila utter a faint scream. As he and Antonio tumbled across the floor, he managed to catch a glimpse of her headed after Patty into the kitchen.

They landed in front of the television set, Patrick on top. He pummeled Antonio's face...only twice. Antonio reached through Patrick's defense and grabbed his jacket lapels, then heaved him away with a grunt of satisfaction. Both ghosts scrambled to their feet, crouched and ready, gazes locked as they circled, effortlessly gliding through the coffee table, the sofa, anything else in their paths. Antonio moved first, but not in any way Patrick expected. He shuffled his hand in a cupping manner, and a heavy book on the coffee table flew at Patrick. Who dodged instinctively. The book hit the top of the television, and sudden sound blasted into the room.

Patrick never took his eyes off Antonio, but he said, "What is that noise?"

"MTV," Antonio answered. "The book landed on that thing they call a remote and turned on the stupid thing."

"My granddaughter listens to MTV?" Patrick muttered. "That scandalous station?"

"So you have seen what a thing that is, too." Antonio and Patrick continued to circle as they spoke. When Antonio's back passed the television, Patrick glimpsed a half-naked man and a woman who was probably completely naked, if they could have seen her behind the man's body wrapped around her. One of those videos the singers today did in conjunction with their songs. He couldn't understand the words, though. The music blared against his senses with only a beat of rhythm recognizable amidst the gibberish.

"Turn that blasted thing off!" Antonio ordered.

"You turn it off," Patrick snarled back. "Your trick to distract me resulted in this racket!"

Antonio lunged. Patrick dodged, and as the dark ghost whizzed by him, brought his knee up into Antonio's nose. But when Patrick followed up with a fist on Antonio's neck, pain ripped through him. The other ghost had his teeth firmly planted in his knee!

"Owwww!" Patrick screamed as the two of them tumbled to the floor again. Some note in the music echoed the howl and intensified Patrick's pain. "Let go of me!" he yelled, but Antonio clamped down harder.

Patrick folded over the dark ghost's back, clenched his teeth against the pain and hammered the back of Antonio's head. Antonio surged upward and then he was on top of Patrick. His ass right in Patrick's face, he snarled and shook Patrick's leg back and forth like a dog tearing at a bone.

The music crescendoed louder, mixed with Patrick's screams and Antonio's growls of rage. Patrick did the only thing he could, the one thing a gentleman would never do. He drew his fist back and uppercut Antonio's balls.

Antonio let go. Antonio collapsed. Antonio curled into a fetal ball and held himself.

Patrick scrambled to his feet. Hand on his throbbing knee, he watched Antonio. The dark ghost never made a sound. He only lay there in silence, shaking in pain, jaws clenched. Not one hint of his agony escaped that mouth.

"Hell," Patrick muttered in embarrassment. "He's a better man than me. I screamed and hollered like a pantywaist."

A movement behind him startled him, and Patrick spun, fists up to confront the threat. Only Twila. She hurried across the room and grabbed the remote from the television. Blessed silence descended when she turned off that blasted show.

Patrick's legs flew out from under him. When he hit the floor, Antonio was on top of him, fist drawn back high over his head. All Patrick could do was thrust his hands up, but he knew he wouldn't be able to defend himself against the power of Antonio's renewed rage.

CHAPTER 34

We rushed in the front door of Patty's house and I skidded to a halt so fast that Carrie plowed into the back of me. For some reason, Antonio lay on the floor. He crashed his fist down, then threw back his head and howled. In pain? Could ghosts feel pain? I'd never asked one.

Maybe it was rage. Antonio rose slowly to his feet, his gaze traveling around the room with vicious intensity. Past him, Twila and Patty stood in the kitchen doorway, mouths open so wide a bird could have nested in each one, let alone any flies zooming about. I cautiously swung my arm backward until I encountered Carrie and, with her in tow, sidestepped toward the far side of the room, away from Antonio.

"Where did he go?" Antonio shouted. He shook his fist in the air. "Coward! Come back here and fight like a man!"

I glanced at Twila as she explained to Antonio, "Patrick dissolved. He was gone before you hit him."

I took another step, but she shook her head at me. Just then Jack ushered Granny into the living room. He set Miss Molly's cat carrier down, but when he bent to open the door, I frantically motioned him not to.

Antonio whirled and glared at us. "Where is he? Did you protect him? I will find him, and the next time, he will not escape my vengeance!"

Before Jack could stop her, Granny tottered right past him, toward Antonio. She thumped her walking stick along with her, and the ghost froze in place. Granny went straight up to him, her head bent back on her neck to stare at his face. Heart caught in my throat in fear, I whispered to Jack, "Do something! He'll hurt her!"

"Who?" Jack replied. "What on earth's she up to?"

I cast Twila a pleading glance, but she shook her head again. How could she not step in? Couldn't she see what I could? The huge, towering dark ghost hovering over Granny's tiny, fragile figure? Despite Twila's silent warning, I couldn't let this happen.

Before I could move, Granny said, "My, my, my. I's been hopin' to run into you again, young feller. By cracky, I don't understand what Alice and Twila see in Patrick when there's a tall, dark, handsome man like you around."

I'd never seen a ghost blush before. Didn't even realize it was possible for them. Antonio's flush overrode his swarthy complexion, though, as Granny toddled completely around him. As she passed his butt, she reached out and patted it, although her hand passed partially through it.

"Mighty fine," she said. "Quite the cat's meow." Then she giggled and pinched his butt.

Antonio flinched, but I suspected it was in reaction, since he couldn't possibly feel the pinch. When Granny stood in front of him again, he said, "I am very charmed that such a flower as you finds me pleasing."

"Adorable," Granny said. "I find you jist adorable. Bet we could've cut a fine rug iffen we'd met a few years ago."

Antonio smiled and held his arm out. "May I assist you to a seat? I would not wish for you to tire yourself."

Granny giggled and wrapped her gnarled fingers around his arm. She only shivered slightly at the touch, and her fingers were visible halfway through the jacket-clad arm. But she ambled over to the sofa and sat

219

with a smooth agility I'd never have thought possible of her. Then she gazed up at Antonio.

"Wish I had me one of them there dance cards. I'd let you write your name on every line."

"*Senora*," Antonio said with a bow. "We would scandalize everyone if I monopolized your every dance. But it would be worth the outrage we would suffer from those who were never fortunate to experience such a love as ours."

Granny sighed and leaned back. Then she craftily said, "Yep. Once in a blue moon, there is such a thing as a love like that."

Antonio flushed again, this time I do believe in embarrassment. "I take your chastisement to heart," he said. Then he dissolved without even a wisp of mist left behind.

Twila clapped loudly. "Good going, Granny!"

Granny grinned in toothless delight in Twila and Patty's direction, the network on her face a road map of intertwined wrinkles. "You gals gotta relearn your flirtin' skills. Man's easy to handle, you put you mind to it." She sagely slipped a glance over her shoulder at me, then Jack.

"Who was she...talking to?" Jack whispered behind me. "All I saw was Granny yammering away like she was sixteen and at some *fais do do*. Thought for a minute she'd gone straight into Alzheimer's."

I didn't bother to explain. Instead, I hurried over to Twila. "What happened here while we were gone?"

She sniffed, then nodded her head approvingly. "I know one thing that happened to you. You got a tomato juice bath. What's Carrie doing with you?"

"She was bound and determined to come with us when we left the hospital. Jack and I found her room and went to talk to her about Mary Ann's murder. Granny was there, too. She said Penny dropped her off. Anyway, Carrie perked right up, and by the time I got out of the shower and back into the clothes the nurse on duty washed for me, Carrie was dressed. And here she is."

"Well," Twila said, "what happened here was something I'd never experienced before. Patrick and Antonio got into a brawl. You should have seen it, Alice. Those two ghosts were actually pounding each other and grunting and yelling in pain."

I stared around the small living room. Not a thing was out of place. "But—"

She read my mind, or my face, because she interrupted, "Their bodies didn't disturb anything except each other. It was quite a show." She shook her head as though in amazement. "But before that, Patrick finished the story about him and Consuela. As we suspected, they made love the last night they were together."

"The baby was a girl," Patty said.

"So the reason he's still hanging around on this side of the veil is to find out what happened to his daughter?"

"No," Patty explained. "Patrick didn't know about the baby until I told him tonight."

Twila nodded. "Then I'm afraid the doppelganger we saw at the hotel has something to do with Patrick being tied here."

Jack snorted and drew our attention, but he had sense enough to keep his mouth shut. He didn't believe in doppelgangers, either. While Twila and I talked, Carrie had joined Granny on the couch, and their gazes were trained on us. Where had Patty gone? Oh, there she was in the kitchen. At the table. Patrick sat across from her, a wounded look on his face.

I raised my voice. "So who won the brawl?"

Twila giggled. "I'd call it a draw."

"That's generous of you," Patrick grumbled. "Especially when I screamed like a girl while Antonio suffered like a man."

"Now, now." Patty reached across the table to touch his arm, but of course her hand slipped straight through it. "Let's just be glad it's over with. I don't care for men fighting."

"Depends," Granny put in. She must have had her hearing aid in, because she'd obviously been able to hear Patty in the kitchen. "They's fighting over me, I sorta take it kindly."

"Why don't all of you come into the kitchen?" Patty invited. "I've got fresh coffee and some cookies on the table."

First I let Miss Molly out of the cat carrier Granny had borrowed from Penny. She stalked out in a snit, tail high, and I knew better than to reach for her. She hated a carrier even more than a leash, and made no bones about showing her displeasure after that offensive captivity. Not that she'd claw me, but she'd been known to hiss and spit to get her point across, and a person who didn't know her could take it as cat bitchiness. Which indeed it was. I'd even drawn back in reaction a time or two.

She flounced past me, straight into the kitchen. As I joined the others in there, she went over to Trucker and meowed piteously. The dog woke up and touched noses with her, then lapped his large tongue across her face.

"I've got some cat food pouches that I feed a couple neighborhood cats with," Patty said. "Do you think she's hungry?"

"That would be great," I replied.

We bumped into each other in the small kitchen as we moved around. Jack and Granny sat at the table with Patrick, Twila poured coffee for everyone—except Patrick, of course—and Patty helped me find her supply of cat food in the cupboards. I chose a pouch I thought a cat might find yummy in an effort to appease Miss Molly. The label proclaimed that it contained fish, crab, and even lobster. I tore it open and squeezed it onto the dish Patty gave me, then set it on the floor beside a dish of water at the back door.

Miss Molly perked up right away. Not that she forgave me, but she did chow into the dish of food that wasn't nearly as appetizing-looking to a human.

"Where'd Grandberg get to?" Jack asked as I settled in the remaining chair at the table and reached for my coffee cup.

"He called Sam to come pick him up," Twila explained. "And before you ask, Alice, no, I didn't get a chance to talk to Sam. I didn't even know he was coming until Grandberg took his leave and went out the door."

"Then what next?" I stupidly asked.

"Why, back to the hotel, of course," she said.

My coffee suddenly fascinated me. I stared at it and examined the beautiful butterscotch hue. Twila had prepared mine the way I like it, milk in the cup first, then add the coffee. No sugar. Just the right mixture, too. About a third milk, the rest coffee. If I had a nickel for every time someone told me there couldn't possibly be any difference in how coffee tasted no matter whether you put the milk in first or after, my bank account would be padded well over and beyond what I stashed in it from royalty checks.

I wonder if I'd have to pay taxes on money I collected on bets like that? I mused.

"Alice!" Twila said insistently. "You need to prepare."

"For what?" Jack asked. "You two are going back to Six Gun."

I sat there torn. Let the two of them work it out. If Jack won, I wouldn't have to expose my cowardice in front of Twila. We could go home and content ourselves with reading about how Jack and Grandberg puzzled out this convoluted mess. No skin off my teeth.

If Twila won...

"Just how are you going to get us back to Six Gun?" Twila asked as some tiny flicker that I tried my darndest to tamp down flared inside me. "Alice's Jeep is at Penny's. And you can't carry both of us on the bike."

That tiny flicker grew into a quite evident flame. Not real large yet, still just the size of a wooden match flame. I mentally tried to blow it out, and succeeded. But like those darn trick cake candles, it winked right back into existence as Jack said...

"We'll borrow Patty's car again."

"I don't think so, will he, Patty?" Twila asked our hostess.

"Not if you don't want him to," Patty said with a stern nod. By then I was slipping looks from beneath my lashes, although I tried so very hard to appear still fascinated with my coffee.

"How are you feeling, Carrie?" Granny asked. I chewed on my inner consciousness, trying to decide just what the heck that flame meant while Carrie said...

"Fit as a fiddle. It was just such a shock seeing Mary Ann down at the bottom of the elevator. Dead, poor soul. After she'd been so brave."

Anger? No, not really. It was...was...

"Then you knew Mary Ann?" Twila asked.

"Oh, yes," Carrie said without a sign of her stutter. "She was such a fine actress. Why, if she had stayed around after the trial, I feel sure she would have succeeded in getting the hotel reopened. She had the ties to do it, and quite a bit of funding already set up."

Resentment? I almost had it. Then my surreptitious glance bypassed Jack for Granny, who sat there raptly munching on one of the molasses cookies from the plate on the table. "Little too much salt," Granny the wonderful cook murmured.

Salt? I swung my gaze back to Jack as he crossed his arms, leaned back in his chair, and said...

"Y'all can just button it up. This is Grandberg's investigation, and the county sheriff's coming in tomorrow to help him out. I've got a couple more days leave comin', so I'll hang around. You girls can get on about your own business."

No, piss and vinegar! The flame morphed into a stinging eruption of stubborn resentment at Jack's high-handed, male dominant attitude.

But I spoke very quietly. "Us *girls* are taking Patty's car and going back to the hotel. We're not about to leave a troubled soul in the hands of a nonbeliever who wants us to shuffle home to women's work and a police chief who finds his comfort at the bottom of a whiskey bottle. We have a responsibility here, and we intend to honor it."

"Way to go, Alice," Twila whispered, and her pride in me stifled the last vestiges of spinelessness I'd experienced since we left skid marks on that seventh-floor hallway. Oh, all right, not all of it, but the scale definitely tipped toward the side of bravery and intrepid heroism. We shall fight the good fight, and all that.

Jack dangled Patty's car keys from his finger, but before our Mexican standoff staring contest even had a chance to erupt into further verbal warfare, Granny grabbed the keys. She stuffed them down the front of her dress and said to Jack, "Wanna go fish for 'em? Ain't had no wandering man-hands on that part of me for so long I forget what it feels like."

"Granny..." Jack crooked his finger at her. "Come on, Granny. Give them back."

"I agree with Jack," Patrick said, and flinched when five pairs of outraged feminine eyes turned on him. "Well, I do. Not necessarily that you need to run off back to Alice's cabin. But we came here with the intention of helping me on my quest for peace and resolution. You and Twila have a responsibility to fulfill that promise, also, Alice. But I can wait a while longer."

Five women stood as one, leaving Jack and Patrick sitting there with a table full of half-empty coffee cups and cookie crumbs. Twila grabbed her backpack from the countertop and we gathered together at the doorway into the living room.

"For one thing," Twila turned and said, "you don't order us around any more than Jack does. For another, the resolution to your predicament is at the hotel. And until you come to terms with whatever it is you're hiding from—hiding from us, maybe—you're doomed to wander." She motioned us on through the door and called, "Here, Trucker, Miss Molly. Let's go for a ride."

Magic words. The two animals beat the rest of us to the front door. I didn't bother with the cat carrier. Miss Molly might decide hiss-spit bitchiness wouldn't do the trick and bring out the last resort weapon—claws—if I tried to stuff her in there right now. Twila opened the door and ushered Granny, Patty, Carrie, Trucker, and Miss Molly out. I let the cat go. She'd stay with her buddy, Trucker.

"You can't leave us stranded here without a vehicle," Jack called, although he had sense enough not to enforce his demand with his presence in the living room and remained at the kitchen door.

"Call a cab," Twila said as she followed me out the door and slammed it behind her.

"I doubt this town even has a cab service," I said to Twila as we went down the front sidewalk toward Patty's compact sedan.

She snickered. "And we care?"

CHAPTER 35

Granny was behind the wheel of Patty's car, the engine already running. Trucker sat beside her, erect, facing the windshield, and I realized I'd forgotten his leash. But I didn't want to go back and face Jack. I'd figure out something, if necessary. Patty and Carrie were already settled in the backseat, the door still open for one more passenger. When we got close enough to the car, I saw Miss Molly. She stood on her back feet, front paws propped on Trucker's shoulder, head turned so she could see where we were going, also.

"We're gonna let Granny drive?" I whispered to Twila.

"Looks like it," she said with a shrug. "We won't be on any freeway, just town streets. She should be all right. She's not night blind. Only her hearing's going."

Agreeably, I scooted in the front seat and pulled Miss Molly onto my lap while Twila joined Carrie and Patty. The cat resumed her watch-cat pose, rear paws on my left leg, front paws on the dashboard. I fastened my seat belt, and without a word, Granny took off down the street. Took off might be too strong a term. She sedately drove down to the corner and stopped at the stop sign, flicked on her turn signal, even though there wasn't a sign of another vehicle anywhere, then turned right.

"No, Granny," I said. I'd been too busy helping her watch out for nonexistent traffic to notice which turn she signaled. "We need to go left here, back toward town."

"Oh," she said. "Okey-dokey. Just let me find a spot to turn around."

We passed two suitable driveways on my side of the road before it dawned on me that Granny couldn't see past Trucker, so she was searching for a turnaround on the left. I wrapped an arm around Trucker and finagled his butt down onto the floorboard in front of me. No way would he fit on the seat if I tried to make him lie down. He sighed at the human override of his desire to keep watch, then propped his muzzle on the dashboard beside Miss Molly. His new stance shoved my legs tightly against the door, but I let him be.

"There's a good wide spot right there." To get Granny's attention, I pointed across Trucker and at the windshield beside the steering wheel. An intersecting road came in there, and we could make the turnaround with no problem.

So I thought.

The white Jeep barreled out of that road with no headlights to warn us it was even flying down it. It ignored the stop sign and zoomed past us at way too high a speed for safety on a narrow country road. Granny jammed on the brakes in reaction, even though the Jeep cleared the intersection with room to spare, given our slow pace.

She and I stared at each other. "That looked like your Jeep, Alice," she said.

"It was!" I agreed. "It's supposed to be back at Penny's!"

"Damn car thief!" Granny shouted.

That was our only warning. She floored pedal to metal and screeched around the corner after the Jeep with a skill worthy of an Indie 500 driver. A chorus of gasps filled the car, but not one of us spoke up. I grabbed the edge of my seat with a crushing grip so tight my fingers ached. Trees whizzed past us—mostly darkness, although I assumed the trees were there. I wrenched my gaze from the road and zeroed in on the speedometer.

Forty. Ever since I'd known her, Granny always said thirty-five was her top speed. Fifty. It crept toward sixty. Trucker kept his eyes on the road, although I doubted it was to help Granny drive. Trucker loves speed. Miss Molly gave it up, though, when we hit sixty. She tends to get carsick if she looks out a window. She scrambled over my shoulder to Twila.

"For Pete's sake, help her drive," Twila whispered desperately beside my ear.

I gulped and jerked my gaze back to the road. Still, a corner of my eye irrefutably kept watch on that tiny figure with her hands clenched at ten and two on the steering wheel.

"Where'd he go?" Granny snarled. "See him yet, Alice?"

"I—" I cleared my throat and gulped in a breath. "Maybe. Isn't that him?"

It was. Through the darkness up ahead I could barely make out the Jeep, and only because it was such a bright white. It continued to race down the road headlight-less. Granny sped up even more and barreled after it.

The Jeep disappeared and I screamed, "Turn ahead!" in warning.

Granny let up on the gas a hair, then twisted the wheel in time to round the slight left curve. The rear tires squealed a hint in protest, but she kept control and mashed the gas feed when the road stretched out ahead of us. On our right now was a large, open field, so at least we had the benefit of starlight and the moon to help our eyes strain for another sight of the Jeep.

"There." Twila pointed across my shoulder. "He's turning left up there."

"I gots him eyeballed," Granny said as she bent her head forward on her skinny neck and continued to concentrate.

"Granny," I offered. "The Jeep's insured. We can let the cops worry about it."

"Yeah," she sneered. "Them cops'll jist wait 'til that thief abandons your car and someone calls 'em to come haul it off. Or strips your car at some chop shop. We ain't gonna let that thief get away with this!"

She wrenched the steering wheel left at the next intersection, and this time the rear of the car skidded and the tires squalled. I didn't dare take my eyes off the road to see how Carrie and Patty were doing...not that there was a blessed thing I could do if Granny did lose control.

"Don't interrupt her concentration," Twila pleaded in another frantic whisper.

So I prayed to the Universe and any underling god or goddess that might be looking down on us as Granny barreled around another curve.

"Ohmigod!" I screamed. "Stop, Granny!"

The Jeep sat in the road in front of us. I instinctively stuck out what a friend of mine calls the Mommy-arm across Granny's slight chest. Tires squalled and the smell of burning rubber infiltrated the sedan. Granny jolted us to a halt a good distance back, a safe distance. She bounced against my arm restraint, then back against the seat, hands still clenched on the steering wheel. Trucker's nose hit the windshield, but he only woofed and snorted, then replaced his muzzle on the dashboard. I held my breath for a second, expecting the airbag to burst free, but it didn't.

"What's he doin'?" Granny muttered.

"The engine's still running," Twila said. "You can see the exhaust smoke."

"That's probably smoke drifting off our tires as well as exhaust," I said. "But I think he's realized that we're following him. Good lord, what if he's got a gun? Statistics say that a high percentage of Texas drivers carry guns."

"Reach under your seat, Granny," Patty said calmly. I guess at least she was taking this all in good stride.

Granny pushed my arm away—I was still protecting her from possible injury—and dug under the seat. She came up with a huge revolver that dwarfed her tiny hand. She propped it on the steering wheel and clutched it with both hands, then growled, "Go ahead, car thief. Make my day." Then she snickered and said, "Always wanted to know what old Eastwood felt like when he said that."

"Give me the gun, Granny," I ordered.

"Git your own," she shot back.

The Jeep still sat there, engine idling. Finally I realized that even this far back from it, the sedan's headlights shone bright enough for us to see through the back window, into the interior. My Jeep has tinted windows, but I'd opted for the lighter tint, just dark enough to protect the upholstery from Texas summer sun. It appeared as though there was only one person inside, the driver. An extremely large driver, if those shoulders meant anything. In fact, the top of his head nearly touched the car roof.

Please don't let that be Delroy, I beseeched every power there was, whether I believed in it or not.

Suddenly a pair of bare feet bound together with some sort of yellow, nylon rope hit the rear window of my Jeep. The feet slammed against the window once, twice...then the Jeep roared off again.

"He's got someone kidnapped in there!" Granny tossed the gun into my lap and roared off after it. "We gots to save 'em!"

"No," I insisted as I juggled the gun and tried to figure out what to do with it. "Turn in at the next house you find so we can call the police! We need backup!"

Granny glared through the windshield, her wrinkled face backlit by the dashboard lights. "I votes we keep on goin'. Might be another dead body on our hands, we wait for the cops. Any other voters?"

"Go," Patty said. "Don't worry about my car."

"Whatever," a voice I recognized as Carrie's agreed.

Not that Granny needed mine and Twila's agreement—hell, we weren't about to try to wrestle control of the car from her at this speed—but she said, "Three to two, even iffen you two think different. Hey! He's takin' off 'crost that there field up ahead! Lookie there! He plowed right through that bob wire fence!"

"Get him, Granny!" Patty yelled.

"Wheeeee," Granny crowed.

She swerved across the ditch beside the road, straight through the hole my Jeep had opened. The sedan bottomed out on the edge of the asphalt and evidently destroyed the muffler. The roar of the engine filled the air. A strand of barbed wire raked down the side of the sedan, and then we jostled across the ruts in pursuit of the Jeep. The farmer had already sown his corn crop, but the plants were only about a foot high.

We had a clear view of the Jeep disappearing into a forest of trees on the other side of the field.

The Jeep's suspension was a lot better suited to make headway and speed across this terrain, but Granny didn't let that daunt her. Bounce, bounce, bounce. The seat belt thankfully held her, but her lips formed another, "Wheeee," as her skinny rump jounced up and down.

I forced one hand free of its grip on the seat and grabbed my neck. Trucker cracked his tender nose against the windshield once too often, then surged onto the seat. He planted his rear end against my shoulder, his front feet braced on the seat and fixed his gaze back on the windshield.

"Reason with her," I begged Twila.

"What?" She bent closer to me. I could feel her breath against my ear as she repeated, "What? I can't hear you over the engine noise!"

I shoved the revolver at her and turned to shout, "Put this thing somewhere it won't go off by accident!"

She moved back, and I could only hope she did what I asked. I wasn't about to look. Those trees were growing at an alarming rate in front of us.

Then we were into the trees. Thank the Universe there was a road there. A trail, really, but Granny expertly guided the sedan down the path. The un-muffled engine roared, so that noise covered up any gaffes Granny made that resulted in tree limbs crunching against the side of the sedan. Then the headlights shone on a huge pool of water in front of us.

"Stop!" Twila screamed in my ear.

Granny did...halfway across the pool of shimmering water. Then she gunned the engine again. The tires spun uselessly, only digging us deeper.

Granny let off the gas and turned to Twila. "Lookie what you did. We'd've made it on through, you hadn't bothered me. Doncha know you ain't supposed to stop in the middle like this? Gotta keep moving, so's you don't get stuck! Which we is."

"I'm sorry, Granny," Twila apologized. "I wasn't thinking."

Granny heaved a sigh and stared back out the windshield. "Now what's we gonna do? He'll prob'ly murder that poor person and it's all our fault."

"It's *not* our fault," I chastised her. "We didn't kidnap whoever that is."

"Looked like a woman's feets," she said in a more reasonable voice. "Had pink toenails."

I hadn't noticed that at the time, but now I replayed the brief glimpse I'd seen of the bound-feet victim in my mind and nodded an agreement. "I think you're right," I told her. "And there was something familiar about that nail polish color, but darned if I can figure it out right now."

"Well, that sure looked like Delroy driving," Twila said.

"Delroy?" Carrie leaned forward. "You've run across Delroy?"

"We ran across him earlier tonight," Twila explained. "He tried to kidnap us, but Mary Ann's ghost ran him off."

"Poor Mary Ann," Carrie said, and I recalled that she'd said something similar a few minutes ago.

But before I could question her, Patty said, "If that's Delroy, I might know where he's holed up."

"Where?" Granny asked as she swiveled. "We's got to help that poor woman. Gotta be a woman, them pink toes and all." Then she frowned and repeated, "Sort've purple-pink toes, come to think of it. Where...?"

"First we've got to get out of the car," Patty pointed out. "How far across this puddle is it?"

"Puddle?" I said. "Looks more like a darned creek across the road."

"Nah," Granny said. "Jist a Texas puddle."

She flicked the lever to turn the lights onto high beam. Good grief, I'd thought she already had them on high. We'd been in low-beam light pursuit! And I saw what she meant. Ahead of us—just about the same distance as behind us, I confirmed with a glance—was the edge of the water.

I opened my door and glanced down. Deep water, though. It was high enough to lap at the floorboard. Wouldn't have been a problem with my Jeep, which had larger tires and set higher off the road. Wasn't a problem for Delroy, if it was him who stole my Jeep. But the sedan...

"Ohmigod," I breathed.

"What?" four voices asked me.

"I left my Jeep at Penny's."

"We knows that, Alice," Granny said. "What's that got to do with— oh my stars," she semi-echoed me in the same worried tone of voice.

CHAPTER 36

"Thought I recognized that toenail color." Granny stared at me in horror. "She said she has it mixed special, to match that lipstick she uses on TV. We gots to save her!"

She floorboarded the gas feed again as Twila demanded, "Who?"

I couldn't answer Twila for a moment. Granny shifted into reverse, gunned the engine, then jammed the gearshift into drive. Again...again. My head rocked back and forth on my neck, and muddy water sprayed up around the sedan as Granny valiantly tried to dig us out. No luck. The tires only slithered deeper in the muck. But the mud eventually silenced the roar, probably because it globbed up the un-mufflered exhaust system. Blessed quiet descended as the engine died completely, but now we were completely without hope of escape from the Texas *puddle*.

Granny flashed me another wrinkled look of fear. "We's got to rescue her. Don't nobody else know he's got her."

"Who?" Twila demanded again.

"Penny," I told her. "Delroy's got Penny tied up in the back of the Jeep. He must have gone to her house and kidnapped her. Drove out of there in my Jeep."

"With all that security?" Twila asked.

"Delroy wouldn't let a little thing like an alarm system keep him from somewhere he wanted to go," Patty said. "He's a horrible man."

"What do you know about men?" Carrie asked, a sneer in her voice. "Just because his daddy wasn't any good didn't mean Delroy couldn't have made something of himself if he wanted to."

"Apple don't fall far from the tree," Patty said. "He had a choice at some point."

"Now you listen here!" Carrie snapped. "Wasn't for that granddaughter of yours, Delroy wouldn't have broken up with my niece. They could have stayed in love. You aren't too damned old to remember what that felt like, are you?"

Patty sniffed. "I was never that *young*. I had sense enough to know men don't buy the cow if they can get the milk free. My granddaughter knew that, too. Leastways, long enough for Delroy to show his true colors."

"You just let your milk bag dry up with the rest of you after that Vietnam war killed your husband," Carrie fumed.

"Why you old biddy," Patty said. "At least I never had to depend on a man for the meals on my table! I finished my schooling with the VA's help, and I never went hungry."

"Never got any meat on your bones, neither," Carrie sneered back. "Probably a good thing you never attracted another man. He'd have had to shake the sheets to find you!"

"Shut up!" Twila shouted. Thank goodness. I was afraid we were going to have a cat fight in that backseat, and not with Miss Molly involved.

"You two work out your differences somewhere else," Twila ordered. "Right now, we've got to find Penny. I don't suppose either one of you brought a cell phone with you?"

The two adversaries both shook their heads negatively.

"Then, you—" She pointed at Patty. "Open the door and start wading. You—" She trained her finger on Carrie. "Get out there after her. And when we get to dry land, figure out where we are and how close we are to a phone. Then we'll call the police in and you can lead them to where you think Delroy might be."

"She started it," Carrie said with a whimper, but Twila shoved Miss Molly into the back window and pitched forward across her and Patty's laps to wrench the door handle. She pushed the door open, then sat back.

"Two choices. You can either both get out of this car on your own and wade through that water, or I'll help you out and you can see if you stay on your feet long enough to keep your clothes dry."

Patty went. She splashed into the water, Carrie right behind her. The two of them waded towards the front of the car, then on through the water to dry land. There they stopped and stood in the headlight glare, waiting for us.

"Here," Twila said. She retrieved Miss Molly and handed her to me, then turned back and picked up Granny's walking stick, which she'd evidently stored in the rear window in deference to the crowded car, and gave it to me. "You can carry Miss Molly. Trucker can make it on his own."

"I's gonna need that stick." Granny opened her door, but Twila laid a hand on her shoulder.

"No, Granny. I'll carry you."

"I's can make it," Granny insisted. "What? You think after that there race I just run, I ain't got enough spunk left to get through a little water and mud? Mud that you got us stuck in?"

"That's what I mean," Twila soothed as I opened my door. "It's my fault you got stuck. Why, if I hadn't yelled out, you'd have made it through the mud just fine. So I'll carry you, okay?"

"Guess since you put it that way..." Granny gave in, although I'd been willing to bet she hadn't been too proud to accept Twila's offer right from the beginning.

I stepped out into the water and sank down well over my tennis shoes in gluey mud, then reached back in for Miss Molly and gripped her tightly. Not that the cat would have tried to escape my hold. Not with water beneath her. The only one I'd ever seen able to give my cat an infrequent but necessary bath was Twila. She has quite a way with cats.

When Twila waded around and leaned in to pick up Granny, then straightened with the tiny woman in her arms, I noticed that Twila had her backpack on.

"Hey," I called. "I could have taken the backpack."

"I got it," she said. Still, I could tell that even though Granny wasn't that heavy, it was a strain on Twila to juggle both Granny and the backpack. Especially when she started off through that glue-like mud.

I called Trucker after me, and he bounded out gleefully. Unlike his cat buddy, he loves to get wet and muddy. He plopped straight into the water and sprayed it all over me. Then he leapt through the water, snapping happily at the spray he raised.

"Meow," Miss Molly complained when a gush of water hit her. She tried to curl up in my arms and wash a spot of mud off her rump, but I lifted her against my shoulder and plunged after Trucker. I suppose I could have used Granny's walking stick, but I didn't want to take a chance the muddy water would ruin the beautiful, varnished finish.

"We should have at least turned the lights off," Patty said in a snitty voice.

"You just wade right on back out there and do it," Carrie snapped.

"That's enough!" Twila put Granny down between the two women. "We need to find Penny before something happens to her! Your battery going dead is not our problem right now."

"Well, if that there Delroy's looking for us," Granny pointed out, "them lights shining there will give him a good idear where we's at."

Twila sighed and started back to the car.

"No, Twila. Here." I handed her Miss Molly. "I'll do it. You rest."

I waded back into the water and made it to the car. Turned off the lights and even shut all the doors before I started back...and noticed a shaft of moonlight flickering on the water. A little dark point illuminated in the moonlight...

"Snake!" I screamed. I lost both of my tennis shoes in the glue-like muck and didn't give one darn. Two seconds later, I stood on dry land in my sock feet and pointed at the water. "There's a snake! We're lucky we didn't get bitten!"

"Rover said the snakes were out," Twila agreed. She juggled Miss Molly into her other arm and pulled her flashlight out of the backpack, then shone it along my finger. The dark point was still there. Still in the same place. Oh, shit. It was just a stick.

"Just a stick," Twila confirmed. When I huffed in embarrassment, she patted my shoulder and said, "I probably would have mistaken it for a snake, too, Alice. I don't like snakes any more than you do."

"Well, the snakes *are* out," Patty confirmed. "And at night they like to lay on trails where the ground's soaked up sun during the day."

Twila just shook her head and pointed the flashlight beam on down the trail. We could see tire tracks from the Jeep, and I caught myself straining to hear the engine, wanting to confirm that Delroy wasn't waiting ahead to ambush us. But only crickets and frogs broke the silence. No scary chitter of a rattlesnake's tail.

"Rattlesnakes live out in the dry rocks, don't they, Patty?" I asked.

"There are woods rattlers," she replied. "But any snake will be long gone. It'll feel our approach through its belly long before we get to it. Or smell us with its tongue."

Twila shone the light on my feet. "Where are your shoes?" I just pointed again at the water. "Well, you can't walk down this trail without shoes. There's sharp rocks in the sand."

It took us another five minutes of wading around in the muck to retrieve my tennis shoes. I didn't really want to put them back on, but I had no choice. Then we marched off. Well, the rest of our group marched. I squished.

"So, Patty," Twila asked. "How close are we to a phone?"

"Not as close as we are to where I think Delroy is," she said, much to our dismay, were the echoing gasps of alarm any indication.

"How far?" Twila demanded.

"A phone or the camp?" Patty asked.

"Either," Twila replied impatiently.

Patty paused and looked around us, and we halted with her. Just ahead the woods opened up again on the right. Another field, it looked like. On our left, the dark woods continued, full of trees, briars, under-brush...skunks, snakes...

"What did you do with the pistol?" I asked Twila.

"In my backpack."

Patty said, "This is an old logging road we're on. Mostly deer hunters use it now. That field up ahead, on the right, belongs to the Yoders. Mennonites. Old Order. I think the only phone around is one shared by a group of them, and I'm not sure which house it's located in. They might be able to pull my car out. They've got those big draft horses they use in the fields. It's a good half mile to their house, though."

"What about the camp?" I asked.

She pointed ahead of us. "There's another intersection up ahead. To the left, about another quarter mile, is an old deer hunter's camp. I know because my daddy used to hunt back there. It's supposedly abandoned now. But I've heard rumors that people have seen lights there now and then."

"Grandberg said something about there being survivalist groups in this area," I recalled aloud.

"Uh huh," Patty said. "The big trial five years ago was supposed to break them up. But most of us around here believe it just drove them deeper into hiding."

"What are we facing with Delroy?" Twila asked.

"He's just a week or so out of prison," Patty replied. "On probation, supposedly, but you already know Delroy doesn't give a flip about the terms of his probation. He's not supposed to associate with known crim-inals or be anywhere around any sort of weapon. Ha! Delroy without a weapon is a man without his penis!"

"And he was in prison for...?" Twila asked.

"Manslaughter," Patty and Carrie both said at once.

Patty continued, "That's what led to the downfall of the survivalists. Delroy was one of them, and he was charged with murder, but you know how overloaded the courts are. He plea bargained. Got five years, out as soon as they needed his prison bed for someone else."

"Who'd he kill?" Granny asked.

"A young woman," Patty said. "Since he never went to trial, all we know is what the papers dug up. That she was his girlfriend...or thought she was. She was pregnant, four or five months along."

"She never proved it was his baby," Carrie said.

"Look, this isn't getting us anywhere," I said. "Which should we head for? That camp or a phone?"

"No brainer," Twila said. "And—" she interrupted when Carrie started to speak, "—no vote. Penny's depending on us."

"Well," I said in a let's-be-sensible tone. "We can split up. Part of us to find a phone. Part of us to go after Penny."

"Good idea," Twila praised me. "Granny, Carrie, and Patty, you go find a phone and contact help. Alice and I will go after Penny."

Well, that wasn't exactly what I'd envisioned, but I had more pride than to beg to go with the elderly. I was doubly glad I'd held my peace when Granny snorted in contempt. She didn't even have to vocalize that she wasn't about to be delegated to the minions of elderly and sent off to safety. She crooked her hand at Trucker.

"C'mon, boy. We's goin' skunk huntin'. Gonna find us one of them two-legged skunks."

Twila only grinned at my discomfort at the word skunk. She ordered Carrie and Patty over to the fence and held up the barbed wire so they could crawl through.

"Left at the intersection," Patty reminded us. "You'll run straight into the camp. Well, the gate first. When you come to it—it's one of those pipe gates—the camp will be a couple dozen yards ahead."

As they started across the field, we caught up to Granny and Trucker. Twila still carried Miss Molly, and guilt stabbed me at her burdens: the backpack and cat. So I took Miss Molly from her and lightened her load that much.

"Gimme my gun." Granny held out her arthritic hand to Twila.

"It's not yours," Twila said patiently. "It's Patty's."

"She give it to me," Granny insisted.

"Too bad," Twila said. "Possession's nine-tenths of the law."

"Huh," Granny said with an indignant snort. "Law ain't done us no good so far. Gotta practice vigilante law, like back in the olden days."

We walked for ten minutes, deeper and deeper into those dark woods. The trees towered around us, in places, branches from either side meeting overhead. Twila was right about the rocks in the path. I could feel some of the sharp points through my tennis shoes. Twila and I could have covered the distance quicker, but despite our fear for Penny, we kept our pace slow in deference to Granny and her walking stick. Finally we saw the gate. As we approached it, Twila centered her light beam on the ground and followed the tire track path. It curved, then went straight through the gate. Then she turned off her light. I knew she had to; we'd be spotted otherwise. Still, I stifled a gasp as the blackness enveloped us.

"Let's wait until our eyes adjust," Twila whispered.

Ha. Fat lot of good that did. Even when my eyes did adjust after a few seconds, I still could barely make out the gate only a couple feet in front of us. Night sounds even seemed muffled. A chitter of a night bird, a slight rustle in the underbrush. "Yip, yip, yowwwwl!" Luckily in the far distance.

"Damn coyotes," Twila murmured.

"They sound sorta purty, don't you think?" Granny said. "Used to be a bounty on 'em, though. Feller we knew nearly cleaned them out around Six Gun. Then he died, and I got to hear coyotes howl again at night."

I knew we were stalling, but I wasn't any more eager than my companions to go through that gate.

"It's locked," I said in relief. I bent down and pointed to the chain with a padlock on it.

Twila leaned down and examined the padlock. Then she twisted it and showed me that it wasn't locked. She slipped the padlock free of the chain, and it slithered from the gate with a jangle.

"Shhhhh!" I said. "He'll hear us!"

"The problem is," Twila said, ignoring my chastisement, "he took time to make the lock look locked, but not brush out his tire tracks.

Maybe he thinks we don't have sense enough to follow a trail. Or maybe..."

"He's waiting in there to ambush us," I finished for her.

Suddenly a scream rent the air. All three of us jumped...and grabbed for the nearest support. We ended up with our arms wrapped around each other, huddled together, Miss Molly squashed in my arms. She hissed her displeasure, and I reluctantly stepped back.

"Oh, lord, we have to go in there," I whispered. "What if that's Penny?"

Granny got a grip first. She pulled back and patted Trucker on the head and said, "Painter. Heard them, too, a'fore. They's a few of 'em left around."

"Painter?" Twila asked.

"A cat," I explained. "Similar to a mountain lion. Puma."

"They ain't mountain-lion colored 'round here," Granny said. "We got black painters in Texas. Seen me one or two over the years."

We stood there silently in the dark for another ten seconds or so. I stared down the driveway, deeper darkness, a barely visible path barely wide enough for a vehicle to traverse. "My Jeep is probably scratched to high heaven," I murmured with a sigh.

What did Delroy's kidnapping Penny mean? How long would he keep her? Would he...kill her? I couldn't begin to imagine what sort of connection there could be between my friend and a guerilla-type outlaw/ex-con. Could it have anything to do with her investigative reporter life? But she'd been confined to politics rather than crime as long as we'd been acquainted.

"We need to get going," Twila said.

We all three heaved a mutual sigh.

CHAPTER 37

W e edged the gate open far enough to squeeze through. Twila
knelt and shrugged off her backpack. She grabbed Trucker's
collar in one hand, then dug in the backpack to retrieve a braided cord
that I recognized as one she used in various ceremonies. I could only see
it because silver threads infiltrated the cord, so it was slightly visible in
the pitch blackness. She tied the cord through Trucker's collar, then
stood and replaced her backpack. But she bent back down and picked up
something on the ground—something she hid beside her leg as she
gripped Trucker's restraint in her other hand.

"Does Trucker know the command 'run silent'?" she asked softly.

I gripped my dog's muzzle and stared at where I assumed his brown
eyes were. "Hush, Trucker," I ordered in a stern whisper. I wasn't sure
he'd obey, but at least I tried.

Not daring to use a light, we ran silent, also, except for my darn
squishy shoes, but there wasn't a thing I could do about that. At least by
now it was a faint squish rather than a blatant squish. Granny actually
took my arm as we slowly eased our way down the trail, using her
walking stick in the other hand. Normally she would bat anyone with
her walking stick who insisted she couldn't navigate under her own

power, even in one of the infrequent ice storms that hit East Texas. But even I had trouble walking on the weed-choked and rutted trail. More than once my foot slid sideways when I stepped in a rut.

Overhead, tree limbs and leaves covered us in a blanket of black. Maybe another storm front had moved in, since it was so dark and moonless. Those blasted fronts came one after another this time of year in Texas. Some brought tornadoes, too, but that last forecast I'd heard hadn't mentioned that danger. Not that our weathermen were ever wrong. Only about all the time. I realized my mind was rambling away from the coming confrontation and steered it back on track.

The trail curved to the left, and as soon as we rounded that bend, we halted. Ahead of us, a cleared area stretched a couple hundred yards onward. Without the intrusion of tree branches, we could see a little better now. But when I looked upward, I confirmed my suspicion that clouds had moved back in and covered the stars and moon.

"What time is it?" I whispered.

"Near daylight," Granny whispered back.

To our left was a ramshackle structure that might have been a camp house. Long, low to the ground, one-story, it was fashioned from varie-gated pieces of tin and wood. A dim light showed through a piece of plastic over a side window. In front of the camp house was a long table with a raggedy tarp overhead. The night breeze had picked up, and one corner of the tarp slapped back and forth.

I swept my gaze around the entire clearing, searching for my Jeep. Then back to the camp house as it dawned on me that I'd seen a trickle of smoke coming from the round piece of tin sticking up from the roof.

"Someone's there," I whispered. "There's a fire going."

Delroy—I guessed it was him, since he wore that same camouflage attire and towered so high he'd ducked through the doorway—emerged from the camp house. We hurriedly eased into the shadows along the trail, Twila and me in front of Granny. Taking no chances, Twila pulled Trucker's head against her leg, hand at ready to grip his muzzle if he tried to bark.

Delroy strode across the clearing and disappeared down another trail that led deeper into the woods. A moment later, a noise I recognized as an ATV engine cut through the silence. He must have had his camp mode of transportation hidden down that trail. Lucky for our peace of mind, the engine noise indicated he'd headed away from us.

"He thinks he lost us," Twila said in astonishment. "That he's safe here."

"Probly figgered no dumb women'd be able to track him down," Granny sneered.

"What if there's someone else here besides Penny?" I asked.

"We'll have to chance it. We might not have much time." Twila sprinted out into the clearing with Trucker, leaving me to follow more slowly with Granny and the cat. By the time we made it through the camp house heavy wooden door, Twila was beside a trussed-up Penny, who lay on a bunk mattress so dirty it made my skin crawl with distaste just to look at it. Twila carefully slipped a large butcher knife blade under the ropes on Penny's wrists, then cut through the bindings around her ankles. On my left was a sink and some dirty dishes, where I assumed she'd grabbed the knife from.

Hands free, Penny jerked the duct tape off her mouth with a rip that made me cringe and said, "We've got to get out of here! He just went out to his hog trap to bring back some meat for breakfast!"

We heard the gunshot even inside the camp house.

"How far away is the hog trap?" I asked.

"How the heck do I know?" Penny surged from the bunk and headed for the door that Granny and I blocked. Her purple-pink toes glittered in the dim light. "Hurry. We've surely got time to get to your vehicle. He took the keys to Alice's Jeep."

Twila caught Penny by the back of the shirt. She was, I finally noticed, wearing a pair of jeans and a red silk blouse with several missing buttons. Penny swung on Twila and the last two blouse buttons popped off when Twila didn't release her.

"Let me go," Penny said. Then she stared down at the revolver in Twila's hand and gasped.

Twila let go of Penny's blouse and swung the pistol back down beside her leg. "We don't have a vehicle. We walked here."

Penny ran her fingers through her disheveled hair. "Then we'll have to walk. He'll kill us, Alice. He's killed before."

But any thought of a clean escape died when we heard the ATV returning.

"Shoot him, Twila," Granny spat. "A'fore he shoots us!"

Twila gulped. "I can't shoot him in cold blood," she said in a tiny voice.

Granny grabbed the pistol and turned toward the door. "I kin!"

I had sense enough to seize the pistol from Granny. It wasn't much of a struggle, since her hands couldn't grip it tightly, given her arthritis. She valiantly tried to take it back, but I shoved Miss Molly into her arms instead. For a moment, I prepared to duck the walking stick, but Granny only huffed and laid it against the door so she could hold the cat in both arms.

"Then you shoot him, Alice," she said.

By then the ATV was roaring back into camp. Ignoring Granny's order to ambush Delroy, I leaned across the dirty sink to the right of the door and lifted a corner of the plastic covering another window to peek out.

Yep, there he was. Delroy had stopped beside a contraption at the end of the awning-covered table. A wooden platform with large pipes on each side of it rising into the air, a tree on each side of the pipes. A crossbar with a winch and cable attached ran between the pipes, and a hook dangled on the end of the cable. Delroy turned a crank on a tree beside the contraption, and the crossbar descended.

"What's he doing?" Twila whispered. She crept up beside me and lifted the far corner of the plastic.

"I'm not sure," I said. Then I glanced at the ATV...and saw the black and white spotted hog lying behind the seat, its poor head dangling down. Delroy reached for a light switch screwed into one of the tree trunks and the spotlight overhead illuminated the scene. Blood poured out of the poor pig's mouth and nose. It looked like it might weigh a hundred pounds. A pair of tusks curved upward and pulled back the upper lip, exposing its teeth.

"He's going to clean that hog," I said with a soft moan of dismay.

"Is that a javelina?" Twila asked.

"Prob'ly one of them fallow pigs," Granny explained, though she couldn't see. "Hogs that escape their pens and breed in the wild. You wouldn't want to eat a javelina, but them fallow ones got good meat on 'em. Feed on acorns and stuff like that."

"Well, he's obviously going to clean and eat it," I said.

"Good." Twila dropped the plastic back in place. "You know men. He'll be concentrating on that." She turned to Penny. "Where's Alice's Jeep?"

She nodded to the left. "Beside the camp house over there. But it won't do us any good. I told you, he took the keys."

We ignored her and I scanned the inside of the camp house. In front of us was a table, obviously not for eating, since cans and empty bottles, tools, and all sorts of hunting and cooking paraphernalia littered every inch of it. On the left was a stove and refrigerator, the right two sets of bunk beds and the small woodstove with a pile of logs beside it.

"Is there another door out of this place?" I asked Penny.

"I don't know," she said as she wrung her hands. "I haven't had a chance to look around. I've been tied up!"

Outside a creaking noise sounded. I lifted the plastic again, and Twila did the same on her side of the window.

"Poor Miss Piggy," Twila said. I stifled a stab of sympathy at the animal myself, although I didn't correct her misinterpretation of the animal's sex. Delroy had it spread-eagled with an iron rod between its back legs, the winch hook attached to the rod. As he cranked, the pig rose into the air until its bloody nose cleared the wooden platform. Then Delroy secured the cable and whipped out a huge knife from the sheath on his belt.

"Ugh." Twila dropped her side of the plastic back into place, but for some reason I couldn't tear my gaze away...until Delroy sliced that knife right down that poor pig's stomach, all the way from his tail to his neck.

I gagged and hid the scene by dropping the plastic. Then I reached for a glass and one of the spigots on the sink before I realized that I'd rather drink out of that Texas puddle than a dirty, stained glass from that dish drainer. But I turned on a tiny stream of water and bent down, cupped some water in my palm and swallowed it.

I straightened and wiped off my mouth, then said, "One of us needs to slip out the door and get to the Jeep while he's busy with the pig." Before Twila could volunteer, I shushed her. "I'll do it. You did put the extra key back in hiding, didn't you?"

"Yes," she replied. "Up under the fender well."

I nodded, licked my bottom lip to catch a dribble of water, took a deep breath, and reached for the door handle.

"Wait," Twila whispered. She moved over to my side of the sink and lifted the plastic. "Ugh," she repeated. "But now's your chance, Alice. He's still concentrating on his butchering job."

I remembered the pistol in my hand and gave it to her. Cautiously I eased the heavy wooden door open as she continued, "But for Pete's sake, don't look at what he's doing."

Of course, I did...just as Delroy shoved his hand inside the pig's stomach and dug out a bundle of glistening, slimy guts, which plopped onto the wooden platform at his feet.

My stomach roiled and I clapped a hand over my mouth. But somehow I controlled the nausea. I had to. The way Delroy was going, it appeared he had plenty of practice cleaning his kills. Whoops, not a word I wanted to use right now. Still, it probably wouldn't take him nearly as long as I wished to do the job. Maybe not long enough even for me to find the Jeep, the keys, get it started...

I whispered to Twila, "Once I get to the Jeep, you need to bring everyone else out and get them in it. I don't think I'll have time to stop here and get you. Delroy's got a rifle on that ATV."

"Take Trucker with you. I'll handle the others."

I nodded and took a deep breath. Then Twila hugged me tightly before she patted my shoulder and said, "We can do this, Alice. Broadcast to me when you've got the keys."

"Okay."

This time I opened the door far enough for Trucker and me to slip out. I kept a wary eye on Delroy over at the cleaning rack, thankfully with his back to me. I also had to make sure I didn't stumble over anything, though. Trucker kept an eye on Delroy and that pig, too, but I shushed him with a bare hint of a whisper and he obediently kept quiet. I edged across the front of the building and made it nearly to the corner before Delroy growled, "What the hell you think you're doin'?"

I froze and clenched Trucker's muzzle. I'd been in mid-glance at the safety the corner represented, and I slowly turned my head, expecting to see Delroy stomping towards me. If he did, I'd release Trucker...unless he had that rifle in his hands...

Delroy threw his knife, thankfully not at me. The small gray coyote disappeared back into the underbrush without harm.

"You can have the guts when I get ready to give 'em to you!" Delroy yelled after the coyote as he strode over and retrieved the skinning knife buried to its hilt in the dirt. He wiped it on his pants leg and returned to the hog without noticing me.

I breathed a sigh of relief and skittered around the corner with Trucker in tow. There was my Jeep. Still making sure I didn't step on a dry stick or anything that would snap under my foot and reveal my presence, I hurried to the Jeep and dropped to the ground beside the front fender well.

A second later, I had the little magnetized box in my hand, then the keys. I checked the driver's door, but for some stupid reason, Delroy had locked the vehicle, as though he were afraid someone would steal the Jeep even here deep in these woods! Keeping a firm hold on Trucker's cord/leash, I placed the index and middle fingers of both hands against my temples and concentrated.

I'm here, Twila. Ready for the rest of you.

I repeated the mental broadcast twice more before I caught the faint sound of the wooden door opening. A few seconds later, Granny edged around the side of the building, with Miss Molly still secure in one arm, her walking stick in the other hand. Then Penny followed her, then Twila.

"Now," I whispered. "The problem is going to be that when I unlock the Jeep—Delroy locked the darn thing!—the lights are going to come on. So we need to be ready to jump in and get the hell out of here. Penny, you go on around to the passenger door. Twila, you get ready to help Granny in the back. And listen. I have to push the button twice to open all the doors, so don't try to get in until you hear two clicks. Otherwise, only the driver's door will open."

Penny quietly went around the front of the Jeep to the front passenger door. Twila took up her stance with her hand at the ready to open the back passenger door. I took a deep breath...and pushed the unlock button. Once. Twice.

The headlights and taillights flared at the first push. The reassuring second clunk indicated that all four doors opened successfully. I jerked my door open, and Trucker bounded in, then on through the console to the backseat as I scrambled in after him. I jammed the key into the ignition and twisted, and the engine roared to life. I didn't even try to back up. With only a brief glance around to make sure I had all my passengers, I slammed the gearshift into drive and hit the gas. I also had sense enough to remember that my Jeep had one of those buttons to disable the airbags on it, and pushed it as we barreled through the underbrush in front of us, past the back of the camp house. I swerved left toward the trail. Lucky for our lives, there weren't any large trees in the way, although I plowed down a few saplings.

I didn't even hear the first bullet. It shattered the driver's side mirror.

"Get down!" I screamed at everyone.

Penny shoved herself onto the floorboard and I crouched as low as I could and still see out the windshield. The next bullet shattered the windshield, but on the passenger side. Probably shattered the hatchback glass, too, but I wasn't about to look. I careened down the trail, fishtailing and fighting for control in the ruts as two more shots rang out. I had no idea if they hit the Jeep or not. I kept going.

Then remembered the gate. The large, heavy pipe gate.

"Screw it," I muttered. The roar of the ATV engine sounded behind me as I slammed the gas feed down to the floor and rammed straight into that gate. Metal shrieked and crumpled, but the gate flew off the hinges and let me through. I jammed on the brakes, but we still slid across the road and nearly into the ditch on the other side. Nearly into a huge tree, also. But I wrestled the steering wheel and somehow got us back on the slightly wider trail, where I drove hell-bent for leather back the way we'd come. I'd lost one headlight in the collision, but one still worked.

"Stay down!" I ordered Penny when she started to get back up on the seat. "He's coming after us!"

A quarter mile doesn't seem that long—didn't seem that long even when we walked it a while ago toward the camp. However, it almost seemed like we were slogging through a wall of water, despite how fast I was going. Especially when I glimpsed the single headlight in the rearview mirror.

"He *is* coming after us!" I warned my passengers again. "Stay down."

Twila didn't. My next glimpse in the mirror showed her leaning over the backseat, the revolver gripped in both hands.

Boom! Boom! Boom!

By then we were at the intersection. I slowed enough to make the right turn, and then remembered we couldn't get back this way. Patty's car blocked that road.

I jammed on the brakes and fishtailed a one-eighty, then yelled to Twila, "Did you hit him?"

"Don't know!" she yelled back. "Maybe. The headlight, anyway."

I floored the gas again. Only problem with that direction was, if Delroy was still after us, he had a straight shot again at the Jeep.

"Do you see him?" I yelled.

Boom-Boom! answered me.

"That's a revolver," I called back to Twila. "It's only got six shots!"

"Okay," she yelled. "I'll save the last one!"

"Don't need to do that." Granny's voice. "Patty had an extra box a'shells under the seat with the gun. Here."

I assumed she gave Twila the box of shells, but I was too busy driving to look into the backseat. The dirt road was still rutted and the tires bumpety-bumped over the washboard terrain, at times wrenching the steering wheel. Finally the road merged into an asphalt-covered county road, and I thanked the Universe and sped up even more.

"Did we lose him?" I called back to Twila.

"I can't tell. I shot the headlight out. But it's starting to get light out, so I should be able to see him if he does catch up. I doubt he'll be able to now, though, since we're on a better road and able to go a lot faster than that four-wheeler."

"Uh oh," I muttered.

Twila must have heard me, because a second later, her head was beside mine. "What's wrong?"

"Look at the temperature gauge on the dash," I said.

The needle was buried way past the "H" for hot. And now the engine started to rumble and clunk. Then it died. And so did all the power to the various other bells and whistles on the Jeep, such as power steering and power brakes. Luckily we were on a straight stretch. Lucky for control of the Jeep—not lucky if Delroy was still after us. The Jeep rolled to a stop right in the middle of the road, steam billowing from under the crumpled hood.

"Busted the radiator," Granny said. This time when I looked in the rearview mirror, I saw her sitting upright on the backseat. "Prob'ly when you rammed through that there gate."

Twila turned around and aimed the pistol out the back window. "We'll hear him first," she said.

"Did you reload?" I asked, as I swiveled around and glanced on the rear floorboard, grateful to see that both Trucker and Miss Molly were huddled there.

In answer, Twila jerked the pistol back and handed it to Granny. "Help me reload it."

Granny flipped some little doohickey on the side of the pistol and it broke open. She shook out the five empty shell casings and one loaded one, and Twila took a new load out of the box on the seat and replaced the shells. Then Twila flipped the gun closed and aimed it again.

Penny stirred, and I said, "You can probably get back up now."

She edged up onto the seat, but stayed crouched low enough to keep behind the protection of the seatback. "Is he still after us?"

"We don't know," I said impatiently. "Hush, so we can hear him if he is."

We waited a good thirty seconds or more, but no ATV engine noise broke the silence, only the ticking of my Jeep engine...after the hiss of escaping steam died out. Then I heard a vehicle, but in front of us. "Someone's coming. I hope they see us before they hit us."

They did. They were watching for us, running siren-silent but with lights flashing. I spotted the lights first, and seconds later, the patrol car braked to a stop right in front of us and the doors flew open. But the cops didn't spring to our rescue. Instead, they crouched behind the protection of the doors and shoved their pistols through the open windows.

"Police!" one of them shouted, although we knew damn well it was a police car. "Everyone out of the vehicle with your hands up!"

I glanced in the rearview mirror again and saw Twila's back. "Drop that pistol into the hatchback," I warned. "If they see you with it, we'll be full of more holes than Bonnie and Clyde!"

A thump sounded, and she slowly turned around, pistol-less.

"Get out of the vehicle!" the cop shouted again. "Now!"

"Mebbe we should ask for some I.D.," Granny said. "Heard on the news they's some phony cops runnin' 'round rapin' poor women they ketch out by their lonesomes."

"Let's don't argue with them, Granny," Twila said. "Just get out."

We opened the doors and just then Trucker decided to jump up onto the backseat. Twila grabbed his collar and slid out the door along with the rest of us, although she could only put one hand on her head, since she gripped Trucker with the other. I faced the cops with my hands on my head and called, "We're not criminals! We're running from one!"

"All of you come to the front of the vehicle and lean against the hood," he ordered.

"Well, by cracky, you jist try to make us, Jimmy John Baker!" Granny said. "Put that there gun back in your pocket!"

She pushed the door Penny stood beside shut and tottered on past her. She thumped her walking stick as she made her way straight to the cop crouched behind the patrol car driver's door. He stood up, as did the other policeman, and Granny shook a gnarled finger in Jimmy John's face.

"Now you listen here, Jimmy John. We's been on the run from that there Delroy tonight. And you get on that there radio in your car and call in some help to go catch him!"

"Yes, ma'am, Miz Chisholm," Jimmy John said. "Right away, ma'am."

The rest of us slowly lowered our hands as Jimmy John slid back into the patrol car. Twila murmured to me, "Does Granny know every cop in Texas?"

"She knows a bunch of them," I replied. "She's lived a long time, and has slews of relatives all over the state. She comes from a large family of large families."

The other cop removed his cap and said, "We're sorry for the mistake, Miz Chisholm. We had a BOLO about that Jeep and that it was in this area with a parole violator and possible kidnap victim in it."

"We done rescued the kidnap vic," Granny said. "All you got's left to do is find Delroy."

"Can we do anything else for you before we take off, ma'am?"

"Well, we needs a tow truck," Granny said. "No, make that two of 'em. Patty Alvidrez's car's stuck down 'nother road back there. And we needs a taxi, iffen there's one somewhere nearby. You can't carry all of us and the cat and dog back to town in your backseat."

"What happened to my Lincoln?" Penny evidently remembered to ask.

"We'll tell you all 'bout it after bit," Granny said before Twila or I tried to explain. "Let's just get these cops after Delroy and find us a place we don't have to dodge bullets to sit a spell."

CHAPTER 38

Within a half hour, things were clicking. The county sheriff arrived minutes before the wrecker, expeditiously gleaned the facts of the situation, and organized the manhunt for Delroy. We gave them directions to the camp, and despite her dishabille, Penny bravely agreed to go back with the two county deputies to give her statement.

Oh, yes, and Jack arrived. In a rental car. A nice, comfy Buick sufficient to carry his three passengers and the two animals. He demanded assurance that each and every one of us was unhurt, then stepped back to let the sheriff take charge.

The wrecker driver examined my Jeep and assured me that he thought the damage minor enough that the dealership could fix it—with authorization from my insurance company, which I handled on his cell phone and through my twenty-four-hour claim service. Granny knew the county sheriff, also, and in deference to her age and exhaustion, he sent us off with the promise to check in at his office later that day for our statements. Armed with Penny's alarm codes and the location of her hidden house keys, an agreeable Jack drove us there through the sunrise. Still, he continued to remain uncharacteristically mute.

At Penny's, only Daisy met us at the door, and she took one look at

Miss Molly and Trucker, then traversed an evidently well-rehearsed route that took her to the top of the entertainment center in the living room. Murmuring about a direly needed breakfast for all of us, Twila bustled into the kitchen while I settled Granny on the sofa and covered her with a beautiful throw draped over the back of it. Her soft snores echoed in the room immediately, about the same time the welcome aroma of brewing coffee drifted in from the area of the house where Twila had disappeared.

Jack's silence was making me nervous, especially when he roamed the cavernous living room and appeared intent on the beautiful artwork rather than questioning me about Penny's rescue. But I couldn't decide whether to try to force a dialogue with him or let things ride. I'd just headed for the kitchen to see what I could do to assist Twila when a phone rang.

I panned the living room in search of Penny's phone, but Jack pulled his cell phone from his shirt pocket, flipped it open and said, "Hello, Katy."

Evidently, he'd retrieved his phone from the Lincoln. Not wanting to eavesdrop—all right, not wanting to have to explain to Katy why we'd been no-shows at her dinner party (was it only the previous evening?)— I scurried toward the safety of the kitchen.

"*Chère?*"

I was the only one here by that name, but I valiantly tried to ignore Jack and make it to the kitchen. He caught me at the doorway, however, and insistently handed me the phone.

"Hello, Katy," I gave in with a sigh, then hurriedly tried to distract what I assumed would be a guilt-trip-laden chastisement on Katy's part and continued, "It was so wonderful of you to send Grandmere Alicia's portrait to me. You're such a sweetheart. You know how much I love it."

"Oh, I knew you would, Alice." I frowned at the unexpectedly cordial tone. "And I understand why y'all couldn't make it last night. Penny called me well in time for me to remove the extra dinner settings and not be embarrassed in front of my other guests. I'm really calling to try to find her—Penny. I've tried every phone number I have."

I didn't have the energy just then to explain everything to Katy. Twila had found her way around the kitchen, and the smell of skillet-fried bacon joined the call of caffeine. Bright and cheery, Penny's kitchen and the odors drew me and my grumbling stomach.

"Penny's...she's sort of involved in something right now, Katy," I said. "Can I give her a message?"

"Please," Katy replied. "I don't think there's anything secretive about it. Just don't tell her current editor. I imagine she spent a fortune couriering that demo DVD all the way to Jefferson last night. Tell her the *Times Picayune* guy really needs to fill that position as soon as possible, and he actually viewed the demo before he left last night. He wants her to contact him immediately and come to New Orleans for an in-person interview."

"Wow," I said. "I'll let her know as soon as she gets back from...uh...as soon as I see her."

"Wonderful," Katy replied. "When do you think you'll be home? Don't forget, you promised to speak at the Daughters of the South meeting Thursday evening. You cancelled the last time."

"You scheduled me before you checked with me, Katy. I had a book tour already planned, and I couldn't fly back from Spokane for one evening, then be in LA by noon the next day."

"Oh, pooh. We offered to pay your airfare. But that's over and done with. I did check with you this time."

"I'll—" Oops. I crossed my fingers. "I'll be there, Katy. Eight o'clock, right?"

"No, seven," she insisted, although I knew exactly what I'd written in my day planner. "We like to chat and relax for an hour before we get down to business."

Gossip about whoever couldn't make the meeting, I corrected her silently, but said, "Seven. Got it."

"Talk to you soon," Katy said, and disconnected.

I handed Jack his phone and he followed me on into the kitchen while I explained why Katy had tracked Penny down through various unanswered cell phone avenues. Twila shooed me away when I offered to help cook, and even rescued the toaster and muffins from me and put Jack in charge. I didn't protest my misjudged cooking skills as much as I could have. Anyway, it wouldn't have made any impression on two people who had experienced my failed attempts too many times over the years. Instead, I poured a cup of coffee and settled at the cozy breakfast nook overlooking Penny's backyard.

The large three-sided window treatment offered a spacious view of the swimming pool and, beyond that, one of those lovely old barns painted what I'd always called barn red. A young man came out of the barn leading a sorrel thoroughbred groomed to perfection, coat gleaming in the morning sun. He mounted in one lithe motion and cantered the horse down a trail that led off into the woods. I finished my coffee and rose to fetch my second cup just as Twila set a plate in front of me.

"I'll go see if I can get Granny up at least long enough to eat," she said as I grabbed a piece of crispy bacon and munched happily.

"Oh, I can go get her," I said around my full mouth. "You cooked."

"No, no." She waved me off and left.

Jack took my coffee cup and refilled it, along with his, then joined me back at the breakfast nook table. "Where's your plate?" I asked.

"I ate at a café while I waited for them to deliver the rental," he said, staring out the window as though he didn't have a thing else to say to me. I shrugged and returned to my meal.

Twila reentered the kitchen and said, "I'm going to take mine and Granny's plates in there."

"Good," I told her. "She can go back to sleep after she eats."

I finished most of my meal by the time she carried the two plates out and left me alone with Jack again. He didn't appear to be paying any attention to me...until I started to rise to take my dirty plate to the sink. Then he laid a hand on my shoulder and gently pushed me back into my chair.

"Nice place Penny's got here," he said when I glanced at him expectantly. "Bet she'll hate to leave it to move to New Orleans."

"Probably," I agreed. "But that's her choice."

"She's got a lot of nice artwork," he went on. "Wonder why she bought knockoffs instead of originals?"

"I didn't know that she had. And where did you learn so much about art?"

"Case in New Orleans. Museum director was murdered so he couldn't report that he'd found a couple forged paintings. His assistant had sold the originals."

"And Penny's paintings are copies? Done by someone impersonating the original artist?"

"Not all of them. Just three that I could pinpoint. The rest are the real deal."

I shrugged. "Maybe she needed the money. We all do sometimes."

"Yeah." Then he changed the subject...or so I thought at first. "How'd someone like Penny get mixed up with a felon like Delroy?"

"She's not *mixed up* with him, Jack. He kidnapped her!"

Jack leaned back in his chair. Drank the last swallow of his coffee, then stood and walked over to the coffeepot and poured a refill.

"Jack," I said persistently. "Delroy kidnapped Penny."

He turned and stared directly at me. "Why? Why Penny?"

"Well...oh...he wanted my Jeep, I guess. He needed to steal a car for transportation."

"Your specific Jeep?" he mused aloud.

"Probably not. He just found an isolated home and took the opportunity."

"Penny's isolated home, huh? How'd he know where it was? Bein' a reporter, she doesn't advertise where she lives, I'll bet. And if he only wanted a vehicle, why take a hostage? Lots of trouble, a hostage, if a man's on the run."

Dread was eating away in my stomach like acid. I wrenched my gaze from Jack's and toyed with my coffee cup. Then I rose and walked over to the refrigerator, opened it and took out a quart of milk. I didn't bother searching for a glass. I poured the coffee cup full and sipped in an effort to soothe the burning in my belly. It didn't work. For a moment, I thought I'd upchuck my entire breakfast in the sink, but I battled the nausea back down.

"I saw another copy of that demo DVD that Penny sent to Katy in the living room." Jack set his coffee cup on the counter. "We're invited guests here right now, but a sharp lawyer might still get it dismissed as evidence if we took it with us without a search warrant first. Seein' as how I'm a cop and havin' suspicions that she might be involved in a crime."

"Which crime?" I whispered.

"Well," Jack drawled, "that's the question. Guess I'll check in and see how the manhunt's goin'."

"You just have a cop's suspicious mind," I insisted stubbornly.

But so did I, I realized, while Jack gazed at me in sympathy. Too many years of writing about crimes. Weaving clues and suspicions together. Dropping red herrings in places where I thought they'd work, and finding out later on in the story that my muse had different ideas about false leads versus true clues.

There were still holes in the logic large enough to drive one of those menacing semis through, however. I could only hope that one of those holes would be large enough to validate Penny's innocence. The acid curdling the milk in my stomach to buttermilk didn't bode well for my desperate mental protestations, though.

I sighed a heartfelt wish-to-be-wrong. "We need to talk to Mary Ann."

From the doorway, Twila said, "Indeed we do. But first we need some sleep."

"We probably don't have time for that," I replied edgily. "What if we sleep through too much?"

"Mary Ann said she'd meet us on the seventh floor," Twila reminded me. "And neither you nor I need to face that without a full-bore well of power. Two hours should do it for us."

Us. I gulped. She hadn't forgotten that she'd placed me in charge, but at least she wasn't making me solo.

"You'll be well up to par with some rest," I insisted. Tried to insist, anyway. My voice came out like a tiny mouse squeaking a protest at a cat's paw placed in front of its escape hole.

As she was wont to do when it suited her, Twila ignored my objection. "We have to follow the entire path. We never did get down in the basement."

I shuddered and pleaded, "Not the basement. We can't possibly find anything to help us down there." Whenever I envisioned places at the hotel that I did not want to revisit, the basement ranked up there in a near tie to the seventh-floor suite. Granted, the seventh floor held the lead by a nose, but the only saving grace of that nasty basement was that I'd met Patrick there. And considering the way things were moving in this ghosthunt/murder investigation, I wasn't so sure that giving in to my utter fascination with Patrick had been a smart move.

Twila tried to soothe me with a compassionate glance. "That's where they found Mary Ann. That's where you met Patrick the first time. That's where it all started, Alice. At least it will be daylight this time when we go back."

"Not in the basement," I muttered. "But there are two large windows in the sitting area of the suite, one in the bedroom."

"Have you figured out whether whatever ran you out of that suite was the same thing we encountered in the hallway?"

I closed my eyes and tried to recall a scene I'd locked away in the corner of my mind marked, *Don't go there.* Wrong move. The impact of that experience crashed straight into a stark visual—and audible. The dire warnings from the entity. The frozen terror on the faces of the others in my group. The mad scramble amidst screams and protestations to obey the entity and get the heck out of that room before whatever we heard took physical action against us.

I'd been in the bedroom—barely. I'd just stuck my nose inside the doorway, took two steps in, when the very walls and ceiling shook in a brief prelude to the real terror. The voice. The words...

Why on earth had I ever thought it a good idea to go back to that hotel? Because I'd be going with Twila, I honestly told myself. I figured that: one, she'd love the place; and two, that no ghost would dare mess with her. Now we were in way too deep to abort.

"It said that it would show us exactly what it was like *over there* if we were so interested in the other side's existence," I whimpered as I stared into Twila's brown eyes. "That the line between the existences was thinner than a spider-web strand."

"It is," she replied. "But it's still a definite barrier. One that's cross-able both ways as long as you're careful."

Jack cleared his throat, and the slight sound drew my hopeful gaze toward him. The basement was, after all, a crime scene. The entire hotel, actually, which included the suite. He was a homicide cop. Surely he wouldn't let us muck around somewhere that evidence might still be gathered. *Not that we'd ever let that stop us before,* I whined pitifully in my mind.

The expression on Jack's face sank any prospect that he would inter-fere. He crossed his arms on his chest and leaned back against the counter. "I'll clean up in here. And stay up while you ladies catch some shut-eye."

"You're going with us?" I asked.

"Yeah," was all he answered.

"Two hours," Twila repeated. "Make sure you wake us up. Before that, if anything drastic happens."

"I've got a feeling the drastic stuff is yet to come," Jack said.

And oh, did I agree with him for once!

* * *

You'd have thought the stress would keep me awake. I didn't expect to sleep a wink. We left Granny on the couch, and Twila and I found a guest bedroom upstairs and stretched out. Both on the same bed. I intended to glean every tiny bit of strength from her presence I could to face what was coming.

I'd barely sank onto the pillow before someone gently shook my shoulder. "Wake up, Alice. It's time to go."

262

I bolted upright. "No," I said to Twila. "You said we could sleep for two hours."

"It's been two," she replied. "I've been up for a few minutes and already took my shower. Granny, too, and I made Jack take his turn. Here." She handed me a bar of quince seed soap. I recognized the color and odor from another time she'd insisted we bathe in this protective measure when we were facing a monumental event.

"We don't have a change of clothing," I pointed out. "I don't like putting on dirty panties after I shower."

"I laid some of Penny's clothes out for you. She won't mind."

I sighed and rose from the bed. Took my shower, and then did mind what Twila had chosen for me to wear. She knew as well as I did that Penny's rear was smaller than mine, and the panties would have cut into me uncomfortably. I wrapped in a robe I found on the back of the bathroom door, then wandered across the hall and into the bedroom I knew from my previous visits belonged to Penny.

And remembered what had been niggling me all along about Mary Ann. Her flapper attire with no logical explanation for it. Still, I had no idea what it all meant, nor the impetus to reason it out, with the upcoming return to the hotel on my mind.

The rest of Penny's house was decorated in the same manner as the living area: earth tones, Southwestern leaning toward Western-style. Here in her bedroom she'd made an island of her own, one that fit with her interest in another era, the one she'd even named her cat from. The Twenties, and Gatsby's love, Daisy. The bed was king-size with a somewhat garish red chenille fringed bedspread and pillow shams. Multicolored, glass-pane Tiffany lamps with prism-cut dangles set on two rather plain bedside tables. Black-and-white framed portraits of flappers and dapper men in suits similar to the one Patrick appeared in at times on the wall, which was papered in an Art Deco–style wallpaper. Yes, even a large portrait of her favorite, Gatsby, leaning against a tree in the shadows, a cigarette between his lips, smoke curling faintly upward past his squinted eyes. He stared at the distant porch on the two-story mansion, where a dinner party or ball was taking place. Light blazed from the story-high windows and illuminated a few couples who had moved out onto the front veranda for privacy or fresh air.

In her white evening dress, Daisy stood off to one side alone, her face turned in his direction. Captivating. The artist had caught them in a way that the two of them were all you noticed after your first glance. The rest of the background faded into obscurity, only a backdrop for the emotions so evident in their stances and expressions.

I started over to the bureau to check the drawers, but another print drew me, one on the wall beside the bureau: a framed show announcement for an off-Broadway performance of *Orphans of the Storm*. I vaguely recalled that as an early talkie, but the poster dated the performance as only a few months ago. Obviously, a theatrical production of the Twenties film. It even proclaimed that the female lead, Marlena Annette, would steal your heart as much as Lillian Gish, the original star in the talkie, did back in her day.

It didn't take a genius to make the connection. Mary Ann—Marlena Annette. Same dark hair, same style, a similar dress, although white, not green. Another piece to the puzzle that I had no idea what to do with.

I opened bureau draws until I found Penny's store of bras and panties, all sexy and matching. Finally I chose a pair of panties that I thought would at least be comfortable, if not an exact fit, then carried them back to the bathroom and dressed. All the while my mind whirled, but couldn't come to any reasonable conclusions. It just didn't make a bit of sense.

Mary Ann and the flapper dress. Marlena Annette. Penny and Delroy. And I'd forgotten Patrick the last few hours. We'd left him with Jack at Patty's house and I hadn't thought to ask Jack when he'd last seen the ghost. Patrick's split...personality? Body? Soul? And what did Antonio have to do with all this? Possibly the two threads we followed—Mary Ann's story and Patrick's—were totally unrelated. Yet somehow they'd merged in this present quest.

The return to the hotel...

"Are you ready?" Twila asked from the bathroom doorway. "Jack and Granny are waiting."

"Granny? She should stay here, Twila. That basement's not a place she needs to try to navigate. And then we'll have all those flights of stairs to climb to the seventh floor."

"You gonna tell her that?"

Of course I wasn't. With a deep breath, I forced out, "Guess I'm as ready as I'll ever be."

CHAPTER 39

We approached the hotel from the back entrance again. Jack started to drive on up to the door, but Twila explained about the unsafe foundation, and he parked down in the tunnel. I didn't like the look on Jack's face when he heard about that foundation, but he only shook his head and turned off the engine. We all got out of the car and gathered in a group in front of the hood. Stared out the end of the tunnel at our destination—that entrance door. Jack's bike was parked near the door, leaning on its kickstand, a ray of sunlight shining on the gleaming gas tank.

"Have we heard from Penny?" I asked to procrastinate. "She should have been done with her statement by now. I'd have thought she'd be back at the house before we left."

"She called while y'all were sleeping," Jack said. "Seems she has an apartment in Fort Worth that she uses when she's on assignment and doesn't want to drive home. I gave her Katy's message, and Penny said she was gonna contact her."

I frowned. "That doesn't make sense. Penny's house here would have been closer for her than Fort Worth."

Jack's shrug indicated he either didn't care to try to explain a

266

woman's decision, or—given the hint of evasion I caught on his face—didn't care to explain his thoughts to the females who accompanied him.

He took a step, but I grabbed his arm. "Now you listen here, Jack. We're going in there as a group just as much as we are individuals. If we aren't forthright and honest with each other, all sorts of unnecessary counters can thwart our success."

"Counters? Y'all gonna cast some spells in there?" He nodded at the hotel.

"No!" I gritted my teeth. "We're going to communicate in there. Channel, talk to the other side, whatever you want to call it. And we all need to be together in it. So what the hell are you hiding from us? Did you watch that demo tape?"

"Yeah," he admitted. "But what was more interesting was what I found on the Internet."

"You used Penny's computer?"

"Closest and most available," he said. "And there were some things I wanted to know."

"So what did you find out?"

"Things," he said flatly. "Are we going in here or not?"

Twila stepped forward and said, "Not! Not with you, anyway, since you're obviously withholding information from us. I'm not about to go in here, or take Alice and Granny in here, with someone who thinks he's just along for the ride. Someone who can cause trouble for us with his nonbeliever mentality, let alone his asinine attitude that the little women don't need to know everything the big bad man does!"

"Your choice," Jack replied grimly. "But you don't have any way to stop me from tagging along."

"We'll just go another time," Twila said.

"Your choice," Jack repeated. "Let's get back in the car and I'll take y'all back to Six Gun."

"I gots a feelin' we ought to finish this up now," Granny put in, and Twila appeared to concede. I didn't believe that for a minute, however. Something was up, and my thoughts were confirmed when she turned her back briefly on the group as though in contemplation, then faced us again.

"I guess we'll have to make allowances," Twila said. "I need my backpack from the trunk."

Since Jack had the car keys, he agreeably ambled to the trunk and pushed the key-lock button to unlock it. We followed him, Twila with Trucker on braided-cord leash, me with Miss Molly leashed but curled in my arms, and Granny with her walking stick. But when Jack reached in to retrieve Twila's things, he uttered an oath and straightened so fast he slammed his head against the trunk lid.

"What the hell are you doin' in there?" he growled as he rubbed his head. "And haven't I told you to be dressed when you're around?"

Patrick slowly stretched his arms and uncurled from his spot in the trunk. He climbed out in all his naked glory and floated over to stand beside Trucker. "I don't recall giving you permission to order me to attire myself to your specifications," he said to Jack.

"Is that the real Patrick?" I whispered to Twila. It was a serious question, given we were back at the hotel where we'd seen the doppelganger.

She nodded, but frowned slightly. "I'm pretty sure it is."

Pretty sure didn't salve my stress one bit, but I supposed it was the best she had to offer. Jack retrieved her backpack, and she squatted beside him to check the contents.

"Darn, I didn't zip it all the way," she said, and gazed up at Jack. "One of my candles is missing. It must have rolled out in the trunk. Could you look for me?"

Jack turned and peered in the trunk. We could all see inside it, and I didn't notice any candle. Yet Twila rose and pointed past Jack's shoulder.

"Is that it? Back in the corner there? Look, that flap of carpet is loose."

Jack leaned on in, and Twila swooped down lickety-split, grabbed his lower legs and heaved. Didn't take me long to get her message. I helped her by slamming the trunk lid down before Jack could recover.

Dead silence. I'm sure we all expected Jack to raise holy hell at the trick. Yet he didn't even thump and bang on the trunk.

"Well," Granny said as she leaned on her walking stick and stared at the trunk. "S'pose we oughta get movin'."

But none of us did.

I bit my bottom lip, then asked, "Is there plenty of oxygen in there?"

"I don't use the stuff, so I wouldn't know," Patrick answered.

"He's going to kill us," I said. Then tapped on the trunk lid. "Jack? Are you all right?"

Dead silence. Even Twila looked concerned. "Maybe that wasn't such a good idea," she whispered. "But darn it, it's going to be hard enough to deal with what we'll find in there without Jack's interference."

"But what if he runs out of oxygen?" I asked.

"Ain't much we can do 'bout it now," Granny said. "Jack's got the keys in there with him."

"There's a trunk release button inside the glove box," I explained. "We better let him out."

We didn't have to. One side of the rear seatback flew forward with a thump, and a second later, Jack emerged into the backseat.

"How'd he do that?" Granny asked as all of us edged back from the car.

"The car I had before my Jeep had a backseat like that," I said. "I'd forgotten about it. You can push the seatback down to carry long items."

"I wish you'd told me that five minutes ago," Twila grumbled.

"I didn't know what you had planned," I defended. "And I'd forgotten about that feature. I traded that car off two years ago!"

By now we were a good distance away from the car, at the mouth of the tunnel. Any minute I expected an enraged Jack to burst out of the car and give us hell. However, he just sat there in the backseat, rubbing his hands over his face and through his hair.

"Mebbe he's gonna do what we want and wait for us," Granny said.

The car door opened and Jack emerged. He closed the door and leaned against it. Crossed his arms and stared toward us with an all-too-calm expression on his face.

Granny cleared her throat. "You gonna waits here, Jack?"

"No." He didn't move, though.

"Then you have to cooperate," Twila said. "And share information."

"I took the damn shower with your soap," he tossed back at her.

"See?" she flared back. "That's what I mean. The power of the quince is as much mental as anything else. And your derision of it will open a hole in our protection!"

He pulled his cell phone out of his shirt pocket. "I can make one phone call and keep all of you from goin' in there."

Patrick sauntered away from the rest of us, straight up to Jack. Finally Jack grew flustered. He shut his eyes, then opened them and gazed anywhere but at the naked ghost.

"You can't keep me out of there," Patrick informed him. "And—" One finger flick on Patrick's part, and Jack's cell phone flew from his hand, towards us. Twila leapt forward and caught it before it hit the ground.

Ghost and man glared at each other. Five seconds. Ten. Then Patrick shrugged and floated back to join us.

"I do believe he has us over a barrel," he said. "He can easily walk to the police station from here."

Granny whimpered, then broke into full-fledged sobs. Twila dropped her backpack and slipped an arm around her, holding onto Trucker's leash with her free hand. "Granny," she soothed. "Granny, what's wrong?"

"He's bein' mean," Granny choked out. "What's we gonna do? We can't he'p these poor lost souls 'cause of him. They's gonna wander and wander. One a'these days, I'm gonna be a soul. What's I gonna do if some'un like Jack interferes with my eternal rest?"

Tears gathered in my eyes at her heart-wrenching words, although suspicion flared when I didn't notice any tear tracks in her wrinkles. Still, I sniffed and glared towards Jack, but he was already beside me.

He patted Granny consolingly on the shoulder. "Aw, Granny, don't. Look, I didn't think of it that way. Jeez, please quit cryin'."

Granny sniffed and dug a hanky out of her pocket. "No, you jist think your cop ways are the answer to everything. You don'ts think beyond slammin' that there cell door on someone. There's lots more to it than that, Jack."

"I know, I know," he conceded. "Well, I guess I'm learning, anyway. Or tryin' to. I can't promise that I'm gonna believe in whatever y'all have in mind, but I'll do my best not to interfere."

"What about sharing the information you have with us?" I demanded.

"That, too," he assured me. "I used Penny's computer to look into the newspaper archives,

and—"

Suddenly the bike's engine roar split the air. And it dawned on me that the ray of sunshine I'd noticed might be something utterly different. Jack raced past us, headed for the bike. Just as he reached it, the kick-stand flew up and the handlebar that controlled the bike's throttle swiveled back and forth. The throaty roar echoed and faded around us. Echoed and faded again as the throttle revved the engine.

Just as the bike started to move, Jack flung himself onto the seat. That beam of supposed sunlight scattered into dozens of pieces. It reformed at the entrance door into Mary Ann—the top half of her anyway—then zipped inside. Jack killed the bike's engine. Then, hands on the handlebars, leaned his head forward and gently banged it on the round object I recalled was the speedometer.

"I think we better get going," Twila said. "We can hear what Jack has to say later."

* * *

We didn't have to use our flashlights as we crossed the lobby. All too soon we were at that basement door. A firmly padlocked door. I'd assumed it would be, like the last time I was here, and hoped the impediment would delay us, if not thwart us completely. I should have known better.

"Shall I?" Patrick asked Jack. "Or do you carry some of those lock-picking tools?"

"Have at it," Jack said, his gaze resolutely on the door instead of Patrick's nudity.

271

Patrick waved his hand at the lock. The tumblers clunked, and it fell open. He grinned and said, "I, of course, find locks no barriers, but perhaps it was Fate that allowed me to meet with your Sir Gary. Have him show me a few abilities that he learned during his existence."

I'm going to have a talk with Fate one of these days. Not that it would do a bit of good.

Twila removed the padlock and opened the door. It squealed on rusty hinges, as it had before, and she led Trucker onto the landing. "At least the tours that used to go through here kept the passageway free of spider webs."

Granny thumped her walking stick with each step and joined Twila. "It'll take me a bit, but I kin climb down there."

"No sense in that," Jack said. "I can carry you." He disappeared into the stairwell, and a moment later, I heard his steps descending. Twila didn't reappear, so I assumed she followed him and Granny. I looked around for Patrick, but he'd disappeared, and Miss Molly and I were all alone in the emptiness. The cat wasn't even antsy, either. She curled quietly in my arms and didn't even purr.

It didn't take a conscious decision for me to figure my next move. I was halfway down the narrow stairwell by the time Jack set Granny down. By the time I hit the floor, Twila had already walked away from the stairwell to examine our cavernous surroundings. She even echoed my thoughts. "Cavernous."

A dank and musty odor filled my nose. Piles of debris littered the floor, some of them disrupted repair jobs. Boards, slats, rusty cans of nails and screws, even pink slabs of insulation, mixed with cast-off trash from the contractors and helpers, empty cigarette packs, soda cans. Other piles indicated disintegrating structure: tangled wires, fallen doors and boards. Here and there, dim streaks of light filtrated in from a few street-level windows. Very dim. Not even dust motes danced in them.

Only our breathing and, in the distance, the sound of water trickling from broken pipes broke the silence. Clear across the basement, a good walk from where we stood, lay the workings to retrieve the underground mineral waters advertised in the hotel's literature. Cold waters, not like the hot springs over in Arkansas. The pipes had corroded over the years and leaked like sieves. A portion of that end of the basement was actually flooded. Overhead, numerous stories, tons of concrete and steel, bricks and

mortar...

"I shall show you around," Patrick said as he visualized again.

"We're not here to sightsee," Twila informed him. "Although I'd love to come back and do that. It must be fascinating how everything necessary to keep the hotel running smoothly and the guests happy was arranged down here." Then she evidently reconsidered. "But maybe that's all part of it. Maybe we need to get a sense of how things operated to understand what's been done, what can be undone."

She slowly moved forward and headed toward the one definite area I wanted to avoid. "Look at the huge ovens and cooking areas," she mused as we followed. Past a humongous steel-topped table, I noticed a yellow flutter, but she didn't break stride. "It must have taken a huge storage area and refrigeration units to keep enough grocery supplies on hand."

"There's a pantry area," Patrick explained. "Even labels on the shelves to keep everything organized. Large refrigerators, also, of course. And—" He motioned toward that yellow flutter—crime tape around the elevator. "That's the service elevator."

"Where Mary Ann was found," Twila said. "Mary Ann, are you here?"

She didn't appear, and I finally spoke. "She said—"

"—the seventh floor," Twila broke in. "I remember. But someone's here. We just have to find her...or him."

"Hope it's that there Antonio," Granny said with a giggle as she clutched Jack's arm. "Like to see him again."

"Not me," I protested adamantly. Not that it would do a darn bit of good.

Patrick floated on through the basement. "The laundry area's over here. This is one service area that doesn't sit right with me. It must have been a horrendous job."

Twila paused and I caught the expression of pain on her face. "How horrible," she agreed with Patrick. "All those machines that could break a woman's physical abilities, let alone her spirit."

She slowly moved over to one huge wooden-barrel-like machine, which was a dozen times larger than a standard whiskey barrel. The door was open, and I remembered what I'd seen before: the inside worn smooth from literally hundreds of thousands of sheets, towels, pillow-cases, and whatever else needed laundering. Suddenly Twila clamped her hands over her ears and hurried away.

"So much pain and discontent," she said. "The women who worked here did so only because they had to have employment and couldn't find other jobs."

Every sense on alert, I trailed behind as Jack assisted Granny around the debris in our paths and Patrick pointed out the other operations: the refrigeration area, the huge power plant room that contained the monstrous equipment necessary to warm and cool the hotel, as well as provide electricity for multitudes of other uses. All silent and powerless now, of course.

We passed a room that held dozens of ceramic pieces, some painted, some yet unfired. Past that lay the far side of the basement, the pipes, the furnaces, the pool of water held back by a three-foot-high concrete wall. An open area where the pipes descended into a deep hole that contained black water from the mineral springs, water that was professed to soothe the real or imagined aches and ailments of people seeking its possible healing powers.

Twila—incautiously to my mind, although I'd done the same thing —handed Jack Trucker's leash and climbed a set of iron steps to a plat-form overlooking the water from the springs.

"Twila," I warned. "Don't lean on that—"

She stubbed her toe on an unnoticed rusty bolt protruding from the floor and grabbed exactly what I'd tried to warn her about: the rusty pipe that emerged from the pool and L-ed beside the platform and into one of the furnace boilers. The pipe broke with a clang and water gushed out in a swift stream as she teetered backward...then forward, toward the water.

CHAPTER 40

"Twila!" I screamed, then Granny blocked my rescue path when Jack shoved her into my arms. I juggled Granny's tiny figure and Miss Molly as he dropped Trucker's leash and took two loping steps, the last one onto the bottom iron step, and grabbed Twila around the waist a second before she plunged into the depths. Swinging her around, he set her down on the floor.

"Who pushed me?" she asked.

"No one," I told her. "You stubbed your toe on that bolt on the platform."

"Yeah, after someone pushed me," she insisted, glaring around the basement, her brown eyes narrowed in warning.

"There's no one else here," Jack said. Then continued before we could chastise his disparagement, "Don't even say it. I will. No one that I can see."

"Exactly," Twila said. "The problem is, neither can we right now."

"We can't leave that water like that." Jack climbed on up to the platform and while we kept careful watch for another attack, he wrestled the pipe back together to cut off the water flow. Shaking his hands, he leapt back to the floor. "Colder than hell, that water."

275

"Where next?" Twila asked Patrick.

"We haven't looked in the men's and ladies' dressing rooms."

Looked in? Although I knew in a corner of my mind that we were searching for...something...someone...something down here, putting it directly into words sent a shiver down my spine.

I gasped. No, it wasn't what Patrick said. The temperature started to drop in a way that I'd never experienced before. I whirled around. Rather than a sudden no-warning plunge, a wall of coldness scurried at us from the other side of the basement. It reminded me of days you could stand outside and watch one of our Texas Blue Northers approach, steadily eating up the sky ahead of it with blue-blackness, the vegetation and trees bowing and waving as it progressed. Around me would be stillness, warmth, yet in the distance an approaching force that wouldn't be denied.

Trucker let out one tremulous howl and scrambled under the narrow ledge on the concrete wall around the water. Some instinct at work made me shove Miss Molly down beside him before I turned to face what was now on top of us. The force surrounded us much like the one Mother Nature founded: bitter cold, rushing wind. And it was invisible, at least to our eyes. Our senses, however, shrieked in defense of whatever it had in mind for us. At least, mine did.

"Stand firm!" Twila shouted as dust and debris filled the air. I grabbed Granny closer and shoved her face into my bosom to protect her from the choking, swirling refuse.

"It's that damn tornado from the seventh floor!" I shouted at Twila. Then thought to see where Jack and Patrick were as she again repeated her order for us to stand firm. I couldn't see either of them.

"That's definitely what it is!" she confirmed, although by now the roar around us nearly drowned out her voice. Twila tried to force herself toward me. Her outstretched hand reached for mine, and I sheltered Granny with one arm while I extended my free arm toward her. By rights the wind that was holding her back should have forced me forward, but it didn't. The tornado swirled, keeping a barrier between us.

For years Twila had warned me that we would sometimes encounter new things during our *adventures*. Still, she'd always appeared calm and confident that we could control any situation in the end. Maybe we'd falter now and then—hell, we *did* falter now and then. But we'd never been defeated. Some situations we left alone, those we strongly felt we had no business interfering in. In others that called to us or threatened those we knew or had agreed to help, we integrated into the fray. Sometimes we retreated to gather our senses and confidence, which was the most important ability we had, and then rejoined the skirmish. Some fights were harder than others. Yet we'd always reached a satisfactory conclusion.

I couldn't help but wonder if the odds were finally tipped against us. Our hands were still about a foot apart.

I mustered strength and bent forward, dragged Granny with me as I edged one foot in Twila's direction. Still at least six inches separated us. Hair flying around her, Twila leaned into the wind. She said something, since I could see her lips move, but the noise masked her words. She faltered, and the distance between our hands lengthened.

"No, damn you!" I screamed. Around me, the blowing debris miraculously never hit me. At the risk of smothering her, I tightened my grip on Granny and lunged for Twila.

Our fingers met...then lost contact. But the wind faltered at our touch. I took advantage and dived forward. Caught Twila's hand just before she was forced out of reach again. Caught it fully this time, not just a finger touch.

We clenched each other's hands and as though both of us knew exactly what to say, screamed in unison, "Be gone! White light, protect us!"

We desperately pulled toward each other. The wind faltered again, and Twila surged toward me. She grabbed me around the waist, and I had sense enough to let go of poor Granny a bit so she could lift her head. I wrapped my arms behind Twila's back, as she had hers on mine now, and we sheltered Granny between us as the wind abruptly ceased.

Eerie silence filled the air now. Amazed, I stared around to see that not one of the piles of debris had been disturbed. Even Twila's backpack sat intact by our feet. Everything, except my pounding heart, appeared to be just as before. Well, not everything. Trucker and Miss Molly huddled against the concrete wall, but neither Jack nor Patrick were anywhere in sight.

The pounding echoed in the eerie silence. We separated and Twila called, "Jack? Jack, where are you?"

A voice called faintly, "Here!"

"Where?" I yelled, although the voice was too indistinct for me to be sure it was Jack. Had to be, though.

"Barrel." At least, that's what I thought I heard.

Recalling Twila's distress in the laundry area, I shoved Granny gently toward her and warily eased my way back the direction we'd come. That large wooden barrel was a long way away—a long, lonesome way from Twila. Sure enough, though, the closer I got to it, the more distinct the thumps grew. The door was closed now, a lever in place to hold it shut.

"J—Jack?" I called.

Thump, thump, thump.

Why didn't he answer instead of only thumping? Maybe...oh, lord, was he suffocating in there? Before I lost my courage, I reached for the lever and shoved it loose. Twila's warning scream—"Don't, Alice!"—came a half second too late.

The door burst open and a swirl of blackness gushed out as I scrambled backward in escape mode. Tripped over something and splatted onto my ass. Pain in my tailbone crawled into my hip joints, but I crawled anyway. I flipped over and skittered across that dirty floor like a baby who hadn't quite mastered walking, heading for Twila, head swinging backward to check for pursuit, forward to check direction.

My black-and-tan and black-and-cream rescuers met me halfway. They skidded to a halt just past my knees and set up a roar and yowl that rivaled the noise of the tornado. I took advantage of their protection to get to my feet, then whirled to offer whatever power I could dredge up to defend them as Twila and Granny hurried over to us.

Beside the barrel, Antonio stood tall and dark, hands on slim hips, head thrown back as his laughter joined the cacophony of dog and cat fury. For a few seconds, Twila, Granny, and I just clapped our hands over our ears. But as soon as Antonio took his first, floating step, it was as though we all five worked in unison. Twila picked up Trucker's leash and I grabbed Miss Molly. This quieted the animals, at least. We each wrapped an arm around Granny's tiny waist and took a step of our own.

A wary expression crossed Antonio's face, but he floated another step forward.

As did we in physical step.

"What did you do with Jack?" I demanded.

He sneered. "You are all so interested in continuing to explore this deteriorating piece of wreckage, I'm sure you'll run across him...somewhere."

In a deceptively mild voice, Twila said, "We want to know where he is now."

He floated nearer. "You are in no position to make demands."

In one swift motion, Twila knelt and unzipped a backpack pocket. She pulled out another braided cord used in her ceremonies—a much longer one—and tossed it in a looping motion worthy of a real Texas cowboy. It flew through the air and curled past Antonio, around him, the end landing halfway between him and us. That left an opening in the circle, but not for long.

"Fetch," Twila murmured to Trucker. The dog raced forward and grabbed the end of the cord, then trotted straight back to Twila and offered it to her. "Good boy," she said as she sealed the circle by placing both ends on the floor behind our group.

Antonio grew silent, contemplative. "What is this?" he asked. "I feel...strange. Somewhat...peaceful."

"I've been thinking about you," Twila said. Granny and I stood motionless, allowing her to take the lead in whatever she had in mind. I thought I knew, but I stilled my mind and concentrated on the here, now, rather than questions or—frankly—fear of what could happen should this dark ghost rebel.

Twila continued, "I think you're tired of this existence. You've made your point for a lot of years. I understand your discontent. You lost everything important to you, through no fault of your own. Indeed, you did your utmost, worked hard. Cared for those you loved the best way you could. You also probably have a lot of guilt because you were partially at fault for Patrick's death. Your un-thought-out actions left your sister without a husband, the child without its father."

He nodded silently.

"You have to understand, Antonio," she went on quietly. "Revenge and guilt are part of the physical existence. Once on the other side, forgiveness is supreme. Earthly matters are not that important any longer, other than the lessons learned during the lifetime."

"Everyone I hurt has forgiven me?" he asked. "My family, who would have regained their land, had I not interfered?"

"The point is," Twila told him, "things you carry guilt for just aren't important once you cross over. That's why you're so surly and discontented in this existence. But yes, forgiveness has been yours for decades now. All you have to do is forgive yourself and cross through the light."

"You can help me do that?"

She nodded. "Very easily. But you must allow me to do it. You still have that much control over your situation."

Antonio contemplated her words for a moment. Then he said, "I wish to go. I wish to be with my family. Those I cared for. Whatever happened on this plane is no longer worth my misguided revenge."

"First you must tell us where Jack is."

"He is all right," Antonio admitted. He hung his head as though ashamed of himself, signifying at least to Twila and me, that the power of the circle was in effect. "You will find him in the men's dressing room."

Twila sighed and beckoned him forward. I couldn't quite quell my reaction. I stiffened slightly as he floated closer, to become more of a part of our group. Twila cast me a cautioning glance, though, and I breathed in deeply, blew out the stress and cleared my mind, grounding myself. Granny leaned on her walking stick and cocked her head, the twinkle in her eyes clearly an indication of her admiration of Antonio's masculine qualities.

"Sit," Twila ordered all of us. And we did, even though the floor was dirty and dusty. I helped Granny down beside me, which left Antonio at my left. Trucker and Miss Molly stretched out on Granny's right.

Twila hardly ever uses the same words in her ceremonies, although she always strives for the same end results. I never tire of watching and listening to her, soaking up new ways for age-old rituals. She walked the circle, murmuring her chant of respect and plea for help from all of her Universe contacts. The elements: earth, air, fire, and water. The guides and spirits. Then she settled down between Antonio and Trucker and reached for Granny's hand, as I did. We left Antonio disconnected from the circle.

"How are you feeling?" Twila asked Antonio.

"Peaceful still," he acknowledged. "Yet...yet...I have a yearning that I don't quite recognize."

"You will," she told him. With a nod at Granny and me, she began, "Envision the light, the white light that we know is both protection and portal, depending on our need for its use. As we begin, spread the light from within yourself to outside yourself. It will brighten, and it will grow more powerful, and then expand to either side of you. The light from each and every one of us will meld and grow ever stronger. Now it is of its own."

She paused, then continued, "It is circling and joining with the Universal light. And we are ready to ask for what we seek." She raised her voice. "I call upon the powers of the Universe to aid this lost soul whose earth name is Antonio. He seeks to leave this earthly plane and cross through the light to join his loved ones. I plea with the powers of the Universe to aid his quest."

She fell silent. Then it began. It will never cease to amaze me, no matter how many times I'm involved in one of Twila's ceremonies to assist a troubled soul. The lightening of the atmosphere, the growing sense of goodwill and joy. The light that descends from above, which begins as a small flare, then widens and grows in height and length until it is a gleaming portal. The door that actually opens in the brightness.

Antonio slowly rose to his feet, an expression of awe on his face. "I can feel all those I love so very close."

"They are," Twila whispered. "Just on the other side of that door. But before you go through…"

"I understand," Antonio said before she could finish her caution. "I thought I knew best, not only for myself, but for others. I made judgments that I should not have. And I wish you all to know that it was not my purpose that dreadful night to cause Patrick's death. The friction and anger between us got out of hand. I left my home and family soon after, partially in cowardice. I could not face my sister's tears and heartbreak, even though she was not aware of what I'd done."

"Then you have learned a lesson during your existence," Twila murmured.

"Yes. Yes, I have." The dark ghost floated out of our circle, over to the door, and the light outlined him. He hesitated, then glanced back. "Thank you. I cannot think of any stronger words than that."

"Save me a dance when I show up," Granny called.

"*Senora,* it will be my pleasure," he replied. Then stepped through the doorway.

CHAPTER 41

"One down, who knows how many more to go," Twila said. She rose and walked the opposite way around us, murmuring to release the circle and gathering her braided cord.

I helped Granny to her feet, and she sighed a disappointed sound. "By cracky, I bets that Antonio was the cat's meow in his day."

I wasn't quite as ready as Granny to dismiss Antonio's formerly human qualities, but Twila said, "He had a lot of good qualities, but his misguided attempts to control others were not those of his finer side. He thought he knew better than what was in their own hearts."

"We have to find Jack," I reminded her, although for some reason I wasn't that worried about him. And Twila didn't appear to be, either.

"He may be having a lesson of his own," she said. "Where is the men's dressing room?"

I led off. We traversed the basement back toward the stairwell, which I yearned to ascend and get out of here. Yet leaving the basement meant facing...I veered behind the stairwell, and Twila and I assisted Granny across some shaky boards that overlay a dip in the floor. A hallway intersected on the right, and I entered it. Our tennis shoes whispered silently on the concrete floor, and we didn't speak. Even Trucker's toenail clicks were muted.

"What are the dressing rooms like?" Twila asked as we walked.

"Your typical locker room, not that different than you find in a health club today."

We'd reached the door to the men's dressing room, which was partially closed, and I steeled myself to push it open. Placed the flat of my hand on it...and shoved before I could rethink. And there was Jack.

"What the hell took y'all so long?" he growled. "Get me out of here!"

To stifle my laughter and avoid antagonizing that six foot of irate male even further, I clamped my teeth tightly over my bottom lip. At least Antonio's tornado of light had a sense of modesty. Jack was jammed back first into the same locker I'd first spied Patrick beside, arms at his side, his shoulders squeezed so tightly that he couldn't escape. Naked, as was Patrick when I first saw him, but a spotless white towel covered Jack from waist to mid-thigh. His clothing lay neatly folded on a spindly chair across the room.

"Can't you wiggle free?" Twila asked.

"If I could have," Jack spat back at her, "I would have!"

"I think maybe there was a force field in front of you before to hold you in place," Twila said, reminding me of the force field Trucker had encountered. "Try again."

Jack did. The strain showed in his body and on his face. He moved his legs, but his shoulders were jammed far too tightly into the locker. "It isn't working," he said unnecessarily.

Twila handed Trucker's leash to Granny, and I set Miss Molly down and tied her leash to Trucker's collar. Leaving Granny to mind the animals, Twila and I approached Jack. Warily, though, at least on my part. Cajun fury emanated from that locker in a force that might even rival the tornado's power.

"I'm not sure what we can do," I said to him. "You're in there pretty good."

We halted a couple feet back, and Twila held her hand out in front of her, checking for the force field, I guessed. She confirmed that it was gone by waving her hand around, then touching Jack's chest.

"Hmmm, damp," she mused. "Like you'd just gotten out of the shower."

Jack glanced over at one of the shower stalls, and I could read the confirmation on his face. "Uh oh," I said. "You've lost your quince protection."

"It didn't keep that…that…whatever it was from picking me up and carrying me!" he gritted.

"Then we'll need something stronger." Twila crouched beside her satchel.

"Get me the hell out of here first!" Jack demanded.

In the background, Granny cackled with glee and said, "Don't be too quick 'bout helpin' him outta there. I's enjoying the show here."

"Then you can handle Jack when we get him out," I said.

"Well, mebbe not," she replied.

While Twila ignored us and dug in her backpack, I ran my hands over Jack's shoulders and down his arms. If I'd been as honest as Granny, I'd have admitted that I was enjoying this, also. It had been a while since I'd touched a naked Jack. That part of our marriage wasn't the problem. There wasn't any hint at all of a space to work my fingers into and help him push out of there. Yet the action did give me an idea.

"Do you have more quince soap, Twila?" She handed me a bar, and I unwrapped the plastic around it.

"That stuff's already proven useless," Jack snapped.

His continued unappreciative attitude sapped away any stirs his naked nearness gave rise to, and I'd had enough. I glared at him and said, "If you don't shut up and let us work, I'm going to leave you here. But—" I dropped my hand to his waist "—before I go, I'm taking the towel!"

Jack shut up. His mouth, anyway. He obviously couldn't control his anger, evidenced by his clenched jaw. I couldn't blame him. It must have been quite a ride.

"Tell us what happened," I said in a calmer voice as I started to work the bar of quince soap across the back of his shoulders.

285

He stared over the top of my head as he said, "That force...whatever the hell it was...came at us. I remember you tucking Miss Molly down beside Trucker, and the next thing I knew, I was airborne. It..." He paused for a moment, then continued, "It wasn't what you'd expect. Not a mad dervish, like you'd think would be inside a tornado. But I was powerless, couldn't move. An instant later, I was in here. Well, in the shower, water gushing over me."

"There hasn't been any water to those showers for decades," I pointed out.

"Let him tell the story his way, Alice," Twila chided.

"Yes, do that, *Chère*," Jack snapped. "Then I was in this locker. Jammed tight, unable to get out."

"Did it throw you in here?" Twila asked as she rose. "Hurt you?"

"No," he admitted. "I was...I was just here."

I finished rubbing the soap over everywhere I could reach, concentrating on the boundaries of Jack's shoulders and arm, then rewrapped the soap in the plastic.

"You're going to have to try to work yourself back and forth," I told him. "See if the soap will help you slide out of there. Twila and I can help, but first see what you can do."

Jack strained once again for escape. Those solid muscles bulged and his mouth tightened with effort. Immediately it became apparent that his struggle only tightened his prison when his muscles bunched. I stepped close again and tried to work my fingers behind his shoulders. I kept my nails short for typing, so I wasn't afraid of hurting him. It didn't seem that the back part of him was the problem, though, and I concentrated on trying to squeeze my fingers along his upper arms.

Touching him should have given me warning, but I reacted a split second too late when his muscles re-bunched again. At first he strained with his right shoulder, the side I was working my fingertips down. Then he relaxed that shoulder, and I jerked my fingertips free from where they'd gotten trapped, and instinctively stuck them in my mouth to suck on the pain. Unfortunately, I didn't step back, and when Jack grunted with effort and popped loose from the locker...

...he popped right into me.

He grabbed for me, but I was already on the way down and slid right through his grasp. Instinctively, I reached for support, but all I got was the towel. And when I hit the floor on my ass, renewing that pain in my tailbone, I ended up between Jack's legs. Staring up at...and it was within mouth reach.

"Oh, my," Twila said. She turned her back immediately, but I guess Granny didn't share Twila's need to give Jack his privacy.

"My, my, my," she said. "Guess bedtime wasn't one of the things that caused that there silly deevorce."

Jack whipped the towel out of my grasp and secured it around him. With a sigh, he reached down and stuck his hands beneath my armpits, lifted me back to my feet. For an instant, we stared at each other, lost in memories, at least on my part. Maybe his, too, since I recognized that look in his eyes. Stormy, dark, a prelude to...

"You hurt?" he asked, which broke the sensation.

"A little," I admitted. I rubbed my rear. "But I'll be all right."

"This will help," Twila said. She handed me a bottle of some sort of lotion. "And it will replace the quince protection."

"Now what sort of supposed magic are you giving us?" Jack growled. But when she challenged him with her gaze, he blushed and glanced away, obviously still embarrassed at the show he'd put on. Well, with my help.

Twila didn't react to his ill-mannered tone. In fact, I noticed a hint of unease on her face, and I didn't think it was a lingering embarrassment on her part at witnessing Jack's nudity. I examined the bottle of lotion in my hand, which she'd already uncapped, then sniffed it. Immediately I stifled a gasp and grabbed Twila's arm to lead her away from Jack and Granny, out into the hallway.

"Is this what I think it is?" I whispered.

"Well, Alice, we've heard that it's supposed to work."

"But we've never tried it! And you said the recipe you found was too faded in places to be sure you could read the exact proportions!"

"I didn't make this," she assured me. "I got it from Cat Dancer a few years ago. In New Orleans. At the same time she was explaining voodoo to me. And Cat told me that she'd added a spell to it, so in addition to the healing qualities, it was an extremely strong protective."

"It's still belladonna," I said. "Poisonous."

"In the wrong quantities," Twila admitted. "But healers used it for years to treat rheumatism and other joint pains. In the correct proportions, it won't kill anyone, as long as the healer is careful. It will help your pain, and in addition to that, give us another layer of protection."

"Us? You won't have any trouble getting Granny to use it, but Jack? Especially if he knows what it is. Lots of Cajuns believe in healers, but Jack's not one of them."

"Let me handle Jack. And don't forget, we'll need to smooth some on Trucker and Miss Molly."

We reentered the dressing room, and only Granny stood there with the animals, a frown on her face. "Where's Jack?" I asked.

"He made me promise to keep my eyes front and center," she grumbled. Then she pointed a gnarled finger and giggled. "But guess he didn't trust me. Since ain't no shower curtains left in here, he went into that there shower that's got a door facing the other way to get dressed."

"Don't get dressed yet, Jack," I called as I walked over to the spot Granny indicated. "You need to put this lotion on you for protection."

"He won't be able to reach his back," Twila reminded me, and I froze in mid-step. That's just what I wanted to do right now—distract myself by smoothing lotion over a body I'd just been reminded had absolutely no flaws. I needed to re-ground myself, prepare for that seventh floor, not let memories erode my concentration.

Jack stepped out of the shower and said, "I'm already dressed. You put quince back on me, so that should be enough. For you ladies, anyway. I still don't believe in this stuff."

I blew out a frustrated breath, but before I could antagonize Jack any further, Twila took the bottle of lotion in her hands and walked straight up to him.

"Either I can put it on you, or you can let Alice," she said. "But you're not going with us without this new protection."

"As I told you outside the hotel," Jack said, "there's no way you can stop me."

"I can damn sure make you think, though," Twila shot back at him. "One of the miracles of protective devices is the power of the human mind along with the device's proven capabilities. Capabilities that have been shown thousands of times over the years to work. And we, the ones that use them, believe in them. But if we foolishly allow someone along that doesn't accept our guidance, it can distract us from our purpose. We have to keep an eye on that person, because we're well aware that he's vulnerable. That can have catastrophic results. And the catastrophe may not happen to the one who was stupid enough not to listen to us. It can happen to someone else, someone who believes in the protection but is vulnerable because he or she has to keep an eye on stupid."

"So I'll be to blame if something happens to one of you," Jack said grimly.

"Yes," was Twila's short answer.

"Give me the damn lotion. But first, tell me what I'm using. And why."

Uh oh. How was Twila going to handle this? I firmly kept my own mouth shut.

"Actually," Twila said, "I'm not sure what all is in it." *Well, she didn't lie.* "A friend who's crossed over now gave it to me, and she didn't tell me exactly how she made it. She just told me that it would work in situations where something extremely powerful was needed."

Relief filled me when Jack only said, "Well, after what just happened to me, I guess I'll take your friend's word on that."

My relief was short-lived, though, when Jack looked at me and said, "You'll have to help me get it on my back, *Chère*. And I'll help you."

"I've got another bottle in my satchel. I'll take care of Granny, and she can also help me with the animals." Twila took a second to wink at me before she left me alone with Jack and that bottle.

CHAPTER 42

Twila led Trucker and I carried Miss Molly. At the basement stairwell, Jack picked up Granny. Up the stairwell. Out of the basement. From the lobby to the mezzanine, then five more stories of narrow, crumbling stairwells...to the seventh floor. Panting slightly from the effort, Jack set Granny down in the hallway. Since it was daylight now, broken doors lining the hallway allowed light from the windows on the outer walls to penetrate. Still, we held our flashlights at the ready.

No tornado met us, only an unsettling quiet. A waiting quiet. I could almost hear it holding its breath in expectation, and I nearly jumped out of my skin when Twila spoke. "Patrick? Mary Ann? Are either of you here?"

No one answered. No one visualized. Not even a precursory chill to forewarn me of an approaching force or specter. The hairs on the back of my neck and arms lay quiescent, rather than standing at attention and waving like tiny headless snakes.

"Are you sure this is necessary?" Jack asked. "There's a legitimate murder investigation going on elsewhere."

"And we're not legitimate?" I snapped before I could stop myself.

He shrugged and jammed his fingertips into his jeans pockets.

"The two of you need to put aside your differences," Twila cautioned. "You're going to need all your concentration, Alice."

Me? She'd warned me, but until then, I'd held out a tiny bit of hope that she might forget. "I'm not ready," I whimpered.

"Patrick contacted you," she said. "You're the center of this. You made the commitment, and you have to see it through."

"I'm ready, willing and..." I bit back *able,* but the unsaid word hung in the air. "I'm totally ready and willing," I repeated, "to assist in any way I can. I just think it makes more sense for experience to take control."

"Control is the problem." Twila frowned that frown of confusion that sent chills down my spine, and my shaky efforts at confidence plummeted. "You can't lose control for even an instant. Or you might not get it back."

"What would happen then?"

"I have no idea," she admitted.

"Don't we haveta go steal Mary Ann's body outta the morgue to put her back together again?" Granny asked. "Like we did with that there Bucky and his head?"

"Don't even think about it," Jack muttered.

"We're not," Twila assured him. "But not because you say so. Mary Ann didn't die here, but something ties her to this place. I think when we reveal that, she'll find peace and cross over on her own. She hasn't appeared that concerned about her disjointed soul, although she claims to be vain. Bucky was adamant that he wanted his physical head back before he'd settle down."

"What about Patrick?" I asked. "He's...for want of a better description...disjointed, too. I thought at first that his condition had something to do with Antonio. Maybe..." Hope filled my voice. "Maybe Patrick's already gone on now. Maybe we're just dealing with Mary Ann."

Twila's brown eyes focused on me in wordless sympathy.

"Maybe not," I muttered. "But why hasn't Patrick appeared again? We can't sort things out on our own."

"We have to try."

"We need another layer of white light."

"Too much will interfere with communication, Alice. You know that. We're still carrying the white light from a while ago, and the belladonna in the lotion. That will have to suf—"

"Belladonna?" Jack interrupted. "You smeared us with nightshade? That shit's poison."

"Hmmmm," Granny mused. "I heard the devil himself tends nightshade plants. But it sure hep'd my arthritis. Ain't got near the aches and pains I had a half hour ago. Mebbe it's better than asafetida."

Ignoring Jack's concerns, Twila explained to Granny, "The lotion needs to be used with care. This I have carries more than the plant in it. It's been blessed."

"Oh," Granny said with a sage nod.

As the chatter around me ceased, I snuggled Miss Molly closer and stroked her while I stared down that hallway tunneled in front of me. It actually did remind me of a tunnel—a long, dark, narrow tunnel. My vision filtered out the available daylight, leaving only that hollow tube. Perhaps I was already focusing...on the goal at the end of it.

Trucker whined and leaned against my legs, his weight comforting rather than a bother. Yet some inner sense surfaced, and I reluctantly handed Miss Molly to Jack and stepped away from Trucker, stepped away from everyone else in our group. Miss Molly meowed faintly, and Trucker woofed quietly, but I stiffened my resolve. I wanted them protected as well as possible. I'd much rather have hit the Internet or a well-stocked library for any research available from other paranormal investigators before I ventured into this. Browse out-of-print tomes in search of answers Twila didn't have. Too late now, though.

A corner of my mind was aware of Twila shuttling Granny and Jack a little further away from me, back down the hallway in the opposite direction. Leaving me the necessary distance to ground myself...prepare myself...without any distracting interference. I drew in and blew out breath, concentrated on asking my spirit guide to intercede for me and bridge my fledgling power to each and every bit of help available from the Universe.

Then I called on the one person I'd always felt I could count on, but never bothered before, and whispered, "Grandmere Alicia? I need you."

I'm here, dear child.

I wanted to breathe a sigh of relief, but it just wouldn't come. Instead, I held out a questing hand, and someone accepted it in a featherlight grasp.

"Are we ready?"

Yes.

First I turned around and sought Twila's concurrence. She smiled at me, and I knew she could see Grandmere. I took a few reluctant steps toward that door.

No fear, child. Fear feeds fear.

I firmed my stride, and everything around me receded until only that door loomed as I walked slowly through the tunnel. Just before I reached our goal, Patrick visualized. I didn't need Twila's low-voiced, "Alice," of warning. I knew it was the doppelganger all on my own. I halted in place until it floated into the suite, then reached for the doorknob.

Turned it. Threw the door open and stomped into the room.

All right, damn it, trip kitty be damned. No sense throwing caution to the wind. I edged in. But maybe that was the right idea. I had time to warily scan the room as well as fine-tune my senses for invisible—or visible—threats.

I frowned. It was the same room. On my left, an open bathroom door: a shattered mirror above a dust-layered sink with gold faucets, a long, claw-foot tub with a shredded shower curtain half pulled around it. The commode slanted to one side. You'd have to have a secure hold elsewhere to sit on it. Ahead of me, the same furniture in place: a dilapidated matching couch and loveseat, two lounge chairs four-cornered around a spindle-legged coffee table, end tables conveniently separating the seating arrangement. The tall armoire in one corner, one door hanging by a hinge. A marble fireplace on the right, the fire pit yawning emptily. Overhead, a brass chandelier similar to the ones in the lobby hung from the ceiling. On the left, that bedroom door...closed.

No color, though. On the previous trip, I could see the coloration of the room, albeit muted with age and deterioration. Now it reminded me of the gray-scale tones when I played with pictures in my photo software. Not even stark black and white, only shades of misty gray.

They all sat there, though. Patrick and his double on the settee, both naked, although no skin tones, only gray murkiness. Mary Ann—the top half of her—hovering in one of the lounge chairs, the green dress washed out to colorlessness nearly invisible against the muted background. And someone else I didn't recognize standing in a far corner. An elderly man dressed in a Twenties-style suit similar to the one Patrick wore at times. The shadows hid his face even with the light pouring in from the curtainless windows. Or maybe it was the wide brim of the hat turned downward over his forehead.

Four of them. I recounted just to be sure. One. Two. Three. Four.

You're recounting to delay things. Grandmere's tone held tolerant laughter.

Twila's gentle shove forced me on into the room so she and the rest of our slapdash group could join me. Our greeting committee sat there without greeting us.

"Well," I said aloud. "Some of us know each other, but maybe those who don't will have the courtesy to introduce themselves to the others?"

Not one damned ghost responded. They just sat and stood there, hovered in Mary Ann's case, faces blank.

"None of them are aware of anyone else," Twila said.

"They don't even appear to be aware of us," I reflected. "What's going on?"

One. Two. Three. Four.

"But you said—" Then I caught Grandmere's meaning. "We have to concentrate on their problems individually." Neither Grandmere nor Twila confirmed my deduction. I wasn't certain it was correct myself, but...*In for a penny, in for a pound.* "Ennie, meenie, miney...mo!" I pointed at the man back in the corner.

He came to life...well, ghost-life. With a whoosh, the man morphed and whirled out of that corner, directly at me. He was also a tornado of light, whoever...whatever he was. Only it in the room glowed with color:

hundreds of dancing circles and stars of red, green, blue, yellow inside a bright white funnel.

"Ah, shit," Jack muttered.

I didn't glance at him to see how he prepared to meet an entity similar to the one that had unclothed him. And despite my trembling knees, I didn't cringe or retreat. Some inner sense confirmed that acting like a yellow-bellied coward would definitely be the wrong move here. I squeezed Grandmere's hand for courage, and actually felt the firm, warm grasp in return. Then I threw my arms up, palms outward. Into the cacophony of increasing wind and noise, I said in a low, stern voice, "Stop!"

Amazingly—to me, at least—it worked. The tail on the tornado curved forward to brake the momentum, skidding and ruffling the shag loops on the carpet like tiny cascading waves on the lake across from my cabin. It halted a bare six inches from my outstretched palms, whirled there for several long seconds as I focused utterly on it, then reformed into the short, chunky man. A full-color man in a wide-lapelled suit, gray jacket and trousers with thin blue stripes, a white shirt and tie with blue and white angled stripes. A white carnation was pinned to his lapel and a three-cornered handkerchief poked from the left-hand suit pocket. Dapper came to mind. Tailored suit, not a wrinkle in sight, starched shirt, expertly knotted tie. But I could actually smell the cloying carnation scent, and I hate those flowers. They always remind me of funerals.

He wore black and white spats on his feet, buttonholed up the sides. The soles definitely could have made those ectoplasm footsteps. And I could see his face now, the sneer on his fleshy lips, the furrowed brow when he clenched one hand and flicked that hat up with his thumb.

He sniffed, then backed up a couple steps. "What's that smell?" I continued to stare at him without answering. If he didn't know what belladonna smelled like, that was to my advantage. "You just can't take a warning, can ya?" he snarled.

"Who are you?" I demanded.

"None of your bidness! Get outta here! Ain't I made that clear enough?"

"Very clear," I told him. "But in your condition, your commands have no power over us."

"What condition?"

I sighed. "You're dead."

"You're full of crap," he spat. "I've been waitin' here for years. And if all you people would just stay away, she'd be back!"

"How many years?" I asked in a calm voice, ignoring the new clue to his presence for now. "Do you have any idea how many?"

"Of course!" But he frowned, puzzlement in his eyes. "It's been...well, I...it don't matter! Get outta here...or you'll be sorry!"

"We're not leaving."

The urge to check my companions grew in me. Just a glance, to assure myself they were still with me, that I wasn't standing here all by my lonesome trying to reason with a ghost that refused to accept his...deadness. I knew better than to break contact, though. But I guess that tricky, nameless ghost had evidently learned a few things over the years. Or brought his deceptive personality with him into this existence.

"Rat!" he shouted as he pointed behind me. "Get it, cat!"

I swiveled in time to see the panic-stricken looks on Granny's and Twila's faces. Looks which I'm sure mirrored mine. Granny shrieked, grabbed Jack and nearly climbed back into his arms. Twila gasped and backed against the wall, her eyes searching for the rat, as mine were. It dawned on me instantly what the ghost had done when I realized that Miss Molly sat unconcerned by Jack's feet, tongue-combing her fur.

"You—" I whirled back. Too late.

The ghost's evil laughter filled the air as he swirled into his tornado form and zoomed back into his corner. When he rematerialized, he held a tommy gun.

Rat-a-tat-tat! Rat-a-tat-tat! The bullets zipped from the gun barrel in flares of flame and the smell of cordite filled the air. "There's your rat!" he shouted, then threw back his head and roared with that malevolent laughter we'd heard in the hallway earlier.

Jack grabbed Twila and shoved her into the bathroom, dropped Granny beside her and slammed the door. He raced toward me, slapping his hand against his hip for his pistol—which wasn't there. "Get down, Alice!"

I dodged Jack's charge, and another barrage of *rat-a-tat-tat*'s smoked from the tommy gun as the ghost waved it back and forth to spray the entire room. With cop instinct, Jack belly-splatted on the floor, reaching for me as he dived. Missing me again.

I wouldn't have been human if I didn't admit that I was scared. Mouth dry, muscles between my legs clenched to hold back the threat of peeing myself, knees locked to counteract the urge to flee and hide in the bathroom with the other scaredy-cat women. Courage came from my mind firmly connected with Grandmere as she soothed, *Steady as she goes, dear heart.*

"Stay there, Jack," I ordered in a firm voice. He gaped at me and I checked on Trucker and Miss Molly. My pets connected with my gaze from where they sat side-by-side a few feet away, calmly taking in the performance. They both rose and sauntered through the hail of ghost bullets, over beside me, as the bathroom door eased open and Twila and Granny peeked out. They stayed in place, though, and my pets and I faced the ghost.

"What the hell?" the ghost muttered, then pulled the tommy gun close to his face to examine it.

When it pointed it at us again, I shrugged and said, "They're ghost bullets, like you. They won't hurt us."

He dropped the gun, and it disappeared into whatever realm it had come from. Pain filled his face, and I sensed the yearning need. "What is your name?" I repeated.

"R—Rocky," he stuttered.

"And her name?"

"Louisa," he whispered. "I told her I would be back. I told her this was my last job. I was leavin' the bidness. Never gonna do another heist. We was gonna go live on one of them South Sea islands."

I turned my head and caught Twila's attention. Motioned her forward. She knew what I needed, and by the time she was at my side, that dreamy expression was in her eyes.

"You were killed in that robbery," she told Rocky. "Someone warned the bank officials about your plans, and the G-men were waiting for you. Pictures of your and your friends' bullet-riddled bodies were splashed all over the papers. She loved you and couldn't handle the pain. She leaped from the window of the next room over and killed herself."

A ghostly tear actually streaked down Rocky's face. "Then that means...she's dead, like me. She won't be coming back here to meet me."

"No," I said in as sympathetic tone as I could manage, given the fact I wasn't real prone to feeling sorry for gangsters. "You'll have to go to her."

"How?" he pleaded.

"Just take my hand," a strange female voice said.

Twila and I stared in awe, as we did at times when unexpected specters that we hadn't called forth visualized. Louisa—it had to be her from the look on Rocky's face—stood in front of the fireplace. She was about five foot, blond hair bobbed, spit curls on her forehead. She wore a low-cut, garish red gown circled in rows of brass bangles, so tight I figured she wouldn't have been able to move in it, had she been in physical form. A gun moll if I'd ever seen one.

She did move, though. Slithered, really. Hand outstretched, she snaked over to Rocky, hips swinging back and forth. Their hands touched, and Twila bowed her head and whispered a low chant. The wall behind Rocky and Louisa brightened into brilliant white, then split open. But when they turned and took a step toward the door, Rocky paused.

"What will happen to me?" he whined. "I ain't real sure I'm ready to face my punishment."

Louisa patted his arm. "You never killed no one, honey. Just took their money."

"I would've a minute ago," he insisted. "I thought they was keepin' me away from you."

"There's forgiveness waiting," she assured him. "It won't even seem bad waiting out your time until you're forgiven. Just like a few years in the pen."

"Guess I can handle that," he replied. And they both stepped through the door, which closed behind them.

"You opened that doorway without your usual preparation," I murmured to Twila in awe.

"No," she denied. "I never completely relinquished the ceremony in the basement. I'm carrying a few necessary things from that with us." Then she continued, "Good job, Alice."

I dusted my hands together. "Two down," I added to Twila's earlier comment. "Three more to go."

She smiled at me, then as Jack rose to his feet with a confused look on his face, started back toward the bathroom. I grabbed a handful of Twila's jacket and jerked her to a halt.

"Huh uh," I ordered in my new, in-charge voice. "You mostly rested that one out. This time you're in for the entire show."

She giggled and snapped me a salute. "Aye, aye, Madame Captain. You're right. This one will be a double-header."

I eenie-meenie'd again and realized she was right. Mary Ann would be our final shot—oops, not a good word again, but accurate. If we followed Grandmere's instructions—which I intended to do—we would confront the ghost twins for the next round.

CHAPTER 43

"What the hell just happened here?" Jack asked.

"We'll explain later," I told him. "Go on over with Granny."

He didn't seem to hear me. He stared around the room, muttering, "I heard a tommy gun, but there aren't any bullet holes anywhere."

I sighed in exasperation, but Twila touched my arm and whispered, "We need to know what all he and Granny are aware of, so we can protect them."

Without any prodding, Jack went on, "Why's Patrick just sitting over there like he's deaf and dumb? He's had plenty to say so far."

"Who else do you see?" I asked quietly.

"Just him," Jack said with a shrug. "Now that that light funnel's disappeared. What was it?"

Twila and I exchanged glances, and while I refocused on the twin ghosts, she gently patted Jack's shoulder and led him over to Granny. "As Alice said, we'll tell you all about it in a little while, Jack. Your job right now is to take care of Granny. And not interfere with us."

Jack obediently slipped an arm around Granny's tiny figure to pull her close to his side. "Ummm, ummm, ummm," Granny said as she gazed up at him. "Mebbe when this is all over, you and me can go ridin' on that bike like you promised me one time. I know's a real nice private spot on the lake back home where we kin go skinny dippin'."

"Whatever you want, Granny," Jack murmured distractedly, and Granny slapped a hand on her knee and cackled with glee.

Quietly, while I kept my main concentration on the couch, Twila asked Granny who she could see. Granny confirmed that she was aware of each and every one of the otherworld beings in the room, and Twila asked her if she'd like a bit more protection.

"No siree," Granny informed her. "You might need my he'p. And I got my asafetida in my pocket." She pulled out that flowered hanky she always carried. Thankfully, it was knotted with a purple ribbon, since the smell of that stuff could rival the skunk smell I'd just defeated.

Twila hesitated, but I held out a hand and crooked a finger at her. She obligingly strolled back over, and we bookended Miss Molly and Trucker between us.

"Do you see the room in black and white rather than color?" I asked her.

"Yes. Strangest thing. It's like we're seeing another dimension, but not actually piercing the veil."

"Maybe it's because of the doppelganger," I reasoned. "Patrick's split somehow even in his ghost state. And it obviously doesn't have anything to do with Antonio, since he's not here now."

"Makes sense," she agreed. "More than one other dimension. One where ghosts can interact with the current world, but another one we haven't been aware of until now. One where entities like doppelgangers exist. Sort of like a person with multiple personalities, but in the afterlife."

"You have any idea how to rejoin a shattered personality? Once it's dead?"

"Research is your bailiwick, Alice. Didn't you use something like that in one of your books once?"

"There's a trigger in a person's life that separates the personalities," I recalled. "It's from abuse sometimes, sometimes from a severe emotional trauma. It's a protective device, a way for a person to shelter him or herself from the pain of the trauma. At times the alter personality can actually take control. That doesn't seem to be the situation here, though. That...that other side of Patrick just seems to...to be there."

"We can't rationalize the other dimensions by comparing them to what we know in this existence. They have their own configuration."

"Still, there is a configuration," I insisted. "A system for being."

"Or nonbeing," she said with a wry chuckle. "And we don't seem to be making any progress here."

"Where's Grandmere?" I concentrated, but no quiet reply thrust itself into my mind. "I guess she's left."

"She's a spirit," Twila reminded me. "Her time on other planes is limited. She probably had to take a breather."

I giggled, partially from nervousness at my now-flagging confidence. "She doesn't breathe."

"Oh, yeah, right." Her reply didn't help my sense of control one bit, since it indicated her confusion as we dealt with a situation we'd never encountered before. My mentor/teacher, my anchor, didn't have the answers here. We were both fledglings, feeling our way.

"Okay," I said. "What do we know about Patrick that could have triggered his...separation? He definitely wasn't abused. The car crash?"

"He only split from his physical body in that."

"Then it had to happen in his next existence," I reasoned. "A deep emotional pain."

Twila snapped her fingers, an astonishingly loud noise in the silent room. "The birth of his child! He claims he didn't know Consuela was pregnant. Yet he's spent this entire existence searching for knowledge of what happened to her after he died."

The vision appeared before us as though in response to the trigger of her accuracy. I had no doubt in my mind that Twila saw it, also, as did Trucker and Miss Molly. Trucker crouched on the floor and whimpered as he plopped his paws over his ears, and Miss Molly meowed that weird meow-ser sound that can set your teeth on edge. The woman's scream echoed in the room, and suddenly we weren't there any longer. Instead, now Twila, my pets, and I were the shadowy figures, lined against the wall in a hospital delivery room.

A beautiful, dark-haired Spanish woman lay on the delivery table, feet pushing against those uncomfortable metal stirrups, a sheet wrinkled over her protruding stomach. Sweat beaded her brow, and the expression on her face was a mixture of physical pain yet joy. A white-garbed doctor leaned between her bare legs, and a nurse in an outmoded, starched cap stroked her damp hair.

"Not much longer, dear," the nurse soothed.

"I...I can't!" Consuela said with an anguished moan. "Make it stop!"

"We can't, dear," the nurse said, then glanced at the doctor. "It's been hours. How much more can she stand?"

"Wait!" the doctor said in a tense voice. "Don't let her push again. I—"

Consuela screamed again and arched off the table. Utter pain replaced the trace of joy on her face, and her agony drowned out the nurse's efforts to comfort her.

"What's wrong, Doctor?" the nurse whispered when Consuela collapsed and her scream died to moans.

"Breach," he replied curtly. "Try to keep her quiet while I..."

Repulsed yet fascinated, since until now my only experience with childbirth had been post-delivery and clean, warm bundles of baby, I couldn't tear my gaze away as the doctor worked feverishly to turn the baby. But when Consuela arched again and screamed, "Patrick!" I flinched and saw Patrick standing over on the other side of the room. Terror and fear marred his handsome face, and he stretched his arms out in a seeking manner.

"We're losing her, Doctor," the nurse said in a worried voice.

I continued to focus on Patrick while Twila whispered, "She's losing too much blood. She's unconscious."

"Wake up, dear," the nurse pleaded. I could hear her hand pat Consuela's face. "You have to help us."

That's when Patrick split. One form of him floated up to the ceiling, the other still stood against the wall. Even in his ghost form his face—both faces—were pale.

"Her soul's leaving," Twila said. "The baby will die, also."

"Patrick!" I called across the room, and the doctor and nurse both snapped to attention and stared at each other.

"Who was that?" the nurse asked.

The doctor shook his head and said, "We've got to at least try to save the baby."

Patrick! This time I mentally called to him so I wouldn't distract the doctor and nurse from their lifesaving efforts. *You have to help her!*

"I can't," he cried in return. The doctor and nurse evidently didn't hear him, though.

I glanced at Consuela. She lay unconscious, and Twila was right. I could see a shimmer over her, a mist that rose in the shape of her body. But then it settled down again and rejoined her.

Patrick! It's not her time!

A stubborn set replaced the fear on the face of the Patrick hovering in the air. "I need her with me." But the Patrick against the wall said, "She's too young to die."

"We died young," the hovering Patrick insisted.

The shimmer over Consuela formed again. This time her form floated out of the pale, unresponsive body and hovered about a foot above it.

The baby, Patrick. Your baby. It deserves its life.

"The baby can come, too," Hovering Patrick said.

"No!" the other Patrick told him.

"Smelling salts," the doctor snapped. "And the scalpel."

"Get back here!" Patrick on the floor said. "We can save her!"

"No," Hovering Patrick said stubbornly. "It's not our place."

The Consuela form floated a foot higher. My mind froze for an instant, then cleared. I laid a hand on Trucker's head and whispered, "Go, boy."

Trucker trotted around the delivery table, Miss Molly at his heels. The dog bypassed the standing Patrick and stood on his hind legs, front legs braced against the wall. His teeth snapped an inch below Hovering Patrick's foot.

Patrick! Both of you! You're being selfish!

"I'm lonely," both of them replied. "So lonely."

Miss Molly jumped up and balanced herself on Trucker's front paws. She braced her front feet on the dog's muzzle and tilted her head back. "Meow!"

"Did you hear a cat?" the doctor asked, but he didn't follow up on his words as a pungent smell filled the room. The smelling salts; I recognized that odor.

Twila whispered, "They're trying to bring her back at least long enough to save the baby."

"What can I do?" I whispered frantically in return. "They won't listen to me."

All at once the tableau in front of me froze. Trucker against the wall, Miss Molly balanced on him, the two Patricks motionless, the doctor and nurse immobile over Consuela's physical body. But the Consuela shape had disappeared and a chill engulfed me, then a strange warmth.

And I wasn't in the delivery room. Instead, I lay on the bed inside that seventh-floor suite amidst tangled sheets, my body in the throes of delicious lovemaking. The man tangled with my sweaty, flushed, and yearning-for-fulfillment body wasn't Patrick, though. Jack joined with me, and he both soothed and stroked me. Ran his hands down my sides and cupped my hips, lifting me even closer to him. He buried his face in my neck and cried, *"Chère!"*

And the climax shattered me into a million pieces. All I could do was hold him, cling to him, legs around his slender hips, arms slipping on his sweaty back and fingernails digging. *Jack!*

And then I was back in the delivery room. Standing beside Twila, who wrapped an arm around my waist as though aware that my unsteady, nearly boneless legs threatened to spill me to the floor. Brown eyes twinkling, she winked at me. Somehow I buttressed both my body and my emotions and tore my gaze away from Twila to the Patrick across the room. He stared back at me, an expression of awe on his face.

"We only had that one time," he whispered. "She was so alive, had her whole life in front of her."

"Is," I told him. "Has. At this point, anyway. Unless you take her away from it. And your child. Unless your fear and guilt over not being with her when she was suffering like this denies that to her."

"But she lived," Patrick said. "I have a granddaughter."

"That's right," I assured him. "So you did make the right decision, even though you've obviously blocked that out. Forgotten it, and been trying to remember all these years. That's why there are two of you, one suffering the guilt, one still lonesome and unsure if he made the right decision."

"Good going, Alice," Twila praised. "I think you figured it out."

"I hope so," I told her, less confident than she sounded.

Patrick stared up at his twin, and Trucker woofed and strained. Miss Molly caught the twin's toe in her mouth and pulled. The twin glanced at Consuela...the Consuela who now hovered upright a few feet from him, a sad expression on her face. Miss Molly tugged, yet the twin resisted.

Go, Consuela said. It's not forever. And our child needs me.

The lower Patrick stretched his arm and moved a step away from the wall, the same yearning expression on his face as that of his twin as he reached for Consuela's spirit.

"I love you," they both said.

I will always love you, she told them both.

The two Patricks joined hands. Trucker backed away from the wall, and Miss Molly balanced on his back now, the twin's toe still in her grasp. With a flash of light, the two Patricks merged. Twila murmured another chant, and a doorway appeared in the ceiling.

"Thank you for everything," the now-one Patrick said as he floated through the doorway. Then Twila and I stood alone watching the doctor and nurse back at work as Trucker and Miss Molly trotted over to our side of the room.

The doctor gave a triumphant grunt and held a blood-smeared baby up by her feet. He smacked her once on the butt, and the welcome first wail of a successful birth echoed in the room. He handed the baby to the nurse, who wrapped her in the towel she held, leaving an opening for the doctor to cut the umbilical cord.

When the baby was free, the doctor and nurse shared a sad look. "Too bad about the mother," the doctor said.

"Can I hold her?" Consuela asked, and both the doctor and nurse stared at Consuela in awe.

The nurse found her voice first. "You sure can, Mother." She placed the baby girl in Consuela's arms. "But just for a second. I need to clean her up and take a couple health precautions."

"My precious," Consuela whispered. She tore her gaze away from her daughter for a brief second and smiled at us.

Then Twila, my pets, and I stood back in the suite. Mary Ann still waited for us, and Granny stood by the bathroom door. But Jack was collapsed on one of the lounge chairs, a flushed look I recognized on his face. Heat blushed up my cheeks.

"Uh...were you always in the delivery room?" I asked Twila.

She winked at me without answering. When the heat of embarrassment flushed down my neck, though, she surrendered and said, "I stayed there to keep an eye on things while you were...busy."

"Thank goodness," I said. "You can explain what happened to me later." Then I glanced at the bedroom door and noticed that it was open a couple inches.

"Opened all on its own," Granny said when I glared at her.

"Before or during?" I demanded.

She grinned so wide her eyes disappeared in her multitude of wrinkles and didn't answer that. "I did's turn off my hearin' aid for a while. Jack, he come out and stumbled over to that there chair. I been keepin' an eye on him."

CHAPTER 44

"There's no time for this," Twila cautioned. "Look."

Mary Ann's half body rose into the air and floated towards the corner of the room where Rocky and the gun moll had disappeared.

"She's searching for the door across the veil," I whispered.

"We have to stop her!"

"Why?" I muttered, but I followed Twila as she raced across the room. "We want her to go on, don't we?"

"Not yet." Twila positioned herself between Mary Ann and the corner, and the ghost descended until she and Twila faced off.

"Get out of the way," Mary Ann spat.

Twila leaned toward Mary Ann until she and the half-ghost were nose-to-nose. "Make me."

Oh, good grief. Just what we needed, a cat fight between Twila and a headstrong entity. Twila wouldn't back down, and although I'd never seen her lose in the end, there was always a first time. She'd run from the first tornado we confronted. But she'd never, ever tried to stop a ghost from crossing over. We'd always both assisted them in any way we could. Would the powers of the Universe abandon us if we pulled a ploy like this? Come to think of it, *we* was the operative word here. Twila had told me all along that it needed to be a joint effort this go-round. But did I dare interfere, even though I thought she might be going about this confrontation the wrong way? Interfere with my leader, teacher, mentor?

"Uh..." I began.

"Shut up, Alice," Twila shot at me. "I'll take care of this one."

"Oh, yeah?" Mary Ann snarled at the same instant I said, "Like hell you will!"

Temper controlling me, I stomped over to the two of them and shoved Twila aside so I could stand in front of the ghost. But I made the mistake of continuing my argument with Twila instead of concentrating on Mary Ann. "You put me in charge this time. Go on back over there with the others."

I caught a nuance in her expression that didn't make sense, and she unexpectedly bumped her hip against mine. I staggered back against the wall. Then she pointed her finger in Mary Ann's face and said, "Get your ass back over in that chair. We've got some questions for you before you leave."

"She doesn't have an ass, Twila." Still angry at her overbearing attitude, I tried to push her aside again. She wouldn't budge.

"She doesn't need an ass to act like one." Twila clenched her fist and shook it under Mary Ann's nose, since she did have one of those.

"Who are you calling an ass?" Mary Ann spat.

"No one," I attempted to soothe the half-ghost. "Twila, she saved us from Delroy. She's on our side."

"She damn sure is," Twila said. "Our side of the veil. And I want to know what she's doing here. Why she's still hanging around."

"Just let her go," I said. "Open the door for her."

"Yes," Mary Ann said. "Open it and get out of my way."

Twila moved aside and waved a hand at me. "If you think that's what you need to do, then have at it, Alice. You've never opened the door on your own before."

Uh oh. Not only didn't I feel competent to perform that ceremony all by my lonesome, Twila's behavior told me in no uncertain terms that she'd block any effort I made. "Look at her," I pleaded. "She's ready. We don't have any right to keep her here."

Twila stepped back and set her hands on her hips. "Yeah, look at her. Here she is, in our time, but dressed like some Twenties floozy. That dress shows her tits. And by the way, sweetie, you need a boob job. Your tits are trying to look at your belly button. Your ass is probably sagging, too. At your age, showing off your middle-aged problems is definitely *not* sex appealing."

Fingers arched, Mary Ann reached for Twila's neck and muttered, "Bitch."

Twila stood her ground, though, and Mary Ann jerked her hands back. "Can't get past the belladonna, can you?" she sneered.

Mary Ann changed tactics. "I need to go. Please."

My heart went out to her. I didn't like to think about my own death, but I couldn't imagine wanting to cross over and being denied. Yet...Twila had to have some reason for acting like this, although I wasn't a bit comfortable playing referee between the two of them.

Referee? Oh, now I get it.

'Bout time, Twila whispered into my mind.

I schooled my expression to lock in the sympathy I'd felt and said to Mary Ann, "We're not going to get past Twila right now." Cupping a hand beside my mouth as though to keep Twila from hearing me, I continued, "She's being mean. Let's go sit down and wait until she isn't paying any attention to us. Then I'll help you cross over."

Mary Ann conceded grudgingly, but at least I got her back over to the chair—the one right beside Jack. He shivered, but focused on me rather than the cause of his unease. That look in his eyes as he stared at me didn't have a thing to do with a nearby ghost. He glanced at the bedroom door, then back.

"*Chère...*"

"Not now, Jack," I murmured.

Granny toddled over and settled on the couch, her walking stick propped between her knees, and Trucker and Miss Molly deserted me in favor of her. Trucker lay down beside Granny with a dog-sigh of contentment, and Miss Molly perched on Granny's lap. Strangely enough, even though Granny had crossed into the inner dimension of this room, she retained her color, as did my pets and Jack. Yet Twila, Mary Ann, as well as the rest of the room, were still in gray tones, as I assumed I was. Yep, I confirmed with a glance down at my body.

I sank to the floor, and despite my tender tailbone, sat cross-legged in front of Mary Ann. I knew this bad cop/good cop routine that Twila was hamming up; I used it in my books often. Somehow I had to carry it off in real life now, though, and I was much better with the written word than as an actress.

"Maybe we can pacify that meanie," I told Mary Ann as I nodded toward where Twila still blocked the potential doorway across the veil. "She wants to know why you stayed here rather than cross over."

"Who are you talking to?" Jack asked.

"Mary Ann," I told him. "And you could help me out here, if you were so inclined."

"What? How? I don't do ghosts."

"You don't do crime very well, either, do you, cop?" Mary Ann said, and Jack's eyes widened as he stared at the chair beside him and shivered again.

"You heard her, didn't you, Jack?"

He nodded slowly, then rose from the chair and backed away. I sighed in disappointment and returned my attention to Mary Ann, but surprising me, Jack sat on the floor beside me.

"Can you see her also?" I asked him.

"No. Just hear. She's the woman from the elevator?"

Before I could respond, Mary Ann spat, "They fooled all of you with that, didn't they? Just like before. You cops are all alike. You're boxed in by a set of supposed irrefutable facts that lead you by the nose!"

"What do you expect when people aren't truthful with us?" Jack demanded. "We're not mind readers. We make our deductions on what the evidence shows."

From the corner of my eye, I saw Twila move away from the wall, a finger to her lips to make sure I wouldn't leak her changed position. She motioned to Granny with her other hand, and Granny dumped Miss Molly to the floor and rose.

"Huh!" Mary Ann crossed her arms and continued to focus on Jack. "Even when people do try to help, you don't make them aware of what the repercussions will be! All you're interested in is closing your case. Getting all your *evidence* in line for trial. You don't care what happens to anyone's life afterwards. Nooooo. You can put them in your witness protection program. Give them another life. Well, what if I don't like that life you pick out for me? What if I want my other life back?"

Granny eased herself into the chair beside Mary Ann and said, "Problem is, honey, you don't have either life now."

"And you know whose fault that is?" Mary Ann pointed at Jack. "Cops like him. They think their only job is to put the bad guys away, then go on to the next case."

"That happens to be the way it works," Jack said mildly.

Twila directed Trucker and Miss Molly into the space beside me, then positioned herself behind Mary Ann's chair. The circle was complete, but I still didn't know what she had in mind. Or, frankly, didn't want to admit my suspicion. I'd thought—hoped desperately— that the ceremony with Antonio in the basement, helping Rocky and Louisa, and the visions that had taken us into their throes when we dealt with Patrick, would be all that were necessary.

"Out in the woods, you kept telling us that we needed to talk to Sam," I prodded Mary Ann. "What was that all about?"

"Obviously," she told me with a stubborn glare, "you haven't done that yet."

"We haven't been able to. Sam's been busy investigating your murder."

"Then maybe you should talk to that bitch of a reporter."

I gaped at the half-ghost. "Penny? She's been nothing but helpfulll-ll..." My tongue stuck against the back side of my top teeth as my mind clicked off points that hadn't seemed important until now. Jack patted me on the back, and I clamped my mouth shut and stared at him in horror.

"Oh, god," I murmured when I could speak again. He had that look on his face that told me he was heading down the path that led to the end of a crime investigation, also: grim mouth, dawning realization that matched mine in his eyes, yet a secretive posture that meant he wasn't quite ready to share anything with anyone else. I'd seen it before, so many times. His total focus at the moment was on just-the-facts, ma'am.

I swung my gaze around the circle. Granny wore a puzzled expression, Twila a similar one. The animals ignored me; they weren't interested in crime results. Mary Ann glared at me and nodded, then lifted her head in a haughty gesture and focused on Jack.

He started to rise to his feet, but I grabbed his arm and pulled him back down. "We're circled. Don't break it. We're not done here."

"I am," he insisted. "I need to—"

"Need to what, cop?" Mary Ann interrupted. "Go off half-cocked again before you know all the facts?"

"He's not going anywhere."

Camo Man/Delroy shoved Grandberg into the room, and the police chief stumbled over beside Jack. But it wasn't Delroy who'd spoken. Sam Peters stood to one side of the door, his pistol aimed at us. I recognized him, even from the few minutes I'd seen him back at the hotel...had it only been the day before? Or maybe recognition dawned because Mary Ann spat, "Fuck you, Sam!" at him.

"Been there, done that, ain't you, darlin'?" Sam said to Mary Ann. "And you just can't stay dead, can you? You had your chance five years ago. Thought you'd done all the damage you could. Got your so-called revenge when you ratted us out, and was out of here free and clear, weren't you?" He aimed that pistol at me. "Then Miz Writer/Ghostbuster had to stick her nose in. Ain't you heard, lady? Curiosity kills cats and nosy people."

"Hunter," I corrected him, surreptitiously laying a hand on Trucker's head so the dog wouldn't mistakenly confront that pistol. Delroy also still had his assault rifle, but right now it hung across his chest while he let Sam handle the situation. "We're ghost*hunters,* not ghost*busters.*"

"I don't give a damn what you call yourself," Sam snarled. "Pretty soon, you won't need to call yourself nothing, just dead."

For an instant, I thought I felt Twila touch my mind. But when I glanced at her, she had her eyes closed as she stood behind Mary Ann, her hands on the back of the chair.

"You won't get away with this!" Grandberg told Sam. "That reporter won't rest until she exposes you!"

"Her?" Sam laughed and sneered at Grandberg. "You still don't get it, do you? She wanted a story. And she's the one who found my ex-lover for us. Miz Marlena Annette, working in that show in New York. Thinking just because she had plastic surgery, no one would ever recognize her."

"You found Penny's story on her computer, didn't you, Jack?" I whispered.

"She'd been hearing rumors that the survivalist group was active around here again," he said. "I'm not sure how Penny found Mary Ann, though."

"It was my Southern accent," Mary Ann said as she continued to glare at Sam. "I needed to stay involved with one part of my life—the theater. She was in New York, attended one of the performances I was in and got invited to the after-party. I agreed to cooperate with her when she figured out who I was and told me she suspected this rotten nest was active again. So I came back to work with Penny. Thought maybe if her newspaper stories got them arrested, maybe I could come back to Texas. It was my home!"

"All you did when you stool pigeoned five years ago was leave room for the rest of us to move up in position," Sam told her.

"I didn't know you were involved...until recently," Mary Ann defended herself. "When you found me at Penny's playing around with her wardrobe of Twenties clothing while she was at work."

"If you'd only talked to me in the office, Mary Ann," Grandberg said.

"Ha!" she retorted. "You had Sam on your payroll! How'd I know you weren't involved, also?"

"That pantywaist?" Sam laughed. "And we knew what that asshole reporter was up to all along. She made the mistake of asking me out to her place one day to talk about her suspicions. Showed me around, and I saw that playbill in her bedroom. Figured you'd show up sooner or later, and we kept an eye on the place. Played her along long enough to get her too involved to dig her way out. We've got ways of looking into people's finances. She'd been over-living her salary for a while, what with trying to keep up with her horse-racing friends. She's going to pack her shit and head to New Orleans. And she'll meet with an accident there...just like all of you are gonna meet with one here."

"You'll never get away with it!" Grandberg repeated. "You'll have the Feebs and ATF after your asses, let alone Homeland Security!"

"Well now, they'll have to find us first, won't they?" Sam told him as a new sound rumbled somewhere deep in the bowels of the hotel. "We'd already started moving our operations way before these *girls*—" He flicked his pistol barrel at Granny, Twila, then me. "—stumbled on one of our camps."

"The one where you murdered me, then cut me in half," Mary Ann spat.

"I said I was sorry for leading them there," Delroy whined.

"Shut up!" Sam snapped. "You just do as you're told. Get out there and wait for Georgie to get that elevator up here."

Delroy shuffled back into the hallway. The noise I'd noticed grew a little louder, and I questioned Jack with my eyes to see if he knew what it could be. But Granny murmured the answer to my query. "Sounds like that there service elevator coming up the shaft. They useta send up meals folks ordered from the kitchen that way."

"There's no electricity," I whispered.

"I can hear you," Sam said. "Ain't you ever heard of a generator? Georgie knows this place inside and out. And between him and Delroy, we've got plenty of particulars on how to carry out anything we want to do. Hell, Georgie even has his own Web site, and if he don't know what we need, he knows other places on the Net to find it. Georgie's also real good at hacking into other folk's E-mail."

I didn't even have to speculate about why Sam was being so forth-coming. He obviously didn't plan for any of us to leave here alive, and couldn't resist bragging before he disposed of us. I couldn't imagine what he was bringing up in the elevator, though. I glanced at Twila to see if she'd come to any conclusions, given that she had evidently been probing around with that well-developed psychic mind of hers, and the look of dismay on her face made me wish I hadn't bothered.

What? I demanded.

She shook her head. Besides, she didn't have to answer. Delroy and Georgie rolled the coffin into the room. They'd balanced it on one of those wheeled creepers like mechanics use to roll around under cars in a garage, but it extended two feet over each end.

Ohmigod!

I think the Universe might be a better place for you to ask for help right now, Twila replied to my silent gasp of dismay.

Me? Damn it, you ask! You're more connected than I am!

There's a bomb in the basement.

"A bomb?" I yelped, and Sam, Delroy, and Georgie all turned on me with a glare.

"How'd she know?" Delroy asked.

"Mary Ann probably told her." Sam glowered at Mary Ann, who was staring at the coffin in both longing and awe. "Well, you ain't gonna be around to cause me any more trouble." He flicked his pistol barrel at Georgie. "Open it. Let's get on with this."

Georgie and Delroy had placed the coffin in front of the fireplace. Georgie backed away from it, shaking his head. "This was your idea, Sam. You open it."

"What are you planning to do with...whatever's in that?" I asked Sam, although I knew exactly what he had in mind. It continued to amaze me at times how many people were interested in the same things Twila and I were. Well, would have amazed me, if I hadn't been so worried about how the hell we were going to get out of this one alive instead of joining the realm of ghosts and spirits in their own dimensions.

"I didn't tell them anything," Mary Ann finally answered Sam. "How could I, since I didn't know myself."

"Yeah, right," Sam shot back at her. "You've been more of a pain in the ass dead than alive."

"Leave her alone, Sam," Grandberg said as he started to move closer to his sister's half-ghost.

"Stop right there." Sam emphasized his order with his pistol, and Grandberg halted behind Granny's chair, close enough to touch Mary Ann, if she could have been touched. Sam continued, "When Boss Lady found out Mary Ann was still around, she figured this was the only way to get rid of her for good. Reunite her, so she'll cross over and get out of our hair. We were gonna force these two to do it, but Delroy failed when Mary Ann showed up."

Boss Lady? There's more to this band?

"Had my way, we'd be gone by now," Sam continued. "But no, we have to make a statement first. But before that, Carrie says we have to get rid of this meddling ghost."

"I've told you not to use my name, asshole." Carrie stepped into the room, an assault rifle of her own snuggled against her side, her finger on the trigger. She now wore camouflage, like Delroy, a suit tailored to fit her tiny figure.

Ma Barker in the flesh, the writer's side of my mind told me before I could stifle it. I knew about Ma Barker from research. That woman definitely had a psycho personality. And now I knew why Carrie had fainted at the elevator.

"You were down there in your ghost form when Carrie looked down the elevator shaft, weren't you?" I whispered to Mary Ann, who nodded an agreement.

"You know what happens to soldiers who don't follow orders," Carrie told Sam.

"Jesus," Jack whispered beside me. "Can this get any worse?"

Sam's shoulders slumped and his expression dissolved from angry confidence into a submissive pout. "Sorry, Ca—Boss Lady," he whined. "But it ain't gonna matter. None of them will be able to rat us out after we get done here."

"You're sure not making any progress," Carrie said with a sneer of contempt. "I'll take care of your disobedience later. Right now..." She swung her rifle barrel toward Georgie and Delroy. "Open that coffin." The two of them scrambled to obey as Carrie pointed the barrel at Twila next. "You. Get on with this and get that damn ghost out of our hair. She caused my organization enough trouble five years ago."

"Alice is in charge on this one," Twila said in a way-too-mild voice in my opinion, considering our circumstances. The coffin lid creaked as it opened, an incongruously loud noise compared to Twila's voice.

"Huh," Granny said. "Hope when they pick out my coffin, they get one that don't need WD-40 on its hinges."

I couldn't help myself. I had enough sense left to keep a strong hold on Trucker, but my gaze irrefutably centered on the coffin. I desperately hoped that maybe I wouldn't be able to see inside it, given my seat on the floor, but the creeper only held the coffin about six inches off the floor. Pale and waxy, Mary Ann's body lay there against a white silk liner, her head propped on a satin pillow bordered with lace.

"Where are my pearls?" Mary Ann demanded.

Delroy reached into one of the multiple pockets in his camo suit, and the pearls slithered out. He held them up and dangled them at Mary Ann. "I called the undertaker and pretended to be the chief. Had him take them off you. And you ain't getting them back."

"Give them here! Now!" Mary Ann screamed. Then she tried to leave the circle...and failed. She couldn't even rise from the chair. "Let me go!" she shouted at me.

I wasn't the one holding her; Twila was. But I didn't feel bound to tell her that. There was no way we could escape this room, not with those rifles and Sam's pistol blocking our way, those itchy trigger fingers straining to scratch themselves on the nearest object. Damn my writer's mind. Mary Ann didn't have to worry about getting killed, though.

"The only way you're getting out of here is to reunite," I told her, not caring that I spoke aloud. Evidently Carrie had this in mind all along, and maybe while we performed that ceremony, someone would figure out what to do next.

"Yeah," Carrie sneered. "So let's get on with it. Get rid of her. Now!"

"It doesn't work that fast." I cautiously adjusted my seat so I could face Carrie directly. "You obviously know a little bit about how the spirit world works, or else you wouldn't be so adamant about us making sure Mary Ann is totally on the other side before you...do whatever else you have in mind."

"I know enough to know that Sam made a mistake when he had Delroy and Georgie cut her body in half. And put it here to throw suspicion on someone who came to the hotel," Carrie spat. "It did something to her. Let her hang around."

"I wasn't dead," Mary Ann said. "The Domitor Delroy injected wasn't enough to kill me, and the knife only nicked my heart. I was only unconscious, still bleeding to death."

"You used an animal sedative on her?" I said with a gasp as I turned towards Delroy.

Grandberg moaned and said, "Ah, Sis," then wilted in agony. Behind him, Grandmere Alicia smiled at me briefly before she shoved her small hands against his back and pushed. Grandberg collapsed over the back of Granny's chair. His chin landed on her walking stick, and gave Granny enough time to wiggle out of the way. She tottered to her feet, and although Twila lunged at her with a shout of "Don't!" Granny yanked the walking stick away and the police chief fell in a heap, his body draped over the chair back.

The circle was broken. Before Twila could repair the damage, Mary Ann realized it, also. She zipped upward, and every gaze in the room followed her progress as she arched across the ceiling and then dove for the coffin. Delroy screamed in fear, dropped the pearls and rushed toward the doorway. Unfortunately for him, Georgie didn't move as fast. Delroy barreled into Georgie and the two of them hit the floor with a thud that shook the entire room. A thud that shook the heavy brass and crystal chandelier from its tentative hold on the ceiling. It fell right on Carrie.

Jack didn't bother with the two fear-stricken men on the floor. He was on his feet in a split second, and the toe of his boot connected with

Sam's pistol hand a split second before his fist smashed Sam's jaw and knocked him a good five feet across the room.

I lunged for Carrie...well, her assault rifle. I grabbed the butt and pulled it free of the tangled mess. Had no idea what to do with it now, since I'd never held one of those nasty weapons before in my life, but at least Ma Barker couldn't shoot us with it if she regained consciousness. It might be a while before that happened, I mused as I noticed the dark knot already swelling on her forehead.

I looked for Twila. She'd evidently decided which direction she needed to go as her part of us overcoming the band of marauders. As Georgie and Delroy untangled themselves and scrambled to their feet, she raced over beside me, the pearls dangling in her hand. Granny left Grandberg lying over the chair and slowly crossed the room to make our group a threesome. But before she halted beside Twila and me, she balanced on her walking stick and kicked Carrie none-too-gently in the butt.

"That's for foolin' me," she said. "You asked me t'come to the hospital so's you could find out what was goin' on."

I searched for Grandmere until I saw her standing beside the coffin, staring down at Mary Ann with a sympathetic look. Evidently, the half-ghost was back in her body, since I didn't see her anywhere.

Georgie and Delroy each took a step toward the doorway. Twila shook the pearls. They cringed backward, then swiveled their heads in one and the same motion toward the coffin, then back to the pearls. Caught between the two fearful devices, they froze in indecision.

By then Jack had Sam's pistol in his hand. "Hold them off a minute," he said to Twila. "Soon as I take care of this one, I'll be over there."

He looked around as though searching for something—I assumed he needed something to use to tie up Sam. "There's a cord in Twila's satchel," I called.

Jack kept the pistol on Sam, who lay on the floor and held his hand against his cheek as he glared at Jack while he searched Twila's backpack. Twila continued to hold Delroy and Georgie at bay with the pearls, but their eyes gave away their intentions the moment they decided the pearls were less frightening than the coffin. Their muscles tightened and they both surged at Twila.

I aimed the assault rifle barrel through the string of pearls, straight at their bellies. They didn't know that I had no idea how the thing worked. The possibility of a bellyful of bullets was enough of a new deterrent. They froze again.

Jack was on his way over to us when that stupid ghost made her stupid move. With a loud moan, Mary Ann sat up in the coffin.

"It's not working," she said. "I need some help here."

Grandmere pushed Mary Ann's body back down a second too late. There was not a bit of indecision left in either Georgie or Delroy. An assault rifle and a string of paranormal pearls couldn't begin to frighten them as much as the possibility that body would get out of the coffin. With twin shrieks, they charged Twila and me.

Granny's walking stick tripped Georgie, who flew end over end into the Carrie-chandelier tangle. Delroy got past us, but just for a second. A black flash streaked across the room, and Trucker beat him to the door. Though Delroy outweighed my dog, Trucker lunged at him and buried his fangs in Delroy's shoulder. For a split second, dog and camouflage blended, then Delroy toppled backwards, Trucker on top of him. Trucker released his hold briefly, then snarled and sprang for Delroy's throat. Only the camouflaged arm Delroy instinctively threw in Trucker's way saved his life.

I laid a hand on Trucker's neck and said, "Stay, boy. Just stay right there." He obeyed, lips drawn back and a rumble in this throat at the attacker he no doubt remembered from the woods. Tail high and back arched, Miss Molly stalked over to her buddy and took up a Halloween-cat stance beside Delroy's head. She hiss-meowed a dare at him to move.

We searched everyone, and Jack found the detonator device for the bomb on Carrie. She'd regained consciousness as Jack tied her up, but mutinously refused to speak except to demand her lawyer. Jack knelt in front of Georgie.

"I hear you're the one who rigged up this device," he said as he held the tiny black box under Georgie's nose. "I just know enough about stuff like this to get myself in trouble. But enough to know you have to acti-vate it somehow for the explosion to happen. You wanna tell us how to disarm it completely?"

"Keep your trap shut!" Sam snarled.

Jack sighed and rose. He motioned to Grandberg, and the two of them dragged Sam into the bathroom. When Sam continued to scream dire threats at Georgie, Twila dug in her backpack and handed Jack a roll of duct tape.

"Duct tape?" I asked her. "What do we use that for in ceremonies?"

She shrugged and smiled at me. "Nothing. You just never know what will come in handy now and then."

Jack ripped off a piece of duct tape and silenced Sam. Then he walked over to Delroy and slapped another piece of tape over his mouth. He and Grandberg dragged Delroy into the bathroom with Sam, then turned their attention to Carrie.

Leave her for now, Grandmere cautioned me.

"She's not talking anyway," I said to Jack. "Maybe you can leave her for last."

He shrugged and focused back on Georgie, but the handyman sput-tered, "I—I don't know how t—to turn it off. Carrie made me fix it up so she could put a pass code on it like she's got on her phone! She's the only one who knows what time it's set to go off!"

"It's already set to explode?" I said with a gasp. "We need to get out of here!"

"I don't know if it is or not!" Georgie insisted. "Only Carrie knows."

Every one of us stared at Ma Barker/Boss Lady, and she glared back at us, mouth clamped stubbornly.

"She wouldn't just lay there not talkin' if she expected this building to explode beneath us." Jack didn't sound quite as positive as I would have liked, though, and he immediately continued, "But let's get all of the rest of you out of here, just in case."

"We're not done here," Twila said. "And I doubt you're thinking of leaving the prisoners behind to get blown up."

"Do what you're told, Twila," Jack ordered, the totally wrong thing to say to my aunt.

She ignored him and both of us looked over at Grandmere. She stared hard at Carrie, the expression on her beautiful face similar to the one Twila used the rare times she stifled her ethics and probed someone's mind.

It's not activated, Grandmere assured us. *But that Carrie woman is a stubborn biddy. You'll have to take drastic action to make her talk.* She smiled at us and nodded at the coffin, where Grandberg now stood staring down at Mary Ann.

Twila jerked the duct tape from Jack's hand and silenced Georgie. Then she grabbed one of Georgie's arms, I took the other one, and we dragged him across the room. The bathroom was rather full now, but we jammed Georgie in, then shut the door.

Jack changed his tactics. "Look, Twila," he said as he held one of her arms. "You've got folks depending on you at home. Living folks."

Granny gently removed Jack's hand from Twila and said, "Now you listen here, Jack. You's outta your depth here. Iffen these ladies say we gotta finish this up, then that's what we needs to do. You jist come on over here with me and take a seat like a proper mourner."

She led Jack over to the lounge chair and stopped. "Tsk, tsk, this ain't at all proper. You and that there poleece chief gotta move things around." She raised her voice and said, "Son, you get over here now." Grandberg obeyed, and she directed Jack and him to circle the couch and lounge chairs in front of Mary Ann's coffin. Then she settled on the couch and pointed at the chairs until Jack and Grandberg took their seats before she called Trucker and Miss Molly up on either side of her. Granny settled back with a proper look of sorrow on her face and then she and Grandmere began: "Amazing Grace, how sweet thou art..."

The room returned to blazing glory, as it had been back in its heyday. The carpet under our feet was soft with padding, the furniture pristine, the windows where a glowing light flowed in clear of dust and grime. Even Jack drew in an astonished breath at the startling change.

"Now what?" I whispered to Twila.

She winked at me and said to Carrie, "You obviously aren't going to talk, so you don't need your mouth free." She slapped another piece of duct tape on Carrie's mouth, then grabbed Carrie's tiny body under the arms. I took her feet, but instead of heading toward the bathroom, Twila headed for the coffin. I had an idea what she had in mind, but my horror at the thought didn't begin to match what I saw in Carrie's eyes when she realized where we were going.

Despite her slight stature, Carrie gave us a struggle. She wriggled and wrenched like a landed fish, doing her best to break free. At the coffin, we laid her down long enough for Twila to rip the duct tape from her mouth and ask, "You ready to tell us how to disarm that bomb?"

"Fuck y—" Carrie spat before Twila slapped the tape back in place.

We regained our holds, and the hymn's chorus swelled in the room to accompany Twila's "One, two, three." We launched Carrie into the coffin beside Mary Ann and Twila closed the lid, except for a tiny slit for air. She jammed the pearls in that space to keep it open.

"I thank you all for coming," Twila said to the mourners. "But there will be a short break in the ceremony."

I don't know how she managed it, but Carrie actually shook that coffin. Fear can give someone even as small as her superhuman strength, I guess. At one point, the creeper even started to slide across the room as the noise of muffled thuds and garbled screams crept out through the slot beneath the lid. I stuck my foot beneath the wheel to hold it into place.

"How long do you think we should wait?" I asked Twila.

"She's probably about done."

Granny raised a hand as though conducting an orchestra and led the opening lines of "Old Rugged Cross" while we lifted the coffin lid. Mary Ann lay there serenely—after all, she was dead. But Carrie pleaded at us with her eyes. Twila pulled off the duct tape again, and Carrie gasped, "Nine-one-one! It's nine-one-one! Get me out of here! Please!"

"Pretty please?" I asked with a snicker.

"Yes! Pretty please. Sugar on it, whatever you want! Oh, god, get me out of here!"

Twila and I lifted her free of the coffin and propped her against it. She struggled and tried to balance herself and hop away, but I laid a hand on her chest and said, "No, no, no. You're staying right here until we know for sure you aren't lying about your passcode."

"I'm not! And it's not going to explode anyway! Not now. I'd have detonated it after we got a few blocks away."

"Well, we'll let the bomb squad look into that," Jack said as he started to rise.

Granny stuck her walking stick in front of Jack to keep him in his seat. "Sit down," she said. "Ain't no proper service without one of them eulogies. I think Miss Carrie here's got a few more things to say."

EPILOGUE

When we got back to Six Gun that evening, we were all too wound up to sleep. We were also hungry. I dug some T-bones out of the freezer while Jack fired up the grill and Twila scrubbed potatoes to nuke in the microwave. Granny sat at the table and peeled some cucumbers and tomatoes for one of her special vinegar-laced salads.

"Nice ceremony for Mary Ann," she mused as she wielded her paring knife.

"I'm just grateful that Grandmere assisted Mary Ann across the veil and I didn't have to perform that ceremony, like Twila threatened me," I said.

"There will be a next time," Twila assured me as she stuck the plastic-wrapped potatoes in the microwave.

Jack came in from the deck and said, "Grill's ready, Alice. How does everyone want their steak?"

"Well done," Twila and Granny answered in unison.

When I started to speak, Jack held up a hand. "I know. Rare. Just leave it on long enough to stop mooing."

"You got it," I agreed. "Same for Trucker and Miss Molly." I handed him a metal baking pan with the marinating steaks in it.

"Alice," he said quietly. "In that bedroom—" His cell phone rang, and Jack's brown eyes promised me that we weren't done with this conversation by a long shot as he juggled the pan of steaks and answered, "Yeah?" He listened for a few moments. "Uh huh. Yeah, I'll let them know." After a pause, he continued, "You call her later and tell her yourself. But don't be surprised if you see a bumbling idiot cop character with your name on it in her next book."

He shut off the phone and said, "Penny came back on her own and willingly told Grandberg all she knew, after he threatened her with being an accessory to murder. She swears she didn't know Mary Ann was dead until she saw Twila's pictures of the murdered woman. Then she realized she was in trouble for withholdin' information. But before she could make up her mind whether to cooperate or write a story on the murder, Delroy kidnapped her to get rid of her, too."

I shook my head. "She was probably hoping she could salvage something and still land the job in New Orleans."

"Well, she picked the wrong people to mess with," Jack explained. "Even Mary Ann didn't know that Sam, Carrie, and Georgie escaped the net five years ago. Carrie's confession said that Delroy met the leader of another group out around Amarillo while he was in prison. They were movin' out there, but Carrie was just pissed enough that she wanted to make a statement before she left. Blow up the hotel."

"Penny'll prob'ly still get her new job," Granny said.

"I suppose," I agreed. "Her notoriety will only help her. But she's definitely off my list of friends."

I caught Twila frowning at me. "What?" I asked.

"You still owe me some money, Alice."

"Damn it, you haven't told me how much."

"Trip kitty," Granny said with a snicker. "Gonna enjoy that there trip to N'awlins."

AFTERWORD

Mineral Springs and the Springs Hotel are fictitious. However, my hotel is based on one in a small West Texas town, a grand old place, abandoned but with still-visible remnants of its glory days. A hotel where I have, indeed, spent time hunting ghosts and chatting with long-passed residents. Efforts are underway to restore the Baker Hotel in Mineral Wells, Texas, efforts that I hope will be successful. There is a Facebook page for information.

I have watched the growth of ebooks for a long while now, and my Christmas wish list last year included a Kindle. My husband saw this wish fulfilled, and I fell in love immediately with the device. It also caused me a lot of work, because I decided to reissue some of my books as ebooks. A natural growth from that was to bring out the multitude of true diaries from my ghost hunting adventures I kept over the years and publish them for others to enjoy. This is an ongoing project, with my plan being to publish a set of diaries in conjunction with each mystery. So far, you can find **Ghost Hunting Diaries Volumes I and II** available in a multitude of ebook formats. **Volume III** is in the works and will soon see life along with **Dead Man Hand**. I also have some fictional short stories I'm getting ready to publish for that wonderful holiday I love: Halloween/Samhain.

You will find out more about what I'm up to and my internet sites, included in the bio at the end of the book. As you traverse to that, I hope you enjoy Alice, Twila, Granny and Jack's latest adventure as much as I did writing it.

BOO!

T. M. Simmons
Author/Ghost Hunter

DEAD MAN HAND
A DEAD MAN MYSTERY, BOOK 3

As I started to turn, my shoulder brushed the door of the forbidden room in this creepy, haunted hotel. It creaked open with an eerie sound, as though the door hinges hadn't moved in a long while. I hesitated, but curiosity got the better of me. Evidently, Granny, also. She shone the penlight in there.

My huge Rottweiler, Trucker, didn't have an iota of curiosity, though. He nearly jerked free as he tried to retrace our steps.

"Just a minute, boy," I ordered. "Sit. This room has a story behind it, and the owner might not let us in here later."

Trucker refused the *sit*. He whined and maintained a strong pull on the leash. I was too interested in the room to chastise him for his disobedience.

The little light didn't illuminate much at a time. In front of us was an old iron bedstead, pillows fluffed and the hand-sewn comforter pristine. Granny moved the beam across the bed to a dresser against the wall. The penlight reflected in the mirror, giving us twice as much light. A half-full bottle of what looked like Jack Daniels set on the dresser surface beside a shot glass, a slim measure of dark liquid in the bottom. Even in this light I noticed the expected layer of dust in a long-closed room was missing.

Glorious, velvety dark-red wallpaper covered the walls. A person would have thought it faded over the years, but it, too, looked as though it had recently been hung.

Still, the room did smell musty...or something. The odor tugged at my senses. It didn't seem to fit with the room's immaculate condition, but I couldn't identify it.

Granny moved the light. The carpet didn't cover the entire floor; at least two feet of polished hardwood gleamed around the edges. But there....

I took the penlight from Granny and focused the beam on the floor. Some of the wallpaper must have peeled off. A red pool of it lay on the carpet over in the far corner of the room. I frowned. It even appeared wet, as though someone had recently spilled water on it. Then it darkened, as though a shadow moved across it.

I climbed the tiny beam of light up the wall. It hit the bare red feet first. Not wallpaper on the floor. Blood caked the naked human toes circling slowly in the glow.

Trucker's nose had told him what we'd find.

Granny gasped. Trucker whined and pulled against the leash harder —not toward the body, away from it. I quickly lowered the light and, heart hammering and nausea roiling—I even had trouble writing about blood—ushered Granny and my pets out of the room. Now my nose, also, identified the coppery scent: blood.

"We got's to call the cops," Granny whispered.

* * *

Available in Paperback and eBook from Your Favorite Bookstore or Online Retailer

About the Author

T. M. Simmons lives in a haunted house on the edge of the East Texas Piney Woods, which she and her husband share with a variety of pets and paranormal residents. In between writing cozy mysteries and other stories, she delights in scaring herself silly during otherworldly encounters and visits haunted building and graveyards during both dark and full moons. Her husband goes along sometimes to protect her from the bumps in the night, although he's been know to spy a ghost and retreat rather than confront. She also pursues paranormal entities with her own real-life Twila, Aunt Belle Brown, and they are Lead Investigators of the Supernatural Researchers of Texas paranormal investigative team. SRT's motto is, "Leave Peace Behind," and the team seeks to leave peace for the people who are dealing with troubled hauntings, as well as for the ghosts. Simmons is extremely willing to discuss her experiences with anyone she can corner.

Sign up here for the T. M. Simmons newsletter and receive a copy of *Thrall Bound, a Short Story;* only available to newsletter subscribers.

https://ghostie3.wixsite.com/index1

www.iseeghosts.com

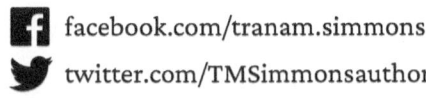

facebook.com/tranam.simmons

twitter.com/TMSimmonsauthor